D1824072

The
White
Book

The White Book

A NOVEL

MAKAVELLI

iUniverse, Inc.
New York Lincoln Shanghai

The White Book

Copyright © 2007 by Makavelli

All rights reserved. No part of this book may be used or reproduced by any means, graphic, electronic, or mechanical, including photocopying, recording, taping or by any information storage retrieval system without the written permission of the publisher except in the case of brief quotations embodied in critical articles and reviews.

iUniverse books may be ordered through booksellers or by contacting:

iUniverse
2021 Pine Lake Road, Suite 100
Lincoln, NE 68512
www.iuniverse.com
1-800-Authors (1-800-288-4677)

Because of the dynamic nature of the Internet, any Web addresses or links contained in this book may have changed since publication and may no longer be valid.

This is a work of fiction. All of the characters, names, incidents, organizations, and dialogue in this novel are either the products of the author's imagination or are used fictitiously.

All excerpts are available at www.myspace.com/thewhitebookpage

ISBN: 978-0-595-42498-6

Printed in the United States of America

This Work

I Dedicate to all True Believers

A prophet wrote that from the clot of the believers would come a grimoire of pure truth,

In every Country

A reminder to all of the events to befall mankind on his journey through the city streets.

And of every Race

In its words would be clues on how to identify the imposters,

For they called it forth and for them it was written

As well as where to find solace after consuming ether from the tree of knowledge.

PROLOGUE

THE HAVANA COUNTYSIDE
Near The Millennium

Imagine this.

"This is the most beautiful land ever seen by human eyes."

Supposedly that's what Christopher Columbus said when he first laid eyes on Cuba. I'll give him that one.

I arrived here an only child, just shy of my teens and impressionable. Like any child, especially one with my genes, I was a rebel.

The first ten years of my life I didn't know my father. I knew of him, the same way as the millions of others who'd witnessed his life or paid attention to his work. I never knew that man was my father. I remember asking my mother if she'd take me on one of those talk shows where they give DNA tests to find the father of your child. I remember her being upset, not angry, more hurt than anything, maybe even a little amused when she looked at me with 100% certainty and said;

"I know exactly who your father is."

She ended our conversation with a promise;

"One day you'll get to meet him."

I did, and that's the one memory that I think I'll keep just for me.

Now we're all here in "the lost city." There's lots of history on this island. I see the places Hyman Roth and Moe Green, Tony Montana, Che Guevara and Fidel used to hang out decades ago. This country is notorious for granting asylum to enemies of the state. These days there's news that "El President'e" had plans to dedicate a statue to an unlikely revolutionary.

As for my father; he's been through it. His days are lazy ones spent processing information, reading, listening to music and screening film while flipping between Bloomberg and CNN, most days from sunup to sundown. Sometimes for fun he

1

takes me with him to the domino games where the wise men meet and weave life tapestries, the fabric of their memories worn thin by time. In the early days he wrote a lot too, in a snow white leather bound journal that he carried with him most everywhere. "The White Book," that's what I called it. I'd watch him and wonder, but I never asked him what he was writing in there, when he was with it he seemed distant. I remember once getting up the nerve to ask my mother; if anyone knew, she would. But all I got from her was another promise.

"He'll tell you when he's ready for you to know."

Then one morning not long after that I was in the kitchen finishing breakfast when he called to me from outside.

"Starr, come here. I got something for you, hurry, run quick see!"

Outside he took my hand and we went walking.

"What do we have here now? Your mother says you've got some questions for me."

"Yeah," I said, "I've got a few."

"What questions could you have with all the information floating around out there?"

Even then I was old enough to know you can't believe everything you hear.

"I checked it all out. Every bit and piece they put out there. I want to hear it from you, your life through your eyes."

"I thought you might." He held up 'The White Book'. "Do you know what this is?"

"Not exactly, mama said you'd tell me that when you were ready."

"I always wanted to make a book out of my life. But this story is not about my life, exactly. It's about my fabled generation and its music, the things that affected them and me; the obstacles we faced during our war and what we did to make it through. In my hand," he said shaking the book, "is history and it helps to know where you came from in the search for where you're going."

He took one last look at his work before he gave it to me.

"It took me a lifetime to put these things together on my own and like any parent I want you to be ahead of the game, so here you go. A few hundred pages on some things you should know."

I remember touching the book and being instantly beguiled. Imagine jewels being handed to an innocent child.

"That's yours now, do whatever you want with it, but if anything should ever happen to me I wanted you to know the truth."

It was early, the sun still on the rise, it was going to be a beautiful day on the island and here we were with nothing to do. I gave the book back to him.

"Read it to me."

"Read it to you?" He smiled, looked around and took in a deep breath of the sticky sweet air. "Ok, I can do that, it may take me a while but I can certainly do that."

"When," he asked?

"Today," I said, "right now. Like you always say, 'nobody is promised tomorrow,' plus I've waited a long time for this."

"Yes," he said, "you have."

He hugged me, squeezed me really. Then he picked me up in a tight bear of a hug. When we part he called to Juan and Carlos who were never far way. Since I'd arrived they'd been like big brothers always looking out for me.

They went to bring the H1's around, and we went inside and told mom our plans. She kissed me.

"Have fun with your daddy."

I could tell she was happy.

From the house we made our way to the restaurant we secretly owned. The manager was already there with his wife.

Dad called to her.

"Dos lemonade por favor, Selma. We gon' be out back soaking up some sun today."

Juan and Carlos took a seat at the picnic table sipping iced coffee and continuing a never-ending game of dominoes. I helped my father take a seat under the bohdi tree. He put his pistol in the grass and loosened the straps on the Kevlar vests we wore whenever we were away from the compound. Selma came and set up a tray behind us. On it was glasses and a pitcher, floating in it, fresh cut fruit and ice, on the side, a bottle of Absinthe; my father's new vice.—It's hard to smoke with one lung—Then to my surprise he pulled from his pocket a stainless steel cylinder protecting one of Cuba's finest. I looked at him.

"Just for the smell," he said. "You already know the drill with your mother."

He lit up then put his arm around me. I could tell he was happy. I was too. We were together and doing the things that families do. There wasn't another place in the world I'd rather have been.

He was ready now and so was I,
Both prepared for the epoch of a lifetime.
An epic tale of heroes and villains,
Politics and religions, laced by providence and design.
I lay back charting my course in the vanilla sky and wondering how,
If at all his epick would tie into mine.

Then he cleared his throat and began his story.

"The Game has changed," he said, "you can feel it in the earth, you can smell it in the air, and you can hear it in the music. Much that once was has now been forgotten, for only a precious few who live remember it."

And then he stopped so abruptly instinct had me reaching for my weapon like I'd been trained to do. He looked at me before he spoke again, a deep and sincere look that bonded our souls.

"But I trust my people, the true believers know, this be the realest shit I ever wrote!"

Then he went back to his story, speaking the words that I'll forever remember as the truest shit he ever spoke.

1971

THE GREAT MIGR8TION

Goodman Game was born in Arkansas in the summer of 1951. Families like his made up the half-million immigrants that settled in Watts and South Central Los Angeles from around the US, traveling miles for the chance at factory jobs left vacant by the war. By the late 50's as the rest of L.A. got richer those areas didn't. Politicians actually raised their taxes to pay for luxuries like Disney World and the intricate L.A. freeway system. In 1958 when the Brooklyn Dodgers were brought to town and their stadium built on Chavez Ravine,—a poor Hispanic community that was supposed to become a housing project,—ghetto residents protested worsening the racial problems there. The police presence increased and with it came police brutality. Newly won civil rights were disappearing alongside the soldiers who'd fought for them. Tensions were high and South Central was about to snap.

It was one of those nights when you feel that anything can happen. Not long after Goodman's fourteenth birthday in the summer of 1965 a car was stopped and three young black males were charged with drinking and driving. That was it.

Goodman, his older brother Bobby, best friend Larry and a few others had gone out to be part of something. Long after the windows had been broken and the store first looted the boys ran through the shelves of Bea's cut rate drug store to see what they could get; that was until Mr. Whitman and his wife Beatrice rushed in with four of LAPD's finest, yelling, "Arrest all these goddamn looters!"

Goodman and Larry ran through the shards of glass and across the street to hide their stash. Winded, Goodman looked around franticly and asked about his brother.

"Right there!" Larry choked on his candy as he pointed and screamed. "He right there!"

Their hearts stopped and time stood still as they watched the officers beat Robert bloody. Goodman wanted to help but the crowd pulled him and his twelve year old friend back. Mr. and Mrs. Whitman cursed Bobby and ordered the officers to "teach the nigger a lesson!" Bobby's brick of Rose fell on the concrete but didn't break, and through the haze of burning buildings and the throes of pain, Goodman Game was presented with a magical moment, something addicts and warriors like to refer to as a moment of clarity. A moment when all things become crystal clear, when past, present, and future merge and the veil you live under is lifted.

The year was 1965 but it might as well have been 1865, or 2065. He was fourteen years old and his veil had been lifted, something usually reserved for much later in life, but fourteen years spent in, "The Life," is equivalent to time spent in any battle or bar. The words to a song his parents often played came to mind and now he understood, because now he too had been changed, and by any means necessary Goodman vowed to change his life. He dropped to his knees and cried, Larry sat beside him and joined in, an enraged community wept, but no amount of tears could stop Watts from burning and by the time the riots were over the aftermath saw hundreds arrested, 34 pronounced dead, 810 wounded and hundreds of businesses destroyed.

1965 also saw the assassination of Brother Malcolm X. In '66 New York rioted. In '67 more riots erupted in Detroit and Newark. 1968 brought the assassination of Dr. Martin Luther King Jr. in Memphis and political unrest at Chicago's Democratic Convention where Richard "The Boss" Daley instructed the CPD and National Guard troops fresh from Vietnam to kill Civil Rights activists if need be. Then at last 1969 closed with a strange turn of events. For Goodman the culmination to a decade of violence arrived in the form a letter from the government.

CALIFORNIA
Compton 1970
Lueders Park

"These chumps got to be jivin' me," Goodman told Larry.

Altogether there were about ten gangsters from their set,—The Lueders Park Hustlers—drinking and smoking three dollar bags of weed.

"These punks want me to fight a war for they sorry asses when they dun' killed every brother I ever had!"

The draft was a real concern in the poorer communities where opportunity was limited, and especially so for children of color. For them a college education was rare, not because they weren't capable like some believed, but because there was no such thing as financial aid back then. For too many underprivileged kids the gangs were everything. The gangs were "family;" and now their families were being torn apart by a bogus war.

Imagine that.

"Man fuck them," shouted one of the Hustlers!

"Yeah fuck them," added another named Sammy, "I aint going if they call me."

They all pretended to agree but Goodman knew game when he heard it and that shit was weak. He'd seen lots of the crew spit it since the draft began, some never came home, others tried to hide but the eye was on them.

Agents hunted them and sent them to a place just as bad or worse, Kansas; 1300 Metropolitan, Leavenworth Federal Penitentiary to be exact.

At seventeen Larry already had a son and could feel the Government's gaze focusing on him.

"Man, what 'chu gon' do," he asked?

Goodman told him what he wanted to hear.

"I'll think of something. But you aint got nothing to worry about, the war gon' be over before they get to you, and if I leave, you gon' help lead this family. Remember y'all," he said to the others, "one man should never lead a crew, that's trouble. One man shouldn't be that powerful."

One month later Goodman left for Southeast Asia and what he believed would be certain death. But even on the other side of the world where the language is different and the faces seemed unkind, to some, he was looking familiar.

WELCOME TO NEW YORK CITY
Greenwich Village
May '71

The radio was tuned to K-Billy's super sounds of the 70's."

"… The rumor is that Morrison's exile in Paris is due to the infamous penis incident. That was probably the first time music had actually gone to trial in the United States, but the way things are going, I can tell you for sure it won't be the last."

It was summer, but her cell was cold, damp and located in the lowest part of the prison where there was no sunlight and day and night was a permanent shade of swirling blues. Drab grey paint covered the brick walls, steel bars and iron pipes that ran overhead spewing boiling hot water that turned to vapor when it hit the air. In spots it dripped continuously making a torturous sound. Ants and centipedes crept on her and mice nipped at her as she slept. She used to wake up brushing them away, but she didn't sleep much anymore. Now they came at all times relentlessly attacking her temple. She'd sit centered in the room searching for their origins. The moment she was sure that she was indeed alone, they'd seem to appear out of thin air, crawling, tickling, and biting their way out of her skin.

"That's just your imagination," she told herself. But too many times the carcasses had proved her wrong. In her heart she knew she was never alone. On this level she saw red eyes piercing the darkness and heard voices calling out to her. She'd answer them sometimes only to find that she'd been fooled. She'd trusted her thoughts at first, but not now. Torture can do that to the mind, and her murderous captors showed her no mercy.

"Shake it off Marian. They can't break you. Keep your head up?"

From far away, she heard laughter.

There were times when she'd thought *Que sra sra,* and given in. It felt good not to care about the outcome. But her imprisonment was about more than her. All her comrades were facing life sentences, she had to keep it together for them, and they for her. They'd taken an oath to be strong for each other.

But breaking her will was a mission detention center officer Eblis Harris reveled in. He'd volunteered for the graveyard shift when she arrived.

"Fewer interruptions."

After months Marian was close to loosing her mind.

"Tonight will be the night," thought Eblis.

Hopefully he'd destroy the body as well, not that it mattered much, once her mind had been broken the matter would surely follow, and then he'd have them both. In her cell he sat squat like a toad beside her, whispering into her ear, taunting her and claiming no fear.

"Why should a son of fire, fear a son of clay. Surrender. This world is ours. We cannot loose."

In her talks with the devils they'd explained to her their plan for conquest, explained how if they couldn't rule in their world, together they'd rule in this one.

But Marian was no fool, she knew they'd been deceived. One way or another they'd serve like all the rest. The lines of time and sanity were faint as they

merged with their opponents and Marian saw for sure exactly what she'd alw[...]
suspected.

"Seeing is believing."

Excerpt 1.

Still hope was fading fast, and darkness was drawing near. Marian's spirit was weak, and so was the child's forming inside her.

NEW YORK CITY
Queens

Excerpt 2.

Les McCann and Eddie Harris recorded the album "Swiss Movement" at the Montreux, Switzerland Jazz Festival in the summer of 1969. A year later it had found its way to America. Strangely, it would be the magic of the 70's that changed the nation. The 60's were all about poets and prophets, revolutions and wars, and *The Movement*, led by Martin and Malcolm had shown a nation of rebels the will and resolve it took to have a voice while under ever-watchful eyes.

Not to mention the newly unveiled eyes of America's flower children who now saw the world in a vibrant Technicolor. In New York city hi-fi color television was in and in Queens NY sharkskin suits in colors like money green, dreamcicle orange, and blood red, filled every corner lounge, and in every corner of the Ritz lounge stood a mack, hustler, or bona-fide player auditioning for the lead role as the real life ultimate hustler.

Excerpt 3.

By the winter of 1971 a true hustler and his newest homeboy sat in the corner of the Ritz lounge breaking from the brutish realities of that foul year of our lord. It hadn't been long since they'd shed blood in the same mud. While Dioses Devine had stayed and finished his tour, Goodgame had used just that to work his magic with a file clerk he'd met during intake at MEPS. Through a series of letters and long collect calls from Southeast Asia he'd somehow talked himself into the heart of Elizabeth. "Lizzie," as he'd nicknamed her. She'd pulled some strings, forged some names, and voila, a medical discharge.

United States government sent me 13,000 miles away from
ier in their bullshit army and I macked my way back to the
ieneral in my own! I'm the first international player from
years later.

Tonight he and his "brotherblood" sipped Martell and reminisced.

"Dioses Devine, yo' ass is wild jack! I never did know how you got away with that shit. Slapped that redneck motherfucker right in front of the Lieutenant.

Me, Washburn and Mac looking at each other like, "this nigga dun' lost his goddamn mind!"

"O'Neil was a lying ass, punk. Even the LT could see that," Dioses said, setting his glass on the table and brushing the ashes from the breast of his grey Johnny Carson Suit.

"Aint that the truth." Goodgame called for another bottle. "But that's bullshit, he said! "You expect me to believe a black Corporal from Harlem gon' get away with smacking the shit outta his Sergeant just cause it's right. Game recognizes game. Don't forget you talking to Goodgame baby. C'mon now!"

"All right." Dioses swallowed his drink. "You remember when I couldn't go on R&R because my father had me on assignments?"

"Show you right."

"Well I was riding with the MP's and we're raiding all the number one spots. About 2am we go into the village and hit that brothel; the one with the fine mama san."

Goodgame imitated her.

"You G.I.'s all beaucoup dinky dow?"

"That's the one."

"Was Debbie there?"

"Which one was Debbie?"

"The one with the good "yum-yum," used to scream, "Oh, me so horny.""

Dioses laughed and nodded.

"We had Duffy from the HK team with us; you know how those crazy fucks got down. So he's tearing mamasan a new asshole trying to find the hiding spots. We find the trap door and ..."

"Which one? O'Neil or the LT," asked Goodgame?

"The LT baby; in there asshole naked 'boom booming' one of them 'ladyboys.'"

The speakers blasted. "Goddamnit ... "

"Ha, ha, sock it to me now!" Goodgame snapped his fingers. "Square ass LT. Edon. I always knew it was somethin' to him."

The barmaid sat the bottle on the table and ran her fingers across Dioses's shoulder.

"Where you been hiding this one, daddy? He's cleaner than the board of health."

Goodgame leaned back in the booth and answered.

"Sup wit' 'chu Brenda? This my man from back East, I was telling you about. Say, where's your cousin, baby?"

"I talked to her a little while ago, she's on her way."

"Good. We'll all rap a lil' later baby-girl, right now I need to holla at my man."

"Ok, Game." She winked at Dioses. "Later 'D'"

Dioses watched her walk away.

"Peace-out baby."

Goodgame exhaled slowly.

"Yeah man, so the LT was a gump? I'm telling you, between that "boy" and these chumps, I don't know which is worse."

"You *should* know! You was moving enough to supply a regiment," laughed Dioses.

"Aww, c'mon, don't be acting like you aint have nothing to do with that shit. Nigga, you the motherfucking man. You got Uptown hustle with Downtown connections.

Dioses objected.

"Those are the old man connections. He won't let me forget that."

"Brotherblood, you need to be making them your connects. With them`, plus mine from Compton, I can make Harlem a nuke bomb bro! Have them out there floating like fucking rice patties and make us some rich ass niggas in the process. I already got some blocks off Hollis that's on fire 'Jack!'"

"What about up in Harlem. No other hustlers out there getting it on," asked 'D'?

"Aw hell yeah, 116th, 'tween Lennox and seventh avenue is a drug bazaar man, but believe me when I tell you its enough money out here and P.K. or none of them other cats gonna stop that. Give me a few more months, forget Isaac, they gone call me black Moses."

"Why," wondered Dioses?

"Cause I'll make it a sea of red out here! Please believe me. We gon' get this money baby."

"I heard my old man talking not long before I left. They say the war is going strong, and '*Air America*' aint letting up. That horse has got everybody leaning; black, white, and yellow, all of 'em leaning."

"Baby you know I aint gaming you, I wouldn't do that to you mack buddy. Besides game recognizes game so believe me when I tell you we aint got much choice. This fuckin' indentured servitude they calling jobs is for the birds and aint no Movement left. I was watching the news where they had that pregnant sister locked up in The House of D."

"Yeah, I heard about that."

"Yes sir," Goodgame hit the table with his fist, shaking the glasses. "They coming back every day turned out on that horse, the chumps and the gumps. You got tennis shoe pimps turning out straight broads. These chicks get dusted and freaky than a son-of-a-bitch and when they get dope sick it aint nothing they won't do. *Yes sir*," He hit the table again, "shit is far out D." He chuckled and slapped hands with Dioses. "W'sup man, partners? We'll be the black Rockefellers baby; _____ *if*, you can get that connect!"

The sounds of the Undisputed Truth brought the speakers in the bar to life.

Excerpt 4.

The men looked inside each other, left eye to left eye. No smiles. No double-crosses. No bullshit. *Veritas ad Mas.*

"I'll get on it," said Dioses pointing toward the exit. "Is that yours?"

Goodgame turned his head to see Lizzie and Brenda standing at the door blowing kisses. At last a smile came across both their faces as they raised their glasses to toast.

On nights like these hustlers everywhere were raising their chalices and downing the elixir of the gods. With these unions one day soon the burden-bearers of this nation would prosper, and unlike the generations before, the offspring of these Americans had their own ideas of freedom; ideas that only money could buy. Some nights you could catch them in front of 30 Rockefeller Plaza hoping that the eternal flame from Prometheus would shine upon them and their seeds, blessing them with fame and fortune. Imagine that; the sons of mortals and slaves borne free; *the sons of liberty.*

"C'mon 'D', let me properly introduce you two," said Goodgame.

They got up and walked toward the door. Outside in the brisk New York morning they climbed inside a Coupe De Ville where the young Brenda whispered more smiles onto the face of Dioses Devine as the naive Bostonian kept them amused.

"Ohh I love this car," she said, "it's so big, like a ship."

Goodgame started the big engine and Al Green's, "*I Can't Get Next To You.*" played on the eight-track.

"That's right baby, now watch daddy make it sail on dry land."

Everybody laughed as the pirates set sail, hunting for a treasure *born in blood.*

1972

THE GREAT MIGR8TION

QUEENS
Wintertime
1971

Not everyone possessed that type of ambition though. Rolo Smith's story was much too common where we were from.

Rolo's night had gone much different from others in the Ritz. It was just after 3:30 am when he stumbled out of the lounge and into winds that seemed much colder. He'd conversed with no old friends, made no allies, and met no beautiful women. In fact his 33 year old mind was so far gone it couldn't conceive thoughts of fame and fortune. His bones snapped and popped as he pulled his ratty wool coat closed and wondered why he could never find one with buttons. Not good, because the way things were shaping up he was looking forward to the coldest winter ever. He shook his head thankful that the ground was dry.

"Could be raining," he thought, as eyes watched him in the distance.

Moe, the Ritz's owner was also leaving the lounge. He stepped out the door and head toward his Lincoln Continental. "Shit!" he shouted before going back inside. Rolo decided to give it one more try and crossed the street. He pulled on the locked door and Moe came out seconds later with a brown paper bag. Rolo startled him and he let out a quick, shrill scream, higher than his already high pitched speaking voice.

"Whaah! Rolo, what the fuck! Nigga, you damn near got ya' ass shot fucking around out here." Moe was palming a little 22.

Rolo waved his hand nonchalantly.

"Shit man, you just looking for a reason to shoot a motherfucker."

Rolo had yet to get used to his relatives newfound wealth and paranoia.

"Seems like ever since you inherited that money you been acting brand new! C'mon man, do ya' cousin a solid and let me crash on that cot in the back? It's colder than a son-of-a-bitch out here! Kind of like you."

He couldn't resist. He knew the answer to the question before he asked it.

"No," answered Moe flatly, smirking and looking Rolo up and down. "What the fuck am I the Red Cross? Does this bag look like a fucking charity bell to you? I run a lounge, not a flophouse?"

"Aww man what the fuck do that got to do with anything? I'm your blood! Help ya' people out."

"People?" Moe looked around. "What people," he asked? "Am I fucking preacher? Where's my congregation? Look man, I don't owe you shit. I let you drink for free and I aint even fucking you!"

"Oh yes you are," said Rolo, disgustedly. "Nigga you gave me two funky ass beers and one shot of whiskey. I'm a motherfucking dope addict son, its gon' take more than that."

Moe said nothing. There was no arguing good logic. He reached into the bag and pulled out six or seven hundred dollars. He peeled off the singles, seventeen in all, and put the rest back in the bag.

"Here. Trip is busy in there now. Come back later and you can mop up."

Rolo snatched the dollars from him with one hand and punched him in the jaw with the other. Moe staggered from the blow.

"You a bitch," Rolo screamed. "You gon' need me one day and that shitty little gun aint gon' help you!"

Rolo ran away at full speed not wanting that shitty little gun to make him a liar. Moe rubbed his jaw almost amused as he watched his cousin sprint toward the subway.

"Ladies and gentlemen the nut has left the building!" He walked off fingering his keys and thinking; *"I wonder if that bitch ..."*

He never finished his thought. A gloved hand covered Moe's mouth from behind and a gun was forced into his back as a voice demanded;

"Be quiet nigga, and give me everything you got."

"Ok, take it easy, just be cool baby."

Those were Moe's last words. The gunman, for whatever reasons squeezed two in his back, grabbed the keys and bag, and then sped off in his car.

In the distance Rolo thought.

"I wonder if that bitch is shooting at me."

After nearly an hour Rolo walked down Fulton Street in the changing area of Bed-Stuy. By the 1970's, generations of prominent families had cut their huge twenty room brownstones into smaller units and were renting to the poorer ones that were moving to Brooklyn. The once noble gentry that lived there kept to tradition and gentrified other areas. Now this borough had a methadone clinic and a liquor store on one corner, and working class family units on the next. The clinics didn't open until 5:30 am but the one thing a fiend will be on time for is a fix. So every morning as the batteries of the city,—bus drivers, hospital and postal workers and janitor types,—awoke before day to begin their shifts, zombies too, crawled out from "under their rocks" as the mayor put it, scratching, coughing and looking for a "lil' pick me up" to get them started.

It was 4:45 on the corner of Fulton & St. James Place when Rolo slapped his hands together and blew into them. He sat on the stoop wondering what blessing God would grant him today. Yesterday he'd hustled up his own.

✳

Donald and Rolo Smith weren't related. They'd only known each other for the few months that Rolo had been at the clinic, but already they'd sized the other up. It rained overnight and was a dreary morning. The patients were glad to be inside even though the entire clinic smelled like a wet half-smoked cigarette. Donald hadn't slept much, at home his mother-in-law had been on his case all night nagging about everything.

"Bitch if you know so much, why you staying wit' 'cha daughter for? Huh?"

Donald had let the truth slip out, and before knew it both women were on his ass talking all kinds of shit. They took turns during the night; one slept while the other one talked. He'd already done a year inside and was in the last months of a parole sentence for a botched armed robbery. He had to be on the grill at 7:00 am and the two wouldn't stop bitching. That morning he saw Rolo in the corner in the clinic talking; they nodded at each other while listening to the sleepy voice of a nurse who'd been up all night bitching at her man. She was calling out names and was still in the E's when Donald dozed off.

"Tay-lor. Tay-lor."

"Right here, baby," Taylor shouted, rushing to the cart and waking Donald! *"Taylor!"* He thought. "Hey sweetheart. Ahh, I was over there talking to my man, 'aand', you aint call my name. *I'm Smith.*"

The nurse snapped.

"I called Smith! I'm on the T's now."

Donald stepped back.

"Alright baby, but I didn't get mine so ..."

"What Smith is you?"

"Uhh D, Donald Smith," he said groggily.

The nurse looked at him.

"What 'chu trying to pull? You checked right here, look!"

Sure enough there was an X in the box next to his name, right under Rolo Smith.

"What kinda shit is this," wondered Donald out loud? "Listen baby, I was talking to my man over there," said Donald pointing to no one. "I aint been up here."

Taylor swallowed his medicine and walked slowly to the door.

"When I looked out there you was sleep," said the nurse, twisting her lips. "However it go and come, it aint no extras." She point to a sign on the wall.

"I-Don't-Want-No-Extra!" Donald said, his voice rising with his fear of going the whole day without his medicine. "I aint been up here, that's what I'm trying to tell you now!"

"Don't be yelling at me! You won't get nothing tomorrow or the next day," she mumbled. "Mess with me."

"Stanking bitch," Donald mumbled back.

"Dopefeind, bitch! Ya' mammy is a stankin' bitch for having you."

Outside Donald saw Taylor look at Rolo and shake his head. A square and a smile were on Rolo's lips while he spoke.

"Playboy. Them bitches giving you a hard time in there, man?"

Donald thought he looked a little higher than he should have.

"Man fuck these ho's," he said sprinting for the bus and spending the rest of the day in pain standing over a hot ass grill.

That evening Donald's mother in law was still bitching. He needed a drink and wound up spending his last two dollars at a hole in the wall where all the down on their luck dudes hung out drinking cheap liquor.

"Man, I wish I had some mo' money. That'd solve all my problems," he told the bartender.

"Look here, I hate to tell you," said the bartender lying. He loved to keep up shit. "Ya' man Rolo was just in here trying to score. That's who suckered you this morning. I heard him telling the story to Barry. Hmph! That's ya' man though."

Donald was mad as fuck and knew the lounge up in Queens where Rolo hung out. He went to the crib, got his pistol and waited till past three in the morning for him to leave. The plan was to teach him a lesson. "It's about damn time," he said when he saw Rolo leaving the bar, but seconds later the sparkling knot Moe pulled out of the bag altered his plan.

"Shiit," he thought, *"my wish dun' come true."*

NEW YORK CITY
Brooklyn '71

It was 5:00 am when Rolo saw the Lincoln pulling up. He knew he'd pay for punching his cousin one day, but he didn't think it'd be this soon. The door opened and Donald ran up on Rolo, piece in hand. He hadn't seen the police car on the lookout for a stolen Lincoln Continental tailing him for the last five blocks. In a flash Rolo saw it all. His whole life. His cigarette fell to the ground as Five-O pumped Donald full of rounds. Donald had bought a bag of "Time Bomb" and gotten so high he couldn't believe his own eyes; he thought Rolo was shooting at him. For the second time that night he unloaded, blessing Rolo with an end to his pitiful existence and proving that the Lord works in mysterious ways. Four hundred dollars found its way into a policeman's pocket and what was left of the bag was entered into police custody.

All That Glitters …

Around the corner Gaietta Neece was startled, she'd been dreaming and thought she'd heard fire clappers, the kind that they'd pop year round on the island of Jamaica. Her boyfriend Paul's snoring reminded her of her whereabouts. She opened her eyes and looked at the clock; it was 5:02 am. Only an hour before her day began. She'd been sick most mornings for the last week and needed her rest. Outside there were sirens approaching, her eyes circled her spacious apartment before she shut them and went back to sleep.

She felt grateful to be there. This island had another kind of clappers, but she'd learned to keep on pushing on because in America the sky was the limit, and one way or another she'd soon have what she wanted.

JAMAICA
Kingston
1968

The time had come for Gaietta Neece to make a choice.—England or the States.—As for England, since they'd invaded and colonized her homeland in 1655 she was already a citizen. She'd visited an uncle who lived there a couple of times before.

"It's a fil'ty mess, Lon'don. Dem folks dere, mighty rude." She told Paul when they'd discussed the two. He, however, had seen things differently when he left for England over ten years before Gaietta would make her Exodus.

ENGLAND
London
1956

Paul was 22 years old and ready for a change of pace. He had a dream and was determined to follow it. He wasn't a soundboy singing songs of freedom and fighting for the honor of his people. Nor did preaching and singing in the church with his father appeal to him. He smoked, but the idea of sitting in the heat sweating and getting wasted on one of the spice plantations wasn't appealing either. Paul was fascinated by the "tele" and was determined to get on it some-how. He truly believed that if he, "work hard enough," and "do da rite ting" he would one day see his face on the BBC. Paul hopped a plane and immigrated to England, becoming one of the quarter million Jamaicans that heard London calling between 1950 & 1960.

On arrival he found that the area where he was to live was not the pristine and regal England that he'd heard about, but an old and dirty city with piss and vomit in every corner where grim looking foreigners called him names and tried to break his spirit. Yet everywhere he went he heard the sounds of marching charging feet. This country was going through a change, the time was right for revolution.

Paul refused to turn back, he was determined to blend in and change with it; his plan was to one day be a star.

He took jobs at hotels and restaurants; he worked all the shifts, when and wherever he'd be more inclined to meet the beautiful people. No matter what you wouldn't catch him leaving on the midnight train back to Zi'on."

Paul applied every few months to the BBC offices and by 1960 had finally been hired as a janitor. He gave his resume and portfolio to anyone who'd see them, but after four years he was no closer to making it than the day he arrived. He never showed it, but inside he was struggling. When Lafayette Ron Hubbard moved to England and headquartered his church of *Scientology* there, it garnered so much attention; Paul began to question his faith. He took his father advice and got on some praise the Lord shit.

"If I should die before I wake. O'ur Faddah ..."

JAMAICA
Kingston
1968

The Caribbean islands are lush and fertile. This one covers over 4200 miles of beautiful land, thick with fruit trees and greenery. It was much different than where we were from. But you know what they say about the color of the grass on the other side.

Prime Minister Michael Manley brought independence to Jamaica in 1962. Finally Jamaicans were to have their own country. Some took advantage of their freedom and began traveling to the neighboring isles. Those who landed in Cuba got a surprise when their passports were seized. It seemed that the Queen wanted to once again rid her territories of troublemakers. She banned American civil rights activists and political organizations from entering the island and Jamaicans began to realize that many times freedom is just an illusion.

"Selassie is Jah." "Ride the Kings highway." "Return to Zion."

In Kingston every wall was lined with graffiti. It was one way to make your voice heard. The voting majority supported the Jamaican Labor Party; they shouted their names from the rooftops and painted JLP everywhere. The party won by a landslide, and in West Kingston where Gaietta lived, a state of emergency was declared. Gaietta loved her home and family but at eighteen she knew there was little future for her there. Already all her time was divided between school and sewing for small clothing company owned by Massau, a longtime family friend. When her father was killed in a fishing accident Massau promised;

"As long as me com'pny run, me door is open to you."

Her mother had been working for the company since she was 14, and started teaching Gaietta at 7, by now she'd developed a keen eye for fashion and was one of their best seamstresses.

Whenever she could, she'd relax with a glass of Booth's rum, her Sensational Mytals records;—she loved Ska music—and her favorite Vogue and Cosmopolitan magazines. Downtown she'd see the women strutting in last season's fashions. They might be fooling their coworkers but nothing got past her. She could always tell the real from the fake and she'd let you know it.

It was that talent more than anything that would help to shape her decision, and one she'd try to pass down.

The television news broadcast the deportation of Dr. Walter Rodney back to his homeland. He was a University lecturer of Guyanese descent and a Movement advocate whose influence had become a problem. It was a hot topic during the days of the '68 fashion expo. As Gaietta and her mother browsed through the rows of garments looking for styles to copy she noticed Emane, one of the few black fashion models of her day chatting with some industry people. He pulled her mother closer to the crowd hoping to of meet her.

"It serves him right. I've recently returned from America and London. The atmosphere there is too fragile there to have an instigator like him stirring up trouble here. He is obviously educated enough to be speaking at the University level. He should have kept quiet and enjoyed Jamaica; that's what I plan to do."

The words were from Samantha a young, rail thin, model with freckles and fiery red hair. Gaietta watched as the others stood around giving similar opinions of a man who she'd come to respect. Emane said nothing. Gaietta let go of her mother's hand and approached the crowd. She wasn't loud or brash and Mama Neece couldn't make out her words, but by the looks on the faces in the crowd her opinion wasn't the popular one. *"She look good, stan'ding dere in da crowd. Na'tural,"* thought Mama Neece, hoping that her daughter hadn't caused a scene.

Gaietta returned and led her to another part of the expo.

Later as they browsed Emane sought them out to congratulate Gaietta on the things she felt she couldn't say. Full of smiles they exchanged information and two weeks later Mama brought home a letter from the Post Office. Gaietta's decision had finally been made, four days later, dressed in her finest; she said her goodbyes and boarded a plane.

NEW YORK CITY
LaGuardia Airport
1968

Her flight landed at 9:00 pm but Gaietta was to busy star gazing to hear the pilot's instructions. The view was far out. Surrounded by thousands of twinkling lights she imagined herself aboard the Apollo making her very own giant leap. On the ground the airport was jumping as the P.A.'s sounded with flight information and people from different countries hurried to catch a flight to somewhere. For nearly an hour she explored the airport, part of her afraid to step out into the great unknown, another part getting a feel for her new home, ___ until.

"May I help you ma'am?"

Gaietta smiled pleasantly at the officer blocking her path.

"No tank you, sir. Me jus loo'kin' around."

"You've been wandering around here for hours. Don't you have someplace to go?"

"What you mean ho'urs? Me plane jus land, not long a'go. Here is da tic'ket, see!"

She held out all her documents and the officer looked them over carefully.

"Jamaica," he said. "Well you aren't in Jamaica anymore lady, we got laws here against vagrants and loiterers. Beat it before I arrest you."

He pressed the papers flat into her stomach just under her breasts. Her hands covered his as she grabbed for them. The officer took the liberty of giving her breasts a squeeze before removing his hand and walking off.

Gaietta was young and attractive and dressed in a two piece Anne Kline knock-off that she'd made. She knew she looked good, far from a vagrant. She gathered her things and hailed a cab. Inside The Chairman of the Board sang, *"That's Life."*

Excerpt 5.

"Who is dis on da' radio," snapped Gaietta?

Like most people, she'd heard the music, but never paid attention to the lyrics.

"That is Frank Sinatra, ma'am. You like it," asked the cabbie watching her through his mirror?

"Who, you say? Si'na'tra. Dat old white man," she asked? She was frowning a little and hadn't noticed the driver at all, but the words to the song would remain forever in her memory. Tonight Old Blue Eyes made a new fan.

"Yeah mon, dey sells him on da se'cond floor at da Times Store. I know you been dere," he said, watching as her frown turned upside down. He grinned. "Is 'dat a smile me put on your face child?"

"What is your name," demanded Gaietta?

"Dey call me Paul," he answered now watching the road.

"Where are you from? How ya' know 'bout da Times Store? You aren't ser'ious, dat's your papa!"

On and on she went, long after they had reached her destination, a hotel in Brooklyn, recommended by Emane. She and Paul parted feeling like old friends, exchanging numbers and promising to keep in touch. It was the start of a long courtship and pretty soon you couldn't separate them. Paul told her all about the years he spent in London and the stars that he'd met. She told him about the JLP and gave him up close information on JLP and The Movement.

He told her about all the rock stars he'd seen play in dive bars and the sex, drugs, and strange behavior that were finding their way across the pond. She told him about how a chance meeting with Emane had led to a job in the Garment District. Paul even opened up to her about his attempts at being a movie star and how he didn't get far.

Gaietta was realistic in her encouragement, letting him know that dreams don't always come true. But as she'd learned, you have to, *"get back in the race."* That night she lay in her hotel room thinking about the incident with the policeman.

"He could not re'sist me. Him jus wan'na cop-a-feel."

BROOKLYN
1971

It was 6:32am; Paul lay awake in bed while Gaietta stood retching in the bathroom sink.

"Gaia, girl what's the ma'tter wit you? You got some'ting you want to tell me?"

"Paul, my love, may'be we better sit and talk."

Paul was excited when he heard the news, at thirty-seven and some change he was glad to hear that his seamen were still swimming. A child would carry on his family name and was perhaps the one thing that could help reunite him with his own father. When he'd left London his father tried desperately to get him to return to Jamaica where together they'd run the church. Again he declined his fathers offer. It was the beginning of fierce argument that would leave the two silent all these years.

Gaietta's love for Paul was true, but not strong. She thought about him and the way they met. She was so young he had to correct her when she mistook all the skyscrapers in New York for cathedrals. Where she was from the largest buildings were always churches. Paul had been a friendly face, one that reminded her of home, and at fourteen years her senior, sometimes the father she'd been missing. She wondered was that what she'd seen in him all along? Or was it the reason she kept her answer to his marriage proposal on hold; that and the fact that lately he'd been hinting at returning to Jamaica. *"Not hap'nin', papa."* The Garment district work was good, but more promising was her nursing classes at Queens College.

By Mid-March of 1972 Gaietta had just come from visiting her mother. She was quiet as Paul drove them home. She had some bad news to deliver.

"Sit down dar'ling, I have sum'ting to tell you," she said unpacking the bottles. One was her favorite Jamaican rum and the other a more precious bottle of Jamaican whiskey. Paul's heart sank when he saw it. His voice was barely audible.

"Gaia, what's go'ing on?"

"Darling, I saw your faddah while I was at home.

He's not doing well. Your mother gave me 'dis to bring to you. She wrote you a letter too."

Tears welled up in Paul's eyes as he read it. Gaietta kissed him and opened the whiskey.

Paul knew the bottle well; his papa had had it since he was twelve when he made his first batch of homegrown. She mixed the two and they took turns taking sips. In April he made the trip back home to be by his father's side.

A month and a half later, Gaietta lay watching a special on the Olympics in Munich. Moms was a month overdue and the baby was ready for the lights of New York, but was New York ready for the likes of him. He was close to shooting his way out when it happened; around 2:15 pm, Gaietta's water broke.

"Mercy, mercy," she cried! Paul was still away but they'd planned for this. She found the keys to the cab and drove herself to Cumberland hospital.

"Just stay calm Gaia, you can do it."

Hours later, she held her son, Thomas. Emane was in town doing shoots and came to be with her friend. Gaietta wished Paul was there; nevertheless she was overjoyed thinking about something his father had said when he'd given her his blessings.

"Come clo'ser me darling. Let me take a good look at you. You look good, heal'ty." He sat on the porch rocking in his chair and smiling. How is dat ba'by? do'ing?"

"Fine Papa, just fine," she answered. "It's me I'm wor'ried a'bout. It is all the time kick'ing, punch'ing, and keep'ing up a fuss. I t'ink he gonna be a bad boy."

Papa laughed heartily.

"Right you are me darling, the child will be a boy. But don't you wor'ry bout a 'ting girl. Jah is watching that one. He will be a spe'cial child, the con'quer'ing li'on. In the city, they will call him, *"King of Kings."*

1973

THE GREAT MIGR8TION

QUEENS

It was 1951 when Pops and his family arrived in New York. Swang was about ten; his sister Peanut, a few years older. Music was in his blood. All those late night sessions with Sonny and the rest of the boys must have touched him in some way. For as long as he could remember he'd heard the sounds of his father's guitar and harmonica. His mother would speak in wonder about, "them boys out back, smoking on Salvia and blowing in the bottle way past late, just'a howling at the moon. You got it in you too, don't think you don't. I'd be sitting out there with my sweet tea, and you be rocking from side to side, keeping time in the womb."

Pops had etched out a living selling swine and shine at a juke joint in the swamplands of Greenwood Mississippi, not far from the crossroad of highway 61&49 and close the town where Emitt Till got lynched.

"Long as they stay down by the river," said the locals, "they can shoot their baby's mamas and do whatever else they want. Just give us ours, and for damn sure don't be whistling at America's future."

The truth was where they were from wasn't the spot for a black man, especially one that had learned the arts, and smoked leaf too. Pops decided it was time they go. Damn them chains. The family traveled north to the city where it was written.

The Prophets

"The reckoning has drawn near for humankind.
As they turn away in heedlessness,
their hearts inattentive,
and keep their conferences secret,

as do those who act oppressively:
Is this but a man like yourselves?
Will you then take to sorcery
with open eyes?
'No,' they say, 'it is a jumble of dreams.'
'No, he made it up.'
'No, he is a poet.'
'Let him produce a sign like what was revealed
by the ancients.'
We have sent to you a Book
in which is a reminder for you all:
Will you not then comprehend?

Pops took to the streets and got busy doing him, hustling the club owners and band leaders. All it took was some talk about credentials, and a session.

"Yeah he played with them boys," they'd say; sure that he was official.

Jobs were plentiful at first, long nights stamping on sawdust stages and earthen floors in juke joints and chitlin' circuit clubs had become long nights of stomping stone in the after hours ceremonies and country homes of the eastern seaboard, Pops strumming frantically as their stars stood beside themselves providing the kind of entertainment that only their kind could enjoy. But in just a few short years playing music would become his hustle, by then every cat was picking up an axe and claiming to be born under a bad sign. Soon Pops had to do something he'd never dreamed of, and if you ask Swang, that's what did it. When his father took that job at Grand Central Station he all but stopped playing music, and when he did play," according to Swang, "It wasn't right no more."

By the time he was old enough to put it all into perspective Pops was just a shell. The only time his music had life now was on those occasions when he'd return home at 5:00am after a twelve hour shift of cleaning and taking shit. He'd sit alone and play Robert Johnson's, *I Put a Spell on you,"* and for a moment, both of them were taken back to the swamp and the placenta.

"I'm telling you baby", Swang would confess later, "The whole house would get cold."

*

Nobody knows for sure the origins of "The Blues"; the best estimates place them somewhere in the rural south of the early 1900's. That the chords, riffs and drunken, smoke filled tales of this nations hungry tired and poor's, violence, superstitions, and sexual bravado were the advent of rock and roll and American music is the one fact that most will agree on. Bluesmen were music's original bad boys. So bad in fact, that one of its earliest and most infamous stars, Robert Johnson is said to have waited on a moonless Mississippi night for Satan himself to come and tune his guitar. Whatever the truth may be, besides having quite the effect on the "byrds", this "devil music" was perhaps the greatest influence in the 'British invasion of the '60's. By 1965, the music, myth and folklore of blues legends like Robert Johnson, Robert Lockwood and their pupils had found a new home in the streets of London. Arriving on the backs of "the greatest recording orginisation in the world" the Beatles crept ashore in the first wave, and while they were surly it's stars with their suits and pretty boy looks, they failed to satisfy the appetites of America's hooligans, mischief makers and thugs. So for them a second wave was formed, and this time they arrived aboard a "Starship", and from it emerged a "golden god."

If Robert Plant was Thor, pounding his hammer and driving ships to new land, then Jimmy Page was certainly "Odin, the supreme god", guiding their fates and pulling the strings.

Described as "'Jimmy Magic Fingers Page, Grand Sorcerer of the Magic Guitar,'" he "grew up almost alone" in a "comfortable house" and "doesn't remember having any playmates until he was five." A self-described loner, he taught himself how to play the electric guitar and by 1960 was considered an "adept." Those two, along with John Paul Jones, and John Henry Bonham formed, Led Zeppelin, a group that for over ten years invaded cities around the globe, putting it down night after night, arguably, harder than anyone else had before them, but rumored tales of decadence and mayhem chased them like wolves out for blood. It's been said that the blokes "sustained themselves" on the road by drinking vaginal secretions direct from the source and by "eating women and throwing their bones out of windows." Whispered were tales of "sex magic and endless orgies" where dimepeices and bustdowns were "publicly banged on tabletops." "One girl raved dementedly about the guitarist's prowess with a whip." "But there was always something else whispered about Led Zeppelin, something more sinister." All this, and "during their decade long prime … they were "the biggest band in the world."

QUEENS
1971

By now both Swang's parents had passed on, and Peanut had married a local barber named Q. She'd learned to do hair and at Q's urging, gotten certified. Together they opened shops a few doors down from each other and did pretty well with their three little girls. Every now and then when Swang had some free time, or when his pockets was low—which was usually one in the same—he would drop in. Q would always have something interesting to bless him with. Even back then the shop was where everyone hung out, putting a hundred on ten, and comparing conspiracy theories. Brothers standing outside selling bean pies, hotter than a motherfucker in them black suits. In the middle, that red and white barber pole, and on the other side, pimps, hotter than two motherfuckers, with a ho named 'polly' on one arm, and 'esther', on the other, both of them selling jiggable pies. But all was well in them days. Swang would step out into the summer heat to smoke his *Kools* and blow his trumpet. That was out of respect, back then it wasn't illegal to smoke inside. Where we were from you just had respect for that man or woman sitting next to you and they had love for you too. "Each one, teach one." That's what Q and his Islamic brothers would say. He'd converted right after The Champ. Back then you had two types of revolutionaries, radicals and teachers. 'Movement' cats they called 'em. Q was a teacher, they got the least action. The pretty brown round loved players, not revolutionaries. So for Swang that was it.

His pop had passed his talents down and Swang had learned to pull strings quick. Hustling was second nature. During his teens he'd learned to play almost every instrument used on the jazz circuit. He'd given blues up a while back.

"I couldn't walk that path with a clear conscious after seeing what I did down south and what it did to my Pop." He'd told that to his wife on their first date.

Besides, blues had long since turned into something else. It wasn't raw no more. The mainstream had taken it and turned it into R&B. Then cats like Fats Domino, Elvis Presley and Little Richard got hold to it and transformed it into something else altogether. Swang needed that boom-bap. Jazz was smooth but it still had an edge to it. There was something spiritual about it, and the jazz clubs stayed packed with prime 'round'. Swang gave props. He studied all the greats, Miles Davis, King Louis Armstrong, Dizzy Gillespie, and Byrd. But his man, the one he learned the most from next to his Pops, was Duke "Elegant" Ellington. "A gentleman, master musician, and more importantly, a traveler and a scholar.

As Swang neared that turning point that blues singers sing about and enlightened men long to reach, he'd managed to put together a tight little house band for a local club.

Duke Ellington was ending a successful tour of The U.S.S.R. and word had it that he'd be performing at the Lincoln Center in New York. Swang had to get on that bill. This was his chance to put it down for one of the greats. He took a page from his pops book and put his mouthpiece and hustle game to work for him but weeks passed with no word. "I'll see what I can do," was all he heard. Then days before the show, he received a blessing.

"This is who calling? You serious? No sir. Yes sir, we will. Thank you." He grabbed his hat and hurried down to the shop to share the news with his family.

"Peanut, where's Q at?"

"He'd better be down at the shop," she answered plainly. She struggled to keep a straight face as she and her client went back to discussing Jet and Ebony magazine founder and Publisher of the year, John H. Johnson.

"Uhh huh, I aint even got to ask now, you could never hold water."

"Ask me what 'Wang Wang'? What are you talking about?"

Swang tapped his foot and looked away. 'Leila', as she was now called burst out screaming and hopping from foot to foot.

"Q didn't tell me until this morning. He said he'd been working on it for a while but he was worried that if he told me it would get back to you."

Her client was worried about getting burned with the hot comb.

"He was right. Damn girl, I didn't know those Fruit of Islam dudes had pull like that. I didn't think this was their type of thing." Excited, he hugged his big sister and took an empty seat across the way.

"Well Wang, they are doing the security and you know your man *is* a Shriner."

"Whaaat? I thought I knew every thing there was to know about the man, you learn something new everyday."

"Who is your man, if you don't mind me asking, _____ *'Wang Wang?'*"

It was only then that he saw her smile. It startled him for a moment, beauty so pure. Any other day that would have been the first thing he noticed. He stayed cool; barely caring that she'd called him Wang.

"My man is the one and only Duke Ellington. Who's *your* man, if *I* may ask?" Her cheeks turned rosy. She hadn't expected that. He stood up quickly and helped her from the stylist chair.

She smiled at Leila.

"Thanks. How much do I owe you?"

"Ten dollars for you," she answered.

The client reached for her sweater and purse hanging on the coat rack. Swang got to them first and handed them to her, accidentally knocking his hat to the floor.

"Thanks again," she said softly through her grin. "Duke Ellington, huh? I guess I should have known from the hat."

Leila chuckled, she'd teased her little brother for years about that hat.

"You *are* a jazz fan *'Ms'*. Fatima? I hope that's right, you never answered."

"Yes, to both questions." She zipped her purse. "How'd you know my name?"

"You work at the bookstore in Harlem," answered Swang. "Q took me once."

"Really, I don't remember you."

"I didn't come in."

"Oh, I see," she said turning toward the door.

Sirius followed.

"Can I walk you somewhere, anywhere?"

"I suppose. If your sister says it's Ok."

They waited for Leila's approval.

"Ya'll both grow," she said waving to them. "That's a lady you're with Wang, treat her like one."

"OK, *mama*. I'll be right back. I still got to see Q and thank him, twice now!"

Three days later the Lincoln Center was in full swing and Swang's set went off without a hitch. His band played a medley of classics that showed his appreciation for the music that he'd dedicated his life to. Fatima stood with Q and Leila, shining, with her hair in a bun and dressed like a queen. She turned red all over when Swang named a number that he'd been working on after her.

After giving Q a thousand and one thanks and showering his queen with hugs and kisses, the only thing left to do on this night was meet the Duke. Swang made his way backstage with hopes of meeting the man he had long admired. Outside his dressing room were some of New York's elite, politicking and waiting to rub palms with the man of the hour. If it hadn't been for Q's connection with F.O.I. he wouldn't have made it this far. He began to wonder if the meaning of life that had escaped him for so long was taking shape before him. He'd always listened to Q and his brothers at the shop. He agreed with some of their teachings but didn't know if he could live by the rules of their faith. *"Shit, bacon & pork chops taste good!"* But the more he really listened to their message the more the beauty and simplicity of Islam became clear.

As he stood deep in thought the dressing room door opened and the hallway brightened as Mr. Elegant himself emerged. The crowd swayed as everyone big and small tried to squeeze in a moment with the man. Somehow Swang got pushed to the back in the crowd.

"Please excuse me, but we must clear this area, Mr. Ellington is due onstage." One of the FOI he'd spent time with at the shop grabbed his hand as he made his way to the front. He whispered something in The Dukes ear and he turned around looking pleased.

After a few words, Swang watched in awe as Mr. Edward Kennedy Ellington ascended the stairway to spend some quality time with his mistress.

"What did you say to him, Singh?"

"I told him the truth. I said that I had a young man who was interested in joining our Order. You wouldn't make me out to be a liar would you," asked Singh as he cleared the hall of hanger-ons?

"Naw, Singh, I wouldn't do that."

Just then Swang noticed the door to The Dukes dressing room ajar. He ducked in and tried to savor the moment. Looking around at all the instruments and clothes, he fought the urge to touch. On the valet table lay three books, The Bible, The Qu'ran and a journal. He fingered through the journal until he came to a page titled, *"GOUTELAS JOURNAL, 1966"*

<u>Excerpt 6.</u>

The clapping of the audience brought him back. He closed the journal, shut the door behind him, and rushed back to the ballroom just as the orchestra began playing, "Sophisticated Lady."

He apologized for the wait as he led Fatima to the dance floor.

"Sorry baby."

"Its Ok, how did it go? Did you meet him?"

"Yeah, everything went just like I prayed it would."

"That's great. I'm glad to see you happy."

Swang pulled her close and gazed into her eyes, loving her energy. At that moment there was no one on the floor but those two.

"Do you ..."

She put her finger to his lips. "Shhh. Yes. You know I do."

QUEENS
March
1973

"Naw Lisa, he didn't show up tonight, I was hoping you'd tell me where he was."

"I don't know Swang. The no good nigga said to meet him here after rehearsals!"

He laughed at the thought of somebody else catching hell like he did and wondered what was wrong with Kelly. It was the second night this week he hadn't shown up for rehearsals. He had no time for screw ups. He'd recently pressed his first album and was scheduled to play some out of town dates. He wanted things to be trump-tight and it was evident he needed a new sax player.

"I could see it in that cat' eyes," he thought, *"he was on some other shit."*

In the meantime, Lisa ran on and on about getting rid of her man.

"Uh, uhhn, Swang. I can't have this. My man is going to r-e-s-p-e-c-t—me."

Lisa was popular and respected around the club scene; clean and curvy with a caramel complexion and a pretty nice voice, she had a reputation for being a straight shooter. She'd been in an on and off again relationship with a married Harlem dealer named Peebles who'd recently been shot during a deal gone bad in Central Park. Everyone felt badly about it. Peebles was a cool brother, but now playas had their sights set on Lisa, and here was Kelly fucking up.

"Hey Swang, how come you never tried to hit on me?"

"Give me a chance," he said, "I'm working up my nerve, slow and steady wins the race."

They laughed.

"Slow down, Lisa, I'm sure Kelly's got a good excuse. But when you see him tell him *we* need to talk."

He moved steadily putting everything in its place, closing up the studio and trying to calm Lisa down. She talked as if she was really through with Kelly and he knew the last thing any man needed was to loose his girl and his gig in the same night, so feeling some pity he tried to save one.

"C'mon Lisa give the brother a chance. Let's go downstairs and have a drink, maybe Kelly will show up."

He turned off the lights and watched as her hips swayed down the stairs, thinking;

"Allah, have mercy."

By the spring of 1973 some changes had occurred. Swang' s name had changed, Swang's faith had changed, and a prophet was developing in the womb of Fatima Ali.

It was late and Sirius's rehearsals were normally over around eleven. Fatima had been pacing the floor waiting for her husband to arrive at their apartment in Queens. She lay down on the couch with the new bestseller, *Dr. Atkins New Diet Revolution.*

"This guy is out of his mind," she thought, *"this will never take off."*

She read some more and struggled to stay awake listening to Bill Withers sing *"Use Me"* on the radio.

Excerpt 7.

Minutes later the sound of keys jingling at the door sprang her into action. She threw the book down and looked at the clock. It was 1:20am.

She didn't know where Sirius had been, but since he'd been fumbling with the keys for nearly five minutes she had a good idea of what he'd been doing. At three months pregnant Fatima was still feisty and wouldn't be made a fool of. Her sudden movements startled the baby and both were prepared for the worst when she opened the door.

"You drunk motherfucker. Where have you been? And don't even think about lying, I can smell that shit all over you! You know what time it is?"

"Baby calm down, I, I …"

"You, you … you drunk and high, that's what you are! You come in here all times of the morning smelling like perfume and shit. I know you aint been out cheating on me and I'm sitting in here pregnant."

She stormed towards the kitchen.

Sirius gave up on explaining and began ducking as plate after plate smashed into the walls.

"Man," he thought, "broads sure do some dumb shit."

He grabbed her arms and begged her to stay calm. Just then he slipped on some broken glass and they both fell to the floor knocking over a chair.

"Damn girl," he shouted, "look what you dun' did. You bout as crazy as a fucking road lizard. You dun' cut your arm up and shit. You gon' mess around and have the police up here." He tried to reason with her between her sobs. "You aint even listening to me, baby. All I did was help that girl Lisa into a cab. Shit! Kelly didn't show up to rehearsal and …"

Yada, yada, yada.

"… so she was drunk and I had smoked one, and that was it. I told her to give Kelly another chance. I flagged her taxi and she gave me a little thank you hug …"

Fatima scowled as she tended to the cut on her arm.

"Lil' 'thank you hug,'" she said under her breath. "Lying-ass nigga."

"I heard that shit. Aint nobody lying to yo' ass."

Sirius was picking up glass and wondering if she'd purposely broken the cheap dishes.

"I tell you something else," he said, "and you can take it as a lie if you want. Tomorrow we going down to the clinic because we can't afford no baby; plus you don't want a baby by a liar no way."

The more things change …

The next afternoon the two sat quietly in the clinic waiting to call the others bluff, Sirius pretending to read the pamphlets and Fatima trying hard not to cry. He wanted to reach out and hug her but it was her jealousy that had brought them here. *"She's gotta learn a lesson,"* he thought, *"I aint gon' be going through this."*

When the nurse called them Fatima didn't move. Her eyes swelled as Sirius got closer to the desk. A veteran nurse who'd seen this game too many times before tore up their forms as she looked at him and said;

"That's somebody's life y'all playing with."

Sirius took her words and ran with them.

"C'mon 'Tima', lets go home."

Inside the womb a prophet rocked from side to side rejoicing at his near miss; he couldn't wait to get out and begin his reign.

Later that year after some complications in July, Fatima gave birth in the month of September. Sirius held his wife's arm and coached her while tears streamed down his face at the sight of his first born son. The hospital staff cleaned him off and placed him in the arms of his father who made a crack about his good looks. The nurses laughed and asked Fatima for baby Ali's name. She'd taken her husband Muslim name but had kept her own faith. She looked warmly at her family and though she'd been reluctant at first, now that she'd seen him with her own two eyes she knew the name his daddy had chosen for him fit.

"His name is Malik."

That evening when the commotion was over the new mother held her child and prayed for a blessing. She lifted the Qu'ran from Sirius's lap and recite:

The Believers

"Successful indeed are the believers.
These are their heirs who will inherit Paradise …
Verily We created man from a product of wet earth;
then placed him as a drop of seed in a safe lodging;
then fashioned We the drop of clot,
then fashioned We the clot a little lump,
then fashioned We the little lump bones,
then clothed the bones with flesh,
and produced it as another creation.
So blessed be Allah, the Best of Creators …"

1974

THE GREAT MIGR8TION

NEW YORK CITY
Cumberland Hospital
1969

The overhead light was bright, beneath it on a cold industrial table Diane laid simultaneously staring at it and slipping into darkness. Her breathing was heavy and the doctor's instructions barely resonating, but she didn't need them. The experience is one that you never forget. She felt sedated, she'd heard the whisperings and wanted out, out of this room, out of this situation, and as much as she didn't want to admit it, out of this life. This time if she crossed over she didn't want to come back. For years her situation seemed hopeless and this was guaranteed to make things worse. She shook her head and shut her eyes tight. She wasn't one for religion, she didn't know any scriptures and had never read any surahs or psalms. She didn't believe in them but for this occasion she formed her own, she had to do something, the pain was unbearable and Diane needed it all to end. *"How the fuck did I get here,"* she thought.

"Goddamn this shit! Lord, or whoever you are, if you think anything about me ..."

BROOKLYN
1949

How indeed? Twenty years earlier Diane had asked her mother about their roots and received an answer that was much too common where we were from.

35

"I'ma tell you like my mama told me, we lost all our history and heritage in the holds of them slave ships that brought us from Africa. And if any pride or self worth did make it across it was beaten out of 'us when we got here. We are the children of free people that were captured and sold into slavery. Violence and bondage were all our people were taught in America, and all that you know is all that you can teach." Florence snickered. "You go to school tomorrow and tell Mrs. Crabtree I said that." Diane nodded, "Now I don't know about no ancestors and all that but I can tell you about me and mine, but this aint for no classroom or no teacher, this is for you and you only. My mother never knew for sure, but she always suspected her father was Mr. Davies, a Mormon man that *her* mama worked for. Now as for your father …"

NEW YORK STATE
White Plains
The late 1930's

Florence Smarter was twenty-three the year she met Aaron Prentiss Wade, He was a good man, educated for his day and full of life. He worked at the Davies owned lumber mill, and fell in love with Florence the moment he laid eyes on her. She was attracted to him too but neither could ever show it. Aaron was disciplined and patient enough to tame what stirred in the pit of his stomach whenever Florence was around. For months he pretended not to notice her, stealing glances only when it was safe too. He'd catch her doing the same. Heated nights twisting, turning, and soiling the sheets were common for them both, but rarely did they speak and each remembered vividly their first kiss. After that tension between the two became unbearable as they await Mr. Davies annual business trip out of town. Aaron's mind was elsewhere and his work around the mill had suffered as a result. None of it had escaped the eye of Mr. Davies.

When the special night came everything went as planned. Inside the mill the two mated like cicadas, this moment was what they'd lived for and for it someone would die. Outside the air was thick and heavy as crickets chirped loudly under the full moon, inside their eyes were watching God. Aaron's droning made it impossible for them to hear the footsteps approaching. The door flung open as the two lay panting and groping one another. Aaron got up and reached for his clothes, never seeing the fire in the eyes of Mr. Davies. Florence knew it well; she ran at him full speed, trying to buy her lover some time. Mr. Davies swung and broke his daughter's nose; she screamed, fell down and lost consciousness. Aaron rushed him. Florence came too as they struggled seeing nothing but red. Red covered her face and the floor. With the taste of blood in her mouth she reached for the wall and a small red axe. Moments later, nude and covered in blood, she straddled the body on the floor. Aaron was watching his life go down. This was not his plan.

"Florence, what we gon' do," he asked? "Somebody had to hear all this, somebody knows he's here. We gotta go baby. We gots to go!"

Florence was in shock screaming and waiving wildly. "Go away! Just go!"

Arron went to console her. He fell to his knees, gave her a series of quick kisses, then he placed his hand on her shoulder. She touched it gently. Aaron put his other hand on her bloody belly and then wiped it in the dirt.

"You've got to run Aaron. Now! ___ Go!"

So much can happen in a moment. A man dies. A child is conceived. A man looses his freedom, and a woman gains hers. That moment was the closest Diane Smarter ever came to her father.

After the incident Florence found herself the center of attention. Aaron was blamed and the lynch mob spent weeks hunting him.

When Diane was born Florence became an outcast. A truck driver named BJ who delivered to the mill took pity on her. He also saw this as his chance to take up with one of the forbidden Smarter women. They moved to New York city, married, and had three children in six years. As they grew so did BJ's hatred of his wife's ways. At sixteen years her senior he was no match for what boiled in Florence's blood. She was tired of her husband's long trips and BJ was enraged when he found out she'd been getting passionate with someone else; but as we know, Florence was a fighter. The out of control look in her eyes when she slashed BJ's arm with his own straight razor assured him that the rumors were true. He decided then that he wouldn't share the same fate and hit the road leaving her and their four children alone.

BROOKLYN

By 1954 Diane was almost fifteen. That year Florence gave birth to her second sister. Diane wasn't happy. She'd become more mother than sibling and with four kids to care for there was no time left in the day for her happiness. Another child meant another mouth to feed, one less item for her at the store, and one more head to do. Diane was through. She'd seen her mother cry and scream herself to sleep at night after too much bourbon, Diane could never be sure if she was longing for the loves she'd lost or cursing them. She decided at the tender age of 15 she'd learned enough to begin her own chapter. She got it from her mama, how to get a man, and the things Florence didn't teach Diane had learned by watching; everything including what she believed were Florence's mistakes.

"My mother cares too much. She cares about the past and the things she did. She cares what these men think about her. She cares if they love her or not."

Diane swore that she would never fall into that trap. The whole world could hate her she was young and beautiful and would make it through. That year she met a Martin, a 19 year old Annapolis naval recruit on leave in New York. She liked him, he was different from the city boys she knew; he was tall and muscular, honest and caring, and best of all, a virgin. A week after Diane gave it up; Martin asked Florence if he could marry her. Even though he was polite and respectful, Florence didn't approve until her daughter explained to her about the extra money she'd be receiving and the one less mouth she'd have to feed, only then did she agree to sign the papers.

Diane gave birth to her first son, Evret, in the summer of 1955 and quickly adjusted to life as a wife and mother. She'd been raising children all her life; now she had her own, and as one of the younger wives, the others treated her special. Money wasn't a problem and they spent most days browsing the local department stores supposedly hunting for sales, but it was really to kill the boredom.

Martin was working long hours and taking on extra duty assignments trying hard for a promotion. When he was home and felt up to it, Diane would let loose on him, three or four times was nothing and Martin was delighted to be on the receiving end. At last Diane was happy and truly missed him when he was gone; she'd get hot just seeing her husband walk up in his uniform, and lately she could even relate to her mother. Then came the birth of their second child in '59, a baby girl they named Shirley.

Just now able to drink legally, Diane had dropped out in the ninth grade and had two kids. Sex, like it often does, had started to loose its hold on the young couple as they found themselves no longer *playing* house. Martin had taken long duty assignments in Hawaii leaving the family alone for months in the small military town. Shopping didn't cut it anymore, and extra money was scarce since Shirley was born. Diane was going stir crazy and in the afternoons when the kids were at daycare she'd hang out in town with some locals who sold weed and such, the whole time getting closer to a young dealer named Anthony. They'd spend days joking and wasting time. Soon he was coming over after she put the kids to bed listening to music and smoking. Then Martin came home with the news.

"Diane we need to talk. You been cheating on me in my own damn house? What the fuck Diane? The neighbors tell me you been in the yard smoking marijuana. What if somebody reported us? I'm up for a promotion, I've told you about that!"

"Martin, I aint never cheated on you. We got kids. I aint gonna disrespect our house like that. Yeah, I had some company and I was smoking outside, but that's because I didn't want it around the kids. What do you want me to do? You leave me here for months at a time, what do you expect me to do?"

"I don't want to hear it Diane. You know this has been a long time coming anyway. You lay around here, you don't work, you don't go to school, you don't do shit. I …"

"You what," screamed Diane, seeing things clearly. The four month duty assignments, the lack of sex, all the little comments since Shirley was born. She hadn't seen it before but maybe that was because she didn't want to. This moment hurt, yet it felt familiar. She'd seen it all before and sworn that it would never be her.

"Who is she," Diane asked calmly?

Martin took the next hour confessing and explaining all the feelings he was harboring. He cared for her and he loved his kids, but he was moving up and he wanted someone who was moving with him. She didn't even have a high school diploma. He was headed places that she couldn't follow but a young woman he'd met in Hawaii could. He'd promised to help as much as possible and take care of his kids, but his admission was inevitable.

"Diane, I want a divorce."

"You uppity-ass nigga, go to hell, and take your slanty-eyed bitch with you. I don't want nobody who don't want me. You just take care of your kids. You can have your fucking divorce. Shit! I can always get a man."

That was true, but there was also truth in what he'd said. Diane put that out of her mind.

"I'll get through."

Diane left the house and went straight to the block, leaving her children and that life behind. That night Tony took her to his mother's house where they got high and had sex until the sun came up. It was like that for the next two months until things were set for her return to Brooklyn.

Back in N.Y. the eight people cramped into a two bedroom apartment easily became better acquainted. Florence was waiting tables at a 24 hr diner in Times Square. After a few weeks she started dating the owner, Melvin. Melvin was an older man; he'd never been married and had no kids so he did for both of theirs regularly. Diane was happy to be back around familiar faces, happy her children were getting to know their aunts and uncles and happy knowing that as bad as New York may have seemed then, it was the city of dreams and anything could happen. Still she couldn't help but think maybe Martin was right, maybe her future was limited; but like clockwork, every couple of weeks Anthony would come to town with the cure for her worries. Diane had written and explained the game to him. After a month or two he decided to open up shop on Fulton. They'd rent a one room spot to chill for a few days and he always left her with enough money and weed to get through till the next time. Pretty soon it was taking more and more to ease her mind. Soon an occasional bump of coke became a weekly hit; then twice a week, "just to get through" she'd say; then more and more until at last it was all she could think about. Now she had two secrets that were getting harder to hide.

Anthony had saved up and decided to move to Brooklyn. He never told her he just popped his ass up one day and said, "Come on, I want to show you something."

"Something," was a one bedroom apartment he'd gotten a few blocks away. Diane had always seen Anthony as just "a young nigga, *with some good dick*," but this move gave her that glimmer of hope she needed.

Now she thought that maybe they could make something out of this. Melvin gave her a job working nights at the diner and the kids would shuttle back and forth between Florence's apartment and hers. One night, after too much malt liquor she decided to break the news about the three periods and the doctors' appointments she'd missed. Anthony had just finished bagging up. He sat there counting money and looking out the window. His back was turned and Diane couldn't see his face.

"What do you plan to do," he asked.

"It's up to you."

"Yo Diane, how you gone leave it up to me?" Anthony sounded annoyed and frightened. "If you was gon' do that you should have told me a long time ago. And what about your sniffin', yo."

Diane was ashamed and put her face in her hands.

Tony scoffed. "Thought I didn't know?"

"I promise I'll stop. I aint gon' do that shit no more, Tony, I swear!"

They made up and for the next few months all seemed to go well as they pre-pared for the arrival. Diane kept her promise to stop sniffing. It was almost easy now that she saw a light at the end of the tunnel. She figured that the sight of her stomach getting rounder with each day would broaden Tony's view on children. In her fifth month he brought home a stroller and crib. She took the night off; they celebrated with some Boones wine and talked about what they'd name the child.

In the seventh month he gave her money for clothes and a bassinet. Florence and Diane spent the day shopping and picking out things before she went to work that night. The next morning when she got home she knew instantly that something wasn't right. Tony was gone, more importantly, the coffee canister that he kept his stash in was gone. It was cloudy that day and Otis Redding's, *Pain in My Heart*, played on the radio. In the back of her mind she'd expected something like this, and in the back of the medicine cabinet she kept her remedy. She reached into her pocket and peeled off a dollar, rolled it up, and sat on the toilet sniffing, crying, and wondering if there really was a curse on the Smarter women.

Less than two months later Diane gave birth to her second daughter. Mallory was just four pounds at birth and the pain of the delivery was unbearable. As soon as she was born she started crying and the crying never stopped. The doctors recognized her pain. They gave Florence custody of the baby and Diane eleven months in a rehabilitation center where everyday she vowed that whatever happened, Mallory would be her last child.

LOUISIANA
New Orleans
Mardi Gras '69

With it's secrets, mysteries, and cultures so thickly mixed; to many it represents the dish that it's most famous for. In the 18th century, French, Spanish, Haitian and Jamaican immigrants came to New Orleans and brought with them what some would call "odd" religious practices. People call it "the wicked city," destined for a fate like Babylon, and *Mardi Gras* is its week long celebration of the rites and practices of the Old World.

"Girrrl, did you see that? It was halfway down his leg."

"And thick as a baby's arm," Diane said laughing and sipping her 'hurricane.'
"But you sure it was a *he*. I couldn't tell."

"Girl you thought I was playing when I told you how it was down here. This is like my fifth or sixth year coming, I love it. I come down here and let it all hang out," explained her girlfriend Pamela, collecting another handful of beads. She'd worked at the cheese factory with Diane for just under a year. She and Diane got along well.

"You need a vacation girl. You got to get out and have some fun. The same ol' thing will drive anyone crazy."

She'd preach that to Diane day in and day out. Soon *that's* what drove her crazy.

Diane had lived a model, albeit mundane life since leaving rehab. The counselors had set her up with a steady job and she'd enrolled in night school. Sometimes she'd take Shirley and Mallory to the movies or the park, but beyond that and the occasional card party at Melvin's place, life was work, school and home. She was glad that she'd taken Pamela up on her offer. She'd only been here for a few hours but already she was feeling the whole southern scene. She was seeing things for the first time with clear and open eyes. Come late afternoon and all the excitement was taking a toll on them. The two decided to stop at *Pat O'Brian's*, famous in the French Quarter for crawfish.

"Pam, you been down here all them times and you aint never tried these things."

"Yeah I tried 'em before, but they aint all that to me. Shit, They aint nothing but baby lobsters anyway and lobsters aint shit but ocean roaches, you ever turned 'em over and looked at them."

"Shut up, girl, I aint trying to hear that. If that's true, these the best bugs I ever had. You want some," asked Diane, tossing aside the shells?"

"Yeah bitch, gimme some, I aint did shit but drink since we got here. I better put something in my stomach. Look at they beety lil' eyes. Ughh!"

They laughed, ate, and discussed the night's plans between bites. Pamela had several friends that she'd hook up with when she came to town. One for whatever zone she was in. She had her swamp friends; she'd slide down there and hang out after hours. Then there were the regulars, tourists who came in each year from cities across America for the festivities, good for cruising the Quarter at all times of the day and night looking for another soul to open up with. It was easier to make friends and drink for free at two in the morning than in the middle of the day. She'd come across some society types too, the elite of New Orleans, with more than enough old money to keep her interested and coming back There was something about them she could never quite put her finger on. The top layer was covered with politeness and etiquette, but underneath the surface they seemed just a little, dangerous. Tonight they were headed to one of their parties.

The mansion was loosely fashioned after Rennes-Le-Chateau in the South of France and it's been said that The Duke of Orleans himself would be honored to reside there. It was equipped with a dungeon and surrounded by gardens, groves and a moat to help accommodate guests or unwanted visitors. It was now owned by *frere Macons* of its Aristocratic designers, *The Valois*,—aka The Kings—and it was a notorious meeting place for a groups ranging from Heptasophs to the Hellfire Club.

Jack Lilly or J.L. as he was known to most was a 31 year old assistant to Pierre de Louis, who headed the N.O. chapter of The Kings. As far back as J.L. could remember all he ever wanted to be was a King cruising around N.O. in a luxury car doing as he pleased. Whatever The Kings wanted they could have.

J.L. knew this for a fact because many times he was the one making the deals go through. A hustler. However things may have seemed to the untrained eye, these were the shot callers in this city. Modern-day Vikings with the bloodlines of Norse and Frankish royalty, there was not a continent on earth where they didn't do business or own assets. The world really was their oyster and unlimited wealth allowed members young and old to buy *anything* with a price. J.I.'s background would never allow him true King status and when his non-society friends questioned his loyalty he'd go on and on about how he resented his employers; but on the down low, he worshipped them and the titles they held. And some would say, "why not!" Not many men with black-blood in their veins could do the things that J.L. did or go to the places that he went. It was the 1960's and he was driving a Rolls Royce; fucking white women, black women, *all* women. His favorites were the ones with olive skin and wavy hair. His wardrobe was top notch and he attended most events with at least one beauty on his arm. For a long time life had been sweet for J.L.; but as he'd soon learn, all success has to be earned.

"Galileo nor DaVinci, himself could not have charted a body as heavenly as hers, yet her walk tells me that she is no angel. Who is that enchanting creature?"

"Her name is Luna, My Lord. During relations she's an equestrian worthy of a Lippizan. I purchased her at a hostel in Palermo nearly four years ago, she was only fourteen and already she'd learn to love in seven different languages."

Lord Ophiuchus rubbed his hands together slow and deliberately. "Yesss, her mother was surely gifted with sight to name her so fittingly. She lights a fire deep within." Pierre agreed and raised his glass to Ophiuchus.

"But I must inform you, My Lord, her appetite is quite voracious, especially when chasing the dragon which she's also developed a healthy appetite for. I couldn't be troubled so I used her as a payment to one of my associates, a Moor of sorts who shares a common taste."

"Mmm. Interessssting. No matter," said Ophiuchus, staring lasciviously, infatuated by Luna's curves, "I must have her."

"As you wish My Lord, I have a hall on the second level already prepared."

Pierre de Louis moved quickly through the crowd greeting guests of the Chateau and making the necessary arrangements. Lord Ophiuchus was not a man to be kept waiting. He was of royal Dutch ancestry and moved the same circles as another royal, "Bernhard Julius Coert Karel Godfried Pieter, Prince of the

Netherlands and Prince of Lippe Biesterfeld who was rumored to head a "nameless" and powerful group.

J.L. was not pleased with his instructions. He knew the things that Luna would be doing and couldn't picture them being done to his favorite.

All of the women were too high to care. J.L. whispered his feelings into Luna's ear as he and the other women he'd gathered climbed the spiral staircase.

Midnight was approaching in the garden of good and evil. Pamela and Diane had been enjoying themselves with the other guests but throughout the evening Diane's attention had drifted to a small tent set up on the far end of the grounds, on it was a sign that read: "Madame Krusemark: Palms Read and Fortunes Told."

She'd always had an interest in the art of divination. But friends and family considered astrology and things of that nature taboo. Krusemark made Diane uneasy, but worse was her assistant, a Creole woman, dark and heavyset with bright grey wandering eyes that never blinked. Krusemark called her, Gypsy. Diane had spotted her roaming the hills and talking to the trees between telling people things that they wanted to know. As far as she could tell Gypsy was fluent in three languages.

"Pamela, I'm going to get my fortune told. You coming?" She tugged at Pamela's arm.

"What's the matter girl? You scared? What the hell, I'll go. I need to know when I'm gon' meet a good man."

The line was long and Diane watched as everyone came out smiling. Maybe that's how it was in New Orleans; maybe everything had a happy ending. When it was finally her turn, Gypsy took Diane by the hand and spoke to her.

"You come with me."

Soon she'd have the answer to many questions.

Inside the Lord's chamber they gathered for a feast of the flesh. All were masked and cloaked. Some wore elaborate costumes made to look like everything from burlesque dancers to farm animals. J.L. was ordered to stay and watch over the activities. He waltzed from room to room in a black tuxedo and green phantoms mask, intentionally avoiding the room with Lord Ophiuchus and Luna until he was summoned there by the Lord himself. Luna lay dazed and confused in the middle of a huge red circle on the floor. The room smelled of incenses and opium and all its occupants stood as if waiting on something. Once inside two members of Lord Ophiuchus's Royal Guard closed the ballroom doors and posted up beside them. Luna's body glistened, reflecting the candles that surrounded her. Pierre and Lord Ophiuchus stood above her reciting verses in Latin as blood trickled from tiny teeth marks on her neck and shoulders. In the corner two platinum blondes, naked and adorned in colorful jewels and angels wings played a harp and violin. J.L. was used to strange scenes at the Chateau and wondered what part he would play in this ritual. One of the guards gave him a mask and instructions. Reluctantly J.L. stripped and replaced his phantom mask with an extremely life like pigs mask, as two Royal Guards lift Luna from the floor. J.L. dropped to his hands and knees and took his place in the circle. Luna was laid upon his back; her thick black hair fell around the mask. He smelled her. She was sticky, bloody, and smelled of sex.

J.L. senses were all distorted; he was disgusted and a little aroused until Lord Ophiuchus opened his cloak and revealed his buttocks above both their heads.

Luna opened her mouth and took him in as the rest of the circle closed in slowly and await the climax. Lord Ophiuchus uttered a phrase in Latin and hit the floor with his scepter. That was J.L.'s que, he closed his eyes and wished he was somewhere else as he raised his head, puckered, and waited to earn his success.

Downstairs the levee had broken and the crowd thinned out. Pam's luck turned for the better. Soon after Krusemark's reading she hooked up with a friend of Louisiana mob boss, Carlos Marcellos.

Diane lounged on a chaise near the entrance to a restroom wondering if there was any truth to the secrets Gypsy had told her that had nearly sent her to sleep. So into her thoughts she never noticed the man enter the rest room. He came out and took a seat next to her.

"Excuse me miss. Is everything ok?"

"Yeah, is it ok for me to be sitting here? What time is it? Is the party over," Diane asked nervously?

"No ma'am. You're fine, but we are clearing these rooms. Are you here alone? May I escort you somewhere?"

"I'm here with my girlfriend Pamela, but she's … I haven't seen her for a while. Were in town from …"

"New York. Yeah, I know Pam. She's been to the Chateau before." He introduced himself. "I'm J.I., what's your name."

"Diane. Nice to meet you." She was stunned as she remembered something Gypsy said. "Your eyes, they're …"

"Yeah, different colors, one green, one brown, I was born like that. Why? Does it bother you? J.L. was anxious to find someone he didn't know and that didn't know him. His mind was full of thoughts that he wanted erased.

"No," said Diane easing back, "I was just asking." J.I. felt the vibe change laid on the charm.

"Listen, I'm off duty now. My place is on the grounds, why don't we go back there and get to know each other. I'll tell a friend to let Pam know where you are. If I know her she might be a while." Diane wanted to erase some thoughts from her mind too and Jack looked friendly enough; he was tall, well mannered and worked for the wealthy owner of the mansion. She decided to get her groove back.

"What the hell, I am on vacation."

The two walked across the grounds, Diane looked away as they past Krusemark's empty tent. When they reached the guest house J.L. sat her down on a swing fixed to the branch of a large sycamore tree. He went inside took a quick hit and gathered some things. Outside he hand Diane a bottle of scotch and some glasses, they talked and sipped as he fixed a pallet on the ground next to the swing. Diane looked through some 45's.

"You got any Aretha Franklin? I love Aretha!"

"Yeah."

J.L. hand her a stack of records. She picked out her favorites.

He put the stack on the turntable, lay on the pallet next to her and did his best tough guy impersonation as he peeled of her slacks. Minutes later they were getting it on underneath the Gulf coast stars while one Aretha song went into the next. It had been a minute since Diane had done this and any touch would've felt good, but she couldn't front; if nothing else, J.L.'s love was king. She was hot, the air was thick and it was hard for her to catch her breath. J.L.'s mind was working overtime; his heart was busy pumping opium through his veins and pushing his realities back and forth. He wished it was Luna or one of the others he'd become accustomed to, but after tonight's events, a change may have been be exactly what he needed to redeem himself. He groped at her skin and thrust harder. Diane whimpered, opened her eyes and watched as the sycamore leaves played hide and seek. Under the light of the full moon Diane couldn't be sure what she saw in J.L.'s one green eye, but again Gypsy's words came to mind and her body tensed. J.L. felt it and instantly switched up his flow. Diane relaxed again as the baseline of Aretha's song "Save Me" began to play. She smiled as she listened and drifted off …

Excerpt 8.

NEW YORK CITY

Cumberland Hospital

1969

"SAVE ME LORD! Please, save me!"

She woke screaming and gasping for air.

"Ms. Smarter, wake up! You've been dreaming," said the nurse. "It's Ok it was just a dream. Congratulations, you're the mother of a healthy ten pound boy."

"Huh? Oh my god! I didn't feel a thing."

"Well then *baa'by*," said the nurse playfully, "I guess your prayer worked. Anyway, you were out for a spell. You're in your room now."

"W-where is he," Diane asked nervously?"

"He should be here; I'll see what's keeping them."

"He's fine; he'll be out in a moment," said another nurse who'd entered the room, "the doctors had to remove that tissue that was covering one of his eyes," she said quietly to the first nurse before leaving.

Diane was terrified. She closed her eyes and struggled to get the words out.

"Nurse?"

"Yes, Ms. Smarter."

"Which eye," she asked softly, "which eye was covered?"

"I believe it was the left one," she said.

Diane opened her eyes and looked out the window only to see a fire red moon looking back at her.

"Nurse," she said loudly! "Keep him out there. I'll see him later. I'm tired. Keep him out there." Then she began to cry as she thought;

"Gypsy was right."

NEW YORK CITY
1974

Five years later, a 15 year old Shirley Smarter walked with her little brother through FAO Schwartz toy store. It was just before closing and all the clerks ignored them. They'd taken one look at them and decided they weren't buying.

"Ok Seth, pick out one thing today and maybe mama or your daddy will have something for you whenever they get home."

Shirley knew better but she wanted to make her brother's birthday as happy as possible. Even at five something in Seth Smarter told him that nothing was promised to him and he should treat every decision as though it were his first and last. He lived for the moment and went for broke every time.

"I want a bike," he said.

A few months earlier he'd amazed everyone when he'd borrowed one and taught himself to ride in one day.

"Boy," Shirley popped him on his head and he dropped one of the dice he'd taken from his brother's car. "Evret didn't give me that much money. Pick something smaller; and you better make it count."

Seth searched his young mind as he picked up the dice. That's when he saw something that jarred the memory of a commercial that stuck in his head. He was always watching TV or day dreaming.

"Pick something the store is about to close."

Shirley popped his head again, but lighter this time. Then Seth made his choice.

"I want a Mr. Microphone."

1975

THE WHIRLWIND

NEW YORK CITY
Marcy Projects

"Hey, ma, look! Mama, look at Seth."

The girls were laughing and pointing to their brother. He was confused but cheesing from ear to ear. He didn't like to be made fun of and wasn't sure if they were laughing with him or at him.

Seth stayed in the girls' room while they ran to the kitchen to get their mother. Mallory lagged behind with dirty bare soles and nappy hair. Her dress was way too big. She was slow to do things and she still cried a lot. It was 12:30 on a weekday in July and she'd just gotten out of bed. The Banana Splits were playing on the TV when Shirley called again for their brother.

"Hurry up, Seth! Come in here and show mama."

The boy didn't move. He stood there with his mic; still in perfect condition eight months and counting; an incredible feat for any little boy, double for one living in the projects. And it wasn't by chance either; he was especially protective of his mic. He'd found a few good hiding places in the family's new apartment. No one was allowed to play with it, and when he brought it out he kept it closer than one would an enemy. He called the mic, his "precious."

"Ok Seth, don't come. I'ma fix you."

Shirley crossed her arms. Her Jelly's slapped against her tapping foot, her gym shorts were wrapped tight around her thick thighs and a yellow tube strapped in her top.

Seth hated for Shirley to be mad at him. He began walking toward the kitchen.

"What's going on," Diane yelled, annoyed and sure that something was wrong? Her voice froze Seth his tracks.

"Aint nothing wrong ma," said Shirley, "dang! Seth was sing ..."

Diane's eyes narrowed.

"Hold up!" Her cigarette dangled over a pot of frying chicken. "Who you think you talking to? I'm ya' mama. Not one of ya' fast-ass friends. You keep talking crazy and I'ma be the one doing the fixin'."

Shirley didn't speak. She cut her eyes and her foot made the mistake of tapping. Even Mallory saw the slap coming. Diane drew back and Mallory screamed. Her mother took the cigarette from her mouth, hugged her and tried to sound motherly.

"Look at my baby, your nose all runny. Come on, come with mama."

She sneered at Shirley.

"You little bitch. When I come out this bathroom you fix this girls hair and get her dressed. Keep fucking with me, ya' ass wont be going to no parade."

Anger and frustration went into Shirley's thoughts.

"I can't stand her. I was trying to make her happy."

In N.Y. the Parade season really kicks off after the 4th of July with the biggest and best; the Puerto Rican day parade. The ones who couldn't make it to the end usually gathered at the edge of Central Park near 59th and 5th. That's where the vendors would set up coolers and grills and the DJ's used to set up their booths and get the party started as Cubans, Italians, Jamaicans Trinidadians, WASP's, Blacks, Arabs and Jews all sweat together in a melting pot of food, music and culture. By the next spring, Strawberry Fields blossomed with tulips and bi-racial babies.

Jose Chavez was the second oldest of six children. His parents were a couple of Puerto Rican domestics. He was pick pocketing at seven, stealing cars at twelve, and now at seventeen he'd moved up from runner to small time coke dealer in the Bronx. He hung out at the lounge next to the supermarket where Evret worked, talking big shit. "I'm next in line bro'." That's where he'd first seen Shirley. This year Jose invited Evret to hang out with him and his people.

"Come to the parade man, and yo, bring your sister too, bro."

Now whenever Shirley saw him outside the bar she'd blush and wonder what dating a Spanish guy would be like.

Seth was standing in the girl's room as Diane and Mallory walked past.

"And you put that damn toy down," she said. Clean that front room. You hear?"

"Yes ma."

He lowered his head. He felt worse for Shirley than for himself. Just like Diane had been, Shirley was more a mother than sister. She and Seth shared a bond that would not be broken. He saw her face from the living room and walked toward the kitchen.

"Naw, don't come in here now. It's all yo' fault," she said sniffling.

Seth was hurt. He stopped and folded the sheet from the couch he and Evret shared. He'd yet to understand what he'd done wrong. Shirley had begun too, Mallory didn't know what was going on, and Evret was planning his escape.

He could remember the days when there was some sort of structure to the household, before the men, the kids, and the drugs. At nineteen he realized the little house in Maryland was better than the projects. The projects were exactly what he'd envisioned when the older cats on the bus talked about jail; a drab, depressing box used to subdue psychotics.

"Man," he thought, *"I was born in a small town."*

After graduating high school Evret had gotten a part time job bagging groceries and had plans of making manager. But his plans meant nothing; there was another who'd pull his strings.

A girl he'd met in school, a tall, thin, double chocolate mocha cutie with big tits and hair that stayed pressed named Filani. When she found out the family had moved to Marcy she decided to school Evret on how things were done.

Soon she had enough of his money to buy a couple of ounces off her boyfriend for Evret to sell. She was helpful; showed him how to bag up and everything. She told her man;

"It's for my sister's guy, baby; some L7 nigga from Flushing."

He gave it to her for wholesale and she pocketed the rest.

LOUISIANA
New Orleans
1969

Jack had no idea what to do about his situation. He and Diane had hung out a little and he'd hit it again just hours before she left New Orleans. He wondered which time it had been; to him it made a huge difference.

He got the feeling his days of being down with the Kings were numbered. No matter how hard he tried he couldn't come to grips with the sacrifice he'd made that night in the chamber. He felt eyes on him wherever he went. Somebody who'd been there had told the tale. Luna claimed she didn't remember anything. For her sake he hoped that was true. However it got out, now when J.L. went to handle business for de Louis he was no longer respected. Some of the dealers had begun mocking, "Deliverance."

"Hey man," one would ask laughing, "how does a pig sound when you stick it?"

"Don't sound like shit with its mouth full," the other would say.

J.I. would pretend not to hear.

"Stupid motherfuckers cant even get the lines right."

Luna had jokes too, and on those nights when she didn't run out on him she'd burst out laughing in the middle of sex. Word was she had a man named Gar in the Magnolia projects. Things were so bad they had started to affect de Louis's money. Customers weren't even paying J.L. right any more.

When Diane called with the news about her condition he tooted all night and screwed up some business. That's all de Louis had been waiting for.

J.L. Pleaded. "But, Louis, you know I been loyal!

J.L. prepared a hit and went to find Luna. It was the last time he or anyone else was going to see her again.

BROOKLYN
1970

When the bus arrived in New York he figured he was home free, but the problem with that plan is always the same; wherever you go, there you are.

He settled in with Diane and tried to get used to a new city; but the game was different there. He didn't fit in. He refused to take a low level position on somebody's team and no one was going to give him a spot without credentials.

J.L. took the last of his little savings and tried to go solo. Like a catfish swimming in a sea of sharks, he aint even move right. 37 years old and still coping ounces. Pathetic.

This year Pam brought back more than souvenirs. Diane wondered for days what had been so important to make her call from New Orleans.

"Hey girl," asked Pam, "is umm, J.L. around."

"Yeah, we watching TV with the kids. I wish we could be there."

Pam found that funny. Across the room J.L. feared the worst. When Diane hung up he started questioning her like he was the police.

"Damn, what is y'all doing it or something?" Diane asked only half joking. "She on the phone acting crazy, talking about telling me something when she gets home, and you here asking all these questions. What's goin' on?"

The night before Pam came home J.L. left the house and didn't come back for a week. That was all the answer Diane needed. After Pam told her the news she quit her job at the factory and they never spoke again. The night J.L. came home was the night the beatings started.

"They saying all kinds of crazy things about you down there J.L. What happened to that girl Luna? Huh?"

"Look bitch don't be asking me about my business. You gon' believe some shit that that whore Pam said. I told you that bitch had been to the Chateu before. Did she tell you what she did," he snickered, "or who she did it with?"

Diane stood in the kitchen amazed and holding a paring knife behind her back. "You gon call me a bitch in front of my mama and my kids; after I just had your son, Jack?"

She thought back to that first night. Twice now it all made sense. A bad taste filled her mouth and she went after him with the knife.

J.L. saw it coming and slapped it out.

"Bitch, you to eager."

J.L. grinned as she lay on the floor spitting out blood and screaming.

"I can't believe I had your baby!"

"Aww bitch please. That boy aint never gon' be shit; none of these bastards will."

Evret came from behind and broke a jug of cherry Kool-Aid over his head and stabbed him in his neck with the handle. A strange feeling of atavism washed over Diane as the blood and Kool-Aid mixed on the floor. She got up reaching for the hot grits on the stove. She remembered the last chick that did that and spit in his face instead. The other kids followed Evret's lead and beat the shit out of J.L.

After that night he moved out and Diane slowly drifted back into her old habits. That night had produced wounds that would never heal.

NYMP
1975

Diane and Seth were the only ones home. She lay in her room smoking cigarettes and listening to her Commodores and Spinners records. She loved them and Seth did too. He'd find a quiet spot and practice for the concert he'd do for her one day. Her favorite song was "One of a Kind, (Love Affair)", it had the power to change his mothers' whole mood, when it was playing she'd sing and be happy. Sometimes she'd grab him and J.L. and they'd all dance. Lately though, "Love Don't Love Nobody" had been on repeat and Seth had noticed her face looked sad; like his when he heard "Ghetto Child." He wanted to see his mother smile. Diane heard a knock on her door and groaned.

"What is it?"

"Look Ma."

Seth pushed open the door and did the whole song in one take. She smiled, kissed him and held him close.

"You're the best," she said.

"Mama that's what Shirley wanted to show you, earlier. Did I do good?"

"Yeah, you did *real* good," said Diane breaking their embrace.

She never held him long enough.

"Turn the stereo back up," she said. She told him to get in bed with her and they lay there listening.

"You like this one Seth?"

"Yep."

He was busy flipping the buttons on the microphone.

"Me too. I think about you when I hear it." Diane started singing; *"Sadie, don't you know we love you sweet Sadie … We should call you …"* Naw, we can't do that; that don't sound right. 'A-D,' she said. That's mama's nickname for you, Ok? Shh. Don't tell nobody where it came from." She put her finger to her lips. "Secrets are important and this one is ours."

A-D was just glad to be having a moment with his mother. A minute later the front door opened.

"Go tell your sister to come here," said Diane.

He jumped out of bed.

"A-D," she said, before he reached the door!

"Yes ma."

"Never forget, Mama loves you."

He blushed, hid his face and kept the moment close to heart.

Shortly after Diane and her family sat on the bed listening to "Then Came you," She hugged Shirley and said;

"You watch after your brother at the parade Saturday."

✳

That's the power that music has to influence and effect peoples lives. However, the results aren't always the same. William S. Burroughs, author of *"Rock Magic"* says this about Led Zeppelin, music concerts, and the musician in general:

Excerpt 9.

✳

SPLENDOR

From sunrise that morning the city was buzzing with anticipation, it started out hot and would only get hotter. Old people were told to stay inside and keep cool, and that was cool with Hector Gonzalez, not many old folks were buying what he was selling anyway. He'd gotten a couple of 0z's of coke from Jose on consignment and was more than a week late paying.

Hector figured with all the people at the parade he could steal enough purses to pay Jose back; if he didn't sniff the money up first.

Jose had his chicas all lined up. His main girl was in P.R. visiting family and his other one he'd see early on. Around 5:00 pm he'd meet up with Evret and Shirley at the edge of the park. She had been on his mind all week.

In the Smarter house A-D was especially excited. Martin had sent the family some money and they'd bought new outfits for today. A-D didn't get many new clothes and always looked a little stale. But today everyone commented on how cute he was. He stayed silent, like a Gregorian, never speaking but forever watching. Not exactly handsome, his looks were a sensitive subject. He had what some call "strong features," Or what mean girls would call, a huge head, wide nose, 'Dumbo' ears, and well, ___let's say he took his lips after his father. He adored girls but had few playmates; a little boy from down the hall, some cousins and his sisters. Evret was hard on him, always roughing him up. He loved his brother but he hated J.L., and often the feelings would get crossed. To everyone else though, A-D was the baby brother that could do no wrong.

Shirley had just finished washing and dressing him. His hair smelled like shampoo.

"Uh oh, watch out here come A-D, all the girls gon' be loving you. You gon' take your mic and sing to 'em," she asked?

He promised to sing to all the girls.

"Good," said Shirley, "You sing your heart out today, you never know, tomorrow the good Lord might take it all away."

She hand him some new batteries. He gave her a hug; he'd been worried about those. Shirley never let him down.

"Mallory made you a sandwich," she said, "go eat."

The parade was like nothing he'd ever seen, all the colorful floats, marching bands, and rowdy people; everywhere people. They held banners and rode in vehicles with signs claiming different organizations. The signs and symbols were everywhere. A-D ate his 'elotes' and wondered about them all. He asked Evret and Shirley question after question. They tried their best to answer him but the little boy was making them feel silly. A float went by seeking donations for a Puerto Rican charity. The square glass machine blowing the dollars around was full, displaying just how much Latinos help their own.

"You see that," said Filani, "that's the only symbol you need to worry about. I know what it means."

Lucky for her, because Evret was starting to forget.

Everybody laughed except A-D. He stayed focused on three symbols painted on a brick wall on the other side of the street; a six point star painted in blue, a red five point star with a crescent moon attached, and a cross painted white. A quick tingly feeling washed over him.

The closer 5:00 pm got, the more anxious Jose and Shirley got. The big drums pounded out bass that everyone could feel and heartbeats sped up all over the parade route. They'd both seen people they knew, hers, from school and Marcy, and his from the block. Then Jose saw Hectors ass lamping in the crowd, up to no good. Jose reached in his sock for his knife and was about to approach him about his cash when Evret called his name. He looked at his watch, it was 5:15. He decided to handle Hector another day.

Evret introduced everybody and Jose and Shirley got to speak for the first time. It was young love as they walked deeper into the park smiling and throwing baby punches.

Jose bought A-D a gang of food and lots of those little glow necklaces. He couldn't wait to show them to Mallory when he got home.

At precisely 9:00 pm Filani started complaining about all the walking and was ready to go. Evret had to be at work early and knew he was going to have to fight to get some. Jose promised to get his people home safe and soon. But when Evret left, so did they; not for home, but for Paradise City. A-D was charged. He loved it in Paradise and figured he could stay there forever as long as Jose was paying.

Shirley wanted to be home before Evret got there, but as midnight neared A-D was still geeked, addicted to the lights and music from the rides. Near the back of the park by the tunnel of love is where they talked over their plans.

Jose had even given A-D a beer hoping to knock him out. Between kisses Shirley told Jose they should pack it up. They both looked at A-D who was too busy chasing rabbits around the city to hear the woman's voice coming from the shadows.

"So, what's the plan children?"

Shirley jumped and Jose reached for his blade.

"Ah, ah, ahh," said a man's voice. "Don't worry about her, familia, she's with me. Did you two figure it out yet?"

Jose relaxed as a tall woman in a short black leather outfit stepped into the light. Her spiked heels were so tall Shirley wondered how she could walk. Her lips were blood red and her strawberry blonde hair was in French braids with beaded ends that rattled whenever she moved her head. The lights of the Ferris wheel came on and A-D turned around. On a bench by the control booth sat a tall sinewy man; pale with black curly shoulder length hair that all but covered his face. He was dressed in what must have been a costume; tight black bell bottoms with designs stitched all over. Suns, moons, and stars; circles, triangles, and squares, and in every triangle there was an eye that shimmied when the light hit it. On his lap sat a guitar; he gave it a strum before he stood and placed it on the bench, picked up a matching bolero style jacket, put it on his bare chest and strut toward the group like a peacock.

"I know what you want," he said, handing Jose a cup of tickets. "You guys ride the tunnel of love, on me. Lilith and I will keep an eye on the child. He can ride the 'Whirlwind,' until you guys get back."

The man smiled and held out his hand. A-D stared, transfixed by the scene. Lilith felt bad vibrations coming from Shirley and tried to soothe her.

"He'll be fine," she said, "I have a few children of my own."

A-D smiled at the lady and she rubbed her fingers over his face.

"You two make sure you're back at midnight," said the man, "We gotta split then. *Comprendes?*"

Lilith bent over to fix her heels and A-D's got an eyeful when he saw that she wasn't wearing any underwear.

The man chuckled.

"You like that?"

A-D smiled.

"You like music," asked the man?

"Yes."

"Me too. Wanna trade?"

A-D had never held a real guitar before. It looked shiny and expensive; but still, this was his "precious."

"I won't break it. I promise."

A-D looked at him sideways before handing him the mic and asking;

"What's your name?"

"People have many names for me," he said opening the gate to the ride and walking back to the bench where A-D sat playing with the guitar. "It depends. What are you, friend or foe?"

The child sat wondering what a foe was as the man took his hand and led him to the ride. He placed him in the seat and strapped him in. The man held his microphone and looked A-D in the eye. Diane Smarter had never thought about blessings for herself or her children, but right now her son was engaged in the ultimate battle and needed all the help he could get. The child looked over at Lilith who was walking toward them with an ornate bottle. The man point to her with A-D's microphone.

"All this can be yours."

"So you like beer," asked Lilith? A-D smiled. "Try this," she said.

The boy knew better than to take things from strangers but the allure of Paradise City had clouded his senses. He took the bottle and drank.

"That," said Lilith "is for your mind, soul, and body."

A drop ran down his cheek. Lilith kissed him and licked it away. A-D felt the wetness of her tongue and the heat of her breath as she whispered in his ear.

"Witness 'Sammael,' in the eye of the Whirlwind my child."

At the control panel, the MC. insert the key as his pupil began the quest. His eyes followed the boy, his mouth moved swiftly, enunciating each syllable of *the secret doctrine* into the microphone. The taste of the bottle lingered in A-D's mouth and the opening chords of *"Stairway to Heaven"* played as the "wonder wheel" raised his consciousness to a new level. There is where he heard a voice.

"… Welcome a new and worthy brother; Seth, creature of ecstatic, magic light …"

He looked out over the ocean and felt freedom on the horizon. He looked at the sky and saw a glittering gold city atop a hill. He felt like he had wings on so he closed his eyes and took flight. He was afraid when the ride descended to earth; afraid of falling from the sky. With every rotation his vision changed. The second time around his ears popped and he was lightheaded. Not only could he hear the rhythm now, he could see it clearly. Again he heard the voice.

"In His name we set your feet upon the Left-Hand Path …"

On the third rotation, through rings of smoke and trees he saw a path to a new beginning guided by the lights and voices of Paradise City.

"In the name of Lucifer we ring about you ..."

The fourth rotation brought about a cold wind; he shivered as he felt the seasons change.

"In the name of Belial we place his mark upon you ..."

His head was humming on the fifth; he felt powerful and full of energy like he could take on the world. Then the wheel slowed and he listened as the anthem reached its crescendo. Below, the voices called to him;

"In the name of Leviathan, and the great salt sea, we dress your being,"

He opened his eyes and instinctively performed the bellows breath. For a split second there was a feeling of infinite peace. Then a flash of lightning created thunder and the tunnel opened, five gave way to six and this spawn of briny heritage was gone; a traveler of both time and space. A tear seeped from under his unveiled eyelid as he experienced the magic and mysticism of seven.

"... images set forth by a childhood fancy ..."

And just into the eighth rotation was when he heard the toast. He opened his eyes and all was revealed.

Through one, darkness engulfed him under a vault of fire, and through the other he witnessed a pale and infinite light; and at nine the two paths unite and became one. Whole.

"HAIL ..."

The ride slowed to a stop and A-D sat stuck from his trip through zones. Shirley returned just minutes after twelve to find her brother sitting in the darkened area weeping to be so alone. The gate keepers had vanished and only the microphone was left resting on the bench.

Shirley and Jose asked if he was Ok.

"You a'ight lil' bro?"

A-D blinked and raised his head, he squinted, and his lips poked out.

"Shirl," he said breathing funny, "I wanna go home."

It felt strange to know the ledge.

1976

THE UNSEEN HAND

BRAZIL
Salvador
1957

It's the third largest city in Brazil, and with eighty-five percent its three million residents black and living in abject poverty, Bahians say it is more African than Africa. Residents of its *favelas* are housed in cement shanties built on the side of large grassy hills; little more than mud packed cinderblocks topped with sheets of aluminum to keep the rain out. It was early evening as Adriana hurried past the others to hers. A young boy stood naked in the doorway throwing rocks at chickens plucking for food near the outhouse, next to them a wood burning stove heat a large pot of water, and from the burnt orange western skies the *Samba de roda* played the outro for the day.

"Stop," said Adriana to her son.

He threw the rest of the rocks on the ground. She took his hand and led him to a tub in the yard. The neighbor's dog barked at them. The boy yelled, "Stop" and the barking ceased. Adriana smiled at her little man as she brought the water to the tub and poured it in. The temperature was right and the boy sat down. Adriana pulled a sheet for privacy, gave her son a sponge and told him to wash himself as she took a seat next to the tub, fished out his foot and began clipping his toenails while he covered his skin in lather. She pretended not to notice him impatiently waiting for her to speak.

"Mami, remember you promised to ..."

"Yes, yes, "Mijo" I remember. Which story do you want me to tell?"

"My favorite," he said splashing about the water, happily. *"The unseen hand."*

Adriana bristled in her seat knowing all along what her son wanted to hear. Believing it was nothing more than a fantastic bedtime story, it had been his only request since she'd told it to him. Adriana questioned if she'd done the right thing by telling him so young. Had she traded his innocence for the knowledge of the workings of the world? Over the years the thought had seemed inconceivable even to adults. A group so influential that it guides world events and policies? So enigmatic that people question their proven existence? So progressive, audacious and relentless in their goals that they've succeeded in designing and building a pyramid of nations? *Really?* Even she'd found it hard to believe until she met one of them face to face.

HARLEM
1976

The man approaching the home was knowledgeable of many things, but how to make peace with his only son was not one of them. After spending the last seven years of his life waging war, he was happy to be home, in *"The Empire State"* that men like he and his father had helped to build. He climbed the stairs and braced himself as he pressed the button.

✳

NEW YORK HARBOR
1906

The bells on the dock signaled an incoming ship. As an urchin on the streets of Edinburgh, Robert had always dreamed of seeing The New World. Now after weeks at sea he was about to set foot on it. "Born again," is how he described the feeling as "the green lady's" light guided the 'travelers' into Ellis Island. On these shores, he'd been told, "everything and everyone moves upward." He felt honored to be there and he owed it all to, *The Craft*.

✳

SCOTLAND
1946

Seven miles outside of Edinburgh stood the five hundred year old Rosslyn Chapel. Inside, dressed in full regalia, several members of New York's Old Holland Lodge number eight listened closely to a Grand Master.

"1118. Our beginning in history is merely a drop in the ocean of time. We owe those beginnings to the visions of men like Priory of Sion founder, Godfrey de Bouillon and his nephew King Baldwin II of Jerusalem, Saint Bernard of Clairveaux, Andre de Montbard, our first Grand Master, Hughes de Payens, and lest we not forget Henry Saint Claire and those original nine Christian soldiers who took the vow of poverty to protect pilgrims on their way to the Holy Land. Taking up residence among the ruins of the great King Solomon's temple, they were recognized as *The Poor Knights of the Temple of Solomon*. From those sacred grounds a glorious turn of events brought to the order good fortune and wealth, and from then on whenever French and English nobles needed money to fund their wars they turned to the order. We were happy to lend it and collect what was called a "crusading fee." If the nobles defaulted on the loans, which they often did, the order gained ownership of their land and property.

When the time came for the order to build their own property they employed the very same stonemasons as the Kings and Popes had to build castles and cathedrals throughout Europe. Those military strongholds eventually became the first safe deposit houses, allowing wealthy travelers to store valuables in one country and safely withdraw them in another,—again for a fee of course. In fact, you'd do well to say that modern banking is the invention of the Knights of the Temple.

By the year 1207 the order had built a fleet of ships that they used for trade during maritime. By 1240 that fleet had increased substantially and could be found haunting established trade routes engaging in what we call *"privateering,"*— the capturing of merchant ships at sea,—others called it pirating, and soon the ships flag, or *"Jolly Roger,"* the skull and crossbones became notorious on the high seas. Sailors and merchants began lodging complaints that fell on deaf ears, for by then we held the deeds to nearly ten-thousand properties in Europe alone and we'd become the wealthiest order in the world, *The Knights Templar*. By the year 1307 even France's King Phillip was indebted to us. Jealousy and spite had grown in the hearts of men and rumors of heresy, including homosexuality and Satan worship plagued the orders 20,000 members. The sitting Pope, Urban II dealt with charges that the order was secretly practicing magick they were accused of learning from the Semites during the Crusades.

Then came that dreadful day, Friday the 13th of October, 1307, when King Phillip ordered all Knights in France arrested and detained, and ordered their assets seized. In 1312 Pope Clement V issued the decree *"Vox Clamantis,"* thereby dissolving the order. Alas, on March 14th, 1314 after years of torture, Templar Grand Master, Jaques de Molay was burned alive in the square of Notre Dame. But as destiny would have it, a large number of our brothers escaped France the holds of their ships filled with what has been called the treasure of all treasures. Some of those brothers built a home here, inside these very walls where they were twice born and in the year 1717 the Mother Grand lodge of England was formed and the Templars were renamed, *the fraternal Order of Free & Accepted Masons."*

✳

The name *Freemason* as well as their symbol of a G imposed between the architectural tools of a compass and square is known by many, but understood by few. The lodges of operative Masons—actual stone working masons—dates back to the middle ages, while speculative Masonry—the process of spiritual advancement based on the study of history, philosophy, astrology, and mathematics— flourished late in the 17th century during the *Age of Reason.* Obligatory questions are often raised as to weather Masonry is a ten million member religion, or a cult, a haven for freethinking individuals, or a Lucifer worshiping conspiracy against Christianity, a fun loving lodge, or a secret society involved in criminal activities that rival the Mafia.

The answers, due greatly to its own duplicitous nature, one that has created schisms between black masons and white masons as well as American Masons and the rest of the world, appear to be forever lost to time. Secrecy, you see is of the utmost importance to the Mason, and according to their own oaths, if broken could result in a number of grisly ritualistic deaths. Secret handshakes and passwords are used to keep imposters out, and even among their own they rely on a complex series of ranks and levels of admission called "degrees" that segregate one from another. Upon completion of the initial 3 degrees—the blue lodge—the celebrant may choose one of two paths of wisdom, *The York Rite,* consisting of an additional ten degrees for a total of 13, or *The Scottish Rite,* which includes an additional 29 for a total of 32 degrees. At that time the celebrant may be invited to join the ultra-secretive, and coveted, honorary *33rd degree.* Researchers have also found beyond it are another set of "hidden grades" and other secret societies referred to as *"Illuminized Masonry,"* that the celebrant may seek admission to, making them essentially "a fraternity within a fraternity." Celebrated Masonic author, 33rd degree Mason and former Grand Commander Albert Pike may have described it best when he wrote, Freemasonry *"has two doctrines, one concealed and reserved for the Masters, the other public."*

*

As both a speculative and an operative mason Robert Devine was a dying breed. He made his living as one of the "skywalkers" that helped construct "the vertical city" after the invention of the elevator. His son Alliouisis could remember watching and wanting to be just like him as he scaled the girders of the Empire State building. Robert though, had other plans for his only son.

Alliouisis Devine graduated West Point in 1942 just in time to join his alum, General George S. Patton's, German campaign. A courageous and decorated officer at the wars end, he was tapped to assist the OSS; a special group of agents devised by the U.S. to combat the manufactured communist threat in Russia and South America. The identities and actions of these operatives were to remain covert, and in 1947 from this group the Central Intelligence Agency was born.

Part of their oath was for "Deus Meumque Jus," (God and my right). Just as Robert Devine had always proclaimed it should be. To Robert, Alliouisis was on track in moving toward his destiny. Today he expressed his appreciation by returning with his son to the sacred grounds of Rosslyn to perform the rites of the sublime degree.

"Let The Brother Receive The Light."

The participant removed Alliouisis's blindfold. He was raised from one knee a new man, and in esteemed company.

"You may now add your name to a list of great men," said Robert. "There's Benjamin Franklin, Thomas Jefferson, Benedict Arnold, Samuel Colt and Harlan Sanders just to name a few, and from this day forth may you do everything in your power to preserve our integrity and traditions."

HARLEM
1976

The sound of the doorbell brought a rush of memories to the mind of Dioses Devine.

✳

August 1967. That's when his mother Adriana passed,—the victim of a robbery gone bad—it was also the year his aunt Dania brought him here to his new home. A week later the sound of the doorbell brought an unexpected visitor. Dania opened the door, took one look at the mans face and was taken back seventeen years to when she and her sister worked for the Church of Our Lady of the Rosary of Blacks, a house of worship founded in the early 1800's by a secret brotherhood of slaves who until then had been unable to pray to their *Orix'as* in peace. One day mysterious men showed up asking questions about the church. Adriana had found herself inexplicably attracted to one of them and soon Dania would wake in the middle of the night and find Adriana's bed empty. Neighbors talked of seeing her and a man walking hand and hand along the beaches under the moonlight. Then one day the man vanished as mysteriously as he'd come and nine months later Adriana gave birth to a boy.

✳

After a brief conversation with the man Dania let him into her home and called for her nephew. "Come "Mijo", she said, "there is someone here to see you."

Dioses was curled up on the bed still mourning his mother's death. He got himself together and went downstairs where he found a strangely familiar face looking back at him.

"Hello son, I don't know what your mother told you about me. My name is Alliouisis, I'm your …," Dioses knew it before the words came out, even so he was in shock studying the mans mouth as he spoke. "… Adriana was eighteen when we met … we were very much in love …" Dioses was picking up only bits and pieces of a story that he knew couldn't possibly be true.

"If you loved her why didn't you stay with us, why no visits, no calls, no letters?"

Alliouisis tried to explain.

"I did those things son; on several occasions. It was your mother who preferred that we not meet."

Dioses thought of his mom.

"If that is true, then she had good reasons."

Alliouisis took a deep breath, sighed and gave Dioses a condescending grin.

"Son, I don't expect you to understand, those were troubled times and we believed our arrangement was for the best."

Dioses flashed a look that could kill.

"Because of your arrangement my mother is dead, and you can go to hell!"

Dioses stormed out of the room. For over a year Alliouisis tried but couldn't reach him. Dioses began hanging out on the streets of Harlem, dabbling in the life he'd left behind as a Pee Wee in the 'city of god'. Alliouisis wasn't having that.

"Ill kill him myself, before I let you," he told Dania's husband Toby during a visit to the family's home.

Then late in 1969 Dioses felt the grip of the unseen hand when Alliouisis and his best friend Benjamin Freidman used their connections to have him drafted and placed under Alliouisis' command. The day he arrived in Vietnam, Dioses was called in to see his commanding officer. After a brief introduction and much to his dismay Colonel Devine stepped from the shadows. Frightened and confused, Dioses asked why his own father had sentenced him to die. Alliouisis answered;

"It's time for you to do the right thing, Dioses. You're *my* son. You owe it to me and this great nation. You *will* satisfy your duty to both."

Dioses wiped the tears from his face before he responded.

"Who do you think you are man? I don't owe you shit. It aint me man, I aint the fortunate son!"

"I hope your time out here brings you some clarity," replied Alliouisis, "maybe then you'll understand just how fortunate you are."

*

Dioses opened the door and came face to face with the father he hadn't seen in years. Alliouisis had been right about one thing, their time in the jungle had forced them to see each other differently and formed a delicate bridge of respect between the two, but Dioses would never understand how his father had chosen his career over his family, and he had no interest in understanding the twisted morals and dogma of The Scottish Rite.

Alliouisis on the other hand had all but given up him ever becoming free and accepted, and at 55 having never married and with no other children it looked as if the Devine family's association with the order would end with him, but destiny sometimes has a will of its own.

Each man nodded at the other as they shook hands, Dioses motioned for him to come in. Alliouisis smiled as Dania took his hat and coat and escort him to the couch.

"You want something to drink," she asked?"

Dioses kissed her on the cheek and answered.

"He's having a Manhattan. I'll get it."

Dania hurried upstairs and Alliouisis stopped surveying the room long enough to admire the man his son had become.

"Dania and Toby have kept the place looking good."—Modest but spotless, with all new plastic covered furniture—"Do you have anything to do with that?"

Dioses said nothing for a moment. He took a seat on the couch and gave his father a drink.

"We both do, but why don't we go easy on the interrogations today."

"Agreed," said Alliouisis holding up his glass.

Dioses touched it with his. They clinked and each took a sip.

"I want to thank you for everything …"

"Please Dioses don't. I appreciate it, but now isn't the time. I'm here today to thank *you* for allowing me this opportunity. It means the world to me. We're going to have a wonderful time. It should be quite the experience for the both of us."

"I'm sure it will," said Dioses. "It's all he's talked about since you invited him."

Just then Dania appeared at the top of the stairs with a handsome young six year old. Dioses called to him.

"Well don't just stand there Fourtunate, come down and say hello to your grandfather."

WASHINGTON
District Of Columbia
The Bicentennial

Butterflies danced in the child's stomach as he looked down from the plane onto Washington Square. They were headed to the Bicentennial celebration where Alliouisis had promised Dioses that Fourtunate would learn the history of the American patriots and the inception of their new world free from the hand of the British Empire. Dioses finally agreed, knowing all along at some point his father would be compelled to include just how much influence a group of Freemasons, had on our Nations Capitol.

"What is Freemasonry Grandpapa?"

Alliouisis reached into his pocket and produced one Federal Reserve Note, he hand it to Fourtune who studied it carefully.
"Now turn it over."

As Fourtune did that Alliouisis reached into his pocket again, this time producing a Swiss Army knife. He placed the magnifying glass over the number one in the right hand corner.
"What do you see?"
"Ooo, look Papa," answered Fourtune. "It's an owl."
"Very good," said Alliouisis as he placed the glass over the Great Seal of the United States and spoke.
"As you will discover, the hand that Freemasonry has played in not only the building of this city but of this nation is clear to all those who are wise enough to see as *he* sees. The Craft is the thread that links the Ancient Mysteries to the modern world. It is *The Light,* and it is what made everything that you see before you possible. In the 1660's the plot of land down there numbered six hundred and sixty-six was called Rome. Over a hundred years later, after the Revolutionary War, a Gaul descendant and *frere Macon*, by the name of Charles L'Enfant began plans for marvels like that there."
Alliouisis motioned to, *Jones point,* where the 1st stone of The Federal City was laid on April 15th, 1791 between the hours of 3:30 and 4:00 pm when "the beautiful Virgin (Virgo) was at her zenith.
"And over there."
He point to *The Washington Monument.* A 550 ft obelisk made from 36,000 separate blocks of granite, the capstone weighing in at precisely 3,300 pounds.
"And most importantly there," exactly thirteen blocks north of the White House on 16th street NW in Lafayette Square, *"the House of the Temple.* It is the North American headquarters of Scottish Rite Freemasonry. Its sacred entrance is guarded by two Sphinxes and secured by 33 stone columns, each 33 ft. tall. Inside its hallowed halls sits the bust of the illustrious Albert Pike.
"And finally, over there," said Alliouisis, "ruling over that large bronze seal of the United States in Freedom Plaza from her home atop The Capitol building is *Persephone.'* She is the 'Queen of the Dead,' 'Protectress of Jesuits,' 'Patroness of the United States,' and the 'Immaculate Virgin of Rome.'"

Hotel California was playing softly in the background as Alliouisis continued explaining the signs and symbols. Up ahead in the distance Fourtune observed the shimmering of the city's streetlights, suddenly his head grew heavy and his sight grew dim as they began to outline a curious shape, from Washington Circle, to DuPont Circle, to Scott Circle, to Logan Circle, and to the east, Mt. Vernon Square, each street connected to form an inverted five point star, known to The Brotherhood as "*Jupiter's earthly abode*," inside of which the mouth of *the Baphomet* rest in the oval office of The White House. Later on this trip, Fourtunate would listen spellbound to its voice as he was absorbed into *Wisdom*, the mind of the he-goat making known to him all that he wished to learn.

1977

CONSPIRACIES

NEW YORK CITY
Harlem

Daddy when we going on the plane? Daddy when we going on the plane? Daddy when we going on the plane?

"We going soon enough man, aint nothing to it," said Goodgame smiling between sips of cognac. "You ready to see Los Angeles, where your daddy is from?"

"Yeah, I wanna go see Mickey Mouse and Daffy Duck and the rest of 'em." The child threw his Mickey toy high in the air. "When we goin' to the park?"

Goodgame pat his head and sent him off to play while he answered the phone and finished his drink.

"Larry, what's to it family? How the game treating you?"

"I can't complain family, things on this side looking lovely. How long before you touch down?"

"Flight is supposed to leave JFK at 1:30, so we should touch down around 1:30 or 2 pm L.A. time." Goodgame chuckled. "Manmade time will always wig me out."

"Always. Hey, I'm sending one of the fellas to scoop y'all up. You put that broad in a taxi cab. We gon' do thangs a lil' different since you bringing nephew."

"Right, right, that sounds like its gone fly. That'll give me a chance to show him some thangs on the ride in. He been bugging the shit out of me about that mouse!"

"I hear you talking man. That's all youngbloods wanna do out here is fuck with the mouse. That freak *"Uncle Walt"* is getting all the cheese."

"Well," laughed Goodgame, "we gon' get some of that too. All in good time baby bro, all in good time. Let me get on outta here, family. I got a little business to take care of and Lynnette is cooking up some chops."

"Now that sounds like a winner; I need to get some grub myself. Give Lynn my love and you have a safe trip. I'll see you when you touch down."

"Solid!"

Goodgame hung up the phone and took another sip of cognac. He reached into his stash, produced a perfectly rolled 1.5, and flamed up. After a couple of long pulls he relaxed on the satin sheets of the king size waterbed. A summer breeze carried the smell of food and the sounds of Salsoul throughout the big brownstone. His thoughts wandered as he inhaled the aroma from two heavy skillets of lightly battered pork chops sizzling atop the stove.

Rice and onions waited patiently in the oven for their rendezvous. Goodgame wanted to chill but there was no time; he was on the clock. It was just before 10:00 am and the streets were calling him.

"Lynnette, how much longer on them plates baby?"

"I'll have 'em ready in a few minutes, bay."

"Alright." He called to Famous. "Lil man, look in the closet and bring my shoes, and get your things together we bout to split."

"Yes," said Fame revving that imaginary engine that all little boys have!

Goodgame put the joint down, pushed up the tile of the dropped ceiling and produced a "Saturday night special" that he never left home without. Tucking it in his waistband he wondered who'd given the pistol that name.

"Had to be a square," he thought, *"cause for a hustler, every night is Saturday night!"*

In the kitchen Lynnette wrapped the food in foil as she listened to her son tell children's stories. Goodgame entered and gave her a long kiss and hug, mentally assuring her that all would go well on this cross country trip that he occasionally took. She'd gone with him before to enjoy the sun and sand but she loved New York, the Harlem spirit, and her home in Esplanade Gardens. She kissed her men and gave them final instructions until the distinct Mercedes horn cut through the music and ended their goodbyes.

"Alright baby, we'll be back in a few days. You know Larry's number if you need anything, and Devine is gon' drop by and check on you so everything's gon' be cool. When I get back we'll check out that *Gladys Knight* show, and I'll bring you some of that sangria you like so much."

Goodgame squeezed her hips while their son struggled to the door with the designer bags.

"C'mon daddy, Uncle D is waiting on us."

Inside the car, the two children, Famous Game, and his best friend, Fourtunate Devine play fought in the back seat, laughing and making bets for penny candy. Dressed in a red Pierre Cardin suit, white button down shirt and white shoes, Famous was already living up to his name. He tried every trick his young mind could think of not to part with the seven pieces he'd just lost.

"Man, how you know they aint married. You aint never been there either, so how you know?"

"I heard it on TV," Fourtune said, "she just his girlfriend; they aint married!"

"They got to be married if they live in the same place, boy."

Fourtune didn't want to hear it.

"Man. I done already told you. You owe me seven pieces of candy, pay up."

Fame blew him off and tried again.

"Daddy, Uncle D!"

"W'sup Fame," asked Dioses turning down the radio?

"Fourtune gon' say Mickey and that girl mouse aint married. Tell him they is. How they gone live together if they aint married? C'mon, now."

Dioses elbowed his friend.

"Well," asked Goodgame, "what about Daffy and all them, Fame? They live there too. Who they s'posed to be, Mickey nem's kids?"

"Yeah Fame, who is they," asked Fourtune, smiling with his hands out?

Famous knew it was a long trip out west and was determined not to be short on candy. He tried again.

"Daddy you know Daffy is a duck. How he gon' be the mice's kids? Them just his homeboys he let hang in the Magic Kingdom while he be running it. Man, why y'all playing?"

Dioses stopped laughing long enough to bring the hustle to an end.

"Sorry man, I think Fourtune's right; they aint married, they just shacking up."

Fame sighed and started counting. When he reached seven he said;

"See there I was gone bring you back all this stuff from Disneyland; but since you gone take all my candy ..."

"Dang Fame," Fourtune pushed it all back on the seat. "Here."

Fame was relieved.

"Good move," said Dioses.

"What 'chu gone bring me," asked Fourtune?

"I 'ont know," said Fame with a mouthful of candy, "whatever my daddy buys us."

NEW YORK CITY
The Bronx

Minutes later at Highbridge Park the two men stood next to a lime green Pinto and talked to the man and woman inside as they chewed on pork chops.

"So y'all got ten hens in them shopping bags in the trunk. Lori, you remember how to stash it," asked Dioses?

"Yeah D, I remember everything to the letter."

The man on the passenger side mumbled something that only she could understand and Goodgame threw his hands up.

"Man, this shit don't make no sense. Lori, what the fuck did he say?"

"Lori tried to hide her smile but her boyfriend Nard was quick as he was self-conscious. It had been just over a week since he'd taken the beating of a lifetime from the NYPD. Some Southern Immortals from off Q5 & Hollis were tired off seeing Harlem players making money in *their* hood and had tried sticking him up after he'd made his collections.

"Its money to be made out here, and a hustler, a real hustler follows the money trail wherever it leads. Be it Queens, L.A., or the doorsteps of Pennsylvania Avenue aint no pooh butt, gangbangers, or no good ol' boy politicians gon' stop us from getting' this money, 'Nard."

That's what Goodgame always said; and Nard wasn't the type to back down.

When they approached him and his bulging black moneybag, he did what came naturally. He unloaded eight shots from his two Saturday Night Specials, *on a Wednesday*, and sent the punks scrambling with a warning and some pissy pants.

"Man, them cats turned tail after the first two shots. I just kept shit poppin' to let 'em know what time it was. Fuck the summer of Sam," he said, "this the summer of Nard."

But the shots had drawn the attention of a squad car. When Nard heard the siren he ran around the corner to stash the bag and guns. Walking down the stoop, two cops questioned and searched him. Mad that all they could find was $1200.00 in his pocket and an airtight story; they taught him a lesson about loyalty, a lesson that cost him several broken ribs and a broken jaw, but saved the bag.

"Uggg, ughhh, wughh...." mumbled Nard through his wired jaw.

"Leonard, calm yo' ass down, man. You gon' have a fucking stroke." Goodgame put his cigarette out. "Niggas can't understand a damn thing you sayin' anyway!"

"Right on," Dioses added. "You gon' upset Lori and make her drop that kid."

Lori smiled and rubbed the pink blouse covering her belly.

"He said don't y'all worry, he aint gone let me forget nothing."

Dioses gave her a piece of paper with the flight information and a phone number.

"Alright, y'all got about an hour to pack them hens and get to the airport. Grab a taxi when you land at L.A.X. Gon' be a dude named Eddie there waiting for you in a cab. He's gonna follow my car. The flight leaves at 1:30. Don't be late."

"We wont," said Lori.

Nard mumbled something and the pinto eased up the block and out of sight.

"Damn baby, even with the short we taking we gon' be able to buy a couple of new blocks when I get back," said Goodgame. "Hey man, I appreciate you rolling wit me on this hook up. Larry's been my man since I was a shortbody. This gon' be good for the families out there. They gon' make at least twenty five grand of each bird." They slapped hands.

"It aint nothing," said Dioses. "Getting this shit for five thousand a bird is almost like getting it free. My old man aint good for nothing else but this."

*

Across the street from them a dull and steady thud sounded as the faded blue racquet ball kept up one. It bounced off the wall in a rainbow like arch as the quiet, inquisitive boy who threw it squinted and judged the distance. He made some adjustments and the ball landed behind his back in his left hand. The crowd cheered while he spoke with the funny talking old man from TV's *Wide World of Sports*. In the middle of the interview he performed another trick. This time he fired the ball into the sky and answered a question or two before he caught it with the bottom of his jersey; just like he'd seen "Mr. October," Reggie Jackson does the week before. Even he had to admit he was good at this.

He pulled off his black and yellow Pirates hat—the one with the three stripes and flat top—and started on his victory lap. Along the way he tripped over his unlaced strings and fell to the ground. The cheering stopped, Cossel disappeared and the park returned to what it was; a vacant lot next to the most recent of the decaying store front apartments that he and his family lived in. His uniform was gone, replaced by his favorite Jimmy Walker T-shirt and his cut off shorts. He stayed grounded for a moment as the dirt clung to his sweaty clothes. What should've been quite embarrassing really wasn't. The clothes were already dusty, and worse than that there was nobody around to see what had happened. There was no pointing or laughing at his fall, just like there were no "ooo's or ahh's" at his tricks. He'd been playing catch by himself. What a sorry sight.

He sat up and looked at the men talking in the park and the two boys playing in the car. They looked to be around his age, but that's where the similarities ended. Everything about their lives seemed better; their clothes, the fact that they were riding in a big shiny car; he'd even heard them arguing about Disneyland and Mickey Mouse. He wondered if his family would ever live so well.

What he envied most though were the boy's fathers. He'd never seen them before, but he'd seen their type. To him they were just like Arnold and Willis on "*Different Strokes.*" He wished some philanthropist would pick him up and give him a stable home in Manhattan. Just once he wanted to run to the door screaming; "Daddy's home!"

All the kids with daddies got way better treatment. At school they had the cool "*Happy Days*" lunchboxes with all the good food. The faculty would talk about this kid's daddy and that kid's daddy; some would give them special treatment based on who their daddies were; like being "*his*" kid somehow made them better than the others. Often the ones being picked up in limos and wearing designer clothes were the worst little fucks around.

The Boy wanted to run upstairs and ask his mother, "*why?*" Why they moved so much, or why they lived so poor, or why he'd never met his father, or why she was never home, why she was always working double shifts or off helping The Movement. But why do that? He knew the answers by heart.

"Look son, I'm not going to lie to you," Marian would say, we go where we are needed, wherever we have members left. We help each other, that's what it's all about. It's not a glamorous life we lead. Look at the neighborhoods in the cities we've been to, they're all poor. That's by design. And it's worse for us because of my past. They won't let me work. They fire me as soon as they find out who I am, and I can't get welfare because then they'd find us." She reached out to him and he watched the cigarette shaking in her hand; a sign of the stress she was under. "I'm sorry baby. I truly am sorry that you have to go through this, but for now that's how it is. They won't stop until they find us. And as for your father," Marian hesitated, "no matter what you hear, he's a good man. One day you'll get to meet him, I promise."

The Boy wondered when that day would be, or if they'd ever passed one another on the street, or what would happen if that day ever came? Would he be able to look him in the eye? Maybe they'd meet one day when he was all grown up and had led his mom out of the hole they were in. They could sit in the house he'd bought her and question each other about the past. At six he couldn't fully understand the sacrifices they'd made because of The Movement but it had to be quite a story. What was so terrible that they wanted him and his people dead?

He had lifetime worth of questions if that day ever came, but right now it was Marian's turn to ask;

"Why on earth are you sitting out here in the dirt, and what are you looking at?"

"Mama," he said, surprised to see her so early, "what 'chu doing home?"

"I didn't work the second shift. Why? You're not happy to see me?"

"Yeah," he said excitedly. He pointed to the Mercedes. "Ma look, the boys in that car are going to Disneyland."

"How do you know?"

"I heard 'em say it when I was playing catch. Ma, look! I got a trick."

Marian stopped him.

"Baby, mama is tired from work. Can you show her later?"

As hurt as he was he rebound quickly.

"Can we go to the park later, I can show you then?"

"Yeah, that's a good idea," said Marian as they started up the stairs. "C'mon let's go inside and get you cleaned up. Where are Yoesef and your sister?"

Inside the playpen Cheris cooed at the sight of her mother. Her father Yoesef, another member of The Movement, was on the couch smoking a joint and reading. He was just as surprised to see Marian home so early.

"Where'd you find her," he asked?

The Boy shrugged his shoulders. He and Yoesef got along well.

"I saw you playing ball," said Yoesef. "Sorry I couldn't come out there."

"That's Ok."

Marian sat Cheris down and went to hug Yoesef.

"Look what I got for you." She gave him a book.

Yoesef jumped up. This excited him; he'd abandoned his original 1972 copy and everything else he owned when the agents came gunning for him. Like others in The Party he'd been listed as an enemy of the state and was making a run for the border. This was just a layover to set his plans and see his baby daughter.

"Hey Marian, I know you aint have no money, how did you get this?"

"I was browsing through the book store on my way home and the owner recognized me," she explained, "gave it to me for free," she said, pleased that her notoriety was good for more than persecution. "And he spoke slowly when he told me this;"

"Nothing happens in politics by chance; if it happens, it was planned that way."
(Franklin D. Roosevelt: 26th President of the United States)

✳

Conspirara: Latin. Meaning to breathe and act in harmony.

Conspire: To plan secretly, an illegal act.

Though the definition has changed some over the years, if we were to believe the picture that's been painted for us, conspiracies are the deluded works of criminals and anarchists; even worse, believers of so called "conspiracy theories" have been labeled as misfits and outcasts or eccentrics with "no life" and "too much time on their hands." Undeniably true in some cases; but I ask you, what are the rich? Insanely wealthy people; some who've never put in a days work in their lives. They live in gated communities; vacation on private, island resorts, and socialize in members' only spas, clubs, lodges and fraternal orders. What are they but a group of people,—society—some with odd views and behavior,—eccentrics— who have nothing else to do with their time but meet in secret? They *are* out there you know; plenty of them. They're everywhere that you aren't. Oh, and it's not by coincidence either, no it's planned that way. Conspired

The 1976 edition of *None Dare Call It Conspiracy* says that one million books were not enough to meet popular demand. The authors ask if you are one of those "persons" that can't quite put your fingers on what's wrong due to the "picture painters." They promised that their book would help you to uncover the "hidden picture" buried by the "Insiders", the Federal Reserve System, the Trilateral Commission and the Council on Foreign Relations; collectively known as, *"The Establishment."*

✳

"This book," said Yoesef "tells you all about the ongoing plan to abolish the constitution of the United States by updating the peoples programming. In the future religion wont matter, science and logic will put an end to faith. Information and technology will turn people into gods. Politics won't matter either. Elections are going to become media productions for the public. Democrat or Republican, both parties will be led by an "invisible government," both of them instruments to promote a New World Order. The book even has a list."

"Who's on it," asked Marian?

"Read it for yourself," he gave it to her, "I promise you'll be surprised." He waved to The Boy "Come over here cadet!"

The Boy rushed over to where his mother and Yoesef were. Yoesef raised his voice to a command tone.

"What do you want to be when you grow up?"

The Boy stood at attention and shouted it like he meant it.

"A General!"

"Let me hear the fourteen signs to slavery."
   "Yes sir!"
   He'd learn the meanings later, but for now he could recite each one verbatim:

Excerpt 10.

"I aint raising no suckers," said Marian proudly hugging him and kissed his cheek.
   "Soldier!" Yoesef shout.
   The boy halted. "Yes, sir."
   "Remember. The only ones who don't believe in the conspiratorial view of history are the ones who don't know it."
   "Yes, sir."
   Yoesef dismissed him and The Boy hurried back to the window just in time to see the men returning to the car. Fame was standing in the sunroof playing. Their eyes met and the lonely look on The Boy's face said a thousand words. He felt sorry for him and flashed him a sign. The Boy had no idea what it meant, but through it he felt a kinship.
   "Fame, sit down and put your seatbelt on," said Dioses, we rolling."
   When the car started "*Harold Melvin and the Bluenotes's*" magnum opus for social change was playing on the stereo;

Excerpt 11.

As the car filled with two generations of gangsters pulled off, each spoke of the future; the elder of one that was nearer and more tangible, and the younger, one more distant but no less possible.
   "I'm telling you Real estate!" Dioses said. "Rockefeller's own tons of real estate that's something safe to invest this money in."
   "What's real estate daddy?"
   "That's when you own land and buildings." Dioses answered. "Stuff like that."
   "Big buildings like The Twin Towers?"
   "Huh, yeah man, you can buy them if you got the bread."
   "Fame," said Fourtunate quietly, "when we get big me and you gon' buy some buildings, Ok."
   "Yep!" Fame replied through bites of candy. "We gon' run New York!"

1978

THE CRUCIBLES

QUEENS
Queensbridge Projects

Mary Hartman, Mary Hartman played on the television but Fatima wasn't watching. The better part of her day was spent cleaning the apartment. She was tired now and lay in bed reading Roots. Kunta Kinte had just lost his foot when there was a knock on her bedroom door.

"Mama, I'm sleepy wit' you," cried her youngest son Bagira. He wiped away crocodile tears. In his room Malik and his best friend Bill played with their *Star Wars* toys and argued about who was going to be Han Solo

"Man," Bill complained, "why you always got to be Han? I only got to be him like one time."

"Nuh, uhh. You was always him when we at yo' house."

"That don't count. When you at yo' house, you can be who you wanna be."

"And when you playing wit' yo' toys," Malik added.

Bill jumped off the bed and slipped on his shoes.

"What is you doing," asked Malik? "Where you going?"

"I'm going upstairs to my house to get *my* Star Wars toys."

"Not at 11:00 at night," said Fatima, on her way to get Bagira's water.

Bill pouted. "Malik won't let me be Han Solo."

"Malik, what have I told you about sharing? Bill is your guest. Let him be Han and you be someone else. What about that guy in black?"

Malik looked at her all crazy like.

Bill explained. "He's a bad guy Mrs. Ali."

"Whatever. You all have about thirty minutes before the lights go out and you go to sleep, so get it together."

"Mama!" Bagira called repeatedly as he pulled Fatima's robe.

"What is it?"

"Malik won't let me play with the toys," he said, evidently not as sleepy as he'd claimed to be.

"You a little liar!"

"What did I tell you about name calling, Malik? Don't make me tell your father you been acting up when he gets home tomorrow."

She looked at the clock. "Baby it's time for you to go to bed anyway."

Malik stuck out his tongue and Bagira started crying.

"Sorry mama. What time is Pop coming home tomorrow," he asked?

"In the afternoon. That's why you all should hurry and go to sleep."

"Where'd cha' daddy go this time," asked Bill.

"Somewhere," Malik opened his eyes wide, "he had to fly on a plane to get there."

"Man, I wish we could fly on a plane and go somewhere too."

"One day," Malik said to him, "we gonna. Don't worry, I got you."

The family was doing well; they'd bought a car and were saving for a house. But Sirius and the band traveled often and made the European trip about twice a year promoting their albums. Performing and meeting new people is what Sirius loved. He told Fatima how he felt like The Duke did when he wrote in his journals. He'd taken her once, making the mistake of letting her see firsthand how European women treat musicians over there. Other than missing his family, the only thing he complained about was the food.

"Man they feed you like you a damn bird. Itty bitty little portions for all that money. Where's the beef?"

Fatima awoke early the next morning with shopping to do for Sirius' special homecoming dinner. Everyone including Bill piled into the Nova to pick up the brown sugar and turnips for the family recipe of chicken tchoupitoulas and greens that Leila had taught her.

It was a little after noon on a late summer day when they got back to Queensbridge. Over thirty-one hundred units made it one of the largest projects in America, and on days like that one all the tenants were in the field trying to soak up the sun. Everyone in every hood lives for the summer. After spending the winter months locked up, summer is their time to shine. On days like that, people were making runs to the aid office or the clinic; and old folks—the brave ones at least—would take walks. If that were a Sunday they'd be going to and from church dressed in big hats with matching purses and shoes. Shorties still in bed clothes would be playing unsupervised in the hallways, as the milk and cereal from breakfast dripped all over the tables. Their parents, if they were still around, would be at work or somewhere recovering from the night before; and the next shift of dealers would be on their way out to relieve the last.

Today Bills mom Sheila sat on the bench in front of their 41st side building in a nightshirt, shorts and some fuzzy house slippers, combing her hair and sipping something that wasn't coffee.

She yelled out when she saw her son.

"Hey baa'by'! Where y'all coming from so early?"

The boys ran ahead to give her hugs as Fatima answered.

"From the store girl, Sirius will be home in a little while and I gotta get this dinner done. What you been up to?"

"Nothing. Sleep. They had a smoke out on the other side last night girl. It was Ok I guess. Same old tired ass niggas. I aint get in till about four in the morning."

She told the boys to go play. Fatima knew what that meant.

"You smiling, where's Rob at?"

"I sent his ass home. Shit, he tired too. Think he can get some then lay up all day. Fuck that. Get a job nigga, aint no love."

"Girl you know you crazy," said Fatima laughing and waving her hands.

"I'll keep the boys tonight if you want me to. I know you trying to do something, Sirius just coming home and shit." Sheila wiggled her ass on the bench. "I'm good for a little while."

"I'll see. I never know what kind of mood he's going to be in when he comes off these trips." Fatima paused. "But could you watch them now for a little while, so I can finish up dinner?"

"Go 'head, I told you I aint doing nothing. Hey," Sheila yelled, "y'all boys get over here and play where I can see you!"

Five hours later the kitchen of the Ali house was on fire. The dish was in the oven and Fatima left a trail of smoke down the stairwell. Sirius was over three hours late when the girl from next door knocked to tell her he was outside.

Sirius was in a good mood and glad to be home. With his suit jacket slung over his back and his burgundy silk shirt clinging to his body, he signed an autograph for the taxi driver. Malik and Bagira were happy to see their old man and were unaware of the trouble that was coming as they pulled on his leg and grabbed at the bags. Some older boys took his instruments to the elevator as Benny, one of the neighborhood wineheads, saw a perfect money making opportunity in it all.

"Si-ri-us! What-up man?"

He held out his fist for a pound and Sirius showed him love, thinking; *"Now this is more like home,"* before he answered;

"Nothing much Benny. What you got for me today?"

"Aww man, I got this sweet camera, man. You should check it out, just like new playa. It's got this scope thang on it and shit. Oops! My fault man I forgot about the boys for a second there."

"It's cool, they've' heard it all before. But I don't need another camera Benny."

Before Benny could open his mouth with a comeback, Sirius hit him with this.

"I tell you what. You take a couple of pictures of me and my boys and I'll throw you a fin.'"

"Show you right." Benny's mind was already adding the bottles. Fatima stood next to Sheila and watched them. Sirius smiled at her, trying to get on her good side. He and the band had stopped at the airport bar and took a few shots with some flight attendants from the plane. Afterwards he'd stopped by the florist and picked up flowers on top of the other gifts. He gave the bouquet to Bagira who ran it to Fatima as Sirius blew her kisses. Sheila folded her arms and mumbled;

"Its gon' take more than that, playa."

The gesture had saved Sirius for the moment; Fatima turned and head for the elevator, calling for the older boys to help her with the bags.

Sirius hugged the boys and posed for a few more pictures. Malik watched Benny fumble with the camera as he thought about selling it at the liquor store. Malik had never quite known whether to laugh at him or pity him.

Benny figured a few compliments would earn him a tip.

"Damn Sirius, these came out smooth. Y'all look good. That's a 'baaad' suit you got there man." Then he stopped. "Damn, this one aint come out quite right."

He continued peeling the back off the picture. No one knew it yet, but his five dollar hustle had produced something priceless; a rare double exposure. Malik stood on the corner between two Queensbridge buildings, his back to the block, his expression pensive. He wore a striped shirt and held a thousand yard stare. The camera's flash had penetrated his head and exposed the thoughts of a smile-less child in a New York state of mind. And at last something other than wine had stimulated Benny's brain.

"Lil' man, what was you thinking on this one," he asked.

"It aint hard to tell," said Sirius, handing him the money. "Come on y'all, let's go inside."

He took his sons hands and walked through the door, greeting everyone and answering questions as all showed love to 41'st sides Ambassador to the world and his little dignitaries.

Upstairs Sirius explained why he was late; leaving out the part about the stewardesses. The family gathered around the table and listened to his stories from the trip. Later, Q and Leila dropped in for dinner with Monique, one of her girlfriends from the shop. When Fatima found out she was Muslim, it put her worries to rest.

Laughter from the boys and their cousins playing in the back room echoed throughout the apartment. After dinner Sirius and Q talked current events while Fatima explained to Leila and Monique how she was looking for a new job. Now that Bagira was older she was seriously considering finishing the teaching classes she was taking when she'd met her husband. The way she looked at it, taking time out to have two children had only added to her resume. Soon she was enjoying the conversation and had forgotten all about Sirius's lateness. But perhaps she had a reason to be worried, she knew her husband, well.

BROOKLYN

Weeks later in the Neece household Gaietta was doing housework. Giving birth had changed her figure so drastically that the modeling career she'd longed for was now just a memory. As that dream faded so did her desire to put in long hours sewing in the garment district because suddenly the beautiful people didn't look so good anymore. When her body changed, so did their attitudes. Now she wanted to do something more substantial with her life, something that would help people.

She realized her new dream of becoming a nurse when she completed her classes at Queens College. She'd taken a job at a clinic not far from her home and was now in school to become an RN.

Her schedule didn't give her many weekends off, but she'd cleared this one so she could spend some time with Thomas who was excited about Monday; his first day of school.

It was early, just another Saturday in Brooklyn as Thomas looked out the window already upset. He was bored and had nothing to do. It was already hot and the radio said the temperature would reach 102. Gaietta had a couple of fans going as Thomas dreamed about school and hanging out with the other kids. His entire summer had been spent sitting under his mom or the babysitter.

"Thomas Ty'ree Neece! What you go'ing to do? Stare out of that win'dow all day. I told you we are going out'side la'ter. Why don't you go and watch the tele' until you take your bath."

"Mommy," he said, leaving the window.

"Yeah pa'pa."

"Can I have a bowl of cereal?"

"Aye yie yie. Boy you just finished ea'tin break'fast. You still hun'gry?"

"Yes mama, cause I always eat cereal when I watch cartoons," he explained.

Thomas was a big boy with a healthy appetite. His clothes were 'Husky' and at age six he wore size twelve, *Incredible Hulk 'Underoos'*, which is all he had on in an attempt to stay cool. He flipped the channels looking for his favorite, *The Superfriends*. That's when he heard it.

"Yes!"

The Emmy winning *Schoolhouse Rock* was a treat; something you didn't get to see every Saturday. Thomas loved it and learned every episode. He had an incredible memory of words and how to manipulate them. To hear it once was all he needed, after that he'd repeat it to you or flip it and make it his own. Today's episode, *Interjections,* was one he especially liked. Geraldine was hot and he was glad she was dissing Geraldo. Thomas thought with his big smile and afro, he kind of looked like the boy on *Verb* and he'd sing along with him;

"… When I use my imagination …"

Excerpt 12.

He was a bright boy who could *say* his ABC's and could count past fifty. He loved when Gaietta would let him practice with money and she enjoyed hearing him recite songs and stories. She believed his memory and cantabile was Jah's gift.

They went out later like Gaietta had promised. Early on they shopped for school supplies and later she took her beloved to see the movie *Heaven Can Wait*. He wanted to see *Animal House* but Gaietta thought the quirky little comedy about a guy dying and going to heaven before his time would serve him better. She'd never know how deeply the thoughts of dying, life after death, and ultimately being bornagain would rest in her son's subconscious.

That night as a rare, "albino elephant" rumbled down the tracks Thomas had a question.

"Mama, what's heaven?"

"Heaven, pa'pa? Heaven is a wonderful place where God and his an'gels live. No'ting but good'ness dere. Peace and qui'et. None of dis riff-raff, or dese sin'ners." She circled her finger around the train car and noticed the puzzled look on her sons face. "But don't you concern your'self wit' such matters, my love. Dat worry is for much la'ter. Every'body has to die some'day, but you've got lots of living to do."

Thomas sank deeper into the cradle of his mothers loving arms and agreed. In his mind though he wasn't so sure. He looked hard at his surroundings; the boombox playing at the far end of the car, the teenagers joking, shooting dice and sneaking beer from brown bags. It looked like a good time to him. If his quiet, sheltered, home life was anything like heaven and this was the alternative, he had some big choices to make.

Monday arrived; the day Thomas had been waiting for. Like anything caged he was ready to get out and do his thing. The first week of school is like the crucible. You have to come correct or suffer the consequences the rest of the year. With every car and bus that unloaded children were sizing each other up. If your parents drove a bucket, you got dropped off around the corner. No new gear? You show up the second week when the major fronting was over.

The first half of the day breezed by for Thomas. The teacher took an instant liking to his chubby cheeks and the goody-goody role that he'd mastered playing at home with Gaia. He passed her tests with ease and earned a few gold stars, but outside in the field was where the real test lay.

Whatever their roll in the classroom, the period of lunch/recess is the most exhilarating of a young students life. Whole days are planned around the schoolyard; it's the proving ground for youth; the place where stars are born.

Thomas maxed his bologna and pb&j sandwiches in less than five minutes. He washed them down with a thermos full of *Tang*. He'd snuck and ate his *Little Debbie's* snack in class and only a Granny Smith apple lay rocking inside the lunch box. There was no way he was eating that when there was playground full of treats to be had.

"That one little cake mom gives me will never make it to lunchtime," he thought.

Knowing this would be a regular thing, Thomas went looking for a supplier.

Circling the grounds in search of a victim, behind a dumpster in the back of the yard is where he found them; a group of kids, mostly third graders, snappin', baggin', shooting dice, and playing the dozens. The hat holding the pot was filled with cakes and money.

The White kid was up first.

"I saw your mother standing on top of the Empire State Building eating airplanes."

The Japanese kid went next.

"Your mother was on *Fonzie's* dick; that's why you were born with one thumb. Heeey!"

Thomas jumped in.

"It's a Black kid, White kid, and Japanese kid; they all in the schoolyard bragging about they daddies. The Japanese kid says; "My dad writes little poems called Haikus and people pay him hundreds of dollars for them. The white kid says, "That's nothing, my dad writes books and people pay him thousands for them. Then the black kid says, "My dad got both y'alls faded, every week he memorizes a couple of pages from a book then says 'em in church and it takes ten people to collect all his dough."

Most of the kids laughed for the sake of laughing, but one stood out.

"Aint 'chu in my class?"

"Yeah,"

"W'sup, I'm Othello."

"What's up, I'm Thomas."

"You wanna get in the game?"

Thomas was embarrassed, he didn't have a dime. He continued watching the other kids, staring at the cakes and about twenty dollars. Othello had just lost his loot. He elbowed Thomas's arm.

"Come on."

They started across the schoolyard.

"Where we going," asked Thomas?

"I know where we can get some money from."

Thomas's face lit up. "How you know all them older kids?"

"My sister *been* going to school here, she in eighth grade."

In another corner they approached a group of girls puffing on one cigarette. Othello slapped one on her butt.

"Gimme some money, Kim."

Kim's girls laughed as she frowned.

"Stop touching my ass Othello. Where's your sister?"

"She sick, she aint coming till next week," he said, "Gimme some money."

"I aint got no money for you," she screamed!

Thomas's eyes were fixed on her bouncing bosom.

"Ooo, you're bad," said Kim's best friend Steevy. "I see you looking at her."

Thomas kept looking. Othello kept begging, and Kim kept repeating herself until Thomas finally blurted out;

"You look good, you wanna make some?"

"Some what," asked Kim?

"Some money."

"How?"

At last Thomas was in the game. He whispered something in Othello's ear and Othello took off. He returned after a minute with the hat.

"I'll give you all this money right here if you let me bite cha' tits," said Thomas.

The girls laughed like crazy.

"You're a little pervert," Steevy said with a big smile.

"Uhh, uhh." Kim's neck rolled. "I don't know what you thought; you got the wrong one baby!"

Othello pulled three dollars from his pocket and added it to the pot.

"Ok, Ok, what about all this; and he won't bite, he'll just kiss 'em."

Kim stopped and looked. "How much money is that?"

The boys counted out twenty-five dollars but Kim still didn't trust them.

"You'll give me all of that just to kiss them?"

They said it in unison. "Uhh, huh."

"Just to kiss them, *that's all?*"

"Nah, to suck 'em," Thomas said quickly.

"Nope nope," Kim waved her hand, "you said …"

"Alright yeah, twenty-five, just to kiss 'em. Hurry up before the bell rings."

Steevy jumped in. "Give it to me, I'll do it."

Some of the other girls agreed and finally Kim said. "Ok, where at?"

The boys led all four girls over to the place they were before. The gamblers were nowhere to be found.

"This good right here," said Othello, unable to believe his luck.

Kim lifted her bra and blouse. Thomas took a long look and wondered what he'd done to deserve this. Kim was nervous and smacked her lips. Thomas touched them softly and circled his finger around the points. She bit down her lip trying not to get aroused before she smacked them again.

"C'mon, you better suck … I mean kiss 'em. I aint got all day."

Thomas kept feeling for a few more seconds before he said;

"Nah, I'm cool with this, kissing 'em costs too much."

All the boys jumped from behind the dumpster pointing, teasing, and laughing. Othello kept the money and Kim cursed them out as she pulled her shirt down. Then they all went at it, boys against girls, until the bell rang.

From that day on Thomas never worried about what he'd eat at lunch. All the kids treat him to his favorites; the milks were chocolate and the cookies, butter crunch.

QB

Malik's first day hadn't gone as well. The week before school started Fatima had found something and this time no matter how hard Sirius tried to explain she refused to hear it. The lipstick on his boxers said it all. She'd never caught him cheating before, but she'd always heard the stories.

"Baby," Sirius pleaded, "if you would just listen a minute I can explain."

Fatima's tone was sullen; she never once raised her voice and Sirius knew this time was different. The sight of her packing a suitcase told him that she meant business.

"Sirius, you need to listen to me. Cause, *I'm serious.* I don't want to hear whatever excuse you've made up. I can't prove it, but then again I don't have to because I feel it. I know you're doing something. You got lipstick on your underwear, perfume on everything. I'm not stupid; I see the way people are looking at me at the club. I've got to trust someone, and since it can't be you, it may as well be me. When you can talk to me without some smooth-ass game coming out of your mouth, do it. Until then Bagira and I will be at my mothers. I need some time for me; so I can get my head together without worrying about where yours has been. She pushed him aside. "You make sure your son gets to school. You can do that, can't you?"

Sirius didn't know what to say. Fatima grabbed some clothes before she tiptoed into the kids' room where the TV was playing;

"Heeere's Johnny!"

She turned the volume down and kissed Malik on his forehead. Then she picked Bagira up and went back to the bedroom. Sirius leaned against the wall as she dressed him.

"Look," he said, raising his voice. "You blowing this shit way out of proportion!"

Fatima never even looked at him.

"Wake Malik up if you want. You want to deal with that tonight?"

He tried a different route.

"It's too late for you to be out there with that boy. Why don't you at least wait ...?"

"I'm going around to Sheila's house to call a taxi. Bye Sirius."

The next several days became a period to remember for both Ali men. Sirius spent more quality time with his son. They took advantage of the dog days of summer and spent long hours playing ball. Sirius had been teaching him to read music and play the horn thinking how it would be fitting if his son would become a third generation musician. In the evenings after hanging out at the barber shop and eating fast food, he'd try out his new compositions on his one man audience. Malik always clapped in approval. Good times were had, but they both missed Fatima.

On Monday morning with his father right behind him Malik took his first steps to school. It was a short walk from the building and all the neighborhood kids went there. Malik was relieved to see Bill and some more of his guys in the schoolyard when they arrived.

"So what's up 'Lik, you gon' be alright out here? I see Bill and Half-Pint over there waiting on you." Sirius waved to them.

"Yeah Pop, I'm Ok."

"Good. I'ma meet you right back here when school let out. Don't go running off cause we going to the shop to see your auntie. Ok."

Sirius took the cigarette out of his mouth and cleared the smoke to make sure he understood. Malik's mind was on something else.

"Pop, when is ma coming home?"

"I don't know man, but you got other things to think about now. You talked to her on the phone last night. Did you ask her?"

"Yes."

"Well."

"She said it was up to you."

Sirius chuckled.

"That's the same thing she told me man. Don't worry, she'll be home soon. Now go on, your boys waiting on you."

He held out his hand. Malik slapped him five and ran over to his crew. Sirius walked across the street and talked to some of the playas from the hood until the bell rang and the kids went inside.

That evening in the barbershop the old timers sat around arguing about everything from the news that smallpox had been eradicated to why Sadat and Begin didn't deserve that years Nobel Peace prize. Malik sat in an empty seat and fell asleep. When he woke Sirius was gone. He looked around for his uncle Q but couldn't find him either. Nobody noticed the child walk out the door and down to the beauty shop looking for a familiar face. The shades had been pulled and the door locked, but Malik heard music and saw a light coming from the inside. He searched until he found a rip in the shade and looked through it. Not knowing what to do, he banged his little fist against the window a few times and gave up. Then he sat on the pavement and began to cry. Inside one player listened as another sang the words he longed to say;

Excerpt 13.

Sirius leaned back in the stylist chair broken hearted and half out of his mind from the lines and weed on the plate next to him. Monique's afro puffs and dark skinned face bobbed up and down between his legs. It took a few minutes before one of the barbers banging on the door brought him to his senses.

Malik was still crying when he picked him up, sat him in the chair and tried to explain human nature to him.

"Come on man, stop crying. Everything's gon' be alright. Tomorrow after school we'll go down to the store and you can pick out anything you want. But we gotta keep this here between us or your mommy aint never coming home. You don't want that do you?" Malik shook his head. "Good. Trust me man. You'll understand one day." Sirius waved his finger back and forth between their chests as he bounced his son on his knee.

"It's like this with all fathers and sons. What's in *you* is in *me*."

1979

THE TWO PLANS

GERMANY
Westphalia

A veil of secrecy cloaked the attendants and the conferences at the Grand Alpine Lodge in the Federal Republic of Switzerland. The last seventy-two hours had been all business, every second by the book as around 100 of the worlds most powerful figures had come together to plan our futures. Just hours after the talks concluded Benjamin Freidman sat exhausted in a limousine watching a steady stream of planes touch down on a private airstrip in the Westphalian countryside; his skin tingling as he anticipated the arrival of the others. This was the one night when internal bickering was set aside as Patriarchs, Knights, and Magus' convened with their Hidden Masters. Tonight's illustrious gathering was only for the *"Aluminados"* all the fools were gone.

Though the group has no name and they surely existed prior to May of 1954, that's when they were discovered at the Bilderberg Hotel in Oosterbeek, Holland. From their Netherlands headquarters—*The Hague*—their three tiered thirty nine member, (13+13+13) steering committee selects the most influential bankers, royals, politicians, scientists, philosophers and media personalities to attend their annual three day summits which they claim are about bettering the world; but over the years many researchers have found the truth to be far less amiable.

In his 1979 autobiography *"With No Apologies,"* former Senator Barry Goldwater had this to say about the goals of one of their brightest members.

Excerpt 14.

Rows upon rows of pine trees whizzed along both sides of the limos as they traveled the cobblestone road to Wewelsburg; the Gothic castle of the Thurn und Taxis. Benjamin kept to himself, loosening his tie and downing another drink to hold back the uneasiness that came from setting foot on this soil; reverberations of his people from *"the night of broken glass."* Even to his colleagues Benjamin was something of a loner. His ancestors were Russian Jews who'd come to Vienna from the Volga mountains. In 1782, through *The Order of Strict Observance,* Jews were officially accepted into the Scottish Rite of Freemasonry, and by 1875 Benjamin's mother had married into a family of wealthy German investment bankers. By 1917 the Freidman family had acquired sizable interests in the Zionist movement and the Belfour Declaration. Four years later in 1921 Benjamin was born in what was to become the state of Israel.

Twenty seven more years would pass before the Zionists dream was realized, during which time Benjamin did his part in Israel's fight for independence by serving with the *Igurn*—the Jewish military underground. These days he'd advanced to key positions in *Shin Bet* and *Mossad.* In the states those credentials made him a supremely qualified member of The Establishment.

Heckler & Koch carrying centurions waved the vehicles past the last of the security checkpoints and onto the grounds where servants were on hand to prep the passengers for the opening ceremony.

"We're here Benjamin," said a friend. "Come now, we mustn't be late for *Le Messe Noir."*

A short time later in the concert hall *Dies Irae* from Verdi's *Requiem* signaled the start of The Black Mass. Under the faint glow of a single gilded scone the litany of over a hundred black hooded and cloaked figures reached a feverish pitch as they closed in around two female bodies; a nude one that would serve as an altar and another, who dressed as a nun would serve as the sacrifice.

"Shemhamforash ..." They shout. *"... And Let Reason Rule The Earth!"*

At the end of the ritual, the palatial and carnal desires of the participants were treated to a diverse and spectacular spread.

On the verge of sixty, neither Benjamin's appetite nor stamina was what it once was. Taking a bottle of *Stolichnaya* as his companion, he went outside the castle looking for a quiet place to collect his thoughts. Last month he and Tzipi, his wife and the mother of his ten year old son, had separated after she'd finally discovered the true nature of his business.

"For fifteen years I've been married to a professional liar."

He was just about to admit that to himself when he opened the Bentley and was startled by the sight.

"Oy! Golem."

Before he could slam the door, a voice called out to him from inside.

"Wait Benji. Come back. It's alright," it said laughing. "You want some of this?"

Benjamin answered instantly. "No thanks. I'm quite alright."

"Hey listen Ben; just give me a few minutes will ya'?

"Sure."

Benjamin closed the door, leaned back against the vehicle and opened the bottle. Forgetting about the glass he took a long swig and wondered what in hell he'd just wandered into.

The voice belonged to the youngest son of his former boss and one time Director of the Central Intelligence Agency.

His code name was "*W* and he'd spent the last five years trying to erase the five party years he'd spent between graduating Yale University and entering Harvard business school; a period that included arrests for drunken driving, cocaine possession, and draft evading. Five years that had also painted him as the "black sheep" of a family at the forefront of a cabal to place at the head of the United States, agents of MI6 and the Windsor Monarchy. Until this evening all accounts had point towards a reformation of W's wayward ways.

Two buxom Swedes with heads full of cornrows exit the car. One said to W.;

"We'll be in the Grotto." The other waved to Benjamin and licked her lips.

"C'mon in here Benjamin," said W.

He had pulled up his pants but made no attempt to hide the copious amount of cocaine sprinkled across his robe, or the dozens of cocaine constructed dollar signs surrounding the Bombay and tonic on the Bentley's bar.

"Look Benji, take a look at this. You think this is Bolivian flake right here, right. Wrong! This is money baby, money in the bank."

W. snorted a few of the dollar signs.

"I'm loaded," he howled, before blowing the rest away.

Benjamin hurried to cover his nose from the powdery mist.

"You've gotta loosen up man," said W. "I'm celebrating, and you should be too. Were all set. Come this time next year The Company will be running the largest corporation in the world and by April 1st of '81 those fools are in for an even bigger surprise. They're about to witness a dynasty like no other. You and Mossad have played a big part in that and it won't be forgotten."

Benjamin looked at him. In that moment he reminded him of Edgar E. Newman, the *Mad* Magazine man-child.

"You haven't spoken with my dad yet have you," asked W?

"Briefly, he told me we'd talk later."

"Yeah, he and Stan are supposed break the news, but what the hell, you look like you could use some cheer so act surprised when they tell ya'. Congratulations, my man! They want to make you Chief of Station in Paris. We need someone over there that can get the job done. Not one of those goddamn pink pansies."

The news put a smile on Benjamin's face.

"There must be something big happening?"

"Benji, big things are happening all over. Like my old man says, 'This thing we got here is a *big* idea.' The New World Order is *here,* and with it came a new global economy. Diversification is gonna be the key to prospering during the coming years. You guys should know that better than all. Just look what we've accomplished in the last year alone. It was our oil deals with the Saudis that caused the energy crisis and boosted the foreign car market in America, we've established the Trade Act, diplomatic relations with China, ousted the Shah and secured agents in key positions in Japan, Canada, France, Italy, Germany, Russia, the UK and the US. Now with a little more help from …"

Benjamin saw the pitch coming from a mile away.

"W.", we rely on a broad coalition of people to keep this thing running smoothly. I have a board I have to answer to and its members like to make the presidents, *dead or alive*, work for them; not the other way around."

Then Benjamin reminded W. of the motto of the old school banking families.

"'Permit me to control the money of a nation and I care not who makes its laws.'"

W. placed a stern hand on his shoulder, a hand meant to steer him in the "right" direction.

"Look Benjamin, I like you, so whenever the truth comes out, and it always does, you'll never be able to say I lied to you. Take some of that money we've been funneling you and your buddies at BCI—Banque du Credit International—and invest it in technology. Information is the future. We've got this guy Jim working on that Web thing over at CERN that's gonna revolutionize the world. What television took forty years to do, this thing will do in ten. Mass media is another good investment; next to the Egyptians you guys have always had the best scribes. Those books were brilliant, but let's face it, intellectualism is dead. Who has time to read a book, less known thirty of 'em, then you got those codes to learn, *"The Zion Protocols,"* and all that crap." W. laughed heartily. "Shit. I hate to admit it, but the truth is the faith based programs are the oldest and are gonna be the hardest to break; but rest assured, one way or another we'll get 'em. I mean the only ones who still believe in them anyway are the poor and the third world nations, and by the year 2000 at least 1.5 billion of those African, Asian, and Latin American undesirables will be gone thanks to good old mother nature and our bio-warfare projects; and with this new GRID virus the WHO has in store, and the Severe Acute Respiratory Syndrome and H#5N#1 bugs they're testing out in Asia, decimation of all the inferior races is inevitable. In the desert, near Fort Meade is an underground lab we call "The I'land," there our eugenics teams are working on The Human Genome Project. That is gonna produce ideal citizens; sons of fire, not clay."

"It's the Thule Society all over again," thought Benjamin. *"Too bad Himmler and Mengele didn't live to see their work completed."*

W. watched as those uneasy feelings rushed forward on Benjamin's face.

"Uhh, ohh, here it comes. Whenever one of your people gets a bad hand or gets it caught in the cookie jar you play the race card; you're getting to be as bad as the ..."

"Regardless of how I feel," interrupted Benjamin, "It's too soon. The programs are too bold, the people will find out."

"So what, that's exactly why they'll work. Blown cover as cover. And whose gonna have enough moxie to say something. You know *our* motto. 'If you're not with *us*, then you're with the enemy.' Get real Benji, who's gonna go against a superpower?"

Benjamin remembered W. had never been to Yemen, never seen ten-thousand AK-47 wielding holy warriors high on *Anima Mundi* and seeking martyrdom.

"War is war, and you and I are profiteers of war," said W. "What your people don't realize is that the ways of traditional warfare are long gone.

To hell with the Geneva Convention. You heard what the Gnomes said in Zurich, you can read between the lines. The days of despots like Hitler and Stalin, hell even Arafat and Belfour; they are history.

Ideas like freedom and uprisings are nothing more than the failed dreams of would-be,"—W. made air quotations with his fingers—"revolutionaries," otherwise our NSA counter-intelligence programs would have picked up on them, in which case they'll soon be ghosts in one of our Black Prisons. From now on we're taking a more proactive approach; *we* will create and eliminate the enemy before they get the chance to do it to us."

"Like in Iran, Iraq and Afghanistan."

"Exactly. They exist as long as we allow them to. And if your friends at the bank have anything to say about that you remind 'em, "It's only murder, all Gods creatures do it." Then you tell 'em W. said this. 'If they back us, I personally guarantee in five years the interest alone will be in the tens of millions, and were talking high nine figures in fifteen years."

"High nines! You'd have to raise the borrowing cap exponentially for that to happen, and with The Fed controlling the interest rates you could make America a debtors nation ..."

Benjamin's voice trailed off as W's plan came into focus.

"If all goes as well, after my fathers run, it's my turn. 1996. W. baby; and that stands for war. By the time I get outta office Americans will have inherited a debt from which they will never recover."

Suddenly the plan seemed less insidious. After processing the dollars signs it all made sense. Benjamin mustered a smile for W's ambitious tale and watched as he pulled two joints from a cigarette case, put them in his mouth and lit them up. "Watch out world," said Benjamin quietly.

W. Smiled and said in his phony Texan twang.

"What do we care if they hate us, Benji? Just so long as they pay us."

W. passed him one and said;

"Turn the sounds up man."

The Doobie Brothers Grammy winning hit was playing.

Excerpt 15.

"You know the saying Benji, 'When at last reason becomes the religion of man, then our problems will be solved.'"

NEW YORK CITY
The Bronx

It was still on and taking place tonight in the gangster zone. The Old Man had sent his emissaries to inform attendees of the rules; nine delegates, no weapons. Not since the sixties had a rally of this size been attempted, but the Councils vote was unanimous. The time was at hand as all the heads had heard the unmistakable whisperings of a nameless fear.

The sun and moon were busy changing positions when the city began its change of regime. From all five points the gangs of New York converged on the spot.

Every organization, from every hood, in every city had been invited. Black Spades, Southern Immortals, the Furries, the Rouges, Dead Rabbits, the Shower Posse, Black P-Stone Rangers, Gangster Disciples, Almighty Latin Kings, MS-13, MS-18, the Mexican Mafia, Vice Lords, El Rukuns, B's and C's, even the Orphans.

"Tonight all beefs are squashed!"

Those were the orders of The Old Man. Imprisoned since forever because the government did not care for his political views; he'd been silent for the last ten, years. Legend was that through his proxies he ran the largest organization in the city, the *Thuggee*, from high atop his prison perch. With a resume that include gang leader, Black Panther, scholar, and General, he was the most respected individual in a world where little respect was given. For years the armies of the street had listened when he spoke, but the vision of the eye was onerous, changing the focus of the people as ideas of community ties and family values were being banned from us, and a sinful decade of decadence called the eighties was being planned for us.

There was a murmur on all nine floors of the abandoned *Alamut Hotel* as the crowd of well over thousand prepared themselves.

"What do you know about the Old Man?"

"What does he look like," asked the younger boppers?

The answer from the older heads was always the same.

"They call him the one and only. No one but Surya has ever seen his face, not even when he was free. But his voice is unmistakable, it flows first through Surya and then through you. Just hearing it is like, MAGIC! *A whole lotta magic!"*

On the ground floor, surrounded by his security force and glowing like a six and a-half foot pillar of fire, Surya, who'd become the voice of The Old Man in all matters stepped into the immaculate garden of the hotel atrium austere; dressed in fatigues and a hoodie, black jeans and boots, when he looked toward the heavens all he could see was troops. Stoically he raised a red knotted bandanna known as a *rumal,* and brought them to attention.

"THUGS OF THE WORLD, STAND UP!"

"Close your eyes, suckers. Now open them. What do you see? The Old Man sees the best of times and the worst of times ahead. Now open your minds and tell me what you see. The Old Man sees what you all are lacking, and that is *vision.*

But worry not suckers, because he has enough of that shit to go around, and he has seen in a dream a future that we will work to make real. A future where we will work to complete the dreams of those that came before us. A future where our voices are heard and where equality is more than an empty word, where our ideas are valued and we are duly compensated for them, a future where every man women and child is free to create his or her own destiny. *Can You Dig It?*"

Boppers young and old shout cheers and applause, until he raised his rumal again and they all paused.

"It will not happen overnight, nothing substantial ever does, but in 20 short years what you now consider to be impossible will in fact, *be*, because The Old Man has a plan, and the vehicle that we will use to drive forward that plan has been set before us. The Old Man has named it,

'**H**armonious **I**nfluences **P**rovided to **H**elp **O**ur **P**eople,' but you brothers may know it simply as Hip-Hop.

Can you dig it? Can You Dig It? CAN-YOU-DIG-IT?"
    The boppers began an extended ovation.

✳

Nobody knows for sure the origins of "Rap," the best estimates place them some-where in the slums of the south Bronx between 1974 and '78. That the break-beats, scratches and smoke induced lyrics of this nations hungry tired and poor's some-times violent and sexual, but always inspiring and poetic visions would become the soundtrack for future generation of Americans is just one thing that its founders had planned on. The others were a brand new lifestyle, a brand new economy, and a brand new way of thinking based around the art form. For them it was totally conceivable that in twenty years Hip-Hop would produce its own party, its own laws, its own army, and its own government *inside* the government. Though what continues to mystify acolytes to this day is that it all began with the pressing of a single record, a 12 inch, candy-coated, aquamarine miracle courtesy of a three man gang from Sugarhill.

✳

With a raise of his rumal Surya continued the promulgation.

"And when I say brothers, know that I mean *all of you;* all the so-called undesirables that they have written off and cast away. All of you soldiers! I call you that because whether you know it or not, there are no civilians left.

We are all soldiers. Agents in an eternal battle against powerful and greedy misanthropists, bent on world domination.

Their Hidden Masters have instructed their "Great Architect" to supply his builders with blueprints for the construction of a new world free from the bloodlines of we indigenous people. For centuries they have employed magicians, ordained kings and deified themselves in order to suppress the knowledge of their agenda, promote a damned ideology, and enslave all who oppose it. Wake Up Brothers! Their malfeasance knows no bounds.

At this very moment the Beast feasts on your flesh, sustains itself on secretions from your grails, and builds it's empires on the bones of your ancestors.

Wake Up Soldiers!

It's the sweat from our brows that fuel this corporation, the beat from our hearts that call its cadence, our spirit that gives it life. And from this day forth, through this blessing called Hip-Hop, it will be *our* culture, *our* ideals, and *our* voices that call for the people of the world, white and black, tan and yellow, red and brown to come together and blend the families, because the color of Hip-Hop is one shade, its goal, one love and one nation amalgamated under one God, and *that* is what those devils fear."

It had started even before he finished, more than just cheers and applause; this time there was a constant and rhythmic pounding that threatened to level the entire structure. A practice started in the prisons known as "the voice of the voiceless." It was the way the Thuggee showed love. The Alamut shook like a packed Coliseum. The Energy coursed through Surya as the ground rumbled beneath his feet. High atop The Mountain the Old Man felt it too, a rush of adrenaline that for him, felt like, victory. Twelve minutes passed and the pounding had not ceased, the soldiers were gone now, lost in a wave of emotion as Surya raised his rumal one last time and brought the conclave to a close.

"To arms Thugs, raise your weapons, and prepare them for the fight for freedom that is on the way. Because although we would welcome peace, the truth is, there can never be peace until we get a piece."

✳

Into the next morning and beyond wherever they went, whatever they did, anyone who'd been in earshot couldn't help cogitating the Old Man's words, trying to decipher what to believe and what not to. A Hip-Hop Nation; who could stop that? In the Caribbean where painting perfect pictures had never worked, the brethren had already chosen sides.

"Dem' either ride wit us, or collide wit us."

"Selassie I!"

With that, Rastas played the tape and took some time to meditate on things.

1980

SURPRISE!

JAMAICA
Kingston

<u>Excerpt 16.</u>

Paul yelled over the radio.

"Thomas you be care'ful out dere play'in, ya hear?"

"Yes papa."

Paul strained trying to pick him up. He opted for a kiss on the cheek instead. Then Thomas ran off to play with the other children. This was a joyous occasion, the first time he'd seen his son in three years.

After his father's health improved, Paul returned to New York City three months after Gaietta had given birth. So far this reunion was going better than that one.

BROOKLYN
1972

Emane came through wonderfully for Gaietta, staying with her and Thomas for two weeks until Mama Neece arrived to help care for them. It was a special time for them as they became each others extended family. Emane would jokingly tell baby Thomas how lucky he was to have a supermodel as his god-mother. Even Samantha dropped in to congratulate the girls on their titles having apologized for the "misunderstanding" in Jamaica long before.

Mama Neece had been to America once, right after her husband died; but that was to Tampa, Florida, nothing like New York. Something about the visit; she never had the urge to return. She'd warned Gaietta before she left home; but as we know, children; people for that matter have their own living to do.

When Paul returned home things had changed. Gaietta's doubts had escalated; she was used to his absence and did little to hide it. As for him, beautiful images of the home he'd tried for so long to forget kept entering his mind. The apartment on St. James was cold. The only warmth he felt there was the summer winds that blew in through the big bay windows.

As the gap between the lovers grew, Paul and Mama Neece grew closer. She noticed that he lacked the rugged good looks and the strong take charge attitude of the typical Caribbean man; nevertheless she believed that she'd found what her daughter had seen in him.

His love was genuine and strong, but somehow he managed to be at once responsible and indecisive. Having known Paul's father for years Mama Neece believed she knew the reason for his dueling natures. Olin, his papa was a serious man and somewhat of a perfectionist. Knowing what was expected from the son of a preacher man couldn't have been easy for him.

As a disciplined Rastafarian priest Olin had been a dedicated 'souljah' of the religious movement as well as Emperor Haile Selassie ever since 1930 when he was crowned in Ethiopia. The Rastafarian faith doesn't stray far from Christianity. They quote passages from the bible as evidence of their struggle and observe Christian religious holidays. There are however, two major differences. They insist that Jesus was a black man and should not be portrayed as a blue eyed, pale skinned European, and also, anyone who would infringe upon their "religious right" to smoke marijuana is considered to be "Babylonian."

While in Jamaica Olin and Mama Neece had talked a few times about the fate of their children. Olin had never given up hope that one day his son would break the spell that the king's magicians had placed upon him.

"What spell, what ma'gician you tal'kin bout, old man," asked Mama Neece?

The religious scholar sat back in his chair and gave a history lesson to his in-law.

"We Ras'ta elders know the se'cret of 33rd degree Ma'sons," he said. "It stems from the o'ccult teachings of master buil'der Hiram Abiff. While con'struc'ting Sol'omon's temple he renounced the Al'mighty in favor of a union between himself and the evil semitic gods Baal and Thoth. Sol'omon ended his days surr'oun'ded by he-goats. Because of dis Ma'sons were banned by Pope Clement XIV in 1773, but we Rastas feel the High Ma'sons had al'ready corr'upted the Va'tican."

Learning things like these from Papa Olin had helped Mama Neece to better understand he and his son's relationship. Some nights while Gaietta and the baby slept, she and Paul would stay up late looking out on the city talking about dreams and life like only people who've experienced some of it can.

"I missed nights like 'dese when I was in Lon'don, every'ting so drab over dere, da sky was always cloudy. Ve'ry seldom ya get to see tings clear'ly."

"I know. Gaia hate goin dere to visit me bro'der'. She say he 'wrader stay home and work."

Mama Neece laughed at the memory.

"Yeah she tell me dat when we first move in," said Paul. "We used to sit here some'time, but Gaietta always want to go out, some'place, do dis, and dat. I tell her, 'Girl, you got to slow down some.'"

He looked warmly towards the bedroom.

"Ya know Mama, I got feel'ins for Gaia. But some'time, I don't know 'bout her. One min'ute she blow hot and o'der times she cold. Too cold."

"Aww, come on now papa, what you expect? She tell me how you two meet. A coun'try girl, first day in da big city, she scared and alone. She act like she big and tough, but she just a litt'le girl, ya' know."

Paul became defensive.

"Mama, you make it sound like I take ad'van'tage of your daugh'ter. She was a big girl, we were in love."

Mama Neece remained calm.

"You say it best right dere. Big girl. Dere is no doubt in me mind you two love each'oter, may'be it's jus' a differ'ent kind of love. Paul, ya' almost fif'teen year older than her, you been pla'ces and seen tings. Don't play crazy wit me papa, ya' know what I mean. I never say you take ad'van'tage of her. Matter of fact, I want to thank you for wat'ching over her. She was luc'ky to have you. But may'be now she ready to be free. I'm her mama and even I had to let her go."

They sat silently taking sips from that special bottle and staring out the window for a long while. Something about the truth when its spoken clearly; there's really nothing more that need be said. Most people can't handle it; they'll do anything not to hear it. Some will cut you off when they hear it coming; others will literally run from it. Funny thing about that though, if they didn't already know it; how would they know when to start running.

Paul was getting too old to run; time had just about caught up with him. The life he wanted to lead was coming to an end and the life he was destined to lead was just beginning.

After Mama Neece left in January of '73 Paul and Gaietta spent the next year making the transition from lovers to friends, all for the sake of their son. Paul was also preparing for the inevitable. Three days after Christmas, in 1974 he moved back to Jamaica and took over the church from his ailing father. It had taken him eighteen years but spell had finally been broken. Olin spent every waking moment preparing his successor until his death in the winter of 1976.

The funeral was a huge and notable event. Gaietta and Thomas were in attendance along with patrons and priests from all over the countryside who'd come to pay their last respects to one of the islands favorite sons and appoint the new pastor. But in a year of increasing political unrest as the CIA wreaked havoc on the country by means of "destabilization" nothing was bigger news that year than the attempted murder in late November of another one of Jamaica's sons.

✳

Four men in black surrounded the home spraying bullets that shattered the windows and walls on the first floor. Two more were in the front yard, one of them shot Rita Marley in the head as she and her five children tried to escape through the front door. Meanwhile another gunman had entered the home and found her husband. One of the eight shots fired at Bob Marley grazed his chest and landed in his arm.

Gunshot wounds and all, the defiant singer and his band The Wailers performed as scheduled just a few days later at the "Smile Jamaica" fest.

The next year was considered to be bad luck by learned Rastas due to St John the Divine's apocalyptic revelations of coinciding sevens. On July 7, 1977 Jamaica resembled a ghost town as many residents stayed locked in their homes.

Many "third world" countries share similar superstitions. In Brazil the entire month of August is said to be cursed. It's said to be the time that the devil deals the cards. They call it, "the month of sorrow and grief."

Even Marley, the once strong and vibrant Rasta whose faith in Jah shielded him from the shadows had begun to feel their presence. In '77 he sat in a tree talking with some old friends while somberly dispensing revelations of his own;

Excerpt 17.

✳

Gaietta received her own share of bad news in '77 when Paul called and informed her that he was engaged to be married. She held the phone at a lost for words. When she found out who it was she immediately remembered Colleen, one of the church's older secretaries. Gaietta also remembered just how much the lady reminded her of her mother. It wasn't until now that Gaietta had gotten up the nerve to visit her ex again.

JAMAICA
Kingston

Excerpt 18.

"Paul, you worry to much, he's a big boy now, and the oder chil'dren wont let no harm come to dey're bro'der."

Gaietta calmed herself. Colleen was right. They were all good kids and excited to see their little brother form the states. From the corners of their eyes she and Colleen exchanged glances.

"You too mama."

Colleen smiled as they went about preparing the conch, rice, plantains and meneudo for supper.

"May'be dis will work out," Gaietta thought.

After the meal they took a stroll around town. It gave everyone a chance to catch up. The sun was like a crooked cop beating on them as they walked peacefully down the street. Gaietta apologized for Thomas's remarks on the meneudo.

"He's jus' not used to it. I don't cook it much at home."

"Don't wor'ry," said Colleen. "Times are chan'ging, kids dese days don't like it much. It's like cabbage or som'ting."

In the distance they heard popping sounds. There was no mistaking them this time, Brooklyn had schooled Gaietta.

"Good God almi'ghty has da whole world gone cra'zy; dey shoo'tin guns in the day'light now?"

Colleen's younger brother Lennox explained how from Kingston to Negril things had taken a turn for the worst in the short time since Edward Seaga had taken office.

"Yeah mon, tings done chan'ged on dis side too, ya' know. A'meri'can sec'ret police come 'round star'tin trou'ble for da Rasta'man. Now dey catch you wit jus a joint, you go'ing 'dung so.'"

"That's right Gaia," added Paul. "Rasta or no, dey say you can't be smo'kin, sell'in, or grow'in'. Dey come t'rough wit big guns and take every'body crop and make it deirs."

Lennox weighed in again.

"Now er'body changin' deir buis'iness to co'caine and her'on; and lot of dem u'sin what dey s'pose be sell'in, ya' know."

They reached a corner store and Lennox asked his sister for fifty cents. He came out with a cold Red Stripe.

"Where ya' manners boy," asked Gaietta? "Go back in dere and get some more," she said, handing him some money. As they walked back to the house, they sipped and talked some more.

"Goodness gra'cious," said Gaia, "shaking her head. "So things here are just as bad as da States."

"Dey're pro'bably worse here," said Colleen. "You know da talk is dat Bob is dy'ing. Dey poison dat poor child. Nobody never get no can'cer from ganja. Tosh don't have can'cer and dey say he smoke more than Marley." Lennox laughed. "Yeah! Bout two pounds a week," he said! "Dem pe'ople takin' out any'body dey tink gon' make trou'ble for dem, any'body who know too much."

He finished his beer and sang Marley's famous line from Rat Race;

"Rasta don't work for no CIA!"

"You really t'ink the CIA is try'ing to kill him? On the news they say it was robbers that shoot up da place."

Everyone spoke at the same time making Gaietta's answer loud and clear. "YES!"

Gaia didn't want to accept the thought that in America, "the land of the free," entertainers were being targeted for simply voicing their opinions. If that were true then who was next?

Lennox told her about how he'd attended meetings with members of JLP and The Movement who'd exposed some information about the ailing stars health.

First they believed that the real source of his sickness could be traced to a visit he received right after the assassination attempt. Secluded in the mountains and under heavy guard, Carl Colby, the son of former CIA director William E. Colby managed to somehow find his whereabouts and get past armed Rastafarian bodyguards with a gift for Bob Marley; a pair of new boots.

Marley tried them on and was pricked. He became sick soon after and was diagnosed with cancer. A source close to Marley and in the house that night had this to say;

Excerpt 19.

Other reported CIA developed carcinogens were MKULTRA and MKSEARCH, both code names for projects aimed at the use of drug experimentation for mind control. STP, PCP, LSD, and MDMA, are all drugs belonging to a group known as "hallucinogens" that have ties to government owned and funded laboratories; labs where they've also developed their own strains of hydroponic marijuana known as G-13.

"Yeah sis'ta, if you don't know, now you know," he said. "You bet'ter take some time out and learn 'bout 'Da A'gen'cy'. Keep your eye on dem, cause dey cer'tain'ly keep'in da eye on you."

Gaietta's head was spinning thinking about all the new knowledge. It was interesting enough, but she didn't have time to waste worrying about things that would never affect her. Still a little voice in her head urged her to dig deeper.

"But why would da CIA care a'bout a reggae sing'er, what can he do?"

By now they were back at the house and Colleen had pulled out some more beers from the icebox. Lennox rolled a few and passed them around.

"What 'bout 'da law'man," asked Gaietta?

"We run 'tings, 'tings no run we," Paul said defiantly! He flicked his lighter and lit up. "I'm a man of da cloth, and 'dis be a house of Jah." He coughed a bit and said in a low voice, "I got what dey call, re'li'gious im'muni'ty."

They all sat on the porch laughing as Lennox began to talk.

"It's an in'con'venient truth, da en'tertain'er of today be da poli'tician of t'morrow. Look at your Rea'gan.____ Da en'tertain'ers got da hearts and minds of da pe'ople. Dey call dem da Rat Pack."

Gaietta and Paul traded glances, remembering that day in the cab. Paul waved to his brother-in-law. "Rat pa'trol! Rat Pack is Sin'atra and Sammy."

Lennox blew him off. "Dem too. A few words from dem can change pub'lic opin'on; *especial'ly da youth.*"

"Dat's true," said Colleen, "dey get all high from drink'in' and smok'in'. Den dey get to feelin' da music and aint no tell'in' what dey'll do. Look at what dey did for Man'son."

Paul nodded. "Not jus dat. More im'portant'ly, da vote! Dey tell Bob dat dey kill him for sure if he comes home be'fore de elec'tion. Seaga is 'Da A'gency's man here. Evry'body knows dat elec'tion was rigged!"

FRANCE
Paris

In the last days of October, high in the skies above Paris, Colonel Alliouisis Devine gave landing information to the pilot of the private Gulfstream jet. He then placed a call to the COS who was just miles below on the tarmac. Even so, this mission was considered "Top Secret", and all communications were being filtered through Langley.

The voice on the other end of the phone answered, "Stat COM."
 "Stat COM, this is "Spartacus," I need a secure line to 'Imammiah.'"
 The operator request further identification. Once it was provided he was connected with a familiar voice."
 "This is 'Imammiah, go ahead."
 "Imammiah, we have the package. ETA is ten minutes. Is there a green light?"
 "That's affirmative 'Spartacus.' Project Takeover is a go. Confirming rendezvous in ten. Clear."
 He relayed the message to his superiors as the plane full of "good shepherds" and the forty million members of "King Georges Calvary" strapped in and prepared for the landing. The jet taxied into a hangar at the far end of the runway. Inside were intelligence agents from France's SDECE, Israel's Mossad, Iran's SAVAK, and Americas CIA. The doors were immediately shut behind them and less than an hour later envoys of limousines and luxury vehicles quietly emerged from the hangar. A short time later the aircraft was once again airborne, this time bound for Washington DC., where at the tony *Alibi club* certain passengers had important matters to discuss.
 Alliouisis steered his vehicle swiftly up Champs Elys'ees on one of the twelve roads that feed into one of the city's greatest monuments, the Arc De Triomphe. Four scenes of valiant and noble soldiers led by sword wielding seraphim and beautiful worshipping maidens were depicted on the pillars of "L'Arc." Engraved on the inside and presented by cherubim is a tribute; the names of the Paris's fallen heroes, Napoleon Bonaparte and family in particular. They'd given the ultimate sacrifice for France during the Revolution. This was The Brotherhoods idea of a joke that Alliouisis always got a kick out of since it was their conspiracy that Napoleon had fought and lost against, and since it was them who'd dedicated the monument.
 And if that weren't enough there were the symbols of a Brotherhood assassination. There was the eternal flame of the Unknown Soldier, and not far from that, pointing to the heavens was "L'Obelisque, where the names of even more murdered revolutionaries adorned the walls. To Alliouisis, L' Arc was more of a warning to

any future dissidents than a tribute. He knew Benjamin would be there waiting. It was ritual for them to meet and go to *The Corronna* when in Paris.

He merged with the traffic and circled twice before he saw his old friend. He threw his hazards on and Benjamin jumped in the car.

They hugged and greeted each other. *"To Strict Observance."*

Alliouisis handed Benjamin a cigar and said;

"I'm getting rusty old friend. I had to circle twice before I saw you."

"I was just thinking, 'I'll remember to bring infra-red glasses next time.'"

They both laughed and got caught up.

"Well, *'Spartacus,'"* Benjamin raised his eyebrow, "how did everything go?"

Alliouisis laughed heartily. "He doesn't need it anymore, so I thought who better to have it than me. What about you?" Alliouisis raised an eyebrow of his own. *"Imammiah?"*

"Well, the more I seek, the more I discover my true nature," he chuckled; besides it fits my promotion to Chief of Station over here"

"You pulled a good one. You've been here about a year now, right?"

"Yes sir. I don't do much these days, mostly pencil pushing or some briefings here and there. I've become a Yeoman."

The two buddies went quiet thinking about their glory days as 007's.

"I'm right behind you," confessed Alliouisis. "Luckily I'd been involved in so many projects with G-2 and ACIS during Operation Phoenix they remembered me; but I thank you. I know it was your outstanding recommendation that sealed the deal. I owe this assignment to you."

"Perhaps its time we go private," said Benjamin somberly.

Alliouisis blew a ring of smoke into the crisp Parisian air.

"What the hell was Carter thinking? He stepped on a lot of toes when he made those cuts; eight-hundred operatives. That nut is the reason those hostages are in Iran in the first place."

Benjamin turned to face him.

"My friend, from what I just witnessed in the hangar the hostages are as good as free, and the Carter administration is history."

THE BRONX
A Few Weeks Later

"MAMA! Come here. Ma! Come look. The hostages is free."

The Boy had finished his homework and wanted his television time, but "tonight", Marian said, "was important."

She was watching the only TV in the house because tonight the results of a long campaign for president would be announced and for months she'd smelled something foul in the air. Tonight America watched as Ronald Reagan, a former B-list movie actor was elected the 39th President of the United States.

The campaign had been close. As each candidate's numbers went up and down in the polls, political strategists saw 52 Americans who'd been held hostage in Iran since November 4th 1979, as the elections X factor. Whoever negotiated their release would most likely be the next president.

After Reagan beat Bush in the primary pressure mounted for him to pick a running mate. When talk emerged of a sort of co-presidency with former president Gerald Ford, Reagan quickly chose Bush; a man he'd expressed a subtle dislike for in the past. With Bush and a secret army of current and fired intelligence officers holding a grudge against Carter on board, the games could begin.

During Reagan's acceptance speech, just moments after mentioning them, an emergency announcement was broadcast. One year to the day they were captured, the hostages had been freed. It was like Mr. Reagan had magically willed their release. If any doubters remained about electing an entertainer as president this act would surly comfort them. Marian wasn't buying it.

"What!"

She lowered her voice; she'd just gotten Cheris to sleep. The Boy should've been in bed too but Marian had gone easy on him since he had missed his programs.

"If you stay up," she'd said, "were watching this."

After a commercial broke the spell of Ted Koppel's voice The Boy went back to playing with his *2XL*, "computer." In reality it was a glorified eight track tape player with dreams of being a computer. The Boy had his two tapes completely memorized and with just one television in the house and Marian watching the news day in and day out, he'd also memorized certain names and phrases too. Sometimes when Marian had been drinking with her friends he'd push her buttons just for fun.

"Ma who is Barbra Walters, Dick Cheney, and Barry Goldwater?"

"Goddamn devil bitches!" she'd yell. "Every last one of them is some Council on Foreign Relations working for, right wing, Republican bitches. Fuck them and that punk-ass Rockefeller act too!"

The Boy would crack a smile and giggle with his sister.

"I told you I can make mama say bitch anytime I get ready."

Sometimes Marian's friends would join in, usually from least drunk to the most.

"Yeah, if any of them get in we all FUBAR," yelled Danny!"

The Boy looked up. "*Fubar*," that was one he hadn't heard before.

"Danny, what the hell is FUBAR," someone asked?

The room quieted some. Danny was a funny white dude who'd become part of the crew. His body had made it home but his mind was still in the war.

"That's ahh, fucked up beyond all recognition," he slurred.

Everybody in the house roasted him that day but tonight Marian agreed.

"Shit was bad enough with Carter, now it's really 'fubar'," she thought.

✳

In the twenty five plus years since the October Surprise numerous people connected to, or investigating it have died under suspicious circumstances. Yet a number of official investigations into the matter have repeatedly found "no evidence" of any wrong doing.

As 1980 came to a close The Agency watched us with a microscope as the other X factor, Generation X, sat watching back with the eyes of a kaleidoscope. In the mid-west the blizzard of '79 had left Chicago covered in a blanket of white. In Washington DC black clouds loomed over the White house, while green, the color of currency and envy ruled as it always had in capitalist New York. In March, Castro opened Mariel Harbor and flooded Miami with a sea of brown skinned Cuban refugees searching for the American dream. And on the waters of the Pacific a tsunami had long been brewing; when it hit an enormous wave of blue and red crashed into the communities of Los-Angeles and beyond, prompting residents to scream for disaster relief.

In a campaign speech Reagan stood waving before a cheering crowd; his wife Nancy to the right of him and George H.W. Bush to the left. At one point he said;

"I am not frightened by what lies ahead; and I don't think the American people are frightened by what lies ahead."

The Boy was also watching. He too was unafraid of what lay ahead, because unlike Reagan he knew the danger was to the side of him.

1981

SANGUINEOUS

MEXICO
Tijuana

Below the border the temperature was dropping. The last week had been upwards of one-hundred degrees; but the tourists liked it that way, if they wanted comfort they'd have gone to Cancun. This is the real Mexico, and just a few miles from America. The crossover at Yasidra California stayed congested. Tijuana is known as a cheap little getaway that college kids and military men keep alive. Boy's Town is street after street of cheap liquor, cheap food and cheap women. Fat or skinny, young or old, it's filled every kind of pussy you could imagine, except free.

Yoesef had been here for a little over a month and would stay until around May when he'd go deeper into Mexico. That had become the routine for the past few years; come here and hustle the vacationers during the holidays and into spring break; sell them whatever they needed, be a guide for fresh faces, and watch out for the girls. He was fluent in Spanish and now spoke English with an intentional accent; with his structured features and the way he'd let his hair grow long most people thought he was a native of Columbia, or the Dominican Republic.

Today during siesta he received two letters; one told him about his family's worsening condition in the slums of New York. Marian had been reduced to performing odd jobs and at times living in shelters. Yoesef was desperate to help. He was by no means well off, but he was well liked by most everyone he met; and because of that he'd come in contact with Felix Ronaldo Barbosa, the writer of the second letter.

*

Rumors about Felix were plenty but facts were few. He claimed to be from Madrid and was thought to be around twenty-five or thirty years old. Not tall, but not short, not light, but not dark, not gay, but not exactly straight either. That like most things about him was rarely mentioned out loud because one thing that everyone was sure of; Felix was a killer. Orphaned by five, he was jailed for robbing and murdering tourists by ten; mostly old males, who'd come to Boy's Town looking for young ones. They'd linked him to more than twenty by his signature; castrated-fellatio. At fifteen he murdered his counselors and escaped from a Mexican youth home. He spent the next few years shuttling back and forth between there and the American west making a name for himself as a hired gun.

He got off on killing.

When Carlos Brigante of "El Cartel De Medellin" needed hits done on some of its members who had been skimming in order to start their own crew, guess who he called. Felix knew it would be best to hit all three at once. He suggested using a bomb. Brigante objected.

"Please, my friend, keep your killings clean."

So many murders Felix had lost count. Yet he still got a thrill from the way peoples expressions changed when they realized the reaper was paying them a visit. He floated off for a minute reveling in the thought. Brigante caught him.

"Felix Pay attention! Two of these men are hitmen like yourself; very shady characters. Do not take them lightly and do not get any ideas."

"Si, si, however jou like. I get paid either way. My price is 100,000 U.S. dollars and two kilos. I have plans on the other side of the border."

Maybe it was the early work with the old men or maybe the years in the prison weren't kind to him. Whatever the case, Felix sometimes required a man's touch. Still he had a reputation to uphold and that was difficult enough with his looks. He had a swimmer physique with a well tattooed torso, the most prominent of which were dog tags with the inscription; *"Carpe Diem."* The tanned skin on his face was smooth and even, except for a scar that ran from his right eye into his 'Caesar' cut hairline. He had no problem picking up 'trade' if that's what he wanted. Just not in Boy's Town. He'd been in the States for a few months; when he returned he stopped in at his favorite strip club, "The Titty Bar." All was in place except for the new bouncer they called, Javier. Felix watched him make moves for a couple of days, always on the low, never bringing attention to himself or his customers. Javier had been watching back, and not just Felix. It was March of 1980 and spring break was underway. Five guys from Arizona University had been hanging out day and night and all had scored except the one they called Rodney. First clue. He was a 6'1, James DeBarge looking cat, complete with jheri curl and neon colors. While his boys slept he'd cruise the strip during the middle of the day when none of the real action was out. Second clue. On his third day there, Felix approached Javier with a proposal.

"W'sup my friend? How 'jou do? I am ..."

"They call you The Barbarian, but some call you The Cat. Which do you prefer?" Javier looked off to the side, scouting the area.

"If jou can do this 'ting for me, jou may call me, friend."

Javier looked at him. Felix smiled and continued.

"I would like a bottle of "Beefeater" Gin, to go. They are all out at the bar. Can jou help me? He opened his hand exposing a folded $100 bill. Javier muffled his laughter. *The Cat*, he thought. "My friend," he said, "I've just the one for you."

Two days later, Felix and Rodney emerged. Felix looked satisfied and Rodney looked beat. He modeled a new outfit and a brand new diamond ring that he admired every time his friends asked him where he'd been.

Javier said nothing as Felix approached him.

"Come with me my friend, we have business to discuss."

Outside in a black Suburban, Felix gave him another $100 bill.

"I already know I have jour con'fidence. Now I want jou to know, that jou have mine. Ok? _____Joesef"

Yoesef looked inside and outside the car for signs of a setup.

"It is Ok my friend. Jou and I are the same jou know. The bitch Rodney; he work in a bank in Tucson. The FBI, they show him photographs of their most wanted. That is how he recognize jou. His kind has eyes like the owl, they can see in the dark. Don't worry my friend; I tell him to hold his fucking tongue or I cut it out. Now I have another proposition for jou." Felix held out two Polaroid pictures.

"Do jou know these men?"

"I've seen them around," said Yoesef relieved, "they're part of the "Primera Classe" crew. They used to be with Escobar and the Medellin."

"Hmph! That's right, jou are wise, my friend. I am going to leave two senoritas with jou. They are very beautiful and whatever dinero they bring jou we will split. When jou see the men, tell my girls. They will know what to do."

Almost a week passed before Primera Classe showed up with a couple more guys.

"Too bad," thought Yoesef, *"babysitting was paying well."*

He'd definitely have something to send to The Boy on his birthday.

The girls went straight for the hitmen leaving the traitor and the other two alone. Yoesef sent more girls over to keep them occupied. A half-hour later a blonde in a large hat and expensive pants outfit strolled up to him and asked for a light. When she raised her head Yoesef realized it was Felix. He walked to the bar and ordered a drink, then scanned the crowd for his girls. He signaled them and when they waved back he walked towards the 'senoritas' room. The girls whispered something to the traitor as they led him and the hitmen to an upstairs room leaving the other two guys on the dance floor. Felix came out of the bathroom and put a few drops from a vial into their "Maxcal de Oaxaca" before heading to Yoesef.

"Room 112," whispered Yoesef. He hand Felix a key.

Little more than ten minutes later Felix,—the masculine version—and his chicas exit the room. They pat him on his ass and giggled;

"Adios Javier."

One went out and brought the Suburban around while the one with the pistols followed Felix to a table where he spoke with the two workers who could barely keep their eyes open.

"Do jou know who I am," he asked? Both were nearly too scared to answer.

"Si senor."

"El Cartel Primera Classe es finito," Felix said! "Jour boss is 'muerto.'"

He sat a bag on the floor and opened it. Inside were three bloody rings with the fingers still in them.

"Jou can follow them to hell, or jou can work for me and follow us to the States. I need jour answers now."

They chose the States.

"Clean jourselves." They put their guns in the bag. "Let's Go."

Felix kept his word and handed Yoesef ten Benjamins as he walked out the door.

"Until we meet again, my friend."

✳

Yoesef opened the second letter and read it. Felix would be in Boy's Town in a week to discuss something important. He asked that Yoesef wait for him. It was luck that he'd caught him. Soon he'd be heading further south, to a place where the water was warm, the drinks were cold, and he didn't know the names of the players. He took a room off the strip, bought some magazines and newspapers and chilled for the next week, catching up on current events.

The headlines of "The Controversy Daily" read,
President Signs Gun Control Act.

But it was too little too late. That year the effects of gunshots would be felt around the globe. People all over were still mourning the loss of another musician by who's iconoclastic lyrics the government felt threatened, Beatle, John Lennon. He'd been murdered in December of 1980 by a figure that had become a trend, the lone gunman. This one, Mark David Chapman, insisted like most of the others that his thoughts were not his own and that he'd been following the instructions of "voices," that "controlled" and "instructed" him. Interesting questions have arisen to weather some of those voices were associated with *World Visions*, a Protestant religious group that on it's board of directors sat the father of another lone gunmen, John Hinckley Jr.

John Hinckley Sr., the CEO of the oil exploration company Vanderbilt Energy Corp., shared a longtime close business and personal relationship with another oilman, George H.W. Bush.

On March 31st, 1981, just days after being sworn into office, Ronald Reagan became the first president to be shot since John F. Kennedy was assassinated in 1963. In the forty years since, most critics dismiss Lee Harvey Oswald and "the magic bullet" theory, and point their fingers at a Mafia/CIA connection. Even more interesting were the alleged reasons behind it. It seems that Kennedy was opposed to the actions of the Federal Reserve Bank and that led to opposition with its "Insiders" in the CFR, and its backers in the CIA.

By 1963 Kennedy had signed a bill that would issue *"more than $4 billion in "United States Notes through the U.S. Treasury*, and *not the Federal Reserve."* By doing that he could effectively reduce the United States national debt by avoiding paying interest on borrowed money from their Bank.

That in addition to his role in the 1961 Bay of Pigs fiasco seems to have been more than enough reason to eliminate the Kennedy threat and produce a family "curse" that stands to this day. Incidentally, in '61 "the Bay of Pigs invasion was actually known as "Operation Zapata." Named that because it was launched from an island owned by a newly formed company, Zapata Oil; owned by once again, none other than George H.W. Bush. The names of the two vessels used in the operation? The Barbra and Houston: Coincidentally these were also the names of Mr. Bush's new wife and home base. Though only speculation it would be fair to say that that this was the second time George Bush had been within six degrees of a Presidential assassination.

Then on May 31st, while waving and addressing a welcoming crowd, the pontiff of The Roman Catholic church and—in their eyes—the embodiment of the Holy Spirit, Pope John Paul II was shot by another lone gunman, Mehmet Ali Agca. Speculations abound, in certain circles it is believed that the assassination attempt was orchestrated by members of the Russian secret police. It seems that The KGB had gained intelligence confirming that The Vatican, the CIA, La Cosa Nostra, and members of Italy's P2 Masonic lodge were in talks to form a "Holy Alliance" in order to bring about the fall of Communism. To quote the Pope;

"In the designs of Providence, there are no mere coincidences."

Everywhere Yoesef turned there was bad news. He hoped whatever Felix had to discuss was better than what he'd been reading. On June 2nd he left the hotel early and decided to get some air. He and some locals spent the day drinking *Bohemia,* and listening to a bad mariachi band. That evening when he returned to the hotel, he noticed two foreign vehicles parked across the street. That sobered him up in a hurry; he put one in the chamber of his gun and got information from the clerk inside.

"Gloria, the cars outside; what's shaking?"

"You mean that Jeep and the Range Rover," she answered, "they've been parked outside all day."

"How many are there?"

"Tres. Mui vistoso," she whispered. "They're across the street in the cantina"

Yoesef slipped her a few bills. She rolled her eyes and put them in her pocket. "Gracias, Javier." He held up a few more. He knew Gloria from around; she was a nightmare to deal with. She reached for the money and he grabbed her hand.

"That was for the information. What's this is for?" She took her hand away slowly putting the money in her pocket as she frowned.

"Damn Javier, I aint saying nada." The look on his face told her she'd better not.

Yoesef had learned long ago not to mix bitches and business on any level. Women were tricky too and it could be a long process finding out which was which. Experience had taught him that it was simpler just to keep the two separate.

Outside he heard familiar sounds coming from one of the two vehicles; he stopped for a moment letting the drums and that timeless voice take him on a voyage back to New York and to his heart. Inside, a high, blurry eyed Felix was murdering the Isley Brothers in Spanglish.

"She mi lady, now and ever, wooe,'oo'oo ... where would I go ... I' AL'WAYS COME BACK TO JOU! _____*I 'Aaalwys Come Back To Jou ..."*

Yoesef waved at the two in the Jeep as he approached the Rover.

"Voyage to Atlantis," Felix?"

"Hey Javieeer, get in man. It's good to see jou mi amigo."

Felix was wasted. He had a joint in his hand but he was high off more than weed. They shook hands and slapped each others back. Yoesef introduced himself to the girls in the truck and they smiled graciously.

"Man, jou know this song," asked Felix. "I love this Is'ley Bro'thers. This song right here, it reminds me of home. Here, fucking, Mexico, jou know." Felix sighed, "What it remind jou of?"

"The same thing; home. It had just come out in '77. Me and Marian played it out the night I left."

"Si. It is a good song for making love to, no?" Felix hit the joint and sympathized with his friend. "Amigo," he said, "I know it hard for jou, not to be with jour family. But I have got good news." He looked at the girls. "Let's go outside." When it was safe to talk Felix filled him in on the last year.

"We stay for a while in California, but esos make things too hot there. Our guy in Tucson, he keep calling; Then I get to thinking, '*This punto works for a bank.*' I go out there and check things out; business good.' So I start to set things up. After about a month we hit it."

Felix smiled, opening his arms wide so Yoesef could see his wealth. He was living the life, designer shirt, the two huge diamond rings, the ostrich boots and belt with the heavyweight championship buckle, plus the Range.

"Now my friend, we going to do it again. George, he no want in this time, so I think of jou,' and this time our guy say there is more money to be made. You are looking at about $200,000."

"You didn't have any problems before," asked Yoesef?

"Nooo! Everything was smooth; like a baby's ass." Felix smiled drunkenly. "We did not even kill nobody." The smile went away. "Besides, all jou have to do is drive, they never know jou there."

Yoesef figured he had nothing to lose. The Agency was after him anyway. With that kind of money he could bring the family down. They could live a good life in Mexico, start a business, and sell the policia marijuana. It was worth the risk.

"I'm in," he said.

"Good!" Felix pat his shoulder. "We leave in three days."

NYMP

It was a gaudy ring that covered two fingers and spelled *"Fresh"* in fancy curved letters with "diamond" cuts. It cost $35 and was made from 10k gold, and whatever else they use to make legends. A-D had hustled hard to get it. He couldn't let this night go by without being fly. Summertime was upon them and Marcy was throwing a party to celebrate. Everyone would be there, including Mallory's friend from school. Rajean was a pretty girl who'd just turned seventeen. A-D loved the challenge. Whenever she'd come to visit he would put on too much Polo cologne, change into Evret's best clothes,—none of his gear ever matched—then find a reason to hang around. Rajean was like Mallory and didn't get out much. She thought A-D's moves were cute but she had her eyes set on something bigger.

Saturday night at the party everyone was grooving. Early on the boom boxes sat on card tables blasting hit songs; by *The Deele, Stephanie Mills*, and *Silk's;* 'Call Me.' Now, the bass pumped and The *S.O.S. Band* clapped and chanted;

"Let's do it ... "

Doing it was exactly what A-D had planned, but he didn't have all night. It was getting late and Diane would be on his ass. But that was the least of his worries, he had to make his move on Rajean soon so he could get upstairs and put Evret's shirt back before he came home. A-D had his cousin Theo looking out for Evret's car.

Theo took a gulp and spit.

"Billy Dee Williams is a lying bastard, man. This shit is nasty. What 'chu' gon' do, man. Hurry up, you been peeping her all night."

Theo had grown impatient, between playing lookout and sneaking malt liquor with A-D he had no time to find his own groove.

"I know," said A-D. "she keeps looking over here too. She must want me to come over there."

"If you don't, I will."

"Slow down gymshoe, I'm waiting for the right time. I aint gon' be out there disco dancing and shit."

Two or three songs later the DJ slowed things down with some oldies, *Average White Band's* "Schoolboy Crush" started and A-D made his move.

Mallory popped her gum when they showed up.

"Nope, you been looking over here all night, she aint goin' wit' 'chu."

A-D stayed cool.

"Shut up Mallory."

When Theo laughed Mallory slapped him and took of running. He chased her and Rajean's eyes darted from side to side looking over A-D's shoulder.

"Ra', c'mon let me holla at you a sec."

"Where we going A-D, you wanna dance?"

"Nah," he mumbled, "I wanna see what's in your Calvin Klein pants."

"I heard you," she said.

"What? All I said was yeah I wanna dance. C'mon."

On the asphalt she couldn't move an inch without his eyes following her. He moved in closer and she backed away mouthing the words to the song;

"Look boy, but don't you touch ..."

She was teasing him and he liked it. He had her attention now and the DJ helped him out when he went deep with the next song, *One Way's* "If you play your cards right." They moved closer together. A-D wore the *Polo* around her so much that it reminded her of him. She breathed in deep and her chest pressed against his, this was it. Their bodies moved rhythmically from side to side as she sang to him. He slid his hands over her butt. She didn't stop him.

"Guess what they say about Calvins is true," he thought.

Things were working out so well that he'd forgotten he planned it like this. Then Theo called him. The dancers opened their eyes and Rajean pushed him away.

Evret put his hand on A-D's shoulder.

"Let's go Casanova. You mother wants you."

People were laughing and A-D heard some girl say; "Damn, homie dissing you."

On the way up Evret dissed him some more.

"Let me see that ring. 'Fresh!'" He laughed. "If you didn't spend your little weed money on shit like this you could buy your own shirts. Take my shit off."

"Fuck you," said A-D before running ahead, "Take yo' shit; and I aint selling weed. Rajean bought me this ring."

"Mama is sleep," yelled Evret, "you better not wake her up."

Minutes later they were wrestling like old times, but now the fights had grown more intense.

"Man, get off me," yelled A-D. "Shit! Get off me, 'E'!"

Diane was asleep in the front room and no one but Theo could hear his muffled cries. He was smaller than both of them and wasn't about to get involved.

"What I tell you about wearing my gear punk? Huh? How many times I got to say it? I done told ya ass nine or ten times to stop fucking with me."

"Evret," Theo said nervously, "that pillow over his face, man; he can't breathe."

"You stay ya' little ass out of this before you get it too," said Evret.

A-D was big for eleven. Evret had a knee in his back and one hand on his head as he punched him. As A-D struggled to get free he kicked over a glass. When it broke he ran for the door and Theo followed. A-D's chest heaved as he tried to catch his breath. Evret stayed at the bed smiling as he and his brother locked stares. A-D wasn't laughing.

"You got one more time to pull it, E." A-D took a few breaths. "One more time and you gon' come up missing."

Evret continued forcing smile even though something gave him the feeling this was more than a threat.

"And you got one more time to be in my shit," he said.

"What the hell is going on in here," yelled Diane? "Y'all breaking up what little we got!"

A-D brushed past her and she yelled for him to come back. It was 12:30 am; he ignored her and walked out the door.

Theo thought quickly.

"Aunt Diane, you want me to go get him?"

"Yeah, and y'all hurry back in here."

Diane looked and sounded tired when she spoke to Evret.

"You too old for this; I can't have this outta you. You supposed to be helping me."

Evret frowned. He was already embarrassed and angry about being back in the house. The move was supposed to be temporary, but almost a year had passed. He'd been gone since '77 when he and Filani moved in together.

That's a whole other story.

When Evret left J.L. moved in full time. He found a job working on an assembly line and gave up on hustling. He was now a customer and wanted to be high, *so high*. Every week he'd take his check straight to the dope man. Whatever money was left when he came home he'd hand over to Diane who'd skim off a little for her a bump. Her job at the dollar store paid the bills and they'd use J.L.'s check to do for the kids. Needless to say they didn't get much. Things went on like that until the factory cut J.L.'s hours in half. It was either his fix, or his family. By October of '80 he could no longer stand the pain and came home broke three weeks in a row. He and Diane got into their biggest yelling match since he'd been back. It opened old wounds. She wanted him with her. He wanted to be free. She went to stay the night at Evret's before she said something she'd regret. That night J.L. packed and left for good. He'd begged, stole, and he'd borrowed. Now he was "easy" like Sunday morning.

"C'mon ma, you know if the store was still open I'd be giving you more money. I'm gon' get a job, it's just taking a while."

"It aint all about the money Evret. I know what you're doing out there to make money. You can't do shit around here without people talking; and I know you blame that girl moving that boy in your apartment on me. I'm sorry about that too, but I kept telling you she wasn't no good. I know you're having a hard time but so is Seth. He aint been the same since his father left. He's acting up in school, fighting and staying in the streets until all times of the night. He's got demons in him Evret, that's what I need your help with. You aint never gon' get through to him beating up on him; that just brings them out."

"See ma, that's the problem, all these women around here; ya'll baby him. I'm trying to make him tougher."

"Don't be surprised if he's tougher than you think."

"That's another thing," said Evret, "y'all always taking up for him. He aint no angel. He's forever wearing my clothes. I caught him stealing change from *your* purse; and if people are talking about me, then I know somebody dun' told you about him out there trying to sell drugs."

"I know all that Evret, *better than you do*. Why do you think you're here?"

A-D and Theo came home late the next afternoon. They'd spent the night around the corner at Diane's girlfriend's house. Her youngest son was around Mallory's age, his name was Charles but everyone called him Chaz.

"Where y'all been," Diane asked A-D?

"We spent the night at Chaz's."

"I told you I saw them going that way," said Shirley shaking her head. A-D looked back and made a face; he hadn't seen her in a couple of days.

"I would have called but their phone ..."

He stopped in mid-sentence when he saw Evret, Rajean, and Mallory sitting on the bed together. He looked at Rajean and she looked away.

"Where my ring," asked A-D?"

Nobody spoke. He asked again.

"Where's my ring? I lost it in here last night when we was arguing."

"We aint seen your ring," said Evret. "Have we Rae'?"

Evret hugged her. She kept quiet and the brothers locked stares again.

"Step outside E."

Evret tried to wave him off, but A-D didn't budge. Finally he grinned and said;

"Fuck it, let's go."

Mallory and Rajean pleaded for them to stop as everyone but Diane raced down the stairs. Shirley promised her she'd break it up. A-D didn't know if it was the blunt he'd puffed on at Chaz's house or if he was high off something else, but each brother had seen the same thing in the others eye a moment ago. A-D hoped Evret would be the bigger man and refuse to go. This was more than a threat and he had to know.

"He lost his job, he lost his broad. Maybe this is what he wants," thought A-D.

Theo's heart raced in his chest. He was with his cousin when he used the spare key to Diane's Regal and took out what was in the video box.

A-D stepped out first, followed by Theo, Evret, and the girls. As soon as they were out the door Evret called A-D's bluff.

"Alright, we out here. So now what's up?"

A-D turned around emotionless. His eyes closed as he pulled the trigger on the 22. Mallory and Rajean screamed. Shirley yelled;

"What the fuck is wrong with you, Seth!"

He opened his eyes in time to see Evret lying on the ground shaking badly and bleeding from his shoulder. Shirley helped him. Suddenly A-D felt naked and ugly; emotions washed over him like waters from a mystic river. He tucked the gun as he ran around confused. It seared his waist, branding him with "the mark of Cain." Theo grabbed his arm.

"Yo, c'mon, let's go!"

They ran around the corner to hide out at Chaz's house.

MEXICO
Tijuana

Three days had turned into almost two weeks. When Felix called Rodney to make the last arrangements he was told to wait a few days because a new guy was snooping around. The next time Felix called, Rodney was sure the guy wasn't undercover; but for some reason the bank was getting an extra shipment of money, about $ 400,000. Yoesef was having second thoughts but Felix assured him things would go smooth.

"Is going to be a piece of cake. I got him trained to handle things. That little bitch will do things how I say do. Think about it amigo, that is almost $150,000 more for you; just for driving."

Yoesef thought again about the possibilities.

The drive through the badlands was peaceful. Yoesef had covered a lot of this country on his way out. This was the America that most Americans never saw; tall mountains, wide valleys, and grand canyons made of orange and red rocks with cactus and tumbleweeds roaming the desert. It was beautiful enough to make a man want to steal it. He'd spent time in New Mexico and Arizona near an Apache reservation learning and listening to the horror stories of murder, rape and disease spread during their war with the English settlers. He'd heard canards before in school but it was different hearing about Geronimo and the ghost dance from the mouth of an original storyteller. The old man who told him was said to have been from a long bloodline of shamans and seers, after sitting under the stars drinking fire-water and smoking peyote, Yoesef knew why. He thought he'd seen a spirit horse galloping toward Mexico. When he left, the shaman told him not to say goodbye, because they'd meet again. Yoesef didn't know about that. He was risking a lot by taking the scenic route, but he wanted to get a good look at America, just in case it was his last.

Now he was back on business.

They parked the Range Rover at Rodney's house and took the Jeep. Pedro was driving a cheap used car that Felix had bought a few miles out of Tucson.

Yoesef dropped Felix off at the bank and parked about five blocks away in the Jeep. The bank used a windowless two door locking system, similar to a prison. The plan was for Rodney to buzz the outside door and let Felix in where he'd quietly relieve the guards of the cash. The armored truck making the pick up was already there, the drivers were coming out. Change of plans. Now they'd have to get it from the truck. Rodney stood at the door as one guard passed bags of money to another one who was standing in the back of the truck. The guard on the ground walked back in the bank. Rodney saw Felix walking up; he signaled to the guard in the truck and closed the door. Felix quickly attached a silencer to his Uzi, and gave the guard in the truck double taps to the head.

He got inside and took aim; the silencer burned his hand through the thin leather gloves. When the door opened he gave another guard two. The agent who'd been sent to watch Rodney's every move saw it. Felix whistled for Pedro who was standing off to the side, he grabbed a couple of bags and head for the car. Felix jumped out of the truck with his own bags and followed him.

"There's no reason for the door to be opening again," thought Felix.

He spun around shooting. Rodney got hit first; the bullets went through his open mouth, tore through his tongue and right into the elderly bank guard who was holding him. The agent fired with precision and hit Felix in his heel. Pedro threw his bags in the car and was on his way back to help Felix when he saw a car speeding up the street. He emptied an entire clip; the car crashed and killed the driver. The agents' pistol was no match for the Uzi's extended clip. He ran out of bullets and Felix nearly cut him in half; but not before he and Pedro caught a few more bullets. Pedro fell dead next to Felix. The agent's gunfire had hit the bags and money blew down the street. Felix stuffed his pockets as he limped to the car, hopped in and sped off to meet Yoesef. He never made it. The car crashed a half block behind the Jeep. Yoesef could hear the sirens as he backed down the street to get him. A steady stream of blood flowed from Felix's chest but he was still trying for the bags in the back of the car.

Yoesef yelled, "Leave them!"

They hopped in the jeep and narrowly got away. Yoesef kept driving as his dream and Felix's life slipped away. Both of them died on the highway. Yoesef took Felix's jewels and close to $ 50,000 from his pockets before he buried his body in the desert. Afterwards he took a nice long look at the mountain range; this time he was sure he'd never be this way again.

1982

KEEPING UP WITH THE FRIEDMANS

MANHATTAN
Central Park West

"**Again, Jere**miah!"

"C'mon dad, I've told you this like a million times. I know it already!" Jeremiah looked exasperated as their housekeeper took the leftover lox and bagels away from the table.

"Well then it should not be a problem, correct?"

Benjamin wasn't giving in. This was too important a day to not have everything, and everyone be *perfect*.

"Jeremiah, I don't know that you realize the importance of this event, or perhaps it's slipped your mind. Son, you're becoming a man soon. The last thing you want to do is embarrass yourself or your family. People are coming from as far as Israel to see you. As a matter of fact I'm off to meet your uncle Alliouisis, he's already arrived. Your mother will be here tomorrow. So I tell you what, just give me a quick run through and I'll listen to your recital and speech later. Deal?"

Jeremiah sighed, figuring he might as well get it over with.

"Quick run through, yeah right."

There was no such thing when it came to the history of the Hebrew race or their faith. Judaism has taken a long and winding road toward righteousness. Theirs is a close knit religion with some distinct differences from its Christian and Islamic schisms. Pre-dating the death of Christ by more than 2,500 years, its followers are still presently awaiting their Messiah. So let us now take a journey through time from the year 5742, to The Genesis.

"In the beginning," said Jeremiah, "God created heaven and earth and all living creatures in six days. On he seventh day he rested. Then God needed someone to work the land that he'd created, so he made man from the dust of the ground and breathed life into his nostrils. He named the first man, Adam. Now Adam needed someplace nice to live, so God created a pretty garden with every tree that man would need and for some odd reason one that he didn't. That was the tree of knowledge; and the garden was named Eden. God forbid Adam to taste the fruits from the knowledge tree. He told Adam that if he did, then he would surely die. Soon God saw that Adam was lonely, so he made him a wife, her name was …"

"Ah, ah, ah." Benjamin quieted his son. "Queen of the *'ha-hitsonem.'* Continue."

"And the Queen and Adam fought because she refused to lie beneath him when they 'knew' one-another. So she cursed him and flew away. God sent angels after her but she refused to return, so God cursed her with the death of 100 of her children daily. Since then she fly's around at night molesting mortal men through their dreams and creating the, *'ha-hitsonem.'* After her came Adams second wife, Eve. Things were good for a while in the garden, but Satan, in the form of a serpent had been trying to get Adam to eat from the forbidden tree. Adam kept telling him no. So the serpent tried his luck with Eve. Once he'd tricked her into eating, she then tricked Adam. Soon after God came into the garden and knew that they had eaten from the tree so he forever punished them and their offspring. Women were cursed with the pain of childbirth and men with work and suffering, after that he covered them in skin and said;

"Behold, the man is become one of us, to know good and evil; and now, lest he put forth his hand, and take also of the tree of life, and eat, and live forever."

"Then he kicked them out of the garden and put up a flaming sword. The sword is the gate that keeps the unworthy away from the *'Sephiroth.'* Do you want me to name the fruit dad?"

"You know them already," asked Benjamin cautiously?

"I told you," Jerry sighed again, "I know all of this already."

"You've been skipping ahead, Jeremiah. That's not always a good thing. You have to be very careful not to drown in the waters."

"Yes father, I know."

Benjamin was pleased. "Do you know about Eve's children, the sin they committed, and how long they lived?"

"Yes."

"Who was it that found grace in the Lord's eyes?"

"Noah."

"Good, so you know of the flood. Who were the sons that repopulated the earth after the flood?"

Jerry was bored and his tone was monotonous.

"Shem Ham, and Japeth. I know about his sons, Gomer and Magog. I know about the gentiles on the neighboring isles, and the tower of Babel …"

Benjamin got it. "Alright, tell me about the first of the Patriarchs."

"Abram was one of Noah's grandchildren; God liked him and talked to him personally. He told him to go to Canaan where he would bless him. After ten years there, his wife Sari who couldn't have children told him to 'know' her hand-maid; an Egyptian woman named Hagar. When Sari found out that Hagar was pregnant, she flipped out and banished her to the wilderness where an angel came to her and told her to go back to Abram because she is going to have a son. The angel instructed her to call him Ishmael. Then, when Abram was 99 years old God said;

"Walk before me and be thou perfect…. behold, my covenant is with thee, and thou shall be the father of many nations. Neither shall thy name anymore be called Abram, but thy name shall be Abraham … And I will make thee exceedingly fruitful … and kings shall come out of thee."

"So after that Abraham and Sari, whose name was now Sarah had a son named Isaac. God told Abraham to take his son to a mountain and sacrifice him, and just as he was about to plunge the dagger into him, an angel stopped him and they used a ram instead. That's why we blow the rams horn at Rosh Hashanah."

Benjamin was laughing loudly. "Didn't you forget something?"

"Oy", Jerry scrunched up his face, it was painful just thinking about it. "Ok, God also told him to circumcise all the men and all the newborn males on their eighth day of birth. That would be the mark of Gods covenant, and anyone's not circumcised will be cut of from his people. Ok?"

"Ok, proceed."

"So Abraham set it up for Isaac to marry his cousin Rebekah. Later on she birthed Jacob and Esau, and Jacob's twelve sons became the leaders of the twelve tribes of Israel."

"Splendid. We've watched *The Ten Commandments* enough times for you to know what happened in Exodus. You seem to have a pretty good grasp of the 'Pentateuch' but you know there's much more to learn once you've mastered those. There are the other thirty-four books of our Old Testament and of course The Talmud."

"When may I begin the *'Sefer Ha-Zohar,'"* asked Jerry anxiously?

"Patience young lamb," said Benjamin proudly, "let's get you through your Bar Mitzvah first." He kissed his son on both cheeks.
"Page me if you need anything Jeremiah."
"Ok. Tell Uncle Alliouisis *Shalom Alechem.*"
Benjamin waived as he walked away.

"I Will."

NEW JERSEY
Teterboro Airport

Alliouisis stowed his bags and settled into Benjamin's Town Car.
"Am I in the right car? What in hell are you listening to my friend?"
Benjamin passed him a memo. "You must not have gotten this."
Alliouisis read it.

ATTENTION! CLASSIFIED! ATTENTION! CLASSIFIED!

Memo: OPERATIONS, COINTELPRO & CHAOS

Subject: "H.i.p. H.o.p. music." aka. Harmonious Influences Provided to Help Our People

Confidential informants in several American inner-cities report a rising insurgent threat. Several groups currently under surveillance have reportedly band together and adopted this genre of music for financial and communicative purposes, enclosed is a cassette recording of known subversive threats and snippets of such material. The exact number of subversives and insurgents is unknown, but their numbers are estimated to be high, and their message widespread. Foreign intelligence sources report this quote from African subversive Fela Kuti:

"Music Is The Weapon Of The Future."

```
Agents   are   instructed   to   begin   surveillance
files  on  all  listed  subversives  and  insurgents
immediately.
```

```
Threat Level: Orange
```

Alliouisis sighed.

"Not again, I thought for sure we'd seen the last of this in the sixties."

"Far from it, it seems that it's cyclic."

"So it seems." Alliouisis listened for a minute and shook his head. "It sounds like a bunch of noise to me." He gave Benjamin back the memo. "Do you think Jeremiah's into this, Hip-Hop?"

"Goodness no, I'd know about that. He's got his head on straight. What about Fourtunate?"

Alliouisis grunted. "You never know about them over there."

Benjamin agreed.

"Maybe its time we set him straight. Why don't you bring him to the Bar Mitzvah, Jeremiah can show him around some and introduce him to the Right crowd."

Alliouisis became teary-eyed at the suggestion.

"That's a wonderful idea, thank you old friend."

"Oh, don't mention it."

"Well," said Alliouisis after a moment, "tell me more about going private and these Orwellian fantasies that you've been having."

Benjamin perked up as he shared his thoughts.

"They're no fantasies; they actually tie into that memo. You're aware of how the goal has been to eventually have extensive files on every citizen?"

"Of course."

"What has been the problem?"

"Too much paperwork, human error; but were working the kinks out. The military is almost fully automated.

"Precisely; and soon that technological prowess is going to reach the private sector."

"It always does."

"*Big Brother'* will soon be a reality. I've heard predictions of personal computers in every home and phones and devices small enough for every vehicle; and therein lays the perfect place for our business venture. I've acquired a small media and telecommunications firm overseas called Manchurian Global. I want you to come in on it with me."

"I never heard of them, what do they make?"

"These." Benjamin held up a small object no larger than a quarter called a *Radio Frequency Identification Device*.

"Bugs," said Alliouisis, chucking. "You want to chip humans?"

"Every last one," said Benjamin. "Make it so we don't have to gather intelligence, we let them do it for us. Soon every citizen will be carrying one type of indistinct pod or another complete with their personal information. We simply add one of these to it and we can gather Intel and track their movements too. It would free up a lot of time for agents."

"That it would; and like Toffler said, *"time is the commodity of the future."*

"Look around," continued Benjamin, "laborers are an endangered species. America's industrial economy is on the decline and that's putting the value of our dollar in jeopardy. The economic future of America lies in knowledge-based wealth, and who knows more about surveillance, intelligence gathering, and national security than us? We'd be fools not to capitalize on that."

Alliouisis was smiling. I'm with you. I feel foolish for not having done it sooner." Then he turned and faced Benjamin. "But it's ironic you know. The key to our survival may also be our downfall."

"How so?"

"I've always said that the biggest threats to our plans were never any army or laws. It's that damn hippie subculture that sits around gathering information and promoting their social, religious, and economic reform. They're nothing more than urban guerillas and homegrown terrorists."

"Yes, and unfortunately they are more like us than we care to admit. They think outside of the box."

"Touché. But what has always rendered them feckless is that they've been unable to come together. They fester in small pockets.

But what if an insurgent threat like these Hip-Hopers took advantage of this burgeoning technology and used it for their cause. I've studied the scenario again and again. If the middle class and the working poor ever come to their senses and join them we are going to have a big problem. There will be anarchy in the USA and ultimately it will come down to us against them; the haves *vs.* the have-nots."

Benjamin stopped the tape and point to the stereo.

"I doubt seriously if these vandals make it that far. But in that unlikely event, always look to history for the answers. We'll simply treat them like we do the C.I.'s. We'll develop them as assets; work them and then turn them. Old friend, it's a fact, once the have-nots become the haves, they will do absolutely anything not to go back."

LOWER MANHATTAN
On Broadway

<u>Excerpt 20.</u>

"**You hear this** nigga on the radio baby? I like that. Nigga say, *'I'm just cool!'*"

Goodgame bucked the seats of his new Cadillac Seville back and forth and laughed with the rest of his family.

"This is the song I was telling you about the other day 'D.' Yeah; we need to go pick this up right now. You think they'll know who it is at the record store?"

"That's *The Time*," explained Lynnette. "He screams it in the start of the song. "They're with *Prince*."

"Prince! That skinny motherfucker with the high ass-voice. Aint *that* a bitch. But you know what? That other shit he had, 'Do Me Baby;' that was tight."

"Uhh, huh," said Dioses, "we were just about to bust you out."

"Everybody listens to Prince, but don't want to admit it," his wife Corinne added from the back seat.

The car left Broadway and cruised uptown. Its occupants going to set their minds free at *Smalls Paradise* on 155th. They'd just seen Jennifer Holiday in the musical *Dreamgirls*, for their weekly dose of New York culture.

"So what did you think about the play Corinne? I don't even have to ask this one here; I already know what he thinks of the theater," said Lynnette, pinching Goodgame's arm.

"Same here," said Lynnette, "this one only takes me because I make him."

Dioses took his pinching.

"I liked it," he said. "The story was uplifting."

"See there 'Nette, I was gonna say the same thing," said Goodgame counting a stack of twenties. "This one was pretty decent. Better than *Cats* and that *La Cage Aux Follies*; aint nobody want to see that old crazy shit."

"Big girl got a set of pipes on her too," added Dioses, "she can blow!"

"That's all them titties she got;" said Goodgame, "they was all over the place."

Corinne and Dioses were in the back laughing while 'Nette shot Goodgame the, "Ok, you're crossing the line" look.

"Don't be looking all crazy at me; you said it in the theater. *'Ooo wee, baby, they know they could've done something better with her chest.'*"

Lynnette burst out laughing while Corinne said to Dioses;

"I liked the soundtrack, while you're out tomorrow, why don't you pick up the album for me."

"I'll get it when I get that *'Cool'* shit," said Goodgame. "I might even see what Prince got new. But why don't you get it on cassette instead of the album; that way you can listen to it in ya' ride."

"Man, she barely drives that car; I told her I'm trading that son-of-a-bitch in."

"Good," Corinne told her husband! "I told you to do that a long time ago. It's too big. I want a little Benz."

Dioses wasn't in the mood for an argument. He called to Lynnette.

"Sweetheart, pull over a minute."

Lynnette eased the Caddy to the curb and Dioses went to the trunk. He hopped back in and gave Goodgame his pistol. The women didn't speak; they knew what time it was. The city was strange like that. Literally minutes ago it was bright lights and big city monuments, well kept buildings, and potted plants. Then gradually all that disappeared as block by block the lights dimmed and piles of garbage littered the streets. Sidewalks crowded with people became scarce for a few blocks as the mood changed, then suddenly on the corners near their homes, fiends hung around under broken streetlights, living the streetlife; the only life they know. Even though the Caddy shielded them they all noticed the change. In their minds they considered themselves the lucky ones. That decision made ten years ago in The Ritz had changed their destinies forever and given their families the means to come and go as they pleased; to purchase inspiration when they pleased; it had given them the freedom to live in both Americas. In their hearts they all knew that their freedom had its limits.

Clarence the doorman immediately called for a busboy when he saw the car pull up. Smalls had no valet service but the club made exceptions for special customers. He ordered the busboy to park the car close to the door.

"What's up Game, what's up 'D', how ya'll doing tonight," he asked?

Goodgame slipped him a twenty as he admired the girls.

"I would hug you two lovely ladies but y'all are sharper than razorblades tonight. Y'all don't hurt nobody in there."

They looked at each other and giggled. "Thank you Clarence, we'll try not to," said Corinne.

She entered the room like a celebrity wearing a sequined top and tight pants. Lynnette wore a tight fitting, low cut dress, with shiny shoes. They were almost opposites of their husbands in style.

Dioses wore a deep purple suit with one of those skinny ties that were popular then. Everyone thought he had a curl, but his hair was naturally like that; Spanish mother and all. Now Goodgame did have a curl, for about two weeks, until he found out the activator screwed up his good shirts. After ruining a few he cut the *Soul Glo* out real quick. Tonight he wore a custom walking suit from *Dapper*

Dan's; maroon shirt and pants with the hat to match, none of that fake print shit; if he wanted *Gucci,* he'd go to Fifth Avenue and buy it. They'd been getting money in these streets for a long time and were respected as old money should be. The intertwined D&G was a logo in Harlem long before *Dolce & Gabbana* was a thought. There'd been some incidents over the years, but they made sure to feed a few wolves whose job was to do nothing, until the day came to do something. They handled any up and comers who got out of line; but these days there were a breed of young cats shooting their way to the top and bringing with them a different set of values. Players and player's lounges like these were becoming a thing of the past as popular clubs like *Harlem World* on one-two-nine and Lennox proved. Game and Devine had been planning for this since day one. They still made a nice profit from the street, but these days a lot of their income was legal. They owned real estate and a few stores. Dioses had his aunt Dania running his. Still it wasn't enough to get them out. It was like anytime as they'd get too far ahead life's little emergencies would pull them back again, plus there was always the extended family calling for aid and assistance. Fame and Fourtune both had siblings now and college for all of them was just around the corner. That was a must; they'd worked too hard to give their kids a chance at a better life. Nah, even if they wanted to the players couldn't leave 'The Life', alone just yet.

"I know the kids better be asleep when we get home. They think they can just run wild when Tish is there."

"It's Saturday, where they got to go tomorrow," Dioses asked his wife?

"I don't care. It's too late for them to be up running around,"

"That's right," said Lynnette.

Corinne's pager went off.

"This is them right here, I knew their lil' asses were still awake. I'm going to the office to use the phone."

"I'll go with you," said Lynnette.

"You always saying, *'Baby, take me somewhere so I can get away from the kids.',* and soon as I do you talk they asses up," said Dioses.

"Goodgame laughed. "Aint nothing wrong with them boys, probably just want some food."

"Shit, Fourtune knows how to order something and my niece Tish is seventeen, she's old enough to cook," said Dioses.

"Man, it aint if she's old enough; it's do she know how. The kids these days can't boil water or toast bread. Good for them they came out with this microwave oven or it'd be a bunch of skinny little crumbs snatchers running around. And on the ordering tip, I didn't tell you because it wasn't that important, but ..."

"This aint funny," said Goodgame rubbing his temples, "but; the last time they spent the night over at the house, them niggas prank called the pizza man."

"Aww shit!" 'Dioses lowered his head.

"Man, I ordered a pizza and the dude was asking me all these questions, so I say, 'Hey, bra. This me, what's the problem?' Then he told me what happened. Man, that nigga was steaming', he said them boys had him running back and forth all night." They laughed. "I gave him a nice tip."

Dioses sipped his drink and asked.

"Man what are we gonna do with them?"

"I don't know."

"Hey, Game; I know Fame was pretty upset about missing that kids Bar Mitzvah." "Don't worry about that man," said Goodgame blowing it off. "I know where that call came from. Fame gotta learn all that sooner or later. He cant go on thinking just cause we got some bread we can go wherever we want, then the truth come kick 'em in his ass. It's still plenty places where racism's alive and well no matter how much money you got. But it's good old 'All-i-wish-is' took Fourtune. Man can't be that bad."

"You know better than to believe that," Dioses said. "He's like any man that's getting up in age, they start looking back on their life and wondering what it all meant. They want their name to live on. Mixed-blood or not, Fourtunate is the only grandson he's got."

MANHATTAN
Central Park West

His weekend celebration had been pleasant at best. Being around his parents and their Park Avenue friends was more work than play; so today, just four full days into his manhood Jerry Freidman started making his own decisions. The first was to skip school. But that wouldn't be any fun alone, and his friends were boring. All their parents said the same thing.

"Take the limo and a credit card and do whatever you want."

How many times could they go see the Yankees or the Knicks play? This year alone, they'd watched the Islanders beat the Canucks for the Stanley Cup and his father had taken him and a friend to see the 49ers win Super Bowl XVI in January. After you've been to that the rest are pretty much just football games. Zoos were for kids, not men, besides; if you've seen one lion you've seen 'em all. Being that there are a plethora of Museums in New York and one could never fully appreciate everything in every one, that was something he did still enjoy, but he was burnt out on that kind of culture. He was fascinated by another kind that for the last few years had been trickling in from the street; a jambalaya of style and music.

At home he'd memorize every word, while in the parks and clubs Dj's like Kool Herc, Lovebug Starski, and Red Alert would spin while the black and Latino kids listened to *The Message* and went crazy break dancing and spitting rhymes. And then there were the girls, such beautiful girls. *"That's the shit."* Jerry thought. And now he'd found just the right tourguide to properly introduce him to it all.

"Uncle Alliouisis said to make him feel comfortable."

The idle mind is a playground …

The phone was still ringing when Fame answered it.

"What's up, Fourtune, why you paging me so early?"

"Is anybody else on the phone?"

"Nah, why?"

Fourtune's voice was barely audible.

"You wanna skip school today?"

"Why," whispered Fame, "what we doin' 'B'?"

"You know that kid, who I went to his thing Friday? He says he's not going to school today and if we cut with him he'll treat us both."

"Why he say me? *I couldn't even go to his weak-ass party*," wondered Fame.

"Yo 'B,' I represent for you at the party. When he called this morning he said to bring you too." Fourtune waited for an answer. "What's up, you going or not?" he asked. "My man got money 'B'. His pops got a limo, *and* they live on Central Park West."

Fame wasn't with it. "Nah, fuck him 'B,' we got money too. I can't see gettin' in trouble for that, plus, you never said where we going."

"Come on," urged Fourtune. "Why you buggin'? It's Times Square or school. We can see that movie Toys.____ I'm not going by myself. *C'mon!*"

"Toys! Richard Pryor! That nigga's crazy. A'ight," thought Fame. "How we gon' do it?"

Fourtunate took a taxi from his house in Dix Hills and met Fame at a store around the corner from his school. They paged Jerry and then tried to duck any truant officers while they wait for him at a cinema in Times Square. Luckily they looked a little older than they were and they always dressed nice. Fourtune had on a striped oxford Polo shirt, and khaki pants with a pair of brown Polo shoes. Fame,—forever fresh—wore a red *Izod* tennis shirt,—he had one in every color—

Georges Marciano jeans trimmed in red leather, and red Pumas. It was around 9:30 am when Jerry showed up and the games got started. They left the show about 11:00. Another movie patron summed it up.

"Man, Richard Pryor is the king of comedy, but that one had to be for the money."

"Man," said Fame tossing back some Dots, "that shit was booty. What's up now?"

Jerry was ready for the real adventure. "You guys smoke pot, right?"

Fame and Fourtune laughed.

"You mean reefer," Fame asked? "What 'chu got man, a tree bag, a nick; w'sup?"

Jerry led them through a doorway and pulled over an ounce of 'Northern lights' from his Eddie Bauer.

"Damn! You selling that," asked Fame?

Jerry's mind was always working.

"No, this is for us to smoke; but how much could I get for it?"

"A lot," answered Fourtune.

"You know how to roll blunts," asked Fame?

"Dude stop," said Jerry nearly ignoring him. "You're insulting me."

They dipped into Melvin's on Broadway, where the restrooms were in the basement. It was around 11:45 when they came out.

"We might as well stay around here, it's the safest place, we might get busted in the park," said Fame looking around.

"Man, you're so paranoid, be cool. Were not gonna get busted. Yo, you guys know anybody in Queens, or Brooklyn, let's go there where the freaks are."

Fame didn't like the sound of that.

"Freaks?"

"Honeys, dude. You know, *girls.* You guys do got girls don't you? You're getting some, right?" Jerry was getting antsy; the weed had created images of sweet black pussy riding wooden seesaws in his playground.

Fourtune tried to talk some sense into him. "Yeah, we get pussy man, but all the honeys are in school now."

"That's why I said lets go to the Bristol, in Jamaica or Crown Heights or Harlem or something."

Fame was starting to see the picture in Jerry's mind.

"Whoa, whoa! What you think, mu'fuckas don't go to school there. Yo 'B,' *I'm* from Harlem. 'Pssht, kill that noise!"

"Ok, cool out dude." Jerry was running out of options. "What about Hunts Point?"

"Man aint nobody fucking with them two dollar skeezers," said Fourtune.

Fame was smiling.

"You wanna fuck a black girl, huh Jerry. You paying?"

"Whatever," answered Jerry.

"Ok. Then we wanna fuck some white girls; no skeezers either. And *you* paying."

Fourtune looked at Fame and wondered how he was going to pull that one off.

Fame figured they were already on The Deuce; with his mouthpiece and Jerry's deep pockets, how hard could it be?

By 2:30 pm their high had worn off and they all realized it wasn't gonna be easy. Every peepshow had turned them around at the door, laughed in their faces, or threatened to call the police when Fame explained himself. They went to the restroom to lift their spirits again. An older guy entered looking suspiciously at them. He said something to Jerry in Hebrew and Jerry told his friends to wait there. A few minutes later he came back smiling.

"Jackpot! That guy that kicked us out at *Show World;* that was his son, Saba. He hooked us up. He said to call this number and talk to them. C'mon lets go find a phone."

"Hold up," said Fame, "we still got half a blunt left."

Jerry reached for it.

Fame passed it to him.

Jerry took a pull and threw it in the toilet.

Fame looked at him like he was stupid.

"What," Jerry asked patting his backpack, "you forgot about this?"

Fourtune chuckled as they ran up the stairs where they ordered burgers and waited.

"So what did they say on the phone," he asked.

"It's an escort service," explained Jerry. "I told 'em what we wanted and gave them this address. They'll be here in twenty minutes."

The table went quiet as each boy became lost in his own fantasy.

Fourtune envisioned doing things to a blonde Playboy centerfold in lingerie and high heels.

Fame saw a Penthouse pictorial with a blonde *and* a brunette who were doing things to each other.

Jerry's vision was like a Players pictorial. He dreamed of ebony, dark and smooth, playing side by side with ivory atop his father's baby grand piano.

"Let's see what's taking them so long." Jerry said, just as a skinny blonde with a thick accent stepped through the door.

"Did someone call forrr' taxi."

The other diners looked around and the girl sighed heavily, put her hands on her hips and raised her voice, aggravating her speech.

"No time for childrrr'ens games. Who here call forrr' 'Shue Paedr', taxicab?"

"Dude that's us, C'mon."

The boys grabbed their things and got in the cab where Jerry expressed his feelings.

"Wow, fucking A, man! We got a lady cab driver. How cool is that? But yo, where's the black girl?"

"Only me. Take it orrr' leave it. My frrr'iend Maya says you sound young. How old arrre you anyway?"

"Eighteen." Jerry said quickly.

"Surrre. I too am only eighteen then. No time for childrrr'ens games." She asked again. "How old?"

All eyes were on Jerry.

"I told you."

The girl hit the brakes on the taxi.

"Ok. Ok. Were all sixteen, we go to school together." Jerry named a high school far away. The girl thought that may have been a lie too, but she said fuck it, everyone had secrets.

"How old are you," asked Fourtune?

"Why," she snapped, "you scarrr'ed of olderrr' woman? Arrr'e you a 'wirgin'?"

"A what," blurted Fame? "Yo, who are you, and where the fuck are you from?"

"I am Nasha," she said, "and I am from Czechoslovakia. What's the matter, you don't like foreign girrr'ls, or maybe you just don't like girls."

She didn't like Fame's attitude or the way he'd been looking at her.

"Never mind him," said Jerry. "Where are we going and what's it gonna cost?"

"That depends," answered Nasha. "What do you want?"

For the first time that day all the boys had the same thought. This didn't match any of their visions. A gamine with a sort of a heroin chic sexiness about her, Nasha looked malnourished. She had big sleepy eyes, pouty red lips and her roots were showing through her dirty blonde hair. As for breasts, little more than nipples poked through her halter top and long skinny legs snaked out of her skirt.

In truth, Nasha was just seventeen; a human trafficking victim who'd been sold to an American businessman for a little of nothing after being orphaned in Prague.

"Head." Jerry smiled.

"Super," she said. "Thrrr'ee hundred for all of you. I know where to go."

She drove to the top floor of a parking garage in Harlem and parked the cab.

"I can smell the pot in your clothes," she said smiling and begging with her eyes as Jerry paid her. I know what you have been doing."

"What have you been doing," asked Jerry digging in his bag. "You look wasted yourself."

Nasha pulled out something that looked like a Listerine strip.

"Whoa, windowpane!" Now Jerry's eyes were hungry. "Trade ya."

"What's that shit," asked Fame?

"It's cool, try it." Jerry gave him the sheet.

"Man, *I'm*-not-doing-that-shit!"

"What the fuck is wrong with you dude?"

He passed it to Fourtune.

"Nah man, I'm cool."

Nasha laughed as she rolled up.

Jerry looked in Fame's direction as he dropped a hit and asked sarcastically;

"Yo 'B,' you scared?"

These two would never get along. In too many ways they were too much alike.

Hall and Oats, "I Can't Go For That" played on the radio. Fame had been waiting all day to give it to Jerry, and again Fourtune stopped him.

"Yo, 'E,'" said Jerry, "put this tape in and let's get in the back."

She pushed it in the deck and they switched seats with the boys.

In the front Fame looked around disgusted. The ashtray was filled with cigarette butts and the windows were smudged with greasy fingerprints most likely from the food containers that stunk up the cab and littered the floor.

Nasha's phony Fendi purse was open, exposing *her* secrets. Condoms, tampons, and strawberry flavored lip gloss next to a Cinderella makeup container. Fame and Fourtune talked while 'his royal badness' did his thing and Nasha slurped furiously in the back seat.

Excerpt 21.

"You want to go to a mansion Nasha," asked Jerry. "Huh, you wanna? Yeah, keep it up; I'll take you everywhere...."

"Fuck this crank. I'm up," said Fame.

Fourtune tried to change his mind. "Man you might as well stay he already paid."

"Nah, you can stay if you want, but I'm up. Call me when you get home."

He gave his man a pound and left the cab. By that time, head had turned into something else in the back seat and Nasha sounded like she was in pain as Jerry sang along to the tape.

<u>Excerpt 22.</u>

Fame wished he had gone to school. He couldn't wait to get off the bus and home to his Atari. When he got there his father was getting out of his car.

"Famous, come over here and help me out," he said. "Get some of these bags."

Fame rifled through them as his father tucked his piece away.

"Prince!"

"Yeeahh, man. That cat there ..." Suddenly Goodgame asked, "You don't be listening to that do you?"

Fame mumbled.

"Um, um"

"Good, cause that cat there is wild Jack!"

1983

THE DRUG YEARS

The message was in the music; it always had been. What was needed was a way to broadcast that message to wider audiences. So when the men in spacesuits arrived with a new technology called music television, The Agency devised a plan. Their media magicians combined Hollywood visuals with the sounds of music to create a potion perfect for casting spells on all who viewed it. The quick editing provided them with the perfect canvases for subliminal messaging. They knew all too well that bombarding the senses would over-stimulate the brain's receptors and lead to millions of cases of ADD. What they didn't know was that through the safety of television and the comfort of their living rooms, each America would begin to discover the other and the effects of that "reality" television is what is presently being uncovered.

You could expect their spell to work on those going through life with blinders on; but how'd they reach the skeptics? The ones who needed to look no further than out their windows to see that things weren't quite right, simple, more science.

Medea entertained the masses with tales from Neverland. That year's favorite was about an unassuming child star that'd grown up, recorded the biggest selling album of all time, won multiple Grammy awards, and had every child begging for his red, zippered, "Beat It" jacket. The kids from one America got the nice leather one and the others got the cheesy vinyl one, and the next year when neither one was popular many parents were happy it turned out that way; but the amazing thing was, *Michael Jackson* had been crowned King, of *both* Americas. At last some began to believe that even though we were separate, we were still equal. As for the others? The Agency's scientists released a deadlier potion to help weaken the stronger minds.

Drop 1 part crack in the *Foundation*; add 1 part MTV, and a little glass pipe.

Excerpt 23.

THE BRONX

"**Damn, shit sure is changing**, even the music sounds different; it's all electronic now, right?

"Yeah, but you know all that's gonna fade away," said Marian. "People are always going to go back to live music, drums and strings, they can't help it; it's in their nature."

She and her friend Eggo sat in her apartment smoking cigarettes watching videos.

"You right," he said. "Give me some George Clinton, 'Maggot Brain.' I can't get with this shit here. Is she a man or a woman?"

"You so silly. That's a woman," laughed Marian. "The Eurythmics"

"Shit, tell me something, you never know these days. What about that, Boy George? I swore up and down that was an ugly bitch. Then they put 'Boy George' on the screen and I said, 'goddamn.'"

Eggo was really in shock, time had slipped fast into the future, and he wasn't used to it. For the last seven years he'd been in and out of jail; a soldier in one of Nicky's crews. He used to do stick-ups; that's how he got his time and his name. He'd run up on suckers grab the purse or the bag, and yell, "Leg-go." Simple as that. Now he worked in the labs cooking up the new shit on the street, crack cocaine. Even the elite were getting in on this. Gone was the chic, sexiness of doing white lines. Fiends needed something harder and hustlers something more practical than powder. By mixing the coke with water, baking soda, and whatever else they wanted it increased the potency and the profits.

Eggo continued crumbling herb.

"What you think about this music television shit," he asked? "Mu'fuckas aint gotta listen to music no more; they can watch it." Suddenly it dawned on him.

"But we was doing that with acid."

"I don't know what to think about it," Marian answered. "It nice to see the singers and everything, but I think it's got too much influence on kids. I can barely get Cheris and The Boy to go to sleep at night. They know every song that comes on this thing." She frowned. "You know they say if you want to teach a child something, put it to music."

"Nah, I didn't know that. See there, that's what I always dug about you, girl. You're a natural teacher, a natural speaker. Little bitty woman like yourself hold a whole room captive with no music, just your voice. I remember the first time I saw you. You was speaking to some people over there at the armory on 168th street."

"It was *Minister Louis Farrakhan* speaking. I said a few words but I was just bringing The Boy to hear him; he was only a few weeks old then. I told you I remember you, Eggo. You was fly. You had on your matching knits and British Walkers; over there hanging with the thugs. Eggo was taken back by the description. He laughed deep this time, choking on the smoke and coughing for a full minute. Marian could tell he was in pain. He grimaced and tried to hide his wide opened mouth and missing teeth.

"You Ok? You want some water or something?"

"Yeah," he said, between coughs.

After he'd calmed down Marian spoke again.

"You know you really need to see a doctor."

"Shit, the doctor can't cure what's ailing me."

"What did they say was wrong?"

Eggo looked up at her. He reached into his pocket and pulled out a couple of glass vials with a white and slightly yellowed substance inside.

"*That* and this," he said raising his cigarette. "They're the reason I'm coughing, but that aint what's wrong with me."

He took another sip of water and leaned back in the chair waiting for her to answer to his riddle.

"Alright Eggo, I aint a doctor now, I give up. What is it? What do you got?"

Eggo looked genuinely disappointed.

"I got a broken spirit," he said. "You get that from giving up, so I don't ever want to hear you say that again. Shit," He took out a small glass pipe and opened a vial. "That aint the Marian I know. I seen you hold your own with every man in The Movement. You was just as good or better. You a hero."

He took a long pull off the pipe and that sweet, sickening smell of burning cocaine filled the room as he made sounds like he was clearing his sinuses.

Marian glimpsed a smiley face in the swirling clouds of smoke that escaped the pipe before Eggo sucked them in.

"What did it get me? What do I have to show for it," she asked as she looked around the room. "If it wasn't for you, I couldn't have paid this months rent. Baby I aint no legend. I'm just a country girl ..."

Suddenly Eggo was full of energy; he was louder and speaking quickly.

"Right, *a girl*, from the country. What, one, two generations from cotton pickers? Self-educated. Never sold nobody out, just fought hard, kept the faith, and won. You the living … ahhh, ahh … the living ahh, _____ 'embodiment', of the freedom fighters this country was built on."

Marian was flattered. She thought he'd laid it on pretty thick but figured *"it's the thought that counts."*

"Well look at you," she said. "You did time. You didn't sell nobody out."

Eggo grinned, "They never gave me a chance to either."

"I used to know this by heart," said Marian, "but it's been so long since I did any speaking. Let me see if I can remember some of it."

<u>Excerpt 24.</u>

"I tell that to The Boy all the time. What it means is that it's never too late. You may still have a roll to play. Not everybody is cut out to be the star but there are all kinds of supporting roles. You fought for freedom when you helped my family out. We love you to death and that's saying a lot because you know The Boy don't like nobody."

"No sir, that lil' nigga's got a temper on him. Shorty's gonna be a thug."

They sat for a while watching the music.

"So that was crack huh," asked Marian softly?

"Yep"

"What's the high like? You don't seem to be going crazy; talked a lot, but that aint crazy."

"Look Marian, you don't want to fuck with that. I know you tried all the other shit, but this shit is different. Please believe me. It'll take away whatever hope a person has left."

"I did a line or two every blue moon. I can handle it."

Marian got up to grab a bottle and heard keys jingling at the door.

Eggo cleared the table and she ducked in the kitchen fanning the fumes as the door opened.

"Mama, where you at? Oh, what's up Eggs."

The Boy loved calling him that. He thought it was funny to be named after food. "Where is ma? What's that smell," he asked, taking off his coat?

"Nothing," answered Marian before correcting him, "and it's 'Where are you?' Why are you home from school so early? You been fighting again?"

"Nah ma, listen. I'm on the playground at lunch, and here come these white mu'fuckas in suits looking at me funny!"

"Ok, watch your mouth."

"Sorry."

The Boy could get pretty excited. He was breathing hard and jumping around.

"So I started walking fast to get off the playground. I got around to the front of the school and they started chasing me."

"Who were they?"

"They hurt you?"

Marian and Eggo's questions were overlapping; both were ready to hear what came next. The Boy knew he had a story and decided to build tension like he'd learned in his drama class where his instructor said; *'he's so gifted at relaying emotions.'*

"Agents," said The Boy relaxed.

Marian and Eggo asked the five W's.

"Nayn one said their names," answered The Boy. "They just showed me their badges and said; 'were Federal agents; we just want to ask you a few questions, that's all. 'So they walked me over to their car. I sat sideways in the front seat with the door open. Then they told me my name, and they told me your name, they called you some dirty names. Punk bitches. Oops, sorry. Then they said they weren't looking for you; they're looking for Yoesef. He's wanted for robbing a bank somewhere in Arizona."

"Whaat? Now that's gangster," yelled Eggo!

Marian put her face in her hands and sighed.

"What else did they say?"

"They said they know he's somewhere in Mexico. Then they tried to make out like we knew where he was. I told them we aint heard from him. Then they started asking where you were and did we still live at the old address in Harlem. I lied. Then the bell rang and I said; 'Can I go back to school now? Y'all messing with my education?' That's when they started laughing and said;

'Sure. We'll see you again soon.' Then I said, 'Not if I see you first.' And I ran in the front door and came out the back. I made sure they didn't follow me."

Eggo grabbed The Boy and gave him a pound and a few dollars.

"This my son right here," he yelled. "My son, fuck the police."

The Boy's story explained a lot. Marian was relieved to know that Yoesef was still alive. Cheris was constantly asking about her father. At least now she didn't have to feel like a total liar when she told her that he was fine. She hadn't heard from him since receiving the big money transfer that they'd used to move into this new apartment. Now the agents were closing in. Soon they'd be forced to move again. Marian was delighted with her son. All her teaching was paying off; and obviously so was the after school class she'd enrolled him in. He was perfecting his technique for his part in a big production that coming up soon.

"You did well today. But you need to stop all that cursing. Calm down and get some rest before rehearsal."

He looked upset; he wanted to go outside.

Marian opened her arms for a hug.

"Now, whose little old angry man are you," she asked mockingly?

The Boy laughed.

"'Aww gaalee mama.'"

QB

The days were getting shorter, autumn had set in. The leaves had turned brown, and the sky stayed a hazy shade of grey, like heroin. Kids were trying to catch the last bit of recreational time before their winter sentences. Nobody was home at the Ali house. Fatima was at the school late, as usual, and Sirius was somewhere playing the streets. The boys had been lockdown in Bill's room doing homework. Now he and his little brother Merlin were begging to get out.

"Mama, c'mon. Were gonna stay right in front. I promise."

"Yeah, Ms. Drew," said Malik. "My mama said it was Ok if you said so."

"Please can we go out," added Bagira."

"Did y'all finish that homework?" Sheila asked, warily and half sleep. Her young daughter Gwen had been home with a bad cold that Sheila was catching.

"Yes!" The lie echoed through the house.

"Right. Ya'll stay in the front so Ms. Versie can keep an eye on y'all. You hear?"

Somebody yelled "Ok," after the door had slammed closed.

The boys pulled on their coats and raced down the stairs into the fall air.

"Damn. It's cold out here," said Bagira.

"It aint that cold," said Bill's younger brother Merlin. He and Bagira were the same age.

"Put your coat on if you cold, 'Baggy.' You know mama gon' scream on you if she catch you without it."

"I aint puttin' that big ass coat on."

"Well shut up then."

Baggy kept quiet but the coat was big on him. Like most project kids his wardrobe only knew two seasons. Project kids are the ones wearing the too big, often dirty, and always passed down, bubble coats when its fifty degrees out. Bagira was wearing Malik's old coat from two years ago. He was skinny and Malik wasn't, so most of his clothes were a little too big and fit him baggy.

The boys wandered out to the middle of the yard kicking at leaves and bottles while trying to think of something to do. No use going around back, the bigger kids on the never let them on basketball courts. Just as well, it was dangerous back there anyway. Wineheads were across the street harmonizing over a smoking garbage can; freezing in their too tight leather jackets and polyurethane and acrylic sweaters. Malik could hear Benny over there talking his special brand of shit.

"Let's go over to the 42nd side and see what's up with them niggas," said Malik. "We'll do it quick; you know your mama aint coming out to look for us"

"Nah, she might've called Ms. Versie's nosy ass and told her to watch us. I aint getting in no trouble before my birthday," said Bill

"True dat."

Merlin and Baggy began talking about their own birthday wishes and all the things they wanted but didn't get. It wasn't long before they were on Christmas and Santa Clause. Malik and Bill laughed under their breaths at the two "tough" little kids who still believed a jolly old white man came down project chimneys. They'd tried to tell them the truth once and their mothers threw them an ass whipping party they'd never forget.

Each boy took a seat on their bench and watched as cars drove by bumping hits, 'Candy Girl,' by *New Edition* and 'Cold Blooded,' by who else but *Rick James.___ Bitch!* The younger two played "that's my car," while the older two named as many as they could. Three cuties walked past the bench on their way in the building from the corner store. The boys fell in line behind them trying to get some play. They stopped at the elevator and Malik went first.

"Hey yo, Shakeisha, slow up girl."

"What do you want Malik, I gotta take my mama this shortening," she asked with her lips curled?

Tasha and Sanitra giggled at Merlin and Baggy who were in the background, pumping the air and licking out their tongues.

"Uhh, you need to get your little brother and teach him some manners. That's just nasty," Shakeisha said.

Bill punched Merlin and told them to go outside where they started up again.

"Why you aint speak to me today in school, 'Keish? What's the deal wit that? I know you heard me."

"And fuck you Sanitra," said Bill, "you don't never speak to me no more. You be acting like you all that and shit."

"Fuck you Bill. You know what you did; grabbing my booty. Uhh uhhh, I don't play that shit, I'm a lady, I …"

"Whatever," said Bill. He'd already felt under her bra last summer on the roof. "When you gonna let me get some trim?"

Tasha was on the heavy side and didn't get much attention. "Come on y'all let's go." She was eating a big peppermint pickle. "We can take the stairs."

"Yo' fat ass know you aint taking no stairs," yelled Bill grabbing his crotch. "Chill out big mama before you get this pickle."

Bill. Merlin and Baggy rolled around on the floor laughing.

"Yo Chill, 'B'" said Malik.

The girls cursed at him as Shakeisha answered Malik.

"Speak to you for what? I told you No, already. I'm with Glenn."

The door to the "freight" finally opened, and the girls walked in. Fish, a four-teen year old clocker who always kept a lil' change from slangin' weed walked out.

"That's a'ight Keisha," said Malik. "Be like that."

Fish pat him on the back. "'Lik, I know you aint trying to get that lil 'cooch.' Leave that ho, alone man."

The boys all gave him pounds and Shakeisha shouted;

"Nigga, you just mad cause you aint get none. Nay, nay!"

They all yelled, "fuck you!" And their deepest voices echoed throughout the hall.

"So, w'sup Fish? How you living black man?"

"Gettin money with this new shit," he said.

Fish flashed about sixty dollars just as two skinny smokers named Pam and Maxine walked pass the gate. Together the two of them made one cold fiend.

"Hey baby, give us six nice ones," said Maxine.

Fish pulled out the potion.

"Yo, shorties go look for 'Jake.'"

Baggy and Merlin disappeared through the door and Fish led the customers to the stairwell. They rushed out a minute later, moving way faster than before.

"Yo, Fish, what's the new shit," asked Malik, "you aint selling weed no more?"

"I already told you!" said Bill, as the younger boys came into the stairwell.

"What 'chu know about this?" Fish held out his hand and Bill smiled as he said;

"This the new shit, yo. Niggas is gettin' money off these."

They studied the jagged rocks for a moment before he folded it back up.

It was dark outside as they walked back to the bench. The shorties were on lookout as Fish broke open a Phillies Blunt and rolled it up. Malik and Bill had smoked a few times before and only the Lord knew what Baggy and Merlin's habits were.

Just as Fish was about to spark it a herd of bodies came rushing off the courts. Fish's big brother Killer Kahn, ran up to the bench.

"Some "Low-life's" just drove through the courts talking shit. Fish, go get that out the shoe box." He turned to the others. "Y'all shorties go home, we about to be shootin'."

Fish took a look at the blunt and tossed it to them.

"That's on me."

They thanked him and ten minutes later the stairwell was smoky and smelled like piss *and* weed. The rancid smell of the incinerator overpowered them both. Through it all the boys giggled as they reminisced.

"Yo, yo, yo, yo, yo, remember, remember ..."

"Remember what;" Baggy asked his brother, "do you remember?"

"Shut up. Y'all go look out," said Bill.

"Nah, we want some too," said Merlin.

Bill made a fist.

"Go look out," he yelled before turning towards Malik and laughing as he asked; "Remember was used to be on the roof making dirt pies and you always put too much water in yo' shit and it always used to drip?"

"Yeah," Malik said, "I remember you put them muddy bowls in the sink and Sheila beat 'cha ass too!"

"Yo, yo. See, there ..." Bill kicked at him.

"A'ight, a'ight, you started it."

"Remember you shot that cat with that BB gun and was digging in its eyes with that stick. It took a whole bunch of BB's to make it die."

"Yeah it did," answered Malik. "I wish we had a real Tec-9 like Mr.T on The A-Team. You see that shit the other night. Son, we'd be jumping out spraying up the block, yo."

The blunt had gone out and Malik tried relighting it. The younger boys had caught a contact and were shadow boxing, swearing pity on all fools.

"I pity all your asses," said Sirius, coming up the stairs. "Give me that." He took the blunt and sniffed it. "What's this?"

It was quiet as each one looked at the other one.

"Come on now. I heard y'all all the way downstairs. Now can't nobody talk?"

"Nothing Pop. Just a blunt, that's all."

"Where did you get it," asked Sirius?

"From Fish."

"Who is that?" Sirius opened the blunt and made sure that only weed was in it.

"That's Killer Kahn's brother, Mr. Ali," said Bill.

"Killer Kahn?" Sirius thought a moment. "You mean Leroy from the 2nd floor?"

"Yeah," answered Bill.

"Bill and Merlin; you two go in the house; and I better not ever catch you smoking. Y'all remember that ass whipping party don't you?"

They ran off.

Walking to their apartment Sirius wondered how to handle this situation. How was he going to tell Malik to not smoke weed when he'd seen him do that and worse all his life? He was glad Fatima wasn't home so he could handle things his way. He asked Bagira if he'd smoked any.

"No."

"Alright go in the front room. I'll talk to you in a minute; and if your mama comes in here don't you say a thing." Sirius closed the door and said;

"Ok Malik, you aint no little baby so I'm gon' give it to you straight? Listen up, drugs aint nothing to play with. They been around since the beginning of time and people been using 'em since then too. Some, like weed, are natural. That means they come from the earth, not some laboratory, they tend to be a little less harmful, but don't let that fool you. You can still get hurt by them; they'll fuck up your heart and your lungs too."

"So if they so bad why do people still use 'em?"

"Different reasons. Why were you smoking?"

Malik's head was boggled, his thoughts still in the clouds.

"Man, why was I smoking?" He hunched his shoulders and made that I don't know sound. "Cause everybody else be doing it," he said finally.

"Like who," Sirius asked? "You know what; that don't even matter. Are you a leader or a follower? Do you do things because that's what *you* want to do, or because that's what you think it's cool to do?"

Malik took too long thinking about it.

"That means you're not ready," said Sirius. "Man, you have to have a strong mind when you're out there experimenting with shit. Not only will it change your perception and make you look at the world different; *they'll open you up, too!*"

"Open you up to what," asked Malik confused.

"Different world's man. Different worlds and the forces that control them. Doctors like to call them hallucinations. That's when people see things that supposedly aint there. I know you've seen them dudes outside pushing around shopping carts and shit; talking to theyselves and waving at the air."

"You mean them dudes with no money, who live on them dirty old couches under the train tracks with all that garbage. They be sleeping in plastic and eating stuff that we throw away?"

"Well, those are called bums son. Some people are just lazy motherfuckers, they aint never had shit and don't want shit. Then you got some who think they gon' get over on the next man for the rest of they lives. They think time is standing still. Them dudes never wake up and realize people is hip to they shit." Sirius stood there a moment, he'd caught a reflection of himself while looking out of his project window and thinking about all the lost souls he'd left behind over the years. He'd come close to being one of them. From the hat on his head to the cigarette in his hand he was a mirror image of a decade gone by. He thanked Allah for his father teachings and Fatima's preaching.

He'd been doing some shit that he shouldn't have right before he caught the kids. Malik looked on silently at his father who was deep in thought. Bagira laughed at the TV in the front room while the aroma of a meatloaf Fatima had left in the oven filled the apartment. The heat was set on "hell" and had the walls and windows sweating. Outside, people started screaming after a bottle was broken; Malik rushed to the window as Sirius opened it and let the demons in.

Malik took a deep breath of the tainted air and looked at his world. Five stories down young boys in hoods scattered as the police chased them. The playground sparkled with colored glass from broken bottles and wasted spirits. They looked like jewels in Malik's young mind. He smiled slightly, anxious to get in their midst. The demons had him hallucinating, making 'The Life,' seem heavenly.

Sirius saw his reaction. He sat Malik on the bed and sat next to him.

"Look man, these projects are designed to drain our energy and keep us tired. I look out this window sometimes I don't want to do shit. Its like 'what's the use.' You gotta want more out of life than this man." He nudged his son. "Anyway; when I was coming up everybody was doing this shit called acid. (LSD or lysergic acid diethylamide) It fucks with the brain makes people see all kinds of shit. I remember one nigga I used to hang around. We was all in this dudes basement getting ready to hit the Apollo and shit ..."

"You used to go to the Apollo Pop."

"Boy please, my daddy hustled Harlem! 125th St. between Seventh and Eighth Avenue, two blocks away from that police station that Malcolm and the NOI posted up in front of; that's my second home, man. Anyway, this cat been 'tripping',—that's what they call it when you high on acid—'tripping,' for two days. I get down there, looking all fly and shit, and this cat throws a whole jug of water in my face, fucked up my threads ... the crazy fucker said my face was melting and he was trying to put it out."

Malik lay back on the bed giggling.

"No joke," said Sirius. They say you can have good trips, where you see flowers and think everything is good and peaceful, or bad ones, where you see shit you don't never want to see again. I guess dude was having a bad one. But another thing is, you can do that shit one time and somehow it stays in you, it comes back again and again whenever it wants to. That's why you see those folks talking and fanning, lots of them are still having bad trips."

Malik started to say something and Sirius stopped him.

"Hold on now, let me finish. Then you got some folks who say that they aint 'trips' at all. They say that some people who hallucinate are really seeing things that we can't see. Other dimensions, they say they can see the spirit world and the spirits know it, so they follow them around fucking with 'em. Either way seems fucked up to me. I never thought no high was worth all that so I never fucked with it. If you ever heard of 'magic' mushrooms or peyote, that's basically the same thing, only they're natural."

Sirius could see he had Malik's full attention; he shook his head and continued.

"Now, what's next? Oh, heroin, I know you heard of that."

Malik shook his head. *"Yes."*

"Heroin comes from these little poppy seeds, like on your hamburger buns."

Malik looked at him funny.

"You can get high from eating hamburger buns?"

"No. You got to do some other things to it, and don't ask, cause I don't know, but that's where it comes from. That's where opium comes from, *and* them *'ine's,* morph-*ine,* code-*ine,* all that, they're barbiturates; downers. They make you feel real woozy and relaxed, then put you to sleep."

Malik jumped in again. "That's why the fiends be nodding and sleep *'aalll'* day?"

"Exactly." Sirius said, "This is just my opinion, but dopefiends are the ones you got to really look out for."

"Why?"

"Cause they some sneaky little bitches, that's why; mostly punk motherfuckers who couldn't make it through life 'cause they can't stand pain and a lot of times, especially where we live, life is painful. So these cats, they escape by shooting junk in they veins and floating all day in they own lil' fantasy world where it don't hurt no more. Not just that, but when they try to stop, they say it hurts physically too. I mean like somebody is twisting your insides and shit. And they right; it does feel like that. That makes it hard as hell to stop when you know all you got to do is get a 'fix' to make it go away. So they just keep on doing it, and that's what makes 'em addicts."

"Why they be all dirty and stinky," asked Malik frowning.

"Cause they don't care about nothing else but getting that fix. They don't care about how they look or what other people think. I told you they be in they're own world. Plus, these dealers mix it with laxatives to stretch the dope out so they can make more money. Man I dun' seen niggas out there noddin' in a pile of shit, flies buzzin' and everything."

Sirius looked him in the eye and made sure he understood.

"They black zombies Lik, don't *ever* turn your back on them. ____Ok. Now you got amphetamines, uppers. Some of these are legal, but that don't make 'em right. People use one every day when they drink their coffee. Coffee's got another, *ine* in it, caff-*ine*. It gets folks all, amped up, excited. Messes with their nerves and keeps 'em awake. If you take too much you can stop eating, and people say they'll make you hallucinate too. Cocaine fits in this category here."

"That's what you had …"

"Yeah-yeah-yeah. Now again, this is only my opinion, but one reason people do this is because they bored. See these are stimulants. There are a lot of people walking around in the world with no hope. The Life has beaten it out of 'em, they feel dead. Cocaine makes the person *feel* something. People say it gives them an *edge* over the competition and inspires them to think up all kinds of new shit. You ever heard of Albert Einstein?"

"No."

"You will. He was one of this century's smartest people. He and his people helped make the "nukes," and he helped discover those other dimensions I was talking' about. He called it *"The Theory of Everything."* And he's said to have used a lot of cocaine."

"But pop, if he was so smart, what did he need the edge for. That's like cheating."

"I guess. If that's how you perceive it." Sirius smiled. "And that brings us to buddah, cannabis, cheebah, chronic, earth, grass, green, hash, hemp, herb, kush, marijuana, reefer, pot, smoke, THC, weed, and whatever else they're calling it these days. "Malik giggled again." I guess you already know what it does. Make your eyes *big*, make your mouth *dry*, and make you *hungry*. But it also opens you up. That's why they call it a gateway drug because it opens the door for all that other stuff."

"People never did nothing crazy off weed," asked Malik.

"'Course they did. Check it out. A long time ago it was a group of Muslims called the Assassin's or "hashshasin," that's Arabic for hashish smoker. They used to throw all this herb over burning coals and sit around in tents just breathing it all in. Then, when they'd gotten as *'hiigh'* as they wanna be they'd go out and kill their enemies in the name of Allah. Now they was some crazy dudes. So like I told you man, people do drugs for all kinds of reasons."

In the front room Baggy jumped up and ran to the door to greet his mother. Sirius could sense the worry coming from Malik; he knew she wouldn't handle the situation quite like this. But he had one more important question to ask

"Hey pop. You tried all these things, right?" Sirius nodded. "How come you never got addicted?"

Sirius took a deep breath before answering.

"Well, I told you why I never tried LSD. As for H, I'm a man; I'd like to think I got a strong mind and can take pain. As for coke, my faith won't allow me to give up hope, and as for weed," Sirius raised an eyebrow and pointed to Malik, "that's how I know you aint ready."

Malik smiled, knowing he was lucky to have a father around that he could talk to.

Sirius gave him another blessing before leaving the room.

"Hey 'Lik, don't worry. This is between me and you. I owe you one, so relax."

1984

VICE vs. THE APOCALYPSE

The next year Frankie said, *"Relax!"* Some tried, but for most hard times had come to their towns. A long running recession coupled with Reaganomics was steadily eating away at the middle class and tens of thousands of "good clean, hard working" people ended up side by side on the unemployment lines with the rest of us. It was the financial backing of The Insiders, the shady dealings of the invisible government, and votes from the red states that had won Reagan the presidency. Now as the 1984 campaign drew nearer, not even the rich flavor from that big block of government cheese could sweeten the sour taste of suddenly being poor.

Throughout his career, Jersey boy *Bruce Springsteen* had appealed to the grass-roots demographic. In 1984 his hit, "Born in the USA," was connecting with more than just the heartland, it conveyed the feelings of many blue collar workers and Vietnam vets feeling abandoned by their country. When the elderly and socially unaware Reagan tried to use the song to rally his campaign, many began to wonder what was going on the president's mind. "War," another *Frankie Goes to Hollywood* song with an impeccable Reagan impersonator proved that they had a good idea.

In 1944, eager to test their new weapon and put the Japanese to shame for attacking Pearl Harbor, America dropped the very first atomic bomb on the city of Hiroshima, six days later, another exploded in Nagasaki. Not be outdone, the Soviet Union quickly produced an arsenal too. After more than forty years the cold war had heated up and the eagle and bear had reached a standoff. Millions opposed to the threat of a real war and the "nuclear winter" that was sure to follow had good reason to think that the end was not near, but here.

The effects of the first nuclear blasts were devastating. By splitting the atom, a bomb the size of a baseball, *"could explode with the same force as twenty thousand tons of TNT,"* and worse, if the explosion didn't kill you, there was always the "fallout." In the days after the blast radioactive 'purple rain' and contaminated air would continue to kill, slower and more agonizingly. Improvements on the bomb were made in the 50's. The blast from the new hydrogen bomb would cause "as *much damage as a million tons of TNT,*" creating winds stronger than hurricanes. People at least fifty miles away from "ground zero" would be burned by intense heat called thermal radiation, and anything in an eight mile radius of ground zero would be turned to carbon and salt. Natural winds could carry another kind of radiation over widespread areas creating deformities and birth defects. Top scientists theorized the same winds would carry debris high into the earth's atmosphere blocking the suns rays and thus changing the climate to that of winter, for an estimated time of "five to ten years."

In short, nuclear war would mean Armageddon.

Finally, in an effort to calm the nation's fears and defeat what Reagan called the "evil empire," he proposed the development of SIDS; or the "Star Wars" defense system. From his broken mind came visions of laser mounted satellites that would blast missiles out of the sky before reaching U.S. airspace.

While the nation's economy was dwindling the president approved the most drastic stockpile of armaments this country has ever known. Pentagon spending peaked at the rate of thirty-four million dollars, *per hour*. The Agency's plan to bring *"order from chaos"* was in full effect. Russia, having greatly underestimated its opposition, had been at war in the mountains of Afghanistan for the past four years. Meanwhile KGB agents were on a mission to destabilize the Nicaraguan government. With Soviet resources and military stretched thin, top officials at the CIA seized their chance to intervene. Reagan secretly trained, funded and provided the *mujahideen* with weapons, including the one that "turned the tide of the war;" the American made Stinger missile; hundreds of which would soon find their way into the hands of both *Al-Qaeda* and the *Taliban*. In South America he supplied aid to the Sandinistas, going so far as to compare the guerillas to "the soldiers of the American and French revolutions." Meanwhile as the CIA continued smuggling into the U.S. certain commodities to help fund its covert operations, friends and family of The Establishment added to their bank accounts by peddling war and its accouterments. What did the masses do? What they always do in hard times; watched and prayed for a miracle. Meanwhile, as teen entrepreneurs were busy raising hell and learning the ropes, word of a mass murderer that had quietly been stalking them was released.

BROOKLYN

"**Ohh girl**, I am go'ing to miss you so much. Who is go'ing to get me in'to trou'ble now," asked Gaietta? Tears ran down her face as she hugged Emane tight.

"Good grief Gaia, you act like I'm not coming back. This is New York City. Wylan has business here."

"I know, I Know. I am sooo hap'py for you, but tings won't be da same round here wit you gone."

The five girls gathered at Gaietta's place all agreed. The previous night, many more had hit the streets to celebrate Emane's engagement to Wylan Vandalay, a handsome and wealthy importer/exporter. Tomorrow they'd be leaving for Bali, where Wylan's family had insisted they be married in Antosari under a flower strewn alter, complete with sashes, sarongs and Malaysian cabana boys catering to their needs. His work in the shipping industry had taken him far away from home, and now that tourism on the island was at an all time high, Wylan had decided to return and base his company there.

How could Emane complain, he was moving her whole family from Monrovia to the islands too. Her modeling career was winding down but with her name still popular they thought a line of "Emane" boutiques would do well on the island.

"Ok, knock it off. You're going to have the rest of us around here crying," said Donna, the youngest of Emane's model friends.

"Yeah, I'm the one who should be sad. Where is my husband," asked Gaia's neighbor Marvela. *"Please Santa,"* she sang, *"Send me a rich man for Christmas!"*

"Just send me one with a job," said Gaietta. "I'm not that picky."

Marvela took a big gulp of imported Chablis and wondered why it wasn't fruity like her *Asti.*

"Girl, he sent you your present early. You got your ex here with you. I know how long it's been since you …" Marvela closed her eyes and began grinding her hips. "You better get some girl."

Gaietta blushed, embarrassed.

"No, no. Dere won't be none of that in here. I want sum'tin' young and strong like da ones dan'cin' in da lea'ther last night. You know at dat rowdy place."

"You mean The Mudd Club," said Donna!

"They were *too* wild at that place for me, honey," said Marvela. "I liked the jazz club in Harlem better."

"What about Xenon," asked Emane?

"That was alright. I used to like disco. We should've gone to Studio 54."

Emane and Donna looked at each other as they sipped their wine. They'd taken Gaietta back in its heyday but they knew that Marvela would have never made it past the velvet rope. Gaia knew it too.

"You wouldn't like it, it's cra'zy as the o'der place," she said.

"Not really. The Mudd Clubb has a lot of artists," Donna explained. *"Robert Mapplethorpe, Jean Michael Basquiat, Andy Warhol* and *Madonna*; they all used to hang out there. That's why there were all the buffed guys. Did you guys notice it was kind of dead in there last night?"

"You know why," Emane answered.

"No!" Donna gasped in denial. "You think so?"

"What, what," asked Marvela?

"The gay plague," said the models simultaneously!

Samantha got up the nerve to speak as the others talked.

"You all know that I've been dating a physician," she said nervously. "Last weekend he took me to the most fabulous party."

"The one for the pharmaceutical companies," asked Donna?"

Samantha took a big gulp of the wine.

"Feyeser and Galaxyo-Smythe-Clyme, exactly. Well I overheard some of the board members talking, they have a new name for the plague, they call it AIDS, (Acquired Immune Deficiency Syndrome) and they say it was created by the US Defense Department for the sum of ten million dollars."

"Oh I don't believe that," said Donna. "What purpose would it serve? Who wants to harm the gays, they're so much fun."

Samantha was usually outspoken but now she seemed hesitant and stammered as she began to speak.

"A-According to the board members it wasn't really meant for gays. I-it was meant to be used as p-primarily against, _____blacks."

"I can't believe that," Donna said, "those doctors were playing with you."

"Girl you better wake up. Everybody in Brooklyn knows about that. They call it HIV or something. They say you get it from being pro ..., promis ..., oh shit, you know what I'm saying. You get it from fucking too much." Marvela laughed at herself. "It's supposed to get in you blood and give you these nasty sores that don't never heal."

Donna squirmed in her seat and looked away as Marvela continued.

"Girl, I know folks who say they spraying that shit on the weed and mixing it with the dope. And you know what? I believe 'em too. I've been around here all my life and I aint never seen the junkies look *this* bad."

Gaietta recalled when she was as naive as Donna. She explained it more tactfully.

"Dat talk has been going 'round the hospital for some time too, since, 'bout '81. Back den it was mostly white homo'sexual men from da city coming in with very bad cases of Kaposi's sarcoma. Dey were calling it da "gay pneumonia, or "gay can'cer;" but da doctors, dey called it GRID. (Gay-Related Immune Deficiency) To dis day some of dem believe dat da CDC, (Center for Disease Control) and the New York Blood Cen'ter are respon'sible for in'fecting thou'sands of men in da late seven'ties trough a pro'ject called op'eration '*Tro'jan Horse.*'"

But of all the women's stories, Emane's had to be the most hard to believe. She found herself hyperventilating thinking about a recent conversation with her family and the state of the world she lived in.

"At home in Liberia my mother told me how millions of people had become infected and also of how the news media says that the disease originated from our people having sexual intercourse with African green monkeys and eating them."

Emane watched the other girls sit silently wondering until she spoke.

"We don't have sex with monkeys, _____ Ok!"

Marvella let out a loud sigh of relief and Emane continued.

"I couldn't wrap my head around the enormity of the problem until I went home and saw it with my own eyes. There were some of the most beautiful human beings grossly atrophied. The whole village smelled like death. And although many people are scared to speak of it, they do believe the story about *the Feasibility program*. They say that a number of doctors working with the WHO,—World Health Organization—quit their jobs and began whistle blowing when they learned that the smallpox vaccine (*Vaccina*) that they were to inject over 1 billion Africans with was rumored to be laced with a virus that genetic scientists had created to reduce the continents population."

Donna was stunned, her mouth open wide.

"My God, that's genocide. Why would they do that?"

There was a long uneasy silence until Samantha finally spoke.

"I really don't know why? But what I do know for sure is that since the disease has no cure the pharmaceutical companies stand to reap limitless profits from legal drug sales to prolong life."

*

In 1984 *The Patriot,* a newspaper in New Delhi India, reported confessions from an anonymous source that AIDS was created as a biological weapon in a Fort Dietrich Maryland lab.

Excerpt 25.

✳

"Damn," yelled Marvella, "they dun' made a bitch scared to fuck!"

They all laughed, breaking the tension in the room.

"That's why I don't mind moving so much," Emane said sniffling. "It's so peaceful in Antosari, it's kind of in the hills and Wylan has some nice land picked out. You guys are going to have to visit once we get things settled."

"Yes ma'am; you can count on me," said Marvela gulping her wine. "Gaia, you aint thought about moving back home?"

"No. *I'm* not rich. How I'm go'in make a living in dere. E'ven when I was out of work last year, me and Tho'mas still make it here. Tings were hard for a while but e'vry'tings a'lright now. I got a bet'ter job, more pay."

She realized she'd been a little coarse in answering and reassured her friend that there were no hard feelings.

"Tank you a'gian, Emane for hel'pin' us." They hugged. "It was rough, but it was nice be'ing at home. I could keep me eye on my boy."

"Where is my little man," asked Emane, rising from the couch. "I wanted to see him before I left."

"He's something else," said Marvela.

Donna smiled politely and gathered her things.

"He is out in da street wit his papa. He calls him'self mad at you girl. I don't tink he could take see'ing you go, so he made you a tape."

Gaietta gave her an envelope off the mantle.

"A tape of what," asked Emane?

"I don't know," Gaietta said, "he made me pro'mise not to o'pen it."

Marvela laughed.

"I told you he said he's gon' be on the radio."

"Ev'ery week'end he's in dere list'nin' to dat noise on WBLS," said Gaia.

"That's, *Mr. Magic and Marley Marl*," said Marvela!

The girls stared at her.

"What? I'm hip. Y'all better get up on this."

They all hugged and walked downstairs to say their goodbyes. As Gaietta went back in some older boys sat on the stoop asking about Thomas. She frowned. She'd warned Thomas about his choice of friends.

The next morning Gaietta was washing dishes Paul and Thomas had gone out early for another round of much needed male bonding. Thomas wasn't enthused and it showed. Time and distance had strained their relationship. Paul saw history repeating itself and was trying to bring his son around. In Thomas's mind the man talking to him might as well had been some cool nigga from off the block. He'd feel bad if something happened to him; maybe even miss him for a minute, but not much more. He was more saddened that Emane was gone, and so was Gaietta. She was cleaning the apartment and thinking of her best friend at the altar getting married when Thomas burst in shattering her peace.

"Tho'mas, what you doing back so soon? Where is your ..."

Paul flew through the door.

"Gaietta, 'damnit! What you been doing? You can'not con'trol dis child?"

"What," she asked sharply?"

Thomas slammed the door to his room while his parents argued.

"I tell you what," yelled Paul. "I just saw old Ms. Ver'sie from down da street, she tell me da boy been shop'liftin. What you got to say 'bout dat?"

Gaietta stayed calm and explained.

"I know a'bout that, Paul. I'm do'in the best I can. Dat hap'pened last year when I was out of work. I've talked to him."

"I don't know. If you can'not con'trol him, I'll take him ..."

"First," snapped Gaietta, "you not ta'king no'one, no'where. Ya uner'stan'. You take your ass back home, dat's what you do. Sec'ond, don't come 'round here yellin' at me, your breath smellin' like old sa'lad ..."

Paul almost raised his hand. He said a prayer before storming into Thomas's room.

"What's da mat'ter wit you boy?"

Thomas ignored him and kept talking. *Run DMC's*, "It's Like That," played in the tape deck. Outside the window Othello yelled up.

"Yo 'T', where da fuck was you last night, I came through around twelve? I had stole a bottle of wine and come up on some dimes; a couple of Puerto Rican girls that was just *dyying* to meet you."

Paul ran over, shut the window and said;

"Turn dat ban'gin down."

Thomas did as he was told as Paul looked around the room at the pictures of early rap icons taped to the wall.

"Why you steal'in son?"

"What 'chu mean, man? We aint have no money. Moms couldn't buy me nothing. We didn't have no heat; the landlord was fussing about the rent. Wasn't no Christmas. Dude, we ate sardines for dinner for a month in this piece. That's why I was stealing."

Paul hadn't realized it was like that. He'd sent money once or twice to help out, but a couple of hundred dollars didn't last a whole year. "Son. I know t'ings was hard, but all Gods chil'dren suffer. Je'sus suf'fer, so did Lot when …"

Thomas cut him off.

"How is God gonna suffer?"

"I said Je'sus, not God."

"They the same person, aint they?"

Paul couldn't believe his ears, this from a preacher's son.

"No. Thomas you don't know the story of Jesus Christ, the foundation of Christianity."

Thomas rolled his eyes at the thought of hearing a sermon.

"Nah."

Paul walked out of the room and returned with some wine from last night and a leftover pancake. He sat on the bed.

"I can be good as the best or bad as the worst, Thomas. Stop test'tin me and move ov'er."

Something in his voice made Thomas a believer.

Paul sanctified the sacrament and Thomas wondered why they always did that in church. In fact he'd wandered about wondering about lots of things. The time never seemed to be right to ask; but there's no time like the present.

"What 'chu you doing?"

"I'm blessing dese tings; dey'll be'come sym'bols of Christ. Once we con'sume dem, we'll be able to com'mune wit him."

Thomas looked at him with confusion.

"We'll be able to *feel* him. Ya uner'stan?"

"Umm, hmm."

"Now, this is Christ's body and this is his blood." Paul gave Thomas the cup. "Drink it."

He complained about the taste.

"It's bett'er than 'dat *Night Train* you been drin'king," said Paul. "Look son, God cre'ated da heavens and da earth. He is every'where and in every'ting. He is all a'round us, son. He is in this room right now, and a little over 2000 years ago he had a son …"

Thomas was suddenly intrigued by the greatest story ever told.

"Who was his wife?"

"He did not have a wife. Save your ques'tions. Any'way, his son was named Jesus. He was born in a horse stable in Beth'lehem, to his mo'ther Mary. His fad-dah was named Joseph …"

"But you said …"

"Wait a min'ute now!" Paul cleared his throat. "So Mary say dat her and Joseph were not doing no'ting, so right there, you have the boys first mi'ri'cle. Joseph was a car'penter, which means one who builds with wood. Jesus was a smart boy, and his faddah teach him da craft. When he was a'bout your age he run off for a few days. When his pa'rents found him, he was in da tem'ple talking bout rel'igion wit some of the Jewish elders. Mary and Jo'seph were Jewish and da Ro'mans were Pa'ga'ns. But listen cause dis is im'portant."

Paul poured them both another glass of wine for a toast.

"Don't let 'dem fool ya. Jesus was a black man, and one day da Al'mighty Jah, come take all his children back home to Af'rica."

After his second glass Thomas had started to feel something. Gradually he was becoming a believer.

"Alright, so when he turns bout t'irty he go to Jordan to see John da Baptist to get bap'tised in da river. Now when John bap'tise him, he heard God say;

"Thou art my beloved son, in thee I am pleased."

After dat, Jesus go off to da wil'der'ness ..."

Thomas had stayed awake in church long enough to hear this part before.

"I thought it was the desert."

"Some say its mur'der, oders say hom'i'cide, _____ no diff'erence. Now, while he out dere in da desert, he fast for for'ty days and for'ty nights, and den, when the devil think he is at his weakest, He come tempting him with da two tongues. Paul was staring out the window. "Da snake be da most cun'ning man, Thomas, ver'y pa'tient. Dat is why it is im'portant to know da word." Thomas shook his head. "Where was I? So, da devil try t'ree time to trick Jesus, and t'ree times he fail. Jesus come from out da desert and start to min'ister. He pick up twelve folks who dey call Disciples, Andrew, Nathaniel, two James', John, Jude, Matthew, Phillip, Peter, Simon, Thomas, and Judas. Dey go from place to place teach'ing to love God and your fellow man. Round dis time is when he start ma'kin' mi'ri'cles, and curing da sick. Da mi'ri'cles get pe'ople from all over to lis'ten to him.

This one time dere be so many pe'ople dat he go on the moun'tain top to speak da word. There he say 'dis:

"Blessed are the poor in spirit: for theirs is the kingdom of heaven.
"Blessed are they that mourn: for they shall be comforted.
"Blessed are the meek: for they shall inherit the earth.
"Blessed are they which hunger and thirst after righteousness: for they shall be filled.
"Blessed are the merciful: for they shall obtain mercy.

"Blessed are the pure in heart: for they shall see God.
"Blessed are the peacemakers: for they shall be called the children of God
"Blessed are they which are persecuted for righteousness sake:
For theirs is the kingdom of heaven.
"Blessed are ye when men shall revile you, and persecute you, and shall say all manner of
evil against you falsely for my sake.
"Rejoice and be exceedingly glad: for great is your reward in heaven: for so persecuted they
the prophets which were before you.
"Ye are the salt of the earth …

And lots of 'dem he speak to were poor folk and crim'inal types, but Jesus don't care. He say that's who he come to save. So he say; "Fol'low me!" and they did. Now, when he 'tirty-tree, he and da Disciples go to Jer'uselem for Passover. He know what's gonna hap'pen when he get dere, but he go any'way.

"Why," asked Thomas.

"Cause ya' must honor thy fadder's wishes. Dose Ro'mans dat I tell ya bout earlier, dey don't like him, and da Jewish priests, they don't like him …

"But he a good dude. If he's teaching religion like the priests why don't nobody like him?"

"*Seek.* Some 'tings you must discover for ya'self, son."

Thomas nodded and went back to listening.

"So da priests con'spire with da Ro'mans, dey con'spire with one of the Disciples, Judas, and he set Jesus up and da priest's a'rrest him."

"Wait, Judas flipped on his man," asked Thomas angrily.

The thought was anathema to him.

This time Paul was less subtle.

"Son, ya must be'ware, 'tings not always as 'dey seem. It be da ones ya run wit, and smoke blunts wit, if ya slip, d'evils make dem sell ya out quick. 'His man,' turn on him for for'ty pieces of si'lver. Da Jews turn Jesus over to the Ro'man Gov'nor, Pontius Pilate. He give the people one last time to set Jesus free, but dey all worked up, talkin' 'bout, 'somebody got to die,' and dey vote it be him. Den, Pilate try to wash the blood from his hands, but it don't work. Him and the 'oder folk try to blame it all on the Jew's, and dat's not quite right either. While dey doin' dis, Jesus is being flogged."

"What's that?"

"It means a *bad* beating son. Den after all of dis, dey make him carry the cross all da way to where he is to be cru'cified."

"What does crucified mean?"

"It means dey tor'ture him and hu'mili'ate him, 'den 'dey nail him to a cross, wit' huge nails, t'rough his hands and feet. Den they leave him out dere to die. But when he died, God was upset, ya know. Da whole Jer'uselum was hit wit' an earth'quake. The fo'llo'ing Sunday, Mary go to his tomb and his body wasn't dere"

"What happened? The Romans stole it didn't they?"

Paul chuckled.

"Nope, he was res'sur'rected! God bring him back from da dead for forty days."

Thomas was starting to see a pattern.

"Why it's always forty this and forty that?"

"Seek," said Paul again.

Thomas sighed. *"That too much work,"* he thought.

"For forty days the Disciples and oder people saw him, after that, he go to da house of his faddah. And all of dat suf'ferin' he did was for you and me. So it's only right dat we do a little suffering."

Gaia stood at the door with her arms crossed as Paul emptied the bottle.

"Good'ness Paul, ya gonna be sleep in a min'ute."

"Where's mine," asked Thomas testing again?"

"I tink you done felt enough this mor'ning," Gaietta said, taking the empty bottle and closing the door behind her.

"So how we know all this stuff really happened," asked Thomas, "from the Bible?"

Paul licked the wine from his lips.

"Umm, hmm. Dat's right," he finally said. "Dere are lots of Bibles. The for'ty-six books of the Chris'tian Old Test'ament, and the twen'ty-seven books of The New Test'ament. Den dere's The King James ver'sion and The Good News Bible ..."

"Why they call it the Good News Bible."

"I don't know, but all they did was take out all da, ye's, thou's, and thee's and put it into modern words."

"That's good," Thomas said, smiling. "I tried to read ma's Bible one time at church. Whew," he exclaimed. "I'll get the Good News one."

"Well, you get what ya' wan get; but I don't recommend that one or The King James version."

"Why not?"

"Be'cause, the Bible is a code book, the "thou's," and "thee's" are part of the code, along with the 40/40's, the ages of the chil'dren and all dat.

That's part of learning doublespeak, *the word*. And sec'ond, you gotta tink about who translate it. How ya know dey didn't put dere own twist on tings.

"They could've done that with all of em," Thomas thought.

"Dats why I say no to the King James version. James' wife Anne was a high witch; and he write book called *Demonology*, plus he a homo'sexual." Paul just about broke his ankle stomping his foot on the floor. "How is dat man qua'lified to write a Bible? You tell me?"

"So which one is right," asked Thomas?

"Which one you 'tink is right?"

Who knows? It's the argument of historians and theologians. Some say Jesus was born in a cave; others say Mary wasn't a virgin, and some believe Jesus—forever the rebel—survived the cross, married Mary Magdalene, went to some far off land and started a revolution. Others say it was all a dream. When you look through history, findings like the Gnostics, *Book of Jubilees* and *The Dead Sea Scrolls* make you question everything. Maybe that's why we should all take time to do *The Work* and verify the facts for ourselves.

Thomas took a few minutes to think it over, but couldn't decide.

"I 'ont know, that's too much to think about at once."

"Nothing is ever too much."

"Why didn't Jesus write it down himself or at least tell somebody?"

"He did tell some pe'ople, 'dere called da *Essenes*."

Thomas looked at him like, *"why didn't you just tell me this before."* Then he remembered there was no time like the present.

"So what did he tell 'em?"

Paul was standing at the door, he turned the knob and the locked popped, he took a step out and motioned for his son to come to him, when Thomas reached the threshold, he looked him in the eye.

"He taught 'dem 'dat 'dey didn't need a tabernacle to talk to dere faddah."

✳

Emane and Paul left in June. By November Reagan and his team had somehow turned the American economy around enough to secure themselves another term by defeating Walter Mondale and the first black candidate to make a serious run for the presidency, CFR member, Jesse L. Jackson. For four years, Vice-President George H.W. Bush's "voodoo economics" had actually put more money into the bank accounts of the rich.

Sitcoms like, Dynasty, Falcon Crest, and ironically, Dallas, about a rich double dealing Texas oil family that eventually moved into politics, topped the Nielsen's, as once again, art imitated life. When this season's programs premiered, one in particular took hold of everyone's vices and has yet to let go.

LUNCH PERIOD
P.S. 521

"No, no. Lookit!" said Victor. "When we first came from Puerto Rico, we used to live there, bro. The buildings *are* turquoise and pink and shit like that, and them birds with the long-ass necks; they call 'em Flamingos. Damn. You mu'fuckas need to get out more.

"Hey," asked Christopher. "What game were they were playing when it first came on. That looked like fun ..."

"Man, fuck all that dumb shit y'all talking about," blurted Thomas, "buildings, birds and shit. What about may man, "Dr. Voodoo," in the strip club. That's how us Jamaican's get down. My nigga had mad dough, big truck chain, and I know y'all saw honey with the fat ass, damn!"

Othello stopped gambling and gave him some dap. "Man that ass was fat, but I never seen a white girl wit' an ass like that."

Thomas laughed. "Yeah, playboy, that's how I'ma live!"

LUNCH PERIOD
P.S. 914

"Yo son, you see that plane that landed in the water? I bet they really got those shits son."

Bills head was in the clouds.

"I'm on that plane, kid."

"What about that gear they was sporting," asked Arthur? "That's that shit they be having in GQ, yo. That shit cost money man."

"True," said Malik. "But did y'all see Trudy's body? That was it right there."

Arthur stopped him. "Hold up.___ Alright, I remember that. Was that really Lionel Ritchie singing?"

"Man, you a dumbass," laughed Bill, "nah that wasn't him."

"What about the cars," asked Malik? "They had Limos, Ferraris, Caddy's and the fresh double R. I'm gon' get that kid, you just wait. I'ma get everything I wish for."

LUNCH PERIOD
P.S. 616

The Boy was looking at it on another level.

"Nigga, everybody had mad heat. That chrome forty-five was sweet. I held heaters before, but nothin' that nice."

Germaine was a hater. "Stop wolfin' son, you a square, yo' skinny ass never held no heat."

"Whatever nigga, you seen that sawed off pump he had. I got that, and trust I bomb first with it."

Parrish tried to keep the peace. "Man both y'all niggas cool out. Yo' where they get that music from? The only good shit they played was at the end when they was goin' to get dude. That was fresh."

"Yeah, yeah, that whole scene was," said The Boy. "The colors and the lights flicking off the car at night, that shit was intense, it had my heart beating all fast."

He banged on his chest. Germaine smacked his lips and laughed.

"Your boy Phil had it on some next level shit," said Parrish.

"Y'all listen to that corny mu'fucker. Damn, both of y'all niggas is squares."

Parrish had had enough. Suddenly he revved the engine on a drop top Daytona Spyder.

"Beat it punk, we bout to cruise down to Park Avenue."

The Boy hopped in and gave Germaine the finger.

"Yeah, later hater. I can't see anything but my dreams comin' true," he said, staring at the cafeteria through his rearview.

LUNCH PERIOD
P.S. 124

Everyone was in the park passing the blunt and drinking. A-D did neither. He leaned against a lamp post, juggling rocks in his palm and watching the long arm of the law. He had one ear on the conversation and the other was somewhere else completely.

Corey made A-D an offer.

"You wanna hit this son?"

A-D turned it down.

"So what 'chu think about that *Miami Vice* shit," asked Corey? "Who you would be like, Crockett or Tubbs?"

A-D was still watching the police.

"Nayn one, holmes. I'm bout to *be* Calderon'."

1985

INTERSTATE 95

"… I see your vision, bro, just stick with me. One day this town will be mine man, and I'm taking you with me."

A-D had listened to Jose repeat that for ten years. He wondered if he still believed the bullshit that came out of his mouth. More and more the only one A-D had any faith in was himself. Even with the scraps that Jose fed him added to his own mom and pop earnings he rarely ate a good meal; and school was something to do if it didn't interfere with his nine-to-five. What more could anyone expect from a child whose own father said he was never gon' be shit? By fifteen he was doing what some twice his age couldn't; surviving the streets. But nine to five's are how you survive, and that wasn't what he was trying to do. He was destined to *live* life to the end of the road. That, he'd always known. His questions were which road to take, and how far to follow it. At this very moment as he gazed at the signs of Interstate I-95 those answers were being decided. Sitting in the passenger's seat of Cline's green five series Mercedes; coming back from locking down some small town, the tempo was rising as *Aerosmith* played. When the speedometer touched seventy an alarm went off, the Benz slowed down, and all the things came back to him.

"He's so ugly, I wouldn't touch him."

✳

Cline laughed, and fed his bitch a little; she moaned and hummed for him. A-D closed his eyes as the needle on the speedometer hit 120 mph. It was summertime, the top was down, and the night winds hit A-D in the face taking his breath away.

"Damn Cline," "what if them people see us?"

"Fuck them," Cline shouted. "We got 160 on the dash and I got a chip in this motherfucker. Trust me nigga, *they can't see us*. But if they do; use this."

He hand A-D a small key. A-D looked at him and Cline point to the glove compartment. He opened it. Inside were two nine's and box of shells.

"It's two of us and only one of him. The game is different where I'm taking you. This a place only a few niggas come back from!"

They pulled into Trenton around 11:30 and the streets were already dead; nothing like the city that never sleeps. A-D wondered how Cline made any money out here. A few smokers were out and about, but not enough to make him rich.

At this rate he could hustle all of third shift and only stack a couple of hundred, _____maybe.

"Look A-D, back there from that Burger King all the way over to this third streetlight right here, that's up for grabs."

"Why the fuck are the street lights hanging on strings out here," wondered A-D?

The farthest he'd ever traveled was Staten Island.

"Most niggas don't want it cause it aint nothing but a few blocks the other side of these restaurants," said Cline. "But they missing the big picture baby, the closer to the expressway the spot is the better. That's prime market for a nigga with some money; one that can wait a little while for his return. Now this area from the light to that school up there is 'six' territory; it's a little strip mall with a *Dairy Queen* about three blocks down."

"Do the blocks go all the way through?"

"Not really. There's a few bars and lot of stores. But that's good for them cause on the weekends when folks get they checks that's where everybody go. From Thursday evening to Sunday evening the whole town is there with that paper, doin' it. They got people coming in from the city shoppin' at the outlet malls. You gotta understand, 'A, these customers aint rich like in N.Y. At home, you got the neighborhood smokers shopping all day, everyday. Then you got smokers coming from close by, walking or in they cars. You got short money hustlers coming from other blocks to shop wit 'chu and don't forget them rich adventuresome motherfuckers coming through every day. You know you can charge them whatever you want."

A-D knew that was true. Jose charged his two or three wealthy customers fifteen-hundred dollars for the same piece he sold everyone else for nine.

"These po' bastards out here living' check to check. They go over to the strip like every two weeks. You know what the name of the street e'rbody goes to is?"

"What is it?"

"Main street!" Cline nudged A-D's arm. "Aint that shit crazy."

"That is some crazy shit," A-D agreed. "Some simple shit," he added.

"Simple shit for some simple motherfuckers," yelled Cline. "They so slow out here they had to spell it out for 'em. That's why it's perfect. Now from the school right here all the way to that fourth light down there, that's 'five' shit. Its two neighborhood bars; one of 'em a redneck joint. Besides them aint no liquor on that side." A-D asked him why. "Cause the people want it that way. Some legal shit called zoning. In the back they got a block or two with row houses. That's like they projects. That's where the nigga who call it for them is set up. It's called Jalalabad.

"One nigga," asked A-D?

"Right! Like he the Lone Ranger or some shit. Look, look! One riot, one ranger." When they finished laughing Cline finally asked;

"Which side you rather have?"

"The blue side."

"Why?"

Cline chewed on a tooth pick and looked at A-D through his fold up Ferrari sunglasses as he waited for an answer. When the light changed he made a right and sped off burning a little rubber.

"Cause of everything you said," answered A-D, "including the shit about being closer to the expressway; they gotta get the most paper. The cats on this side is getting it all through the week, when smokers run out or if somebody pop up at the crib and wanna party; but they loosing too because it aint no traffic. Plus not everybody in them houses back there smokin'."

Cline smiled.

"What's past the fourth light? Who got that," asked A-D?

"Nobody. It's a police station, some stores, and a hotel. Then about four blocks of woods and big houses, and that's it, that's the end of the town. The next town is rich, they got the College further back, don't nobody fuck with that. That shit is like a commonwealth back there, they'll lock ya' ass up for talking wrong."

A-D tilted his head and Cline laughed.

"That's why I fuck wit 'chu, 'A'. Plus you serious; I like that in you man. I know you don't like talking about it." Cline chuckled. "But when I heard that shit man … I had done a week for a warrant and had just got home. People was like, *"Evret Smarter got shot."* and I was like, "Straight up. For what? He don't even be out here like that. Then they said you did that shit and I was like, A-D a shooter? Oh shit! *Lil' A-D a killer.* I knew it though, I seen you nigga."

"What 'chu mean?"

"Nigga, I was fucking with Filani; that ho' your brother used to fuck wit. You know how sometimes I'd drive through there real late in that black cutlass I had?"

"Yeah?"

Cline laughed. "Man, 'Lani would be ducked down in the back seat stalking yo' brother. She's a dirty bitch. What was wrong wit Evret, man?" Cline laughed some more. A-D forced a smile and tried to take up for his brother.

"Man, Evret's from a little town like this."

"Straight! That's right; I think she told me that," said Cline. "You was born there too, right?"

A-D never broke stride.

"Nah, me and 'E' aint even got the same fathers. My father; he was in the Air force. I was born in Missouri." Cline snickered lightly. "But I was raised in Marcy son, aint nothing nice!"

Cline laughed and nudged A-D again.

"My nigga! Yeah, but I used to see you dipping in and out of the Buick all night."

A-D wondered when that could've been.

"You aint even gotta think about that one. Somebody always see you even if you don't see them. It's they job that you don't see them. But check it; I'll prove it."

"How?"

"Remember one night when you had left everything in there. You had like $220.00, around bout, 11 bags, and the 22. Am I right?"

A-D didn't have to think hard. Only once had he ever left money in the car overnight. One night right before his father went away. J.L. had caught him out late and had a talk with him. That's the night his father told him that he was a descendant of royalty. But there was something else about that night.

*

NYMP
1980

A-D knew what his father had been out doing, but he loved having him around. It was the one thing that he had over his brother and sisters. Martin called but never came around, and the last time anyone heard from Anthony he was in jail, begging Diane to bring Mallory for a visit. There were times, like tonight, when J.L. had found some good shit; he'd sit back and tell his son stories about his glory days in New Orleans working for the Kings.

"Boy let me tell you about some of the shit I've seen. Before I met your mama *I* was a King."

"You mean like on TV, with money, sittin' on a throne," asked A-D, puzzled by where all the wealth had gone?

"Huh, almost. Let me tell you something about money, power and respect son. First of all what you see around here; these so called hustlers; them niggas aint making no money man, they at the bottom of the pyramid. Real money people, *old money* people laugh at them."

"Uh, uhh. Not Nicky and Fritz, they got money. Evret said ..."

"Listen! I don't care ... J.L. had to calm himself and remember he was talking to a child. "Fuck Evret," he mumbled. "Man, listen. What I'm trying to tell you is these niggas around here is *hood rich*. Yeah they got a little dough, little cars, little jewelry, and shit. But I'm telling you none of 'em can fool with these people. I've seen Kings man, real royalty. These people got twenty or thirty cars and they all Mercedes, Beamers, Ferraris, and shit. Man where they're from that aint nothing. They use them as cabs."

A-D laughed at his father. He thought he was telling a joke. He couldn't imagine some musty cab driver stinking up his dream car. J.L. eased up on him and rubbed his head playfully. He was trying to stay in his zone.

"Ok, you over here laughing. I drove a Silver Spur."

"Is that better than a BMW or a Porsche?"

"Is it? Boy I wish I still had my pictures. One day I'll take you to Manhattan or out to Montauk and show you how they live. You know them castles that you read about in school.

Well the guy I used to work for; his family had thirty and forty room mansions! Look out the window at those skyscrapers man. Somebody owns them."

Something clicked in A-D's mind.

"I thought big companies owned buildings like that," he asked?

"They do. But who do you think owns the companies?"

J.L. could see the wheels begin to grind in A-D's mind.

"When I lived in Louisiana my boss would have people come through, friends and business partners. I met some that own resorts and islands; countries even!"

"Islands," A-D was getting the feeling that J.L. wasn't making this up, "where?"

"Pick a place. Some are right here in America where the discussions are big oil and politics, and some in the tropics where narcotics are the only topic."

A-D knew lots of people had more money than them. Sometimes he'd see the wealthy ones driving around in their suits and big cars and wonder how they got it.

"Dad, how they make enough money to buy an island?"

"They robbed and stole, sold dope, slaves, and whatever else they had to do for it."

"Not the Kings."

"Especially the Kings." Let me tell you something, son. When you see a wealthy person out there do a little research, follow the money trail. *It don't lie.* And always remember this. *'All great fortunes were built on some great crime.'* Those crooks smartened up. They took that money and opened other markets up with it."

"What kind of markets," A-D asked bemused, "you mean like Evret work at?"

J.I. calmed himself again. "Nah, Seth, That's a supermarket, for buying food. *But it is sort of the same."* J.L. thought out loud, "Except how at one market you go from section to section buying different foods. In these markets you start out selling one thing and then you branch off and sell other things that come from you selling the first thing." A-D understood but J.L. was on a roll, and he decided not to break his flow. "Alright look, say I opened up a weed spot in this house, and then I start selling papers, and jars, and bags too, and then lighters, then shit to snack on and ..."

"I got it."

"Fuck that shit man. That's just good business, you gone need all that to go along with the weed. See, that's what's wrong with these complacent welfare nig-gas. That and affirmative action aint nothing but government handouts; scraps from the white mans table. But believe me son, don't nothing last forever. It's all out there for you man, all you got to do is figure out how to make them give it to you. Don't let no A'rab, or no lil' I 'ching chang do it when you can be getting that money. Them corner store owning motherfuckers is over here sending that money home, building up they countries, and getting they people right!

You aint got no country to send it to. That Marcus Garvey back to Africa shit is dead, understand! Get yo' M's, son. Money buys power and with that comes the respect."

A-D listened attentively and J.L. realized he was looking at one smart black boy.

✳

NEW JERSEY

"**Yeah, Peggy** Sue only had one lollipop the next day. What happened?"

"Man it wasn't nothing really," admitted Cline, "I was going to drop off some work that night but I ran into these cats in Queens. Fucked around and bust all the lead in my steel. My stash piece was a lil' 22 just like yours. So after I lost them niggas I went right for your spot, it was 'bout five in the morning. I had to do it. Them cats was on me and I aint have nothing. But I left you one. You saw that, right? You don't take a nigga's last. I swung back through there the next day to give ya' girl some candy but y'all had moved."

"I figured something like that," said A-D.

There supposedly was the answer to one of his life's little mysteries.

"That's all you remember," asked Cline.

A-D searched his mind.

"Yeah, it's more to it?" he asked impatiently.

"Slow down baby, I told you it wasn't nothing. You had only left $ 210 and 12 bags. I needed to blow something after all that so I bought one off you. You know, saying thanks."

Right again. A-D had always put that to the back of his mind. He figured the missing shells were more important and had made himself believe that he'd screwed up the count.

"So that's that. No hard feelings, right? We cool?"

A-D figured, *"Fuck it."* It had all worked out. No harm done.

"For sure, good looking on the bag," he said.

"Good, because I'm paying you back again tonight."

They pulled in the parking lot of the redneck bar.

"What we doin' over here," asked A-D.

"I get money like a Rothschild, baby. C'mon."

Inside they got crazy looks from the customers but Cline didn't seem to notice. A-D was glad he'd picked up a new outfit that day; denim shorts, Air Force Ones, and a brand new white Izod shirt; his third one. He was on a come up.

In the back of the club four brothers from that side were hanging out with their dates waiting for the mud wrestling fights to begin. They all pretended not to see Cline and A-D. A-D couldn't keep his eyes off one girl working the dance floor; nothing fancy, she was a natural cutie in a short white tennis dress with a black bunny's head on the chest and white K-Swiss.

A-D was taken by a small patch of grey hairs sprouting from her forehead. Her man busted them checking each other out and they left quickly.

Cline started laughing hard.

"Damn 'A'. You dun' stared the girl down and got her in trouble and shit. That was the Lone Ranger."

A-D was sure he'd fucked up.

"My bad, why you aint say nothing?"

"Say something for what," asked Cline belligerently? "If you want that ho, go get that ho! These dumb fucks can't do shit with us! We'll murder these niggas, 'B'."

The owner, a Greg Allman clone came from the back and waved. Cline got up and finished his drink.

Just then two hood stars around eighteen came over and kissed him before they entered the ring.

Another riddle solved. New fits each week. Every garment district purse there was. No jobs. All the around the way girls hated them. Cline turned to A-D.

"Sit back baby, enjoy the show. I know you seen them hoes Paris and Nicky around the way," he grinned, "They staying with us tonight."

✳

INTERSTATE 95

He'd heard a rumor that Paris had said that, but last night she didn't seem to remember. In the motel she and Nicky and the champagne had made him forget all about the girl in the white dress, until now when the guitar snapped him back.

<u>Excerpt 26.</u>

His reflection had sparked a realization:

"*I've never in my life, felt more alive than right now.*"

This trip had shown him the way.

"So what you think I can make off an 0z," asked A-D.

Cline filled him in for a few minutes until state troopers rolled down on them.

"Pull over to the side of the road and stop the vehicle. Stop now or you will be fired on!"

Before the cars had come to a complete stop one trooper jumped out and rushed them with his gun drawn. The other, standing 6'5 and weighing at least three hundred walked up slowly. His eyes were shielded by red tinted shades and his lips by a bushy red moustache that stayed still when he spoke.

"Alright boys, where are we off to in such a hurry?"

The speed control on the Benz had gone off earlier. Cline had been doing the limit. He held out his license and registration then jingled the keys in the ignition with his finger. A-D gripped the key in his pocket.

"If I was speeding officer, I apologize; but I shouldn't have been. I had the cruise control set for the speed limit. I'm trying to get my cousin here home. He's got school tomorrow. One officer circled the car with his gun in hand while the other one called the papers in.

A-D watched Cline's finger for what seemed like an hour before the call came over the radio.

"You mind if we search your vehicle, son."

Cline politely declined.

"You know officer, if it was another time, sure. But right now that would just make us later than we already are. I heard the radio say that my papers cleared. Can we go now, sir? I need to be getting my fathers car back to him."

"What does your father do," asked the trooper?

Cline smiled.

"We own an apothecary."

The officer grunted and ripped off a ticket.

"This is for following to close to that truck back there."

Cline was still smiling when he thanked him and drove off. A-D started breathing again.

"You did good 'A'. Get used to that if you plan on coming back. That's all part of the game."

A-D remained quiet but that hadn't deterred him one bit. He'd already said good-bye to the straight and narrow and chosen his route. It was time he got his weight up, even if it meant lives were lost.

They returned to a regular Sunday night in Marcy; dead and alive at the same time. Banality had begun to set in after they'd crossed the bridge. He wondered how or when he'd be able to go back. He wanted to ask Cline about it but that might not look right. Then again, closed mouths don't get fed.

"Yo Cline, good looking on everything, I'm gon' hit this plate when I get upstairs. You sure this lobster shit is alright?"

"Trust me, all that shit is the bomb."

"So you know when I triple that Oz a third of that is yours, right?"

"C'mon 'A', I aint trying to tax you like that, I …"

"Nah, I know, I know. I'm just sayin'. If you …, I mean, if I, *could* get a block, you'd be good with that?" Cline rubbed his chin for a moment.

"Yeah, 'A' that's tight," he turned and faced him, "You sure the Volvo gone make it there?"

Theo had a sister named Mandrian. Her boyfriend had gotten locked up around Christmas. Mandrian and his family were forced to sell everything he had. Eight months ago he'd paid $ 10,000 for a 1982 Volvo.

Mandrian and the family dogged it for five months before he broke down and told her to sell it so he could try to make bail. He couldn't get anywhere near his asking price. He was lucky to be getting the $ 2,500 that A-D offered. A-D had planned on waiting him out another month and another $500, but it was already May and hustlers in every hood were preparing for the show. The car needed some work, and A-D did too.

"I'll get baby tuned up. She'll make it there."

"Alright man, I'll slide through 'bout Wednesday and tell you what's up."

They gave each other a pound. A-D got out wishing it was a Saturday so all the hood could see him. When he got upstairs the apartment was quiet. Evret had moved out again and he'd seen Mallory out front before he'd come up. Shirley was hardly ever there; she had her boyfriends and her job at Macy's, and there was still Jose to deal with. Come to think of it, that was probably the only reason A-D still dealt with him. Jose ended up being Shirley's first and though they weren't technically together, you know what they say about your first.

Diane was home drinking Pink Champale and watching the news.

(Newscaster) "When we return, we have new information on that hijacked TWA airliner, and the terrorist drug cartels from Columbia who are accused of executing over one hundred people, including eleven judges. Also, Americans are asking the President, 'Where has our money gone?' As the United States finds itself curiously in debt to the World Bank."

"Who there," asked Diane?

"Who you think, coming in with a key, ma?"

"Shit all y'all got keys, that don't mean nothing. Where've you been?"

"I spent the night with some friends; sorry I aint call but you know how it is."

He kissed her on the cheek.

"Not really, I know how to call though."

"C'mon ma, get some of this food. I got red snapper, lobster, shrimps, and spicy rice. Oh yeah, this too." He pulled out a bottle of Moet Chandon. "C'mon lets eat."

"Where you get all this from," wondered Diane. "What friends you been with.

What have you been doing A-D? I know you better not miss no more school."

"Ma, I'm gon' be in school tomorrow. My friend took me to his people's house in Jersey. He bought all this stuff. Now come and sit down so we can eat."

Diane smiled; she hadn't eaten food like this in a long while. No ones stomach would be rumbling tonight. And this was only her third time ever drinking Moet. It was the best brand of champagne she'd ever had. A-D set out two plates and washed out the good glasses.

"Ma, I never had none of that. How is it?"

"Good," she said between bites. You gotta try crawfish sometime, they're like baby lobsters. Your daddy could've told you all about them."

Diane regretted saying it. No one had heard from J.L., in five years. A-D ignored it. He sat down and ate. Mostly rice and a few bites of the other just to taste it. Diane was enjoying herself and that was good enough for him. They sat at the table dining, Diane laughing as the bubbly tickled her nose and A-D showed off his skill for banging out beats on the table. Sometimes when it was just the two of them he'd still perform for her; just to let her know he still had it. But moments like these never lasted long. Jose and his sisters came barging through the door.

"I told you he had something good in that bag," said Mallory poking him in the arm. "Stepping out of Benzes, mmm, mm. Where you been A-D? Huh. Where you been all night long little boy?"

Diane tried to keep the peace. She yelled for Mallory to stop just as A-D spoke.

"What up, Jose? I was gon' page you a little later poppi."

Jose looked at him funny. It was unintentional; the hater in him was showing through.

"Yeah? I hear you took a vacation this weekend," said Jose. "Maybe you should've let someone know. We were worried about you, baby bro."

"Who is 'we'," asked Shirley? "I wasn't worried. He knows how to take care of hisself." A-D turned in her direction. She was waiting with her tongue stuck out. "So, what's next," she asked? "You gonna buy a new car now? You gotta keep up if you hanging with Cline."

The girls were snatching food from their mother's plate as A-D rose from the table and eyed Jose back to Mallory's room.

"Yo, man I need a lil' favor. I need some extra work by this weekend. I need to make some paper so I can get the Volvo fixed."

"How much we talking about," asked Jose?

"I need like two grand to get her riding right. But I can take a couple of 0z's and work 'em off. Whatever's good for you."

"Aww man, I'll have to see. I got you making moves for the next few days. Maybe I can throw you a few dollars, but after that I don't know bro. What about your man Cline? Maybe he can help you out?"

The conversation ended exactly where A-D figured it would. This cat was like camp; trying to make him miss summer.

"Poppi, you got an eighth sitting in the closet there. Two 0z's from that aint hurting you. I'll get it right back."

"I know what I got in there. I got this too …" Jose handed A-D a brown paper bag with another eighth in it. "People are waiting for this and I need it *all* to be here when I come for it."

A-D was seeing Jose for all he was worth this evening and it didn't amount to much. He was hurt. There was blood between them in more ways than one.

"C'mon man? I aint never did you wrong, how you gone act, ___ *bro?*"

They stood there looking through one another for a moment. Jose hadn't been on the trip with him, he didn't know exactly what he'd seen or learned, but it was it was probably more than he'd shown him all these years. Jose had taught him how to make moves for him. Perhaps now he'd learned how to make them for himself. A-D felt like he did that night in Paradise. He'd taken another bite from the tree. *Sathariel.*

"Look bro, I don't like fighting. I'd help you, but you know Shirl's pregnant. You got to think about stuff like that. We're family now for real, you know?"

A-D wondered why Shirley had to get pregnant by this loser.

"Fa' sure. You're right. It can wait."

They opened the door to music from the top ten videos. Careless Whisper by *Wham* filled the room.

"Ma, that's the cute guy I told you about," said Mallory; "with his two earrings."

"Don't be foolish, Mallory. That man is gay."

An old video by *John Mellencamp* came on; *"A lil' ditty, bout Jack and Diane …"*

Diane changed the channel. Jose said his goodbyes to the family, Shirley walked him out, and A-D stayed up until the wee hours toiling over his revised plan.

The next day A-D brought together what would eventually be *The Commission*. His cousin Theo; right hand, second in charge. They'd been around each other since the beginning and could read the others thoughts. Once shop was set up Theo was capable of running shit without him if necessary. Then there was Bebop. The happy go lucky type. Ready for whatever. Good or bad, he was always like, *"whatever!"* But this time when A-D and Theo laid out the plan he had doubts, but it was nothing a little common sense couldn't work out.

"Bop, nigga c'mon. E'rthing gon' run smooth. Summer is here. What else you gone do? You gone ride ho's around on your bicycle?" Theo laughed and A-D giggled. "That mu'fucka aint even got no seat on it."

Theo jumped in. "You gotta keep ya' eyes on the prize, 'bop."

A-D drove at him again. "That's what I'm talkin' about, right there. Roll wit a nigga, it's a done deal, New Jerusalem's locked."

Once he was in, they focused their attentions on a segue. Ais was the same age as A-D, born and bred in BK, but niggas swore up and down he was from Queens. He was smooth when he moved through the boroughs, dropping jewels on those who could hear him and razzle-dazzling those who couldn't. In his travels he'd learned some scriptures and was trying hard to crack the code. His family was middle class, and truthfully he could've chosen another route, but teaching the babies was his calling. The other truth was; he loved the dough.

Never the average, he copped his first navy blue Pumas in '82. Now he was sporting Armani jogging suits and Gucci sneakers with the skinny laces. $125.00 a pair back then. With his flair, and knack for speaking their language he could move undetected on the other side. A-D swung the Volvo over to the curb as Ais stood in front of the barbershop holding session.

"… You know I do this right here because I love my black people. I'm out here trying to teach y'all, about yourselves.

We Asiatic kings, y'all better wake up and take your place in this thing we got going on. The Movement son. This the *new* American Revolution right here. We gettin' a piece of this American pie before it's too late. Ya'll 85% wake ya' asses up and feel what we trying to do."

"That's right. That nigga Ais be spitting that real shit; that god body shit," said someone in the crowd.

"What's up, minister? You got the mosque open early don't you?"

Ais chuckled. Ok, 'bop. You know how some cats be out here misleading the block. I'm just trying to put 'em back on track, you know."

"I know Ais; I'm just fuckin' wit 'chu."

He and Bop slapped hands before he greeted the others.

"What's up, Theo. W'sup, A-D?"

"Nothin' to it. Yo Ais, where you headed son?"

"Nowhere this minute. Just bullshittin' with the fellas, trying to finish this brew. What ch'all on?"

"We on a paper chase," answered A-D. "You should be on it too. Hop in and let me run it to you real quick."

"That sound like a winner."

Ais hopped in and they rolled through the city for a minute waving to the troops on point and smiling at the old heads sitting in front of the bodegas. They could hear their stomachs rumbling and stared cautiously instead of smiling back. Ais listened carefully as Bebop and Theo took turns finishing the others sentences as they ran down the play by play.

"So far, so good. It all sounds like love to me, but who we working for? It aint no spots open out there. Niggas got that shit locked down B."

"You know me Ais. I aint never been a worker and I wouldn't expect you to be either. We all enterprising, entrepreneurs you know. No doubt you got some work put up. We'll each bring an ounce and take turns working that on the block we get from Cline, while we sending clientele through the motel, were well be working this weight off. After a minute we can say fuck that block. We gon' open up a new market for *anybody* who wanna shop."

"That's right," said Theo. "This aint L.A., we colorblind. We honoring green, and whoever wants it can get it. But you know how your people get sometimes, all sectarian and shit. That's why you should holla at 'Sheik' Omar; let 'em know word on the street is we got some good shit, and if his guys a lil' short wit they cheese we'll work wit 'em."

"That's all good," said Ais, "but where we getting this weight from? What we working with …"

"Today we got an eighth of a key," interrupted A-D. "But who knows what tomorrow gon' bring. We doing straight math son, twenty gon' make forty, forty gon' make eighty, eighty and eighty one-sixty. Dope boy magic, son. I see mad paper before the summer is over. What about you?"

A-D's eyes were constantly shifting from the road to the rearview looking for Ais's reaction. Ais's own eyes were off working an imaginary calculator, calendar, and cash register. He figured a crucial part of this venture relied on him, but A-D had only answered one of his questions. Maybe the other one was none of his business. The car was quiet as everyone waited for his reply.

"What if the 'Sheik' don't wanna do business; what I'm supposed to be doin'; sending a message or offering a blessing?"

"Blessing, for sure," said Theo. "Shit, everyone knows you can't refuse blessings."

"Fuck it. Sounds like a plan I can live with. When we leave?"

"Next Saturday," said A-D.

They all shook on it and Theo yelled; "The Commission, baby!"

A-D met up with Cline on Wednesday and worked out the who's who and the what's, what's. Thursday afternoon he left school early and didn't show up Friday. His mama and sisters hadn't seen him and Bebop and Ais had a million questions for Theo.

"We straight," he told them, "he does shit like this sometimes."

Deep down Theo was worried too. He waited at the apartment Saturday night wondering. *"Now where would he go without his car?"*

Sunday evening Theo spotted him walking up to the building like he didn't have a care in the world.

"Where the fuck you been, man? Niggas throwin' questions at me. Your moms worried; that fuckin' Jose all over me, lying and shit, talkin' bout;

"Yeah you should roll with me; I just bought a boat man."

"I spent the night over here yesterday waiting on yo' ass. Where you been?"

A-D touched him on his cheek.

"Aww that sweet. You was was worried about me cuz."

"You play too fuckin' much, man. Yeah, we all was worried about you. We aint know if you was locked up or what."

"That's nice, but y'all don't worry bout me. Especially Jose. 'Pssht.' I'm gon' be a'ight." A-D gave him two large rolls of bills secured by rubber bands. "I been making moves, 'T.'"

Theo's voice was lustful as he fondled the money.

"Damn nigga, you went out there by ya'self, how you get there? Cline took you?"

"Nah, I had some shit on my mind so I left the driving to Greyhound." A-D chuckled at himself. "I came back here 'bout 4 am. Saturday morning, grabbed some more shit out the car and broke out again."

Theo looked at him all crazy like.

"You lying 'A'. You sold out and came back!"

A-D smiled.

"You got the proof in ya' hand, count them stacks cuz. I's outside hugging the block all night. Ya' heard me! I talked to this chick who works at the motel. We all set. It's gon' be beautiful. I'ma use this to get the Volvo fixed this week, *and,* I know how I'm gettin' that eighth a key."

A-D took the money and put it in his pocket. Theo was amazed.

"I'ma put this up and we'll go eat," said A-D running up the stairs. "Close your mouth and smile 'T', _____ we rich."

1986

THE APPRENTICE APPEARS

The City

"... And We showed them the two highways.
... But lo they have not embarked upon the steep road.
Emancipating ... an orphaned relative,
or a pauper in misery.
They are the company on the Right Hand.
But those who repudiate our signs,
They are the company on the Left Hand:
over them will be a vault of fire."

From the Whitehouse to the crackhouse and from Wall Street to Crenshaw capitalists were busy doing what they do; getting money, expanding, and making names for themselves. But no matter how hot they get there will never be another summer like that of '86. At least not in our lifetime. The heat was out 'en force, sending cats across the nation either up north or down state. Lives were lost, fortunes were made, and titles changed hands as the synergy of a brave new world swept across America. Word up, she was in her zone and *you* should've been there.

QB

<u>Excerpt 27.</u>

"Yeeah."

KRS ONE played on the radio as Malik laced up his new Adidas just like JMJ would have if he'd worn laces in his. He bent down to cuff his Lee's. His La'tigra shirt was a lil' young but, *"fuck that,"* he thought.

"6:32am."

Thirty-two minutes could've been thirty-two dollars. Summertime or not he was turning in early tonight. He had to hustle harder. To Malik the world was looking crazy. Daily he'd hear the Arabs in the liquor store say, "you niggers aint shit." The only one they got a kick out of was Benny, and he'd died last year. They joked for a while about how much they missed him, now that had played out. *"Let them kill themselves, they're animals anyway."* That's what the Italians in The Godfather said, and everyone including the "animals" swore by it.

In the evening when he went to the pizza parlor for a slice and a 7up he'd hear the owner's son say, *"You gold teeth, gold chain wearin', mulinyan. Take your ass back to Africa!"* After awhile it all began to sink in. Malik was thirteen going on thirty, his mind was forming impressions that he'd carry with him for the rest of his life. Sirius and Fatima kept drilling it in. *"There's more to life than these projects."* But after all their years of hard work they hadn't found a way out. *"Money is the only way out,"* he thought; *"and this is how everyone is getting it."* Malik wanted to be a kingpin; an American gangster like Supreme and Fat Cat, or "Freeway" Ricky Ross and Tommy Montana. Tommy owned a whole block and you'd often see his 560 Mercedes or his Rolls Royce parked in front of his nightclub, or his sneaker store, or his mansion in Dix Hills. At twenty-one he was an inspiration to every kid in Queens. So every morning Malik would quietly sneak into the closet, unscrew the fake Pepsi can, tuck his stash in his underwear and go out into the hazy morning. He thought about waking Bill up but that would cause too much fuss; he'd be out in a couple of hours. If there was one thing in his world that remained consistent it was him and Bill; two lil' ill motherfuckers that stayed representing for each other. Death was the only thing that might come between them. Malik started through the buildings listening to birds chirp and making sure to keep out of Ms. Versie's sight. A few clockers were already out. He threw 'em the peace sign and kept walking, trying hard not to hate on the next man, but that was money he could've been getting. The courts were empty now but a little later the area would be filled with a hundred niggas in QB tournament shirts. Today was the last day of the *Hoops* summer games and players from every borough would be there. Some crazy-ass dudes from the boogie down Bronx were liable to show up even though they and QB were at war. It dawned on Malik that he'd never known a single year without war. He surmised that from overseas right down to his borough all the wars were somehow connected. War. It was a joke; one borough against another one, this project against the other one, the cops and agents against all of 'em. Shit, when it came down to it people were at war with themselves. Malik sat on the backrest of his bench and sparked up thinking about yesterday when he and Bill had gone to see *The Color Purple;* 'Harpo,' 'Suge Avery pee,' and, *'that aint my mama, ___Smack!'*

He laughed.

"That shit was crazy."

He wondered why they named it that. Perhaps it had something to do with purple being linked to spirituality and purification. He wondered why he was thinking about it; maybe God was trying to tell him something, right now! It had to be now because it couldn't have been yesterday when he and Bill were pick-pocketing foreigners and ripping up their green cards. He hit the blunt, slipped his head-phones over his "X-Clan" hair and pressed play.

"Got to elevate the mind."

He rewound track 8, again and again as he count along;

Excerpt 28.

"The Police?"

Malik hadn't seen "Jake" creeping anywhere, but he hadn't seen Ais either until he was standing in front of him mouthing; "The Police."

"Where son," Malik jumped of the bench paranoid and looking around, "where they at?"

Ais laughed and pointed to the walkman. Malik took the headphones off.

"Yo, 'B'. Not 'Jake.' I meant *The Police;* you listening to their greatest hits joint, right? 'Jake' aint around here, we cool," explained Ais still laughing.

As Malik came down he found it a little funny himself.

"Yeah, son, I listen to everything. I see everything too, just not right now," he muttered.

"Yeah." Ais bumped fists with him. "I like that, that's real. You keeping it real 'B'. Yo, I came to grab one from you."

Malik tried to place his face. He was sure he'd never served him.

"C'mon, shorty, I know you seen me around this way before. I used to kick it with Kahn and 'nem before he got locked. Ais? My wifey is Iesha out on the 40 side."

Malik realized he had seen him before. He'd heard niggas talking about this ill-spittin', god-body-cat who kicked science with his lyrics.

"Right, my bad. It's early, all the herb sellers still in the crib, and I aint holdin' nothing but some personal. What time is it anyway?"

"Almost eight."

"Damn, it's that late."

Ais chuckled.

"You ought to let me get some of what you got there. It seems like some kill; it's got you all in your zone."

"Yeah it is."

Malik studied him one more time. He was dressed in an official Magic Johnson Lakers championship jersey, with matching Converse sneakers and shorts, high top fade and nice size gold chain. A sign of respect for high rollers. Malik finally agreed. Ais paid him and broke out two Phillies. Malik filled them and rolled an 'oowop.'

Ais could tell Malik was special for his age. He wanted to see where his head was. "So who else you listen to?"

"I try to take a lil' of this and a lil' of that. My pops is a musician. So I do a lil' jazz, a lil' rock; H.I.P.-H.O.P. is a must." They smiled. "Right now Rakim is the man."

"That's the Allah of the microphone," declared Ais as they slapped hands. "What's your name shorty?"

"Malik."

"King, huh? Yo, you Muslim?"

Malik nodded and inhaled, so deep.

"Biz MeAllah El Rakman El Rahim"

"Islam's a beautiful thing," replied Ais; pleased to find a brother to build with.

Malik squinted; holding his breath he asked;

"What's the pillars that hold up our building, son?"

Ais laughed. "You testing me? I'm the source for seekers. The earth and the moon are one and we the 'suns.' I only call you that if you shine like one, so you tell me."

"It's five. The first is, *'Shahadah';* faith in one God, and the Beloved of God. Second is, *'Salat';* prayer, towards the East five times a day. Third is, *'Zakat';* charity, purification, and growth. The Fourth is, *'Sawm';* fasting for closer union with Allah, and The fifth is, *'Hajj';* the trip to the *Kaaba* or the 'square house' during the 12th month."

Ais was impressed and clapping his hands.

"Ok, Ok. You know a lil' somethin'. So who's "The Beloved of God."

"The Prophet, Muhammad, the Joy of Creation," answered Malik. He'd been studying and before Ais could ask, he bowed towards the East and hit him with the knowledge.

"Muhammad, 'born around 570 in Mecca; the jewel. They call it that 'cause the white stone that turned black because of mans sins; that's where it is, and that's where Hagar gave birth to Ishmael.

Muhammad was orphaned around six. Then he went to live with his grandfather. When he died he went to live with his uncle Talib." Malik stopped. "Man that had to be rough, you know?"

Ais, was puffing on the Phillie; he bobbed his head.

"Yeah, but he was destined for big things. The angels said it, and when he was around 12 a Christian monk prophesized it too."

Malik took over. "Right, so when he started hustling with Talib he met this vet named Kadijah. They got married, had some children, and then when he was around forty the angel Jabril came to him on Mt. Hira and told him to; *'recite!'* Muhammad asked; 'what shall I recite?' And Jabril said, *'Recite in the name of thy Lord.'* But he was flipping out 'cause he didn't know how to read or write. So he went and told wifey and she told him to talk to her cousin, _____I forgot her name …"

"Waraqah."

"Word, that's it. After he told her the deal, she told him that his messages had to be coming from Allah. So he'd go into these trances where these verses would just come to him and his peeps would write 'em down. Later on the verses,—110 or 114, depending on the translation—became The Holy Qu'ran. He started teaching submission to Allah around 613, and in 620 he had another 'true vision.'

This time Jabril sent him to Jerusalem, from there he rode on a winged stallion all the way to heaven. By 622 AD, the year the Muslim calendar starts, a lot of the leaders in Mecca got fed up with him and ran him off to Yathrib, or Medina.

That's where Islam really took off. Muhammad made a few calls, gathered an army of around 10,000 and in 630 they rode into Mecca and took they shit back. The Meccans had all kinds of idols and false Gods at the Kaaba until he came in and cleaned that shit up. Then he told all believers in Islam to pray toward the Kaaba instead of toward Jerusalem. After that he forever closed the city to non-believers. He died two years later in 632."

"That's when all the trouble started," said Ais.

They gave each other a pound and hit the blunt.

∗

It's been said that Muhammad died without appointing a successor. In his final days his father-in-law Abu Bakr led Salat. A man of high character and one of

Muhammad's earliest converts, Bakr was responsible for bringing many nobles from Mecca over to Islam. He was elected *Caliph* and ruled until his death in 634 when he appointed Omar as leader of the Abbasid caliphate. Since then they have come to be known as *Sunni* Muslims.

Both Abu Bakr and Muhammad's cousin, Ali, had been with him on the first *Hajj* in 622. Supporters of Ali—the fourth and last of the "Righteous" Caliphs—believed that Muhammad chose him as successor, and they refer to sources which state the same. In Muhammad's first public sermons he is reported to have said; Ali is; *"my brother, my executor, and my successor among you. Hearken unto him and obey him."*

Ali was the second Muslim convert following Kadijah and was married to Muhammad's only surviving child. Their bloodline is known as the Imams or, "People of the house." They are the Fatimad caliphate, and more commonly known as *Shiite* Muslims.

✳

Malik knew he'd passed the test and began asking his own questions.

"So what are you?"

"I follow the heirs to the *ilm,*" said Ais, "but I aint a Sevener or a Twelver, I'm a Fiver."

"Yeah, Kahn used to rep them too. I asked Fish what they were all about but he never said."

"That's because he aint know. Yo, I heard what that cop Rocky did to him though, that shit was fucked up. He was cool."

"Walk this way." Malik jumped off the bench and point to the scene of the crime. "It happened right over there. Wasn't no accident either. He had the choke hold on him, trying to get him to cough up his work. Turned him to vapors right there in front of everybody,"

Malik looked around before he served another customer.

"Life's a bitch, aint it?"

"For real," said Ais. "You never know when you gonna go."

They stayed silent a few seconds until Malik's curiosity got to him.

"So what about Fivers?"

"We teach science, supreme mathematics, and supreme alphabet," explained Ais. "Clarence 13X, founded the "Allah" school. He based it on principles from The Nation of Islam, W.D. Fard, and The Honorable Elijah Muhammad. The *Lost found Moslem Lesson No. 2* basically says that the 85% are those without the knowledge, headed for self-destruction. The 10% are the agents, they got knowledge and power, but they use it to cast spells on the 85%. The remaining 5% are us, the poor righteous teachers. Our mission is to rescue the 85%. But those numbers are shifting, the 10% is growing, and ten years from now they'll be agents everywhere."

"Damn, that's deep," said Malik.
  "It's true too. All you gotta do is remember this ..."
Just then Bill strolled up and took a seat on the bench.
  "What's up 'B'?"
Ais looked at Malik.
  "Yo, he's good," said Malik. "This is my nigga when push comes to shove."
Ais and Bill slapped hands.
  "A'ight, I'm gon' drop this and slide 'round back, I know Iesha is waiting for me." Bill had heard about Ais too. They both listened intently.

"Africans are the original people of *this* planet; the fathers and mothers of civilization, and *Islam is our original monotheistic religion.* Science is the key; teach that to your seeds. They the future, they need to be nurtured and protected so they can grow to be self-sufficient as a nation. That's what we tryin' to do. Y'all feel what we tryin' to do?"

They slapped hands and backs.
  "Yo, you Ais?" Bill said, more so telling than asking him.
  "Yeah."
  "What's up 'B'? Iesha keep your name ringing around here. I heard you was somewhere stacking paper with a tight crew; you got an Audi, *and* you be ripping mics." He elbowed Malik in his arm. "This nigga here is ill too, but he act like he scared to spit." Malik punched him. "Yo, 'B' how can we get on?"
  Ais thought, *"Ish, be letting that reefer talk,"* before he smiled at them and said; "If you got the gift you better use it. What you waiting for, Malik?"
  "This nigga just yapping, I aint scared, I do my thing. What's up with gettin' on though?"
  Ais answered truthfully. "I did a few capers with The Commission, but I don't roll wit them no more."
  "What happened," asked Bill?
  He chose his words carefully. There was a delicate amity between him and his former crew.

"Son," he said pointing to Malik, "tell him 'bout *"The Men,"* before its too late. Peace God's, I'm out. One love, one nation."

"One."

Malik watched him walk away. "Yo, he a'ight, he good people."

"Yeah," said Bill, "he got that funny kinda slur in his voice, but he cool. I'm starving, 'B', walk with me to get a slice."

Malik pointed to a bag lady pushing her cart down the street.

"Walk wit Sheila, there she go right there."

Bill picked up a brick and chased him towards the parlor, yelling;

"That aint my mama!"

MARYLAND

Marian was right thinking her family would soon be uprooted. The Agency's harassment worsened over the next year, especially after she'd gotten a call from Yoesef confirming he was still alive. He was still on the run, as free as a wanted man could be, but the Federales were on to him and were tapping his line. After the call Agents may as well have bused The Boy to school as much as they came around. When he graduated in the spring of '85, she moved the family to Maryland. No one liked it. The instant Greyhound pulled into the station The Boy could tell this was not the spot. Despite bad memories, all the blocks from 112 & 7th avenue, to 183 and Morningside were his. Unlike here. Here no one knew about his roots. A catch 22. He'd escaped the eye for the moment. Now he could go out, mingle, and live like a normal teen. That's when he realized that his family wasn't the only one struggling; financially they were poor, but they were rich with love and a sense of purpose, unlike here.

He complained to Marian.

"We all brothers, we all going through the same shit."

"Well, do something about it," she answered.

He hit the corner of Decatur Avenue and tried speaking with the dealers. He tried showing them some love but they gave him none in return. Instead they dissed the way he spoke and dressed. "Fuck you, Mr. New York. Ya' broke ass hippie."

The struggle had turned their hearts to stone. Sadly, he closed his eyes and pictured home.

But the time for shedding tears of was short. Marian's harsh punishment of making him read everything from the dictionary to military journals was about to pay off.

That, with a letter of recommendation sent from his theater group had won him a spot in a school for the gifted. There he slowly began to feel like he'd found a place where he belonged. In a city of bad statistics he'd found a haven for elementals; those with a different take on the world. It was here that the shy could find a voice, the anxious could find patience, and the lost, if they were alert, could find their way.

Still used to covering his tracks, he'd leave school and hang out for a while after class before sneaking up to the back of the library where he'd spend hours bouncing from book to book, reading for himself all the works that Marian had told him about; W.E.B. Dubois, Paul Lawrence Dunbar, LeRoi Jones, Fredrick Douglas, Margaret Walker, Gwendolyn Brooks, Langston Hughes and so many more. Then on to the ones he'd heard about, John Dryden, John Milton, Jean Paul Sartre, William Blake, and Heratio Algeir, they all had their own special charm, but Shakespeare was his favorite. He found Henry the VI poetic.

> *"I'll play the orator as well as Nestor.*
> *Deceive more slyly than Ulysses could,*
> *and like a Sinon, take another Troy.*
> *I can add colors to the chameleon,*
> *change shapes with Proteus for advantages,*
> *and set the murderous Mac ..."*

Ding!—She tapped the bell on the book cart and caught him off guard.

"Get up, it's time."

He stood anxiously. This was the moment he'd been waiting for. He knew her name the first day of school, by the end of the week he knew her life story. The girls he'd heard talking about her never had a kind word. They made her out to be a monster.

"Her mother is from Goa and her father is African."

"Ughh, she's a slut, I think she's got something."

"No one hangs out with her, she's like nineteen and she believes in weird stuff. Zoro ... something; birds eating people and shit!"

Just another crazy New York baby dreaming about living the goodlife but already behind when she got there. The next year she was always out sick. This year the school gave her a job that none of the teachers wanted; staying late, closing the library. It had taken him three days just to get a good view of her. She locked the library door behind them, and with a blank expression rushed down the stairs leaving the scent of hyacinth in the hall and a mass of curly reddish—brown hair bouncing behind her. Her complexion was about the same.

Looking down the stairwell he made a wish as he glimpsed just more than a handful, bouncing up front. She looked up and caught him peeking. Her expression still blank, she had a little gold hoop sticking out of her nose.

He could tell she used to be thicker and had lost some weight; her skin wasn't perfect either; but neither was his.

"They think I dress like a hippie," he thought.

If beauty was in the eye of the beholder, he was sure he'd seen it hers when theirs met. To him she glowed like an angel with broken wings. She'd been staring at life through an empty shell. She was fading fast and somebody had to stop her.

"Why are you always reading this stuff?" She closed the book. "Hmph, Sir Francis Bacon."

"First let me make sure you really here." He held her hand and rubbed his fingers over her bitten nails. "Damn," he said sarcastically, "you actually talking to me today?"

She smacked her lips. "That's why you're here isn't it?"

"I'm here," he answered nonchalantly, "to learn."

She rolled her eyes. "And I'm here to teach; so when you're ready, I'll be back."

"Alright, you got me. I wanna be an honest man, so yeah, that's why I'm here."

"I hope you're getting something out of all this reading."

"I do to," he mumbled.

She turned and walked away.

"I'm sorry, I'm sorry. Don't disappear on me, _____Maya."

She turned back smiling.

"I don't have time for children's games. Who told you my name; and what else did they tell you," she asked, coughing and placing some books on the cart.

"You remember a long time ago this show called *"That's Incredible!"*

"I think so."

"Remember yogi Kudu?"

"Who?"

"They had this seven foot black guy who used to fold hisself up in this itty-bitty glass box and stay in there for the whole show. They called him yogi Kudu or somethin' like that."

She hunched her shoulders.

"Anyway, I got a cardboard box and tried to fold myself up and stay in there like him. My mother woke up and asked me what the fuck was wrong with me. I told her I was yogi Kudu. She asked me what a yogi was and when I couldn't tell her she made me read all of Siddhartha while I sat in the Box."

Maya laughed.

"I like your mother, she sounds interesting."

"Yeah, she a'ight."

Not long ago he would have gone on singing her praises, but no more. The last time was at the interview to get in here.

"So what should I be reading?"

"Something lighter," she said, "you always pick the heavy stuff. Look how big this book is."

He placed it in the cart for her.

"Thanks. Your story was cute, but you're still playing. I asked you *who* told you my name. Not who told you what it meant."

"I aint playin', you know how people talk."

"People should mind their business. What else did they say?"

"All kinds of wild shit. It would take me 1001 nights to tell you all the stories going around about you."

She pointed to her watch.

"The *Swatch* is ticking. Let me hear one now and well see about the other 1000."

"Ok, let's see. They call you 'the black one.' They say you're a monster and that you drink blood. Rumor is you can swallow a man in one gulp. You used to be a dancer out in Cali until you almost killed your husband. Now you're running from him; that's why you came out here."

She laughed and coughed some more. "Close," she joked, "but I've never been to California. I heard aint nothing like it. I'm from New York, near Broadway and the Avenue of the Americas."

"Stop bullshitting," he nearly shouted, "me too. I'm from Harlem, the Bronx, all over."

"I know. I know all about you."

"How?"

"People talk."

"Tell me something about me then."

They took their seats and she bent forward, gently opened his hand and rubbed her fingers across his wrist and palms before she said;

"You're a seeker; an explorer of everything. You're volatile too, but that's because you're sensitive and you try to hide that side. You like danger. You're forever talking about getting riches and bitches but I don't think you really know what you want. I think you're lost. But trust me," she breathed deep and closed her eyes, "you're barely fifteen, there's still time for you. When you learn some patience it'll all come back." She exhaled and opened them. "*And* you're in love with that skinny little girl you're always with, Synical."

The Boy snatched his hand away.

"This chick aint right."

But of course she was.

He'd met Synical the first day of class. Pretty and petite with chiseled features. She wanted to do anything, dance, act, sing. When she needed a partner for a class project,—doing a music video—she picked him and the song.

"Yo, that song is corny."

She insisted. He figured she had a crush on the artist or something. No matter. Anything to be near her. Months passed, she became his conception of love. He wrote poetry to her. She read poetry to him. They shared commonalities.

Two poor black kids in a school that catered to rich white ones. Her father was gone and so was his.

When Marian left N.Y., Eggo was locked up. She never wrote him or told him where she went. New Years Day 1986, some friends called and told Marian that he'd died from a broken heart.

He and Synical could relate to each other, but her friendship came with conditions.

"That's just my homie," he said to Maya. "Aint nothin' goin' on between us."

"The way you act when she's in here; I don't know. I think you'd get with her if she was feeling you."

The Boy was embarrassed and lowered his head.

"Why don't you just find somebody else, a lot of the girls here think you're cute. They say you've got nice eyes and a nice smile. They're right."

He flashed them both before rushing to Synical's rescue.

"You don't understand Synical. She's looking out for me. She's forever telling me how I need to get my shit together, sign up for this and enroll in that. She's always on my ass about my smoking and drinking. I remember one time I showed her a picture of this girl I liked when I lived in the Bronx." He laughed hesitantly. "She talked about the girl so bad; she said that I'd do better if I got straight." He imitated Synical. *'A real woman wants someone that's doing something with their life, and until you do those are the kinds of tramps you'll get.'* She's right too. I gotta get paid cause all that cute shit don't mean nothing if you aint got no car or no ends. That's all the females around my way care about, fuck that sensitive good looking shit. Unless you got jacks, like L.L. or something." The Boy stood up. "Look at me, I'm stone broke, I stay on the bus, and I'm skinny as fuck. I aint shit, that's one reason I spend so much time in here. What else I'ma do?"

Maya looked him in the eye.

"What is your reality," she asked, "when you dream what do you dream about?"

The Boy thought for a moment then something came over him. He got angry, his eyes narrowed and he spit his answer out.

"Nothing! When I sleep I don't dream no more. I aint got time for that shit, I gotta make a living. That's why my family is where we at now, cause of a fucking dream. My mama used to tell me about all the dreams her and her friends had about equality and independence. The American dream," he snickered, "man we got suckered. She had me believing in that shit for the longest, but this a white mans world, it says it right there in the Constitution. '… Endowed by *their* Creator, with rights to life, liberty, and *the pursuit,* of happyness.' And when *those* men talk about, 'governments are instituted among men, deriving their just powers from the consent of the governed,' that shit don't apply to me. If we the ones being governed why we couldn't even vote on it 'til twenty years ago. And the most fucked up part of the dream; the shit about 'whenever any form of government becomes destructive of these ends, it is *the right,* of the people to alter or to abolish it, and to institute a new government. It is, *their right,* it is *their duty,* to throw off such government, and to provide new guards for their future security.' Please! Don't you believe it. My mama believed that shit and look at her now; she cries all the time and dreams with her fucking eyes open."

Clenched fists held back his tears. "I love my people, but damn, we gotta use our brains before we all be some victims."

He was angry and hurt. He'd been lied to and felt abandoned. Maya felt for him. The sun was shining brightly outside the library window, but inside she'd opened Pandora's dark box.

"What's done is done, I can't take it back."

She watched him dry his eyes. Then she picked up her chair and sat it behind his. He tried to rise but she pressed down on his shoulders as she straddled her seat.

"Shh. Sit down. I'll take it from here." She massaged his shoulders and told him a story to ease his troubled mind. "Normally I keep to myself, but I think we've both said a little too much today, so here it is. My mother's Indian; a Hindu from a lower caste family. I don't really know much about my father. He died when I was around two. But his people were from what used to be Persia; he was a mix of African and Iranian. They met in New York in the sixties; my mother was always worried about cash because it's really poor where she's from. She says my father would comfort her with the story of Zurvan Akarana, which means 'Infinite Time;' similar to The God of your bible. He created these two lights;

the greater one, Ormazd, is wise and kind. He presides over all that is good and he wanted to make Persia and the world into a paradise. But Ahriman, the lesser light tore his way out of the Zurvan's womb to begin an evil reign. They say whenever people have doubts and fears, or wherever there is laziness, or poverty, that's Ahriman or "Angry Man."

"Who?"

"Ahriman's, other name is 'Angra Mainyu,' I couldn't pronounce that, so I called him 'Angry Man.' The Amesa Spentas, or Holy Immortals are like angels, they help to keep us on the right path. But Ahiriman has his Devatas, and they're always out to get you. If you let them, they'll have you believing that the sun doesn't shine and that the sky is never blue. There's a war going on between them. Both sides use whatever means they can to influence people. You have to know which one is guiding you. So, the story says that there will come a day when 'Ahura Mazda' or Ormazd will come back to power and sink 'Angry Man' into the darkness forever. There are 17 songs called *gathas* that you're supposed to sing to praise God, but my mother never learned them, so I made my own."

The Boy was in a much better mood now.

"Sing 'me to me," he said.

"I don't think so. Tell me one of your poems."

"I don't write poetry."

She recited a few of his titles.

"Stick to honesty, you're a lousy liar."

The Boy looked at her long and hard.

"You're starting to freak me out for real, how do you know all these things about me. You a jogan?"

Maya laughed hard for a moment. He laughed with her before she stopped and punched him in the back.

"My grandmother was a jogan. My mother doesn't have the gift; but she swore up and down that I'd never last."

The memory bothered her. She heaved and struggled to catch her breath.

The Boy asked affectionately.

"Are you Ok?"

"Yeah, I'll be fine." Maya was quiet a moment. "I went through your files in the office, Ok. I watched your interview tape and everything. He looked violated. "Hey, I had to know who this guy hanging around here was. As far as the poetry goes; close your notebook when you go to the bathroom."

The Boy breathed a sigh of relief.

"See, I knew it wasn't nothing to that psychic crap."

"You don't have to be a jogan to see things. You should know that if you read about yogis. Yoga means to *yoke*. To bring together the mind, body, and spirit. When it's done properly the veil of illusion is lifted. After that, anything is possible. It would be good for you, help you to relax, help you with your energy, and your focus."

"Teach me."

"You want it all don't you? It can take years to cross the ocean of Samsara. I don't have that long. Besides, what do I get in return?"

The Boy didn't need to cross the ocean to see Maya. Outside sunrays had turned to raindrops. The Boy listened to them hit the window pane as put his words together. He knew this girl. Reading people is a numbers game. If you know their character and their history, odds are good you can figure them out. She never had a father, part time mother, she'd grown up way too fast. He remembered N.Y, and the faces of all the young girls on the Avenue, Maya didn't need another dream.

"She needs a friend."

He spoke from his heart.

"I can make you a promise. I promise not to leave, and to take away the pain if you let me."

Maya stopped massaging his shoulders and held him silently from behind for a long while until she pushed away.

"It's time for you to leave now, *for real*. You've got class tomorrow. Don't be late."

The Boy got up and eased toward the door. Maya thought of something and chased him down.

"Hey, I got a question. What should I call you?"

He looked up the stairwell and smiled. "You can call me daddy."

✳

Week one. They searched The Upanishads for *Atman*.

"Ommmm …"

"So these are just thoughts …" interrupted The Boy.

"Not thoughts," said Maya, "mystic visions."

"Sorry. Mystic visions, that people experienced and wrote down."

"Yep, just like me with my songs, and you with your poetry."

Week two. They studied 112 mysteries from The Book of Secrets
   "Oh, this is the real shit here. When we gon' practice this?"
Maya pushed her chair back from the table and raised an eyebrow.
"We? That's Synical's department, not mine."

Week three. They kicked it. "Let's talk about sex."
   "I only did it once …"
He remembered how Eggs had gotten it for him, gave him condoms, and paid
for it. He never dreamed loosing his virginity would be like that. He'd dreamed
of love and a red rose swaying in paradise, waterfalls, heaven, and the whole nine.
Instead he got six minutes of pleasure and five minutes of game from a prostitute
while she sat on the toilet and got right.
   "Baby, never trust a 'ho wit cha loot, __and never pull a gat that you can't shoot."
   "… it wasn't nothing," he answered, "what about you?"
Maya cracked a coy little smile. "I been known to clown and get around."
"You ever been in love?"
The smile disappeared before she answered. "No."

Week four. She sang seventeen jewels to him, about girls and boys, birds and the
life. Dreams of angelic fathers who'd make it alright. She prayed for peace in the
ghettos and for soldiers out west. She sang of how weeks went on forever for those
who say they aint blessed.
   The Boy clapped and whistled.
   "Shh! This *is* the library. They used to sound better but I can't reach those highs
anymore." She sat next to him. "Why don't you do something with your poetry?"
   "Like what?"
   "I don't know. Why don't you *flow?* I saw you in that video. I know you want
to."
   He admit he did.
   "Well," she asked.
   "That's with somebody else's stuff," he said. "What would I write about?"
   "The same things you write about in your poetry. Write about what you know,
what you see, that's the truth. Those things are going on everyday and people
want to hear about 'em baby."
   "People don't want to hear the truth. I told you, they want fairy tales."
   "Why are you thinking so small? It's a big world out there how do you know
what everybody wants to hear. Don't *you* be fooled; most of the world is a ghetto,
not Neverlands. Look around this school. How many kids like us have access to
this?" She waved her hands around the room.

"Take that stuff you said from The Constitution, outside of here none of my friends know that; flow for them, they need to hear your words of wisdom."

Week five. He wrote.

Week six. She read, and he wrote some more.

Week seven. Maya got his wheels spinning by studying the petals of the lotus, but she'd yet to unlock his heart. "BREATHE!" She said loudly. "Deep, expand your chest, hold it, _____hold it. Don't let it out." The Boy's eyes bulged, his chest was about to explode, then his lungs fizzled oxygen like an untied balloon.

Maya sighed.

"All this will be for nothing if you don't learn to breathe. *Prana* and *bindu* are your life-force. You have to learn to conserve them."

"What's prana?"

"Your vital energy, your *flow*, The Boy perked up.

"You mean *The Force?*"

Maya rolled her eyes and kept talking.

"Every culture has a version of it. In parts of Africa they call it mulungu, Christians call it, The Holy Spirit, but it was discovered in India where it's called prana. Hatha yoga teaches, 'Life is the period between one breath and the next; a person who only half-breathes, only half-lives. He, who breathes correctly, acquires control of the whole being.' Maya shook her head, disappointed. "All your smoking is killing you."

The Boy looked.

"I know you aint talking."

Maya smiled. "I don't smoke cigarettes though. Thank you, come again." She instructed him to take in more air. "Deeper, you can do it. One-twelve, one-thirteen. That's good, that was almost two minutes."

The Boy panted. "How will I know when I'm doing it right?"

Maya smiled. "Oh, believe me, you'll know."

Week eight. The Boy complained.

"We been at this almost two weeks and I aint felt nothing."

"That's because you're waiting to see something. Revelations come when you don't expect them. Clear your mind and your senses. Don't hear, don't smell, don't feel, don't want, and most of all, don't think. Just let it be."

They sat cross legged trying for another fifteen minutes.

"Ok, it's getting late," he said.

Maya was upset. She jumped up and cleared the last couple from the library then locked the door.

"What are you doing?"

She led him to one of the big wooden tables.

"Get up there, lotus position."

He climbed on the table.

"It's ashamed when somebody wants more for you than you want for yourself." She put a tape in the deck. *Pink Floyd's*. "Shine on You Crazy Diamond."

Excerpt 29.

The Boy tried to talk.

"Shhh! Breathe and stay calm," said Maya. "Whatever happens I'm with you." She circled the table contracting her abdomen with air from deep within and holding it in her cheeks. "Wssss." She continued blowing it out slow and steady until a blue mist hung like a cloud around The Boy's head. He pulled it in through his nostrils and down into his own stomach as she said softly,

Excerpt 30.

Slowly she lay him down on the table and pressed her lips tight against his. She opened their mouths and they began to breathe one breath; the breath of the eternal, out from her torso into his, there and back again. Waves of vibrations rolled across his body and heat moved upwards through his spine as he floated in the tide of the ocean. He tried to rise but she stopped him, took her lips away and said;

Excerpt 31.

Then she pressed her forehead against his. Beads of sweat rolled down from his hairline. Shapes danced and took form as visions began to materialize behind his closed eyelids. His breath was suspended; his eyelids fluttered, and through her his own mystic visions became perfectly clear.

"That was me," he asked when he woke?

Maya hovered over him. "What did you see?"

"Shit," his voice was filled with wonder, "what didn't I see? I saw everything we talked about. I saw me rolling in a five hundred Benz. I had a big ass house, fly clothes and jewels ... Oh," he'd almost forgotten, "I was somewhere on a yacht too! Can you imagine, a fucking yacht; I'm drinking champagne and margaritas with models and counting hundred stacks."

"How did you get there," asked Maya?

"I did what you told me too; I spoke the truth. I let my poetry flow through me. How did you know?" Maya smiled quietly as he continued.

"And the love, the love I was getting ..." He blinked, swallowed and struggled to catch his breath. "It was beautiful."

"Love always is," she said, "but there are laws to the universe. Always, where there's one, there is the other. Love can't exist without hate on that plane.

Where you were successful, there were those in your vision that weren't. In some, that success will breed envy, others are devoid of love. Did you see or feel that?"

"I did. At times I was paranoid; always looking over my shoulder and peepin' 'round corners. But there was nothing there. Just shadows and whispers." He opened his eyes wide. *The void.* Like it says in the Upanishads; *'Where heaven and earth meet there is a space wide as a razors edge or a fly's wing through which one may pass to another world.'*"

Maya took over. "Right. In the void lies the gate to another realm. Your true calling lies on the other side of that gate. The Golem,—those who dwell without form in the lower planes—are there to frighten you. They claim to possess the keys to the gate, but they lie. The key is available to all who are brave enough to use it."

The Boy had another question.

"There was something else. When we kissed, I saw ..."

"I know what you saw. Our dreams and fears; they're connected now. But be careful with that. You don't want to know some people that well."

One and a half weeks later. Synical's chest heaved up and down as she listened to The Boy's plea.

"I swear we aint doing nothing. I'm gon' prove it to you. Before you get home, I'll prove how serious I am about you; how much I love you."

"Love me? You got a strange way of showing it. You spend more time with her than you do with me. In the library by yourselves all the time; and y'all just talking and reading. Right! If you want to prove something to me leave now. It's the last day of school. What are you staying here for?"

He tried honesty. "Syn', you're my heart. But I can't lie, I care about Maya, and she needs me right now."

Synical stormed towards the bus stop. "That's who you be with then."

With a long face, The Boy made his way to the library. Maya had been at the fountain taking her medication and saw it all from the window. She was in the library stacking books when he reached her.

"What's wrong with you," she asked?

"Nothing, I'm straight."

They sat silent for a while in the empty library.

"Go with her."

"Nah, I'm hanging out with you today, she knew that."

He changed the subject. "So what 'chu doing tonight? We aint talked about how were gon' k.i.t.?"

Maya smiled. "Stop by my place tonight. We can talk about all kinds of shit there."

The Boy looked up. "Yo' place. All this time you never even gave me a phone number; and shit like what?"

"You know," she said provocatively, "shit like me being a dancer and swallowing men in one gulp." She grabbed his had and wrote a number on it.

"What's this?"

"My room number. You know where the Alexandria Hotel is?"

"No".

"You're smart, you'll find out by nine tonight." She held his cheeks. "I'll be your friend until the end of time." Then she kissed his lips. "Go catch your girl."

Outside Synical's bus had come and gone. The gift of a lifetime was waiting for The Boy, but still he couldn't get her off his mind. He wanted to go to her house but there wasn't enough time.

"I'll call before she gets home and set things right with her mom."

At home he spent more than an hour putting his outfit together. Cheris helped him get dressed and Marian gave him a sample bottle of cologne and a few dollars. The bus ride was long one and he wasn't in the best of moods when he arrived. It was nine-thirty; the building was tall and ancient and drizzle hit him in the face as he looked up at the sign. He approached the front desk, nervously watching as the pimped-out front desk clerk kissed a centerfold while the wild haired bellhop stood by watching. The Boy listened to the action behind the red doors as he made his way to her room. He was scared to knock when he got there. Inside he heard Qawwali music playing as the scent of chamomile and lilac seeped under the door. He checked the hall; it was empty. He kneeled and peeked through the key hole. The inside was decorated in rich velour. He watched Maya close the curtain. She took off her shawl and laid it on the couch.

"Damn!"

He blinked and gasped. She immediately focused on the door and moved towards it in a dress that fit her curves like a crimson sheath. She winked at him, then floated back and did a dance worthy of the temple, her body rolled and her petals reached for the sun. Weak in the knees, he braced himself to keep from falling to temptation.

"The door is open."

Feeling blessed to have found a true love at last; he opened it, and let himself in.

When he woke it was morning, the rain had subsided and sunlight shone across his sleeping face. The clock on the wall read two pm. He immediately felt a pain deep in his chest. Maya was gone. He rushed to the mirror where in his reflection was a message written in lipstick.

"Dear Daddy,

The seed of the future has taken root in the present. Believe in it, and follow that path to your destiny. Many will wish death on you. But many more will come to love you. Love is God. God is your Strength. Don't give in to 'Angry Man,' or The Devatas, and look to 'The Immortalz' for guidance, as we've looked inside each other. Remember, I've seen your spirit, yours is the greater light. What are you waiting for? Shine, diamond, be the legend you were born to be."

1987

DOPE MEN

"California, aint nothing like it."

Her voice echoed in The Boy's head as he pictured her in flight pursuing her own dreams. Maybe he'd catch up with her one day, maybe not. One thing was certain; if she did make the trip out west she'd learn quickly, "Cali was more than just fun and switches, and everyone in LA's got a lil' bit of thug in 'em."

That mindset was a must if you were out chasing currency. Conditions hadn't improved much since '65 and the gang epidemic had worsened around the U.S. and had reached epic proportions in California. It had long been an open secret in both Americas that The Agency was instrumental in supplying drugs to urban communities. Paragraphs and pages had been leaked for years but as this one came to a end, The 'Contra' scandal was shedding new light on the secret wars of the C.I.A. Drugs became the leading source of revenue in the South Central area, helping to divide neighborhoods and create dissension in gang ranks. The demand was high and the supply limitless. Hydras formed as brother battled against brother for the control of dope spots that they believed would one day get them off the block.

CALIFORNIA
Compton

Legend has it Raymond Washington and Stanley 'Tookie' Williams founded the *Cribbs* around 1970. By the summer of 1972 they were known as Crips. Soon after a set of theirs from Compton and the Piru street Crips had words. The Piru's were defeated and sought revenge. Needing allies they turned to a number of other smaller gangs that included the L.A. Brims, the Bishops and Lueders Park Hustlers sets. This alliance quickly became known as the Bloods.

Quincy McDonald was neither. As a lanky, soft-spoken 19 year old he'd spent his younger years among Bloods. He now he lived in Crip territory. Like most neighborhood kids he'd learned two things; to walk it like he talked it, and the best way to escape joining a gang was to have a skill they respected. Athletes were generally left alone and so were musicians. Quincy was every bit a chemist at mixing sounds as the drug chefs had become at cooking crack. Part of a small time band that was going nowhere, he earned most of his money making mix tapes and Dj'ing at gang parties. He'd done a few for a paid lil' G from the Rolling 60's Crip set. When Quincy ran into some trouble, he gave his homeboy Edgar Evans a call.

"Good lookin' cuzz. I aint wanna hit your old girl's house collect but I figured she was at church this morning and you'd probably be over there."

It was a little after noon and Double E had just bailed Quincy out of the county jail. He walked inconspicuously in front, a royal blue Dodgers cap was pulled low over his jehri curl and a white T-shirt and blue Levis were his only disguise. Quincy followed closely in a *Member's Only* jacket, t-shirt and tight slacks. At 6'2 he loomed almost a foot taller than Double E. They left the building and jumped into E's powder blue, custom, 1964 Impala.

"Yeah, you figured right. I had just crept in right before you called. What up though; what happened over there?"

"Man some old crazy shit. You know how these pigs be trying to jack a nigga for any old thing. I had a fucking warrant on some old parking tickets. 72 hours I was in that bitch on some bullshit."

Double E laughed.

"Damn that's some old bad luck shit. I better knock on this motherfucking wood. I aint never been in that bitch."

Quincy couldn't believe his ears.

"All these years you been slangin', you aint never been to County?"

"Nope, I guess I'm lucky like that."

Quincy shook his head thinking.

"All the dirt this nigga do, and I'm the one they put in jail."

"Well you need to pass me some of that good shit," he said, "cause I'm sick of this here. I was with this honey right; bad bitch, big ass. I'd met her at the swap meet."

"What 'chu get over there," asked Double E?

Quincy poked his chest out.

"I copped me some hundred spoke Dayton's for the ride. That's why I couldn't make bail. I had just spent all my cash on them; but back to honey. I aint have no money for a room so I slid by the homeboy Killa Bee's house and waxed it. Now we in the room chillin' with the *Erk and Jerk* and *Old E'*. I fucked around and fell asleep listening to a lil', Bootsy ..."

<u>Excerpt 32.</u>

"At six in the morning somebody come knocking. I knew who it was, don't nobody else knock like that. I heard Killa' Bee in there tapping his girl. A couple of his boys is in the front room knocked out. Nobody got up to answer the door. They knock a couple more times then all of a sudden, Boom! The C.R.A.S.H. team kicks down the door and rush the motherfucker. The niggas in the front room cut out the back door. The bitches is screaming and shit. Killa Bee reached for his drawers and cuzzzz," Quincy closed his eyes. "They let his ass have it. Hit holmes with a whole clip."

Double E chuckled and shook his head.

"When I go that's the way to I wanna do it, deep in some pussy."

Quincy raised an eyebrow.

"Man, the ho' I'm with cussing me out. Police got shotguns to my head and shit.

"Who did they want?"

"Man, Killa Bee. Cuzz was wanted on a 211 and a couple of 187's. They caught them niggas who ran out the back. Bee's bitch caught a uuw. Lucky that greedy ho' I had smoked all the chronic or they would've put that on me."

"You lucky they aint give you none of they unsolved cases."

Quincy hadn't thought about that.

"You aint lying. Man the po-po's had us locked in these little cells, fifty and sixty deep. Niggas was stacked on top of each other. Cuzz' on one the right, Slobs on the left. Man, I damn near went blind all the bustas talkin' shit and throwin' up gang signs. Everybody's breath stankin' like they ass ..."

"Yeah, I was gon' tell you to have a tic-tac."

Quincy tried to play it off.

"G'head nigga, you know how we do, beer drinkin', breath stinkin', sniffin' glue."

"Yeah I know, but for real have a tic-tac."

He popped a few.

A luminous sun had broken through L.A.'s infamous smog. Glossy low-riders kept warm under multiple coats of carnauba oil, sweetening the air as they passed by. Shorties rode custom bicycles down side streets, knuckleheads shot hoops, and families had cookouts in the park. The *Bacardi 151* and *St. Ides* flowed, blowing back the drinker's curls like the palm trees on the bottle. G's in plaids and khakis chased after sisters in bright neon spandex; so far only one person had taken a bullet from an AK, and that made it a good day.

Double E' had been digging the scene with a gangster lean when he spotted some prospects in the park. He flipped the switches on his six-four and got front to back and side to side before he pressed the button on his Alpine.

"This is Dj A&M, you're listening to radio station 103.787. None of that rap shit, straight R&B, straight R&B, straight R-&-B."

"Man turn off that bullshit. Play the tape," yelled Double E!

<u>Excerpt 33.</u>

"I see you got that Rhyme Pays huh, that nigga Ice-T is gangsta."

Double E got all excited.

"Did you see the bitch on the cover? Woo! That bitch got my shit on bone."

The picture did nothing for Quincy.

"Man don't even talk about it. My shit been killing me every since the dick doctor juked me."

"Dick doctor," Double E yelled over the music?

"Hell yeah," Quincy shouted back. "After they take blood and DNA and what not, there's a fat bastard sitting there with a long metal Q-tip just juking niggas in they dicks all day! Big bitch stuck me so hard I'm still scared to piss."

Quincy winced and grabbed his crotch and Double E laughed loud.

"Uhh, uhh, you can best believe I won't be going there."

A tricked out El Camino pulled along side them at a Compton stoplight. The driver rolled the window down and started to say something but Double E beat him to it.

"Kay Gee, what's up Westside?"

Kay Gee was so high he could barely keep his eyes open. He had that real California 'G' drawl.

"Suup 60's? A G' out here looking for some of them Slobs off fake street to rollll 'onnn." He held up a Mossberg 500 'Cruiser' shotgun.

"Fa' sheezy. I got that mack in the back for they ass. I just bailed out my man 'Q'. He told me about Killa Bee."

"Yeaahh. We got a lil' somethin' planned for them crooked ass Rampart bi'atches though. You know we gots to pull they ho' card. But what up Quincy man? When you gon' make some new tapes cuzzz. Yo' shit be tight. You be cutting up the tracks like a doctor. I'm still bumping the last one."

Kay Gee pushed the bass boost on his JVC, rattling the bed of the El Camino.

"I'ma mix up a new batch when I get back to the lab," said Quincy

Kay Gee blessed him with a forty of 8-Ball. Q cracked it and started drinking.

"Good, niggas in the street is dying to hear some of that gangsta shit."

The light changed. Kay Gee did some sort of twisted shit with his fingers, screamed "Westside" and peeled off. Double E saw an undercover cop in a Chevy Nova and thought.

"If Gee catch another case he gon' do some time."

'E' did the smart thing; he laid low and crept up the block before taking another swig from the forty.

"Dumb ass cops roll around all fuckin' day tryin' to catch a nigga ridin' dirty."

"I'm tired of they motherfucking jacking," said Quincy. "If niggas grabbed some nines and started pluggin' they asses; that would put 'em in line."

Double E stared him down.

"I'd do that shit. I don't give a fuck. I been telling you man; you need to leave that old sissy ass band you with alone. Niggas aint checking for that no more. Homeboys out here thinking the same way we is. They wanna hear songs about how they living; some real gangster type shit. You know it's damn near two hundred different Crip sets out here, and over fifty Blood sets. When they go rollin' on suckers they aint trying to hear no love and R&B shit, and they aint with that pro-black shit so they aint yelling that either."

Quincy thought about it. Ice-T was the hottest thing out; and even though the West hated the East they were bumping Criminal Minded from BDP. But still.

"Man that kind of music aint getting no radio play E', I'm trying to get paid."

Double E stared harder.

"Man who the fuck listens the radio? Is we listening to the radio now? We can get rich selling tapes outta the trunk. I'm talking to some people about a distribution deal for a record label I just started. Plus I got a couple of homeboys that write rhymes. We can start a group. With you making the beats; it's a wrap! When that money starts rolling in them bitches on the radio will play this shit."

Quincy was skeptical about going into business with a gangster, what he really wanted to do was pay 'E' back the bail money and ride his Dayton's into the California sun. Double E point when they pulled up to Killa Bee's house.

"Hey 'Q,' check it out."

"Damn!"

Quincy yelled at the top of his lungs. They sat in the '6-4 for a few minutes. The sight of 'Q's car sitting on bricks instead of chrome erased any doubts he had left. "What's the name of the group," he asked?

"Gangsters In Black," said Double 'E.'

Quincy looked at him.

"What time you want me at the studio cuzz?"

Double E laughed as they gave each other a pound.

"C'mon cuzz, I'll take you over to Slauson and get you some wheels."

Quincy didn't know it, but a bad set of circumstances had led to him making one of the best decisions of his life. Double E turned out to be more than a gangster. At heart he was a business man who'd watched and learned from some real OG's.

Two months later Edgar 'Double E' Evans and his group did what the others were afraid to do. They released an EP exposing the world to the reality of life in South Central LA., and after that the game would never be the same.

CALIFORNIA
Beverly Hills

By 1987, Oranthal Laurence, a Bounty Hunter Blood OG, had become a high roller in Los Angeles. At 34 he head an empire that distributed coke and dope to a number of states throughout the U.S., including, Nevada, Chicago, and New York. Standing an intimidating 6'6 and dealing directly with top members of El Medellin Cartel, he had no problem commanding respect on the streets of South Central. That stature served him well again on Rodeo Drive where he was fitted for the two-thousand dollar suits he wore while running a number of legitimate businesses and lounging at Hollywood premieres.

It was opening night at Mann's Chinese Theater and limo's lined the street of the black tie event as the paparazzi scurried to get a shot of the elite on the red carpet.

Inside each sat with their Playbill in hand as they tried to unravel the mishmash of pop culture surrealism that had been branded art.

After the show, Oranthal and his wife Juanita were at the bar sipping Glenlivet and parleing with Judge Patricia McMullen and her city councilman husband, Daniel.

Oranthal voice was low and steady like rolling thunder and he spoke in slow measured intervals with precisely the right mix of humor and sarcasm.

"I understand about the city budget Dan, in fact, *I overstand*. That money is sup-posed to be for the *entire* city, not just the communities that house friends and business partners of the mayor. There are lots in that area that have been vacant since I was twelve years old. South bureau looks like a third world country. No offense Patricia."

He pointed his glass in the judge's direction. She took a sip and point hers back. "Oh, none taken Oranthal, please," she said, "speak freely."

"While I know it's not your personal position," confessed Oranthal, "many of your, uhh, associates, would love to see me and mine behind the walls of one of those state of the art detention centers, instead of behind the scenes of an art premiere. I can read the Wall Street Journal. Major corporations are investing shitloads of revenue into every aspect of the prison system. Big businesses have got interests in prisons. The more prisoners there are, the more food they eat, the more uniforms they wear, the more free labor the state gets, and so on. All I'm saying is this Dan; while the politicians that run this city are spending all that money fronting like they want to stop me and people like me. They could put some of that money into the schools or some youth activities for the children in Jordan Downs or Baldwin Village. *That* would stop people like me; but instead I see they've repaved the streets and put in new planters in Brentwood and Baldwin Hills, *and* they're steady building up the Hispanic areas. That's why there's no money left in the city budget." Daniel took a convenient sip and Oranthal con-tinued. "Oh I see it clearly, Blacks will be the minority. A mass naturalization of illegals will mean taxes and loyal constituents. As for the Mexican Mafia and any others still talking that Pancho Villa shit, well, there's a cell at the pen waiting for them."

Daniel seemed to agree as he wiped his mouth and cleared his throat.

"Oranthal, you know like I do that the ethnic numbers in prisons are dispro-portionate. You also know that next year is an election year and people are going to be looking at the mayor to see what he's done for them lately. No taxpayer wants to see their money go to someone else's community, and frankly the major source of revenue in the areas you're referring to is, *non-taxable*, as you know all too well."

Juanita caught herself before she sprayed her drink; but this was a friendly debate and the couples smiled knowingly. Oranthal was preparing his comeback when he was distracted by the approach of four well dressed men.

"Excuse us Mr. and Mrs. McMullen but we would like to have a word with Mr. Laurence. Perhaps you'd like to step outside Mr. Laurence, we have some questions we'd like to ask you?"

Oranthal smiled politely.

"I can tell from your suits that you aren't from the state, but regardless I'm gonna have to refer you to my attorney. You can ask him all the questions you like. That's what I pay him for."

Oranthal raised his glass and winked at the agent.

"Then Mr. Laurence," he said, "I'd suggest you give him a raise, because you're under arrest for conspiracy, trafficking and murder!"

The agents cuffed him and Patricia comfort Juanita with a hug before she opened her purse and slipped her a business card.

"You all do a lot for the community," she whispered. "Contact this man. Tell him I referred you; he specializes in cases like these."

Then the McMullens got ghost.

Juanita was embarrassed and nearly in tears trying to provide damage control to the stunned theater goers. Their special night had been ruined; but the worst news had yet to come. Sam, Oranthal's right hand man should've been at the premiere had he not cancelled at the last moment. Juanita phoned him and found that The Agency had him in custody too. With her back to the wall, Juanita called on the one person she knew Oranthal could trust. Two days later he received a visit.

CALIFORNIA
Los Angeles
Metropolitan Detention Center

"**Larry-O, what's** to it lil' brother?"

"Bro, trying to maintain in this dirty game; that's all Blood."

Goodgame took a pull from his square and looked away from the glass. His gators snapped steadily at the floor.

"Damn Blood! I hate to see you like this man."

"You know our business. The cave or the grave aint never far when you chasing the almighty dollar." Larry-O managed a smile. "Forget all that; it's good to see you bro', how is everybody?"

Goodgame regained his composure.

"Everybody sends their love. Lynnette aint been feeling well, but the kids alright. Fame's bad ass is outside with Juanita. You know he got his own lil' thang going back home. I'm gon' nip that in the bud though, his ass is going straight to college next year."

"I know that's the last thing you wanted. Tell him 'Uncle' said get it together."

"I will. Hey how is Uncle Sam treatin' my nephew?"

"He love it man. He told me he was doing what he was born to do."

"Aint that somethin'. Well long as he's happy. Hey look here, man, I know about them people and they phone lines.

I'm right here now so lay it on me; whatever I can do for you family. My man back East has got some godly connections. I might be able to call in a favor."

"Thanks bro, but this is political. I got this connected attorney. A high powered 'yarmulke' named Francis Kleinfeld. He's on his shit. Juanita's been handling things pretty well the past few days. There are a few moves you can help her with. Business that punk bitch should've been doing."

Larry-O had forced the last sentence through his teeth. Goodgame watched as blood vessels turned his eyes red. He wasn't alone. The visiting area reeked with strife and the sadistic jailers got pleasure from the prisoner's pain.

"Take it easy, baby," said Goodgame, You know the rule; 'Thorough niggas don't take the stand, they make a stand, and do they time like a man.' Sammy's gon' get what's coming to him. All things will play out in time."

"Huh, well I got plenty of that. These motherfuckers trying to hit me with a fifty piece. That fucking judge denied me bail; they scared of niggas with passports. These Uncle Toms out here was so glad to get me off the streets that the mayor rode with them people when they seized my property; like *I'm* public enemy number one! The shit's been all over the news."

When Larry-O was taken into custody, the headlines read;

"Mutiny on The Bounty!"

"The Agency scores a point in the war on drugs as alleged kingpin and murderer, Oranthal Laurence, is placed behind bars when childhood friend turns CI."

"Don't believe the hype," explained Oranthal, "It's crazy out here Blood. They coming after us like this, what about Lehder and Sosa and 'nem? You know I've been down there; they own that shit, all of it. Dope dealing cartels run South America. You remember last year in April they had that news story about the plane full of coke the Costa Rican police caught going to Nicaragua?"

"For sure," said Goodgame, "that's what got Oliver North in hot water and kicked off the Contra scandal."

"Right."

"You know the guy they caught, *Adolfo Calero?*" Oranthal nodded. "They linked him to this dude *Richard Secord.* He used to run Air-America back when I was in 'Nam."

"Huh. No shit."

"Yeah man. They've got papers from Ollie' on file saying he was doing business with one of the Contra leaders who wanted to fly in 1,500 Kilos."

Oranthal couldn't hold back his smile.

"That's long money man, looong' money."

"You know it," said Goodgame.

"I bet 'chu any money it goes deeper. I bet it goes all the way to Washington too."

Excerpt 34.

Goodgame replied with a knowing candor.

"Blood, you know it do. Drugs are running North America too. And you know they gotta blame it on somebody so I guess that's where brothers like you and me come in." Goodgame placed his palm to the glass and bowed his head. Oranthal did the same. "Just be courageous and strong. When the kingdom come and all these colors bleed into one; maybe then we'll all find what were looking for."

✳

In 1972 there were an estimated 18 gangs in the greater Los Angeles area, by 1982, that number had reached 155. In L.A. alone, combined Blood and Crip factions reached 275 by 1996, with an estimated 150,000 soldiers, at war with not only each other, but also the biggest, and best equipped gang in the city, the 40,000 member Los Angeles Police Department. Some of them knew what they were up against.

Excerpt 35.

1988

APOLLO KIDS

BROOKLYN
October

Thomas's crew watched him search every pocket anxious to find what *he* was looking for.

"*HAH!* I got close to six dollars left, that's two cheeseburgers for me. "*HAH!*"

"C'mon 'T'," Julius whined, "chill with that shit. It's bad enough you always screamin' it when we playin' C-Lo."

"Stop your blood'clot cry'ing." Thomas did his best Jamaican accent. "I like Alf, he a funny little nigga. _____*HAH!*"

"Yo' big ass be buggin'," said Julius, sockless and irritated, "and all this walking is hurting my feet, lets get there."

His soaking wet British Knights had rubbed blisters on his heels. Othello was doubled up; he took a pair off and gave them to his boy. No one had train fare and they were miles away from their block where Thomas was known as 'The Kid'. At fourteen he'd hit a growth spurt, expanding steadily upward and outward. Othello had his own nickname for him, *The Titan*; it was a play on his initials and his size. The other kid, Wesley was fifteen, black as night, and wanted to be The Mack. Julius—chubby and short for thirteen—was the hype man; usually popping more shit than he could back up. Eighteen year old Victor had been locked up almost a year. The twins—Warren and Allison—were both sixteen and at home. Together they were known as, the 'Yung Gunz'. All decked out in hunting gear and Dickies from the army surplus they looked more like construction workers than regulators.

It was just after 10:30 pm, and the Gunz had just picked up a fat dime on Nostrand and St. Johns. They told jokes and stories while marching through an

218

autumn sleet on their way to Alex's, 'mystery' meat market where they sold giant sized cheeseburgers, fries and a soda for $1.99. Julius and Wesely were hungry and broke after they'd spent their combined $3.25 on the weed.

"He be killing me trying to snap off. You should've rode your bike if your feet hurt, Pee Wee Herman." Thomas imitated Pee Wee dance and all.

"I've got a Silver Shadow. Ha, ha!"

"You see that nigga on 227 the other night." asked Othello.

"I seen that freak," answered Wesley. "I seen Sandra's big ass too. I'd hit that ass so hard she'd be calling my name in that screechy ass voice. *'Weesleey'.*"

Julius jumped in. "Word to the mutha, I'll hit that too."

Othello hit him with a right.

"Ya' lil' ass would get swallowed up in her shit. You'd be in there like; 'Maary! Help me Maaary; I'm inside Sandra's big ass!'"

Wesley struck with a left.

"Right, right and Mary would be like; 'Sorry Julius, Wesley's coming in. You should've beat Calvin's punk ass and got with Brenda instead.'"

Julius stopped laughing.

"Uhh, uhh. Her grill is tore up. I'd be like Ice T, dissin' LL. 'Nah, nah man, I don't want none of that man, you can keep that man!'"

Thomas went for the knockout.

"Quit lying. She look as good as Vanessa on *The Cosby Show*, and you love her Gumby afro wearing ass." He peeped Julius getting upset. "Nah, but this my nigga," Thomas said before imitating him.

"C'mon 'T', Lemme hold the tech, let me hold down the tech?"

Othello was doubled over in tears laughing and begging.

"Oh shit. *Please* tell it again 'T'. Why I had to miss it. I'd pay to see that shit." Wesley joined in, imitating Julius as he smiled proudly.

"Where the cash at, where the stash at?"

Thomas liked to see him that way.

"Julius, lace up your shoes and roll another L; and hurry up, I got a story to tell."

NEW YORK CITY
New Years Eve
Morning Rush 1987

The number four train squeaked along the tracks, worming its way through the shit brown core of the 'Rotten Apple.' Traffic on it was lighter than usual at seven in the morning as many had the day off. The unlucky passengers kept to themselves, nodding or reading their papers while a family of British tourists marveled at the great bridges that connect the boroughs. Their young son, off in his own world, blasted Queen through his headphones, leaving an old lady who sat behind them with whiplash from scowling at the music in front of her, and Thomas and Julius drinking and cursing in the back.

"Damn 'T', why ya'moms be bugging like that?"
   "She crazy," said Thomas angrily. "I'm sick of this shit. I'm a grown ass man."
   Gaietta had become the crazy mom on the block who didn't take any shorts. She'd done everything from flushing Thomas's work down the toilet to pulling knives on his friends.
   "Word, I don't know what my mother would do if she caught me fucking in the crib," said Julius, "probably nothing as many times as I dun' caught her doin' it." "Mine shouldn't say shit either; it aint like I was in her bed this time."
   Julius turned to Thomas.
   "You be doing it in your old girls bed?"
   "She don't. That's why she so mad. She need to go out and get her some dick."
   He heard her voice in his head.
   "*Tho'mas, you better check your'self.*"

Unlike her mother, Gaietta couldn't accept the fact that although she'd brought Thomas into this world he did not belong to her. She could give him her love but not her thoughts.

"Fuck that bitch," Thomas said.
   He'd been mad at her since Christmas Eve when she'd come home early to find him drunk and his girlfriend hiding naked in the closet. She took his keys and kicked them both out. He'd been wearing the same pin striped Lee's and sleeping on the roof of their building ever since. Each day he'd call home begging Gaietta to let him back in but she refused talk. That hurt. She'd always been there for him and the feeling of being a motherless child was not something Thomas was used

to. At the same time it struck him strangely funny; all those instances where he'd let the sound of her voice go in one ear and out the other. Now as the train crept toward Strong Island his ego and id did battle while his super-ego refereed.

"Tho'mas, look at me ba'by, I love you ..." pled Gaietta with tears in her eyes. *"Leave the riff-raff a'lone, they're no'thing but trouble. Fo'cus on your dream. The sky is the limit."*

Thomas was only sixteen and already he despised looking ahead. He had a feeling his best days were behind him and there wasn't much left to see. In grammar school he was the cute, chubby kid. Now the teachers looked at him with disgust before telling him he was a crook who'd never amount to anything; and as down as his girl Nikki was, she couldn't resist taking cheap shots at him.

"You Jenny Craig eatin' motherfucker."

"You crazy 'T'," said Julius. "Stop fuckin' around and tell me who was up there?"

"Me and my bitch," said Thomas. "Damn! Why you need to know who I'm giving dick to?"

The train came to a stop. A three man crew made their way through the car carrying a radio. Thomas knew one of them from school. He talked too much; the kind of nigga whose mouth moved fast, but brain moved slow. As they passed he point to Thomas and said;

"Yo check it son, you see that big ashy nigga right there in the red and black lumberjack coat. Duke a bum, he be sewing tags on his shirts and shit."

Julius snickered.

"You gon' let him punk you like that?"

Thomas answered instantly.

"Nigga please. Gimme the tech."

Julius reached inside his bubble coat and hand it over.

Thomas jumped up, aimed it at the clowns face, and with no hesitation. *"POW!"*

"Motherfucker! Stay in your place."

The train was in an uproar as passengers panicked. Thomas grinned as the body dropped to the floor. The sight of a screaming child who moments ago rested peacefully in his mothers arm shook him up. It was like stumbling on an old photograph, one that took him way back to the happiness and pain that had always haunted him. The British boy, firmly seated in his world, stared calmly at 'The Kid' through limpid blue pools. Imbibing them, Thomas realized the choice he'd made.

Excerpt 36.

But that was just fantasy, the part of the story he never told. Thomas's id had managed a comeback. This was the real life.

The train came to a stop. The Brits got off and a three man crew made their way through the car carrying a radio that played *'Top Billing'*. The old lady threw a fit. Thomas knew one of them from school. He talked too much; the kind of nigga whose mouth moved fast, but brain moved slow. As they passed, he point to Thomas and said;

"Yo check it son, you see that big ashy nigga right there in the red and black lumberjack coat. Duke a bum, he be sewing tags on his shirts and shit."

Julius snickered and asked.

"You gone let him punk you like that?"

Thomas thought for a moment. He watched as the crew took seats the other end of the car. Julius was holding a tech and a nine that Victor left at Thomas's crib when he turned himself in. He followed his intuition.

"What 'chu think? Gimme the tech."

"For what? What 'chu gone do?"

"This nigga wanna be a comedian, I got a joke for his ass."

Thomas whispered something to Julius.

"You gon' rob him on the train," asked Julius, "aint nobody never robbed no train?"

"So what! Nigga we dead broke. Aint nobody giving us shit; fuck this clown, I'm 'bout to get paid."

Julius was something like a hybrid, it didn't take much gas to fill his tank up.

"A'ight." He put his hand in his coat and said, "Yo 'T', lemme hold the tech?"

Thomas viewed him askew. What he saw surprised him. In Julius's eyes was that glaze; the same kind of you find in a fiends eye when they crave.

"A'ight. But if the cops come bustin' you better bust back, cause I aint running and I aint wit no fucking asthma attacks."

Julius gave him the Beretta. Thomas cocked it.

"Is you wit me," he asked? "_____*I'm ready*! Is you wit me?"

Julius had nothing to loose and everything to prove. He put one in the chamber and let thirty-two snooze.

"Nigga please, I cock and squeeze for you Kid."

Thomas smiled.

"My nigga, let's make it happen."

NYMP
October

"**Give Up** The Loot!" They all shouted in unison.

"So I pops one through the roof and I'm like; 'Everybody get on the mother-fucking floor,'" said Thomas.

"What the old lady say," asked Wesely? *"Lord have mercy, the devil is alive and breathing!"*

Othello was still laughing.

"You niggas is crazy, robbin' trains. Billy the mu'fukin' Kid." He hit Julius. "That's ya' hero, huh Bobby Brady?"

Thomas corrected him.

"Yo, how many times I gotta tell you; that was Jesse James."

Julius wiped the smile off his face and went to work.

"Big 'T' was stickin' niggas like, 'What! What! What! Give that shit up.' We was snatchin' purses and chains, leaving whelps on niggas necks. I started to get the old lady for her shit too. I told her, 'sit 'cha old ass down lady, before we take yaw' hat.' 'T' got the pregnant bitch for her baby bag. The baby wouldn't fucking stop crying so I went in there, grabbed a bottle and was like, 'here bitch, shut that little bastard up.'"

Thomas laughed.

"This motherfucker playin' step daddy in the middle of a stick up. The next stop was coming so I yell; "C'mon motherfucka'!"

"By the time I get to the other end," said Julius, "'T' done made the niggas with the radio come outta they pants. Them bitches was 'bout to piss on theyself. I'm like, "Where the cash at, niggas where the stash at?" I snatched they loot up, 'T' kicked the one nigga dead in his face. POW! And was like; 'Motherfucker, stay in your place.' And we was 5000 G!"

Located in the heart of Marcy, Alex's wasn't the same stage as *Willies Burgers* in Harlem, it was sort of an off-Broadway thing; but the game don't stop, so even on nights like this the show must go on. When the Gunz turned the corner the production was in full effect. Headlights reflected off rims like *"bling"* as Maximas and Mustangs with low profile kits passed by gli-*ding*. Behind the grill the Mexicans kept it business as usual with *EPMD* and got the job done with *Big Daddy Kane.*

Ten or twelve niggas were out front kidding and playing around, a few of them listening to bad lil' shorty no older than eleven as he split a Dutch Master with his fingernail and boast about how no rapper could rap quite like he could.

"Don't me and that nigga be flowing alike? Nah but for real. Nigga, I'm bad-der than batteries and I'm comin' up with this." He pulled his first gun from his sleeve, an FMJ Dillinger with two bullets. "I'ma cop me that 944 bubble back Porche. Shit, y'all playing. I'm out here till the sun come up. This is real life and I'm serious."

They laughed, not knowing what to make the flashy lil' nigga dressed in all black, rocking a too big Troop jacket and Air Force Ones. Julius hated on him a little as he and Wesely split Thomas's second cheeseburger. A red 325i cruised by and some hotties hailed it like it was a taxi.

"Check it out, yo." Othello pointed. "Big money whip."

"Yo I know dude," said Thomas, "he a senior at the school." Thomas laughed. "But he aint never there. I remember we was in study one time and he gassed this bad bitch to show the class her tits. His crew is from Marcy, The Commission."

"I heard about them cats," said Othello. "They went outta town and blew up. A few months later bodies started showing up.

NEW JERSEY
Trenton
August

A-D was over an hour late and normally that would've been fine. It'd been two months since he'd checked in and Jessica was used to not having him around. She'd hoped that today would be different; come morning she'd be leaving for her freshman year at Tennessee State. Too upset to speak, she sat in a booth of a New Jersey Bennigan's picking at her gray patch and jotting down her feelings.

"Probably for the last time you are on your way to meet me and as usual you're late; and as usual I'm upset; but unlike usual this time I'm saying "Fuck it because after today I don't have to go through this shit with you anymore. I don't have to be disappointed by you being late as hell, only to call hours later and tell me you can't come. I don't have to throw away my pride by waiting patiently until you can make time for me. I don't have to be on pins and needles around you, worried about the consequences if I make one wrong move. I don't have to worry about planning where to go, what to wear, or what to do. On the other hand it's probably the last time I'll have to kiss you, touch you, and be with you. Am I happy to be leaving you? No. But it's for the best. Who would've thought the way we met that I would fuck you, fall in love with you, and be fucked around by you? Maybe you're not to blame. Maybe I should blame destiny or some shit like that.

Whatever the reason, it's just another chapter in the book titled life, one ends and another begins. Still, I had hoped that my book would end; '.... and they both lived happily ever after.'

It's strange. When I was little I always read fairy tales and I always knew that I'd end up in one."

Following Jessica's white haired wisdom through "the Garden State" had led A-D to a wonderland of success. By the '86 summer The Commission had done it. The summer of '85 they'd been no shows in the 'hood, their faces rarely seen. After Sheik Omar was taken care of all went as planned in Trenton. *"Like butter baby."*

There was that one incident at the Turnpike Motel, but, *"C'mon, holmes had to know he was wrong."*

Once the Volvo was fixed Bebop got a seat for his bike and more. As expected, Theo superbly handled the day to day operations of the crew and Ais, whose small part was instrumental, had been a perfect liaison.

A car accident in May of this year resulted in the demise of another son of Marcy.

But one mans loss is often another mans gain.

Danny Dan was well on his way to becoming 'major,' when his career ended on the same stretch of highway that A-D's began on. Those who talk say he went out fast, the way he lived. They say at 160 mph the impact would've torn anything less than his Mercedes in half. They say he predicted that's how he'd go and wouldn't have had it any other way. Brooklyn showed its love by throwing him a Bed-Stuy parade. Not one for funerals, A-D didn't attend. Instead he left Bebop with an envelope to put inside Dan's sports car shaped casket while he and Theo took a trip to Virginia.

Like most niggas who was "doin' it," Danny Dan would spread love the Brooklyn way by bringing up a few carloads of honeys from the south. Niggas in Marcy would run through 'em and send 'em back to the country with stories to tell. Theo, slender and handsome but still minus six of six feet, had matured well. What he lacked in height he made up for in energy. He'd kept in contact with one girl named Bonny. When he heard about Dan's death he gave her a call. The next day he picked her up at the bus station in a Toyota Celica.

NYMP
May

"'Sup baby, how was the ride.

"Fucked up," said Bonny with an attitude! "I was sitting next to some old men. The one next to me snored the whole trip and the one behind me kept sweating me for my number. Shoot, you know you could've came and got me."

"Slow up love, I told you we been handling business. Shits been hectic with everybody buggin' on this funeral. Plus you aint gotta worry about all that no more, because this is yours. You like it? A nice little hooptie for you to get around with. See, aint I always there for you?

Bonny was like a race car in the red. She blushed and jumped back in her lane. "Yeah, you is."

"Right. So now I need you to be there for me. What's the 411? I need to know the business out there. Who's been talking? Who's making moves? What's up with your brother's crew?"

"Nothing Theo, everybody's kind of messed up about Dan crashing. Most niggas can't do anything with his spots because they broke and the others are just worried about finding another supplier. But mostly everybody's just getting ready for the funeral. I guess after that they'll start making moves. And my brothers is on a paper chase, they wit' 'chu. Whatever."

"That good, cause this is how it's gon' be. Tell your brothers we want thoroughbreds that's gon' stay outside; I mean even when the heats out, *stay outside.* Tell 'em to let niggas know, they want us on they side, ____alright."

Later that evening in Newport Beach, Bonny—a self proclaimed "down bitch"—paced the floor while her brother's crew rounded up the natives and escort them through the basement where they all got her speech.

"Check it; y'all know how it's going down. The Commission has got a proposition where y'all can all make dollars. But they man aint selling quarters, so y'all need to get cha' weight right. Bonny dropped a half a key of soft white powder on the table. "He got jobs for ya."

Niggas faces lit up. Most of 'em had never seen uncooked coke.

"You hitting us off of that," asked the brave one?

"This shit is the best," she confessed, "I aint got it to give, but I'll give you a test."

After that most left happy, but there's always a problem nigga. Caesar was a Danny Dan holdout. A 28 gram copping, minor league nigga with a minor league connect. He laughed in Bonny's face.

"I got my own thing going. I aint wit it, and my man aint either."

Bonny put her hand on his shoulder and personally led him to the door.

"That's cool too; A-D will be here the day after tomorrow for you."

NEW JERSEY
Trenton
August

A half an hour later A-D strolled into the restaurant and gave the hostess a name.

"You're in *trouble*," she said flirting with him.

The look on Jessica's face said it all. He'd been expecting the worse and that's exactly what he got. She gathered her things when she saw him approaching.

He grinned and said somewhat sarcastically.

"No point in leaving now Jess; I'm here."

"Aint nothing funny Seth, you know how important today was to me."

"I know, I'm sorry, but it's just one day. I'll make it up to you."

"Not this time Seth. Money won't make this problem go away."

She tossed him the letter and the check then stormed towards the bathroom.

He looked at the waitress.

"Add a *Monte Cristo* and two rum punches to this."

He gave her the check and followed Jessica to the bathroom. When they returned to the table she sat silent as A-D munched on his food.

"You gon' drink that," he asked? "It's your favorite." She pushed the drink aside.

"W'sup with all this drama Jess? What? You think I was out fucking around? I was taking care of business; for both of us. When I'm off track you supposed to keep me focused."

"Focused on what?" She waved her finger and spelled it out a little too loudly. "Seth, you-are-a-drug-deal-er! What do you do that's so important or stressful that I need to keep you focused? How much focus do you need to stand on the corner?"

A-D kept munching like he didn't know her and Jessica apologized.

"I'm sorry baby; I didn't mean that, it's just sometimes I trip on how happy we could be. You're not stupid Seth. You went to school and got good grades when you wanted. You could be a great thinker or a philosopher. You don't have to go to 'Sidewalk U'. Get your GED, apply for financial aid, and meet me in Tennessee next semester, we could get an apartment on campus and ..."

A-D rolled his eyes and cut her off. She'd had finally gotten a little rise out him

"I aint going nowhere, this is my kingdom, *I* created it, and *I'm* comfortable here."

Jessica got frustrated and questioned him again.

"And what happens to those who go against the king? What, off with their heads? How long is that going to last? You really think people don't know about you? Trust me baby, *they're talking*. You're making more money than everyone here and since you showed up in Trenton, people have come up dead, or missing, or in jail. Do you have anything you want to tell me, ___ huh? What *really* happened to Omar?" A-D didn't blink. "All my girls think I'm crazy or some kind of monster for talking to you. I had my doubts at first; I mean _____ I still do. It's like I tell them 'The A-D I know would never do that.' But now I've got to wonder, just who is the real A-D? Don't you care what people think?

Over the years A-D had become virtually unreadable. One could look into his eyes and find nothing, no love, no hate, no fear, no anger; he kept a barrier up that prevented most from getting inside. Outside of Shirley and Theo, Jessica was the one person who'd come close to knowing him, and at times she still felt like a stranger. What she did know was that he had a ruthlessness about him. He was controlling with a knack for silently instilling fear in the most formidable opponents.

He could become almost sociopathic when his authority had been threatened or when something stood in his way. Jessica knew she'd crossed a line. She felt something inside him shift, his face went totally blank and the tension she felt in the restaurant was like a knife in her windpipe taking a little bit of life from her as he uncharacteristically tried to convey his feelings on our America.

"You know Jess it must be easy for you to sit there telling me all the things that I could be doing, but you can't judge what I do unless you lived my life. You try looking at the same four walls everyday cause it aint no money to go outside, your stomach always rumbling 'cause your mother is out getting' high with the food money. Then when there is money and she's at home, you wished she'd just take it and leave. Pshht; believe me, you aint never felt pain until you've heard your mama yelling and crying night after night. You choose between those two, because that's what I had to do. At nine I saw a seven year old boy with his brains blown cause two kids had just thrown him out of a fifth floor window."

Jessica winced.

"That's horrible."

"You think? I used to play with that kid, he was like the only friend I had, and when I saw him, I didn't even feel sorry for him. I felt sorry for *me.*"

"Why?"

"Because he was gone. He'd found a way out. Now *I* found a way out and I aint never going back. I don't need college; I got my MBA from Marcy, so why don't you go find ya'self a doctor or a lawyer or somebody, cause I aint ready to be what you want me to be."

Jessica gave in. There was no fight left in her.

"Fine then, take me home. You won't see me anymore. But you know what Seth? I think the real problem is I'm not what you want me to be."

The short drive to Jessica's house was turning out to be the longest of A-D's life. The hum of *Pirelli* treads gliding over even asphalt was the only sound as shocks and silence held the two in suspense. A-D enjoyed the ride.

"You could roll a set of rims forever out here."

He turned to see if Jessica was as hurt as he thought she was. Deep in his heart he felt something too, but pride wouldn't let him show it. He watched as the tears rolled down her cheeks. He couldn't see them coming down his eyes, so he played the stereo to let *Guy* do the crying.

<u>Excerpt 37.</u>

Parked in front of her house he passed Jessica a tissue, put his arm around her, and asked entreatingly that she change her mind.

"Things aint gon' be the same without you, but I told you it was a few things about my life that I couldn't explain. Stay with me. We'll get somthin' to sip and go to our spot; you left some stuff over there anyway. C'mon Jess', we can work it out."

Eventually she surrendered. Regardless of what happened Jessica couldn't bring herself to hate him, even though she had tried. For her, love was stronger than pride.

NYMP
October

A-D stepped out of the car onto the block. A single gold tooth and a cobra medallion sparkling as he traded pounds. He'd gained respect not only as a hustler, but his friend Chaz had entered the music game. A few weeks earlier he'd released a single with him and A-D trading verses. Now the hustler was gaining notoriety as a rapper too. He eyed Thomas's crew as he bought a few quarter juices.

"W'sup Yung'uns? Y'all a long way from home aint 'cha?"

The gang nodded and Thomas answered.

"We over here trying to peep life like you know it, rich and famous."

He and Thomas smiled and slapped hands.

"'Sup 'Kid? I seen you in the halls and round the way, I like ya' style."
Thomas couldn't believe it.
"Stop frontin' nigga, you the man. I saw Heather in study that day."
"You saw that? You see her later on when she gave me head by my locker."
"What?" Thomas could only fantasize. "I'd love to be gettin' it like that."
"I rather be gettin' it like you, the fast way, ski mask way. 'Knowhaimean?'"
Thomas was enjoying his fifteen minutes of fame when A-D motioned to the car.
"Yo, if you got a minute let's ride around awhile."
Thomas turned to his boys.
"Y'all cool out here for a few, I'ma talk some business with my man."
Inside the office he studied the interior as A-D fired the ignition.
"Whoa'hoa, you got a CD in here, car phone. It's tight. Who's that playing?"
"That's some bootleg shit," A-D took out '*The Black Album*' and popped in
GIB's first full length disk. It was the hottest thing on the streets.
"I heard all the coaches wanted you for the football team. Why you aint join."
"Not my thing," Thomas answered, "aint nobody fucking up my spleen."
A-D laughed.
"I know a niggas time is money, so here."
Thomas took the roll of money and counted it.
"Whoa, a 'G,' that's love, but I'd take this ride for free." He gave it back.

Thomas knew that loyalty couldn't be bought, and that it played a big part when
making new friends.

"Nah," A-D replied, "that's love right there."
    A-D figured they were off to a good start. He got busy explaining to him the
usual things he did when coaching *his* team.
    "I feel all that," said Thomas, "and no disrespect man, but a nigga can't tell me
nothin' about these corners. I wrote my team a fucking manual so you know, *I*
know the rules."
He had A-D's full attention.
"Lemme hear 'em?"
Thomas blessed him with his flow and the ten crack commandments.
"How you like that," Thomas asked hyped? "I can make *you* famous."
A-D was convinced that 'The Kid' was coming of age.
"You hired. When you wanna start?"
With the major business out of the way they turned to small talk.
"I heard you flowing in the hallway a few times, you got skills."

"Huh, skills don't pay the bills unless you on wax," Thomas said. "Now that you got that single out, you gon' be leaving this shit alone pretty soon aint 'chu?"

"Shit, even on wax these rappers be getting jerked," explained A-D. "Aint enough cash in that game to keep me around. Besides, I aint a rapper. I'm a hustler. It just so happens I know how to rap."

Back at the burger stand they sat in the car wrapping things up.

"But really Kid, your flow is unbelievable. If you want to get on I might be able to help you with that. I'm going to London next week ..."

"London!"

"Yeah, Chaz's label is sending us over there to hype the single."

"I thought the white boys over there was all about *Guns and Roses* and that freaky-ass 'house' music; that *Frankie Knuckles* and *Ron Hardy* shit. I aint know they listened to rap."

"Man rap is the truth and the truth is universal. They love this shit over there. It's making the white boys at the record companies look like Ritchie Rich."

A-D had seen where the money trail led at meetings with Chaz. Sitting behind a desk was really where he wanted to be, but he'd dismissed the idea.

"Not in my lifetime."

He wasn't in his right mind.

"I know you goin' to the big concert at the Apollo in a few weeks."

Not waiting for an answer he passed Thomas back the 'G'.

"You on the team now," he said. "You'll be there." He knew Thomas was too hungry to refuse and not hungry enough to bite the hand that fed him. "Real recognizes real. That there's crew love."

A-D honked the horn.

"Yo Ptah!"

The shorty in all black rushed over to the car as they got out.

"Park the car and keep the keys. And don't let me catch ya' ass at McDonalds."

HARLEM
November 7th

The Event

"When the event befalleth,
There is no denying that it will befall,
Abasing some, exalting others,
There will be three kinds:

Those on the Right hand …
Those on the Left hand …
And the foremost in the race …"

After eight years of Regan's rule the winds of change had spread the dark clouds of DC's *Thaumiel* across the U.S. In January of 1989 one of the most corrupt of leaders would claim his throne. But tonight, Malik lay perfectly still, witnessing the flight of a lifeless crow through a broken sky. Rings of smoke from weed and hash erode his ozonosphere, the way hairspray does in Spanish Harlem. Through one of the holes an eagle clutching a serpent glide in on a ray of light that came to rest atop his head, 114 jewels sparkled and a true vision occurred. Atop the wings of the eagle Malik climbed and away they soared, to glimpse a future that he couldn't quite comprehend. A destiny that would be lost, found, and then lost again. But not before he learned that he was the man.

"Eagles!"

Malik lay sprawled in the cargo area of the Mazda MP3, his eyes moving rapidly under closed lids and uttering something about eagles.

"What the fuck is up with 'Lik," wondered Half Pint from the middle seat? "You hear him back there? Let's wake his ass up."

"No," Bill said with authority. "Let him chill. He aint really had no sleep since about Wednesday."

XS was driving and Dooney was riding shotgun. He shouted.

"Wednesday! What the fuck he been on?"

Bill laughed. "Some of everything, check it, he say 'Sleep is the cousin of death.' I guess food is too, 'cause he aint been eatin' either."

"What's the deal," asked Half Pint, "he still buggin' about his old man?"

"Yeah I think so. Plus his moms still buggin' about him droppin' outta school."

"Shit, my moms wanted me gone; she wondered what took me so long."

XS shot Dooney a confused look.

"You stopped going after the eighth grade."

"I know."

They laughed and passed back a fifth. It was always the same before a show; Hennessy and a barrel-o-blunts.

Malik, no longer scared to grab the mic and start sparkin', had earned a rep for being one of the best in QB, and while he nor the four carloads of soldiers were officially performing, this was one of the biggest concerts of the year and when that many crews came together; put it like this, Apollo kids live to spit the real.

"That nigga will be a'ight when he sees all these 'hoes," yelled XS!

Blocks away from the theater coatless women moved briskly toward the door, big doorknocker earrings weighing them down, big bootknocking asses busting outta their clothes, big glossy lips glistening under the marquee lights. The music played as they swung into positions to get chosen for dates, while carloads of horny niggas rode by beating their chests and throwing 'em lines. The 80's had 'em all acting like apes.

Girls found Malik good looking and hand him the pussy; but he wasn't on that tonight. His sights were set on Karma. Cafe au 'lait complexion, medium build, she remind him of Whitley from A Different World, without the accent. They talked and hung out all the time but she considered Malik "just a friend." Her man Chico ran with a crew called The Bricklayers. He was a few years older and was never around. Malik's crew was deep but their pockets were shallow. Karma kept him around to ease the boredom. She loved shining and wasn't giving it up.

"Yo 'Lik, yelled Bill, wake the fuck up, we here."

He awoke slowly, stretching and brushing the ash off his number 56 Giants jersey.

"Word? How long I been out, son?"

"A minute," said Bill passing him the fifth."

Malik looked outside.

"Damn its a million niggas out here. Koch got the police blocking off the streets and shit."

"Yo' ass back there dreamin'," said Half Pint, "you missed *Salt and Pepa* and *Heavy D* getting' out the limousine."

"You lying."

"No he aint," said XS.

"Word up. Magazines is out there taking pictures and shit," added Dooney.

"Damn."

They stayed in the van getting bent, waiting for Bagira, Merlin, Tiny, Stone, and the rest of the niggas to show up. Inside the building was on ten. Even though The Messenger of Prophecy had foretold the coming of the Dajaul, he was mad as hell about the election of the 41st President. Tonight he'd promised to bring the noise. The scent of weed was heavy in patches all over the theater, especially the balcony. The show hadn't started yet and niggas up there were already high, gladiating, swinging razors and chairs. The promoters sent an intern from their street team on stage to calm them down.

"Ladies and gentleman, my name is Dizzy; I'm speaking on behalf of the promoters of this event, we not with none of that standing around, looking hard and shit. That's why we as a people can't have nothing. Do y'all even know what it means to be black?" He stopped and looked around.

"We all came here for a party so I wanna see y'all stand the fuck up and have a good time!"

His voice cracked under the pressure.

The crowd went silent and needless to say, Dizzy was booed off stage that night. But he was driven and determined to make the world love him, eventually he'd get it right.

Next, a legend in a grey retro suit, bowtie and dark glasses was escorted to the stage to show him how it was done.

"Hey, hey hey, now. It's Alright."

There was a murmur in the crowd. Those in the know stood and applauded. Someone yelled. "It's the raisin man!"

Grinning from ear to ear and rocking like a chair, he said;

"Oh yeah, that's right, that's right. If you folks want this show to go on l-let me hear you say yeah!"

The crowd shout; *"Yeah!"*

"That's good, because you all know the rules when you come in here," he said enthusiastically. "If, if you know me, you know I believe it aint no harm in having a little taste."

Laughter erupted throughout the crowd.

"But don't loose your cool and start messing up the man's place. Alright? Now some of you might know that but I'm a Florida boy myself. What you probably didn't know was that I used to live r-right around here at The Hotel Theresa."

The crowd recognized.

"So I see you in Harlem."

Every seat on the main floor of the Apollo went empty as Harlem stood up. Fame and Fourtune were there with some live chicks sporting ice and matching furs.

"I see the girl with the diamond 'rang,' she know how to shake that thang. I see Brooklyn and Queens up there in the balcony with they mind on they money. Y'all stop thinking pennies and start thinking dollars."

The Gunz and the rest of BK bust their heat in the air while the mobb from QB bust theirs back. A-D was in the VIPs section, talking slick and whispering in the ear of all the girls, including Karma.

She smiled and whispered back the things that groupies say. She and Malik made eye contact and she wondered if he'd look at her differently tomorrow.

"I see the Bronx and everybody in the ghettos with a big stack of bills that get bigger each day. Any man can go wrong when he's busted. You all gon' have got to clean up some of this shit, but I still love you and I aint giving up on none of you."

Love begets love. His love brought a standing ovation from all five boroughs.

"A-Alright now. No one came hear to hear me preach so I'm going to pack my things and go, but before I do, who did y'all come to see?"

The lights went down and the air raid sirens blared. The theater reached a frenzied pitch as The Cold Lamper, dressed in a top hat and bright yellow track suit rushed the stage and cleared the way for The Prophet of Rage.

<u>Excerpt 38.</u>

Ninety minutes later the lights came on, and the streets were crawling with pretty cars and women. Made niggas were networking and discussing future enterprises while aspiring Dj's, producers and rappers passed blunts and got the ciphers started. Ais rode up with one of his baddest stallions. He introduced Malik to the Gunz and another group called L.A.I.R. When the Commission approached with Karma and her girls behind them, all the crab MC's in the crowd bailed.

Ais asked Malik discreetly.

"Son, you holding heat?"

Malik was ready to ride for him.

"Yeah. You a'ight god; what's the deal?"

"You know my style, baby bro'. *You* stay cool."

A-D slid up, slapped hands with Thomas and whispered something to him. Ais and Theo gave each other dap while Karma gave Malik a nervous hug.

"Hey Malik."

"W'sup."

She introduced him to A-D. They traded pounds and began the cipher.

Thomas went first; he threw an ill verse in, about Madonna, virgins, young girls and high men.

Ais was up next, he was all about his dean, spitting knowledge for the Asiatic, by any means.

Next up was A-D, who was living 'That Life', he warmed the crowd with cashmere thoughts, for those stuck living 'trife'.

And after sixteen rounds some lines had escaped unnoticed, but naked eyes had seen what was about to go down and stayed focused.

A-D said a verse, loaded with double entendres about those who squeeze first.

Then with one thing on his mind and one hand on Karma's behind, he lift up his mink and revealed a Tech-9.

Theo hyped up the crowd. "Y'all niggas know who's winnin'!"

A-D was spittin' venom into the minds of the women.

A broke nigga without a pot to piss in, Malik's thoughts were spinnin', he looked up to A-D and his big chain glistened.

Son's dome was aching, his heart was breaking and all this amidst snakes, faking and perpetrating; the index finger of his hand just inching towards the trigger that was tucked in his waistband.

"Remember The Clot."

"I'm here to teach man that which he knew not."

To the voices he listened, continued with his mission, put his pride on the line, and shot back half-a-bar, that he ended with;

Mankind

> *"In the name of God, the beneficent, the merciful.*
> *I seek refuge in the Lord of men, The King of men,*
> *The God of Men. From the evil whisperings of Satan,*
> *who whispers into the hearts of men,*
> *from among the jinn and the men."*

A-D gave Malik dap; he smiled and pretended to be a fan. Ais gave him some advice;

"Just because a nigga press palms wit' cha,' don't make him your man."

1989

THE YEAR OF LIVING DANGEROUSLY

QB
August '89
3:00 am

Every lesson learned brought the wonder years closer to an end as this generation's survivors came of age. The Reagan Era was over. The Soviet Union was crumbling and from as far away as Berlin bricks were tumbling from the wall. While The Agency was giving the enemy a new face, some like Fame and Fourtune climbed the masonry on their way to higher learning. Others like Thomas—who'd later this year get caught with a pocket full of stones—were trapped in the court system, and many on their way to rocks like Rikers Island counted the days until they could get back to life, as those who'd ignored Nancy's plea to "Just Say No" fell back to a frightening reality. And then we had Malik and Bill, who already at the halftime of their lives stayed getting by however they wanted; mainly drinking, smoking, and enjoying the ride.

"No! Damn, how many times do niggas gotta tell you, no. You acting like you 'ont speak English or something."

Malik raised his voice.

"NO Mu'Fucka! NO!"

Bill was calmer when he spoke.

"You crazy Rob. What's the deal; you think we got a Coinstar machine in the tip or somethin'? You wild; first you come short, and then you come with change, no quarters or nothin', fuckin' pennies. And why the bag wet Rob? Tell the truth, you got this shit out the fountain didn't 'chu?"

Rob had on overalls with high-tops shoes and shirttails. He looked like he'd bathed in oil; his odor burned the nose, and his voice sounded like he'd been gargling gravel. His wife Nip was a little thing, a fast talker with pigtails held in place by caked on Ampro gel. Her sneakers squished as she rocked from side to side. They were made for each other.

"What is this," he asked undaunted? "You aint gotta count shit, they all there, this me baby, Robby. I been knowing y'all …,"

Rob sighed and smacked his lips.

"Shit y'all niggas making all that money in the hood and y'all gon' trip over a dollar. One fucking dollar …"

"But that's the thing," said Malik, "you aint got dollars, Rob. You got pennies." Bill snickered and gave him a pound.

"Lik, why is you …, why y'all trying to play Robby shady baby? Do I play y'all like that when I come through with the merch'. Huh? Robby be the man then, so don't be cruel and let me be the man now. Hook a nigga up with two nice cracks so me and my old lady can go on the roof and do our thang."

Malik scoffed at the baseheads.

"You serious? Dion looking for you right now for selling him them broken amps. Then you come 'round here yesterday trying to get off that bullshit …"

He stopped short and asked Rob a question.

"You lived in QB all yo' life, right?"

Rob squinted.

"Yeah."

"Who you know got a fireplace in this bitch?"

Bill snickered and gave Malik another pound as Rob stuttered.

"H-Hey, I didn't hook … I aint know them amps was broke … a nigga gave 'em to me like that, you know? If I knew they …"

He paused a few more seconds then gave up.

"Fuck all that, man. I'ma take care of you on the first. I'll pay you *double* on the first. C'mon y'all, do the right thing. I'm sick baby, I'm hurtin'."

Bill was sick of the games.

"We doin' the right thing. You come at the Rastas with this shit they gon' whup yo' ass with that bag. Get the fuck outta here and go get some dollars, nigga; ten of them shits."

Nip stepped in to rescue her man.

"Baby,y'allisactinwack.Ionlysmoke*nice*rocks.Ifyashit'sgoodI'llbringyoucustomers outtheass.Youwonthavenotimetocuttityou'llbesellingstraightoutthemeasuringpot!"

Bill and Malik looked at each other.

"What the fuck?"

Malik shouted.

"English mu'fucka! English!"

"Lik, Bill, ya' ... y'all lil' niggas is like family to me. I, I practically raised y'all and this is how you do me, _____ *family?*"

Bill jumped up and shoved the two out into a cool starry night.

"Bye! BYE! Y'all get the fuck outta here, come back with some paper."

He waved to the lookouts on the roof, they signaled back before he went back in the building. Rats ducked inside the elevator shaft as he walked past the graffiti up to the first landing. He moved an empty bottle and sat in the dim, pissy staircase. On the way down to get his slinky, Malik sparked a blunt and passed him the E&J. The O'Jays played behind the door of a first floor apartment as they got bent and struggled to stay awake.

Excerpt 39.

"This cat hit my old girl like ten years ago and now I'm 'supposed to give him props for that. Man where these niggas head be at son?"

"Gone," said Malik, "they zombies, kid."

Bill agreed.

"You ever sit and wonder where all this shit is going; where we headed?"

Malik imitated Kool Mo Dee.

"Self destruction, we headed for self-destruction!"

"I'm for real. How long you think this drug game gon' last man? Them people aint playin' no more, you see how they doin' Noriega and Gotti."

Malik stopped playing with the slinky. He was about two sips away from being an alcoholic so he slurred a little when he spoke.

"Ok, last time. This is drugs. This is your brain on drugs."

When Bill didn't laugh Malik got serious.

"A'ight, a'ight. I meditated on that shit, son. It's like this. Remember what my 'Pops' said when he caught us smoking? The more I look at it, the more I can see the whole shit; especially when I dun' blew one."

They laughed.

"Man, drugs aint going nowhere. No matter what they tell you people need that shit. Your whole ... Like your brain ... niggas whole bodies is made outta drugs. Cause dig it. You ..." Malik tried to get his thoughts together. *"People ...* they come from the earth, so when they die they going back to that shit. Earth, son! That's it right there. All the shit that grow, herbs and plants, and *'seeeeds,* and shit. You know how if you fuck with enough of 'em or mix 'em together you get a high. Well, we God's seeds, son. Our bodies our minds, everything supposed to grow like plants and crops. It's just some of us is roses and some is weeds. As long as folks been living they been doing drugs. That shit is nature, man. It's natural."

"You think so," asked Bill?

"Most definitely," said Malik assuredly.

Bill put his thoughts out there.

"On the real I think one of the reasons they be telling niggas not to fuck with shit is because it get you to thinking deep. That long term, goal planning type thinking. They don't want us thinking like that cause man ... The more people be thinkin', the more thinkers would link up and peep they plan. They'd see that we aint nothing but slaves. We be payin' taxes and living all fucked up while they rich asses be lying back on yachts and sending they people to the moon. If niggas knew that I bet 'chu they'd stop sleepwalking and start making moves. You know, planning they futures, starting they own businesses, and stacking they paper. Shit, them people *cant* let niggas know they still slaves cause if they knew, fa' sure they'd get live on some Nat Turner shit like *Paris* be spitting."

Malik scoffed.

"They'd come right back on some Executive Order 11490 shit, FEMA, martial law, black helicopters and black prison shit."

Bill ignored the liquor talking.

"Whatever, that's some Willie Lynch shit right there. Straight up and down, that's what I think. I'ma tell you something' else I thought of when I was zoning."

"What, that the world gon' blow up?"

"You aint know?"

Bill threw some change at him.

"Nah, son. I'm going to job core."

Malik got real serious.

"What? So what 'chu sayin'?"

Bill said it again slow and loud for the people in the cheap seats.

"I'ma go-to-*job-core*, get my G-E-D, then I'm going to the Na-vy."

"'B,' you buggin'. When you think of this?"

"I been thinking about it ever since we seen *Top Gun*. You know 'I don't feel right unless I'm mach 10 with my hair on fire.'"

Malik had mixed feelings like a mulatto. He forced a smile but he didn't know what he'd do without his wingman.

Bill dropped him a hint.

"You aint thought about goin' back?"

"Nah, son. I promised my old earth I'd get my GED but I aint goin' back to high school. Schools are all fucked up. Niggas only go to fuck hoes and hoes only go to show off for niggas. The teachers be on some bullshit, they just go there to get paid. And some more shit I was thinking about. After you learn reading, writing and math, and I aint talking about that calculus and trig' shit, basic math, the rest of it you can learn yourself."

"True," said Bill, "but you gotta have that diploma or aint nobody gon' hire you."

"That's Sheila talkin' right there. Aint nobody hiring us no way. It's million's of niggas trying to get jobs and the people in them corporate offices hire one black face so they can make a quota. What the rest of us supposed to do? Niggas gotta make they own jobs. Shit, we on the clock right now. I wanna do something different anyway."

"Like what?"

"I 'ont know," said Malik looking the other way, "make movies, write books. Moms said to choose one and when I get my GED she'll get me a camcorder or a typewriter."

"Get the typewriter, you forever writin' them little stories."

"Yeah, that's what I was thinking."

They sat speechless for a minute.

"But that camera would be tight," said Bill. "We could make our own pornos, like 'New Wave Hookers.'"

"Yeah, that's what I was thinking."

They slapped hands and Bill pointed the bottle at him.

"Ahhh, 'Lik wanna be a moviemaker."

Malik took it and sipped some more brandy.

"What kinda shit you gone make," asked Bill, "some action shit like *Die Hard* or some of that corny shit you always dragging me to see."

"Stop frontin' nigga! You know you like that shit. You was tearing up when Sophia got her ass beat and when Goose died."

Bill kicked him.

"That shit was ill, B."

They settled down and Malik said;

"Yeah son, that's the move. It aint nothing else left for us out here."

Bill put out the last of the blunt.

"For you it is," he said. "In your heart you know what you supposed to be doin'. Every since that night, maybe before that. I knew a long time ago. That's why when you was scared to rock in the park I pushed you. That shit sounds crazy right? You always been the quiet type and somethin' just told me my part was to play the back and push. That's why I never tried to steal none of your light son. Especially when it comes to rhyming. That's your time to shine. That night at the event, I seen it 'B', like I was one of Dionne's psychic friends or somethin'. Dude had it all and still couldn't pull it off. The way you gave it to him that night was real. Them niggas couldn't do nothin' with that. That's why he tried to pull that crab ass move, and that's why the shorties had to get at him. Ais had already told us about his crew."

"They faith is with Satan. Everything them cats into is underworld related."

QUEENS
November 8th
1988

When the ciphers broke after The Apollo that night, they divided into three groups. Malik was exhausted. He took it in and laid it down. Bill, XS and some of the others found something to get into, while Bagira and Merlin's crew plotted as they followed A-D and Karma. Hours later they still hadn't made up their minds whether to steal him, peel him, or just kill him for the name. Luckily he spotted their car as they sat in front of her building.

"Yo, you know them cats back there?"
   Karma looked and recognized Baggy.
   "That looks like Malik's little brother and his friends."
   A-D smirked as he watched the streets through his mirror.
   "You mean them lil' niggas from earlier?"
   "They young," said Karma, "they aint nothing. You want me to say something cause I don't want no trouble?"
   "Pssht, I aint worried about them cats. They aint worth my shells."
   "Still," Karma picked up his car phone. "I'ma call Malik and see what's up?"
   She dialed the number but no one answered.
   "Ma, don't even worry," said A-D. "I'm good."
   "*You sure,*" asked Karma? "Alright, thanks for the ride. I'm gon' call you, alright?"
   "Fa sure."
   A-D pulled off followed closely by the car. When they hit Linden shots rang out and he was chased to the bridge.

QB
August '89
3:28 am.

"Yeah, that cat calling my crib at two in the morning talking bout, *'Just calm your boys and I'll give y'all a pass.'* I'm like, 'first of all nigga, how you get my number?'"

Malik chuckled.

"Man, keeping an eye on these snakes is a full time job. I miss lamping and just wildin' out like we used to."

"Me too," said Bill. "Let's hit the show after the 3rd when the money is slow."

"Word, what 'chu wanna see," asked Malik?

Bill kept quiet and looked at his watch.

"Uhh uhh, I'm late, I gotta go do 'S'."

"A'ight, tell me when we off the clock."

"When is that," Bill asked more serious than ever? "You just said it 'Lik, we aint never off the clock. Sky's getting dark, life's but the twinkling of an eye. All that good shit; plus we seen too much too soon, its got you scared to go to sleep like if you blink you gon' miss something. I see it like this; either we get busy livin', get our props and our clout, or we get busy dyin'. Meditate on that. Yo, I'm out."

Five minutes later at **3:33 am.**

"POW." One shot broke Malik's meditation. Then there was silence. Six shots quickly followed. Malik's heart skipped and his eyes widened as he leapt to his feet. He ran and pushed open the door with the music, reached under the cushion of the couch, grabbed the nine and raced out into the dungeon to face hells men. He was barely able to see as high as he be. He tripped and called out to Bill who'd gotten the Mac 10 from the tall grass. Whistles and shots filtered down from the roof. Shadows scurried across the courtyard toward Malik. Bill fired but the Mac hadn't been cleaned in a year and wouldn't spray right. It spit some shells that way then jammed. He looked.

"Damn! Three shells caught in the chamber!"

The flashes from the Mac had vanquished the shadows. Malik got up running. When he reached Bill he was on his back breathing heavy and his eyes were fixed on the stars. There was no blood and Malik didn't see a bullet hole. Relieved, he smiled and lay down next to him.

"You had me worried, God."

Bill coughed. When it gurgled Malik realized the mud was warm and sticky. He grabbed Bill's shoulders, raised them and fell back in the mud.

"Shit!"

So many times they'd witnessed this scene secretly praying that it would never be them. Bill was silent. The beginnings of a smile creased his lips as he raised his hand and tried to focus. Malik was on his knees and took his palm as he bent over to hear last words. Seconds ticked by slowly as troops gathered around. Someone took the guns and stashed them. Ms. Versie had already called upstairs. Malik saw Sheila running toward them barefoot and braless in her nightgown; her and the sirens wailing wildly in the distance. There was no wind that night, the air was heavy and still; yet she felt a gust blow past her as twenty-one grams fled her son's body. He looked down on them ecstatic; his lifelong wish for wings had finally been granted.

QB
The Funeral

The organ grind as the choir sang *Randy Crawford's* "Knocking on Heavens Door" to the capacity crowd.

<u>Excerpt 40.</u>

Young and old alike had come to pay homage to one of QB's finest making the small parlor hot and uncomfortable.

"Pay your respects and move to the side," they said.

Malik couldn't hear them; he knelt beside the casket refusing to let them by. He realized he'd never really known murder until that night and wondered what Bill had seen when he looked down on his body. He stood and looked at his brethren who was to be buried in his class A's. A Fila suit and heavy chain—Malik blessed his forehead.

"Respect all, fear none. You were the baddest motherfucker in the valley."

Bagira and Merlin finally coaxed him to his seat but his mind stuck on the moment his best friend became a casualty of war. He fought back tears as the preacher gave a sermon laden with treacle remarks on what a waste of life this was. Malik could no longer stand to see his man that way.

He asked Allah for forgiveness before he left. Fatima started after him and Sirius took her hand.

"No baby let him go."

Outside Malik borrowed a car. The first stop was the liquor store; the second was his building, then up to his room where from under the bed he uncovered two guns, a mask and a flashlight. Not knowing where he was going he went speeding off to wherever. Minutes later lights were flashing in his rearview. He pulled the Cougar over, spilling tequila on his suit as he tried holding the steering wheel steady. The patrol car sped by and Malik continued on his quest for redemption and amends; both were elusive, and when he was unable to find them at the bottom of a bottle or in the chambers of his guns he took his drunk ass home. Fatima threw down her copy of, *"The Satanic Verses"* and opened the door as he fumbled with his keys.

"It's almost one o'clock Malik, where have you been."

"Out."

He headed for his room and Sirius said calmly;

"'Lik, get 'cha ass back in here and answer your mama."

Malik stopped. He reeked of liquor.

"I'm sorry ma, I just been driving around."

Fatima sighed and hugged her son before saying her piece.

"Malik you know that we're all upset. Bill was like family to us. I'm not going to lie and say I know how you feel because I've never gone through anything like this. I can tell you that I'm really praying for the Lord's forgiveness because I'm *so* relieved that I am not Sheila. I don't ever want to feel what she's feeling now."

It was too late for that. Fatima was filled with empathy as she felt the loss of mothers everywhere.

"That could've just as easily been you, bullets don't have names. Malik you have got to get yourself together, focus on the positive. If you keep putting all that poison in your body you'll be moving on to harder things real soon. Let this be a wake up call. Don't let Bill die in vain."

She hugged him tight, filling his chest with sunshine.

"I love you," she said.

"I love you too Ma."

Sirius stood up.

"Come with me Malik."

They went in his room and shut the door. Malik sat quietly as Sirius's look burned a hole in his head.

"What did you do out there tonight?"

"Nothing Pop."

"Don't lie to me!"

"I swear. I was by myself, just riding and thinking. I had a head full of ill thoughts, but I aint do nothing."

Sirius's stare masked his relief. He placed the shoebox on the bed.

"Where are they?"

Malik tried to think of an answer. Sirius was more forceful when he asked again and Malik placed the pistols in the shoebox.

"I'll take these for a while. They're the last thing you need. Now," Sirius said, "Now tell me about those thoughts."

Malik took a seat on the bed; he didn't know where to start. He began yesterday with questions but today he had answers.

"I wanted to represent for my man so I came home and grabbed those. Then I went outside looking for the suspect in his killing,"

"Would that have solved the problem or brought Bill back?"

"No. But people been whispering things like it was my fault; and at the funeral it seemed like everybody was looking at me. Besides, I figured Bill would do it for me. That all sounds silly, right? But I was mad-hurt. I aint know what to believe."

"You study the scriptures. We taught you right from wrong. You believe in what you heart tells you is right."

Malik perked up.

"In the end that's what I did. All while I was driving I heard Bill saying that if I went through with this it would make me; and that's not who I am."

Sirius agreed and Malik continued.

"But when I looked in the mirror I hated me."

"Why?"

"Because," he said shrinking, "I felt like a coward."

"Ugliness is jealous of beauty," said Sirius, "like *Togarini* is to *Tiphereth.*"

After a minute Malik said.

"I thought about you and Ma and Baggy. I realized you were right; street glory and ghetto fame aint worth it. I decided it was time for me to rethink my plan."

"What did you come up with?"

"Something Bill said right before everything happened. It's like he was trying to push me in the right direction. Now it's time to destroy and rebuild.

"Transformation is tricky, 'Lik. When you deconstruct your world you never know how long it's going to take to rebuild it. I hope you understand it aint easy."

Malik responded quickly.

"I know, but neither is living a lie. Life is too short for me to be afraid of what people think or say. I'm sorry Pop, but fuck 'em if they can't see my vision. From now on I'm doin' things my way."

Sirius beamed as he hugged his son.

"That's my boy. Now you're ready."

Malik pushed the shoebox toward him.

"You can keep them. I promise y'all aint gotta worry about me no more. I'ma work hard and get rich so we all can eat."

"How you gon' do that?"

"I'ma do like you and grandpa; do the music thing."

He laid his book of rhymes on the bed.

"I heard these two girls, Wendy and Lisa, say *'Only fools and kings make real their wildest dreams.'* What 'chu think about that?"

Sirius reached out to shake his son's hand before Malik sealed the door to his atelier.

"I think "smart boys turn to men and do whatever they wish.""

THE AMAZON
July '87

They'd traveled from the coast of one sea to the other still looking, but sweet dreams were turning quickly to street dreams for the family. In Maryland The Boy had gotten way too wild and for Marian the stress had gotten major. She shipped the children out west to a friend of the family who'd taken them in for the summer.

It was a Tuesday when the bus pulled into the station and this time there was a different feeling; like life was set to move at an accelerated pace.

"This might not be so bad after all."

That was The Boy's first thought as he admired the homes of the folks who lived on the hill. Foliage camouflaged them from their neighbors below making it hard for them to see the jungle's ills. The Boy couldn't take his eyes off the view; it was the kind of view that wanted to be seen.

Aunt Audrey's car had just passed the police and fire stations when she stopped at "the front" for a few bottles of Cisco. That's what gave it away, in every hood the storefronts were the same; dealers on the corner trying to fatten their pockets and dishing out dimes for the thoughts of old men. Suddenly The Boy was startled by the sound of Blue Thunder. They'd told him it never rained in southern California.

"Aunt Audrey, what's that?"

"That's the ghetto bird." She laughed. "Stay out of its way; you don't want it to drop a load on you."

As she opened the door a group surrounded the car searching for a plate or a face that looked familiar, all swearing they could place the nigga that was gonna kill them. Cheris gripped her brother's arm; he gripped his nine and comforted her.

"Don't worry 'bout nothin'; these niggas don't know my style."

The helicopters spotlight dispersed the crowd and a squad car rolled down on them. The cops jumped out with an attitude.

"What the fuck are you waiting for, move this piece of shit."

The Boy tightened his grip, thinking;

"Fuck tha police."

One cop knocked on the driver's window and repeated himself. Just then Audrey came out of the store followed by one of the dealers. She was totally relaxed as she brushed past the officer and into the vehicle.

"This is a legal space and all my papers check out so watch it sucker!"

The cops moved on to harass someone else as the dealer leaned inside the window and peeped what The Boy was holding.

"Y'all straight in here?"

"We fine," Audrey said to him. "I'ma see you Friday."

"A'ight. Yo shorty, don't hurt nobody."

Audrey drove off as he and The Boy silently traded crooked smiles.

The next day the children set out to explore things on this side. At fifteen Cheris was ripe and the neighborhood accepted her but nothing had changed for The Boy. This block was like all the rest. Men called him a 'pretty nigga' and the Amazon women called him gay. Still he wasn't giving up on the hood. Again he prayed, and after three days of sipping Thunderbird and grape Kool-Aid the dealer from the front showed up with a fifth of Hennessy.

"Sup homie, you drinkin'?"

Cheris had told him that he was part of *"The Clique,"* and the man to see if he wanted to get on. He was a big nigga; twenty one with a wife and a baby's mama, two kids, a Caddy, a crib and a fat pocket. That made him a baller in the Amazon; everyone called him J.I.

"You know them other niggas don't think you really down. They say you aint from the West so fuck you. I say it aint where you from, it's where you at; so if you want to you can roll wit' me on the night shift. Same deal as the others; you get a dub off every hundred you serve. That cool, lil' homie?"

The Boy sat on the step of Audrey's apartment looking dismal in a crumpled hat turned to the back, and no name shirt, shorts and run down work boots. J.I. towered over him. The Boy had met his kind before; some on Decatur, plenty in New York; flashy niggas full of pride and arrogance. Smalltime; but they were the cream of their ghetto blocks and they knew it. They had no time and only one use for broke niggas like him. But by now it was obvious that Audrey and Marian were on similar paths. On top of that he was eighteen and responsible for a little girl whose empty stomach had seduced her to fuck the world.

"I'm cool wit' that," he said to the dealer.

"You know," said J.I., coming at him again, "I got family back East. I been here since I was seven but I go there at least once a year to parle'. What about you?"

"Don't ask me 'bout my past, it was all bad."

"I hear that, but it's some shit you got to know, *partner,* 'cause things is different on this side."

He pulled a pack of *Newports* from his pocket. The Boy asked for one. J.I. passed him two.

"For a 'G' to get ahead out here," said J.I., "he gotta be the first out the gate and stay bubbling, cause the next man is always looking for that come up. But you know that." J.I. winked. "I caught what you was holding that night in the car. It aint look like you was backing down for one-time either. That's good cause these niggas is scared of the them punks. We got crooked cops from as far as L.A. coming through robbing the homies for they bread. It'll be good to have a 'G' who'll pull that thang."

"I aint never scared."

"Good. Stay away from the bangers. Most of 'em is bitch niggas with no heart." He looked down at The Boy's feet. "Next thing you do is get some *Nikes*; cause out here when we fight it's in the middle of the night with no lights on; and speaking of that I hope you can box, cause aint nothing but killers in the park where we be."

The Boy sat back sponging up J.I.'s spiel and wondering; *"Why me?"* What forces had brought them together and more importantly what price would he have to pay? J.I.'s kind did nothing for free. Even he knew *"the game is to be sold, not told."* But as wrong as it seemed this was his means to an end. He decided whatever the price he was going to have it. Each morning he was up before the sunrise and every night he was the last one to leave the block; all part of his plan to make a killing, straight ballin'.

THE AMAZON
Two Weeks Later

"Man let me get that."

J.I. confiscated his pack ending The Boy's career. It was just as well; dealing wasn't his thing. No one had bothered to explain to him the fundamentals of that game. Some of them he'd learned early on through the beat downs he'd taken before he got his boxing game right. Only his reputation for keeping a gat close kept the killers off him. After winning one fight in particular against The Cliques champion brawler they reluctantly took him in, showing him the same kind of love that you'd show a stray dog. The dealers gave him a new job making food and liquor runs, but most of his nights were spent rolling blunts, cheifing, writing rhymes and entertaining the homies on the set with his crazy dreams.

"Y'all niggas watch what I tell you I'ma have more money, more weed, more rhymes and more platinum records than any other rapper!"

Once the laughter was over and the haters had finished hating themselves there were always the few who managed to look past The Boy's appearance and the hubris of his words to mine for the truth; and the truth was *he had some tight shit.* Plus when it came to his music he was determined. He may have been on the bottom any other time, but when he performed it was clear that nobody or nothing could stop him from shining.

Unlike the others who put their energy into more conventional hustles, he ate, drank, and slept, rap; and though it took some time The Amazon found that the skinny, bummy little dude from the East coast who couldn't play ball or sell dope *could,* rap his ass off. He developed a following and like a twentieth century troubadour he gave his listeners a little positivity for those long nights slangin' in the alleys of Cali.

THE AMAZON
July '88

J.I. was a traveler too. He'd been up north in Portland for a few months having things his way. When he returned pushing a Cadillac Escalante the other members of The Clique jumped on his dick and filled him in with the gossip like they always did. But this time he had to share his shine.

"What up boy," asked J.I. enthusiastically?

The Boy was happy to see him.

"What's up cousin; when you get back?"

"I rode in late last night. But fuck me. I hear you 'round here rocking shit like them quakes do. Folks tellin' me you a star now."

"I'm trying. If you think them drugs got 'em feinding wait till they get a hit of me."

J.I. perceived that as an insult.

"Nigga it's takin' you long enough. You been on that bullshit forever."

The Boy took it in stride.

"Man shit don't happen overnight. If you wanna make it in this game you gotta work at it."

"Uhh huh, that's why I rather use my gun 'cause I get the money quicker. But I see you on a come up. When I left you was wearin' silver, now I come back and you sportin' some gold."

They laughed and showed each other love.

"You still holdin' them thangs," asked J.I.

The Boy raised his shirt and showed his gun.

"Well what 'chu on man? I gotta check a few traps. Why 'ont 'chu roll wit' a nigga. I got a lil' something we can break down and roll up."

They hung out the rest of the day showing off and kicking it with the homies in the hood. That evening J.I. was feeling so good he let him ride on a short trip to one of his girls houses. Driving home that night they were buzzed and swerving down the 405. The top was down and the stereo was pumping the Isleys *"For the Love of You,"* when a car full of white boys damn near wrecked their shit checking out J.I.'s ride.

The Boy loved every minute of it.

"Damn J', you did a nigga right today. I had a ball. That's my word."

"That's your word," said J.I. smiling.

"My mama always told me; 'Without your word, you a shell of a man.'"

"That's good advice."

"You think that's good advice? I got tons of that shit," said The Boy. What about putting some of that money on your boy? All I need is some studio time for a good demo and I'ma blow the fuck up.

The money gon' come and I'll be able to pay you back with a quickness."

J.I. didn't know a thing about the music business and the word from his homies back east was that even good rappers got jerked around. That meant a lot because he never really felt The Boy's style.

"Man I can't just throw paper at you like that, but I tell you what. You can earn that shit. I'm bout to start grindin' in The Amazon again. I need a homie with a strap watcthin' my back. You do that for me and I think you can make your demo money."

The Boy had no problem with the work ethic. Holding the strap was better than being a runner. They bumped fists.

"It's a done deal."

J.I. laughed inside. It was funny to him, broke niggas and they dreams.

"I rather use my gun, cause I get the money quicker."

THE AMAZON
August '89
2:45 am

Yesterday afternoon The Boy received two letters, what looked like a mural covered the envelope of the first. The contents told him of Yoesef's worsening condition at the hands of Federal Authorities.

"To my brother, friend, and son;

I hope this letter finds you in the best of regards. It's funny how things turned out. All the time we lived under the same roof to have to talk this way. It's been a while since we've conversed. Let me stop bullshitting; we never really have. There was so much I wanted to say; so much you needed to hear. There never seemed to be enough time before but there's plenty now. What a man has to come to when he's facing sixty years. Growing up I never gave it much thought as I'm sure you haven't, but since your family tree consists of drug dealer's thugs and killers maybe it's time you did.

As a young black male and a soldier in this ongoing war, maybe you should.

From the cradle to the grave our lives have never been easy. You had no choice. Born when you were yours was destined to be a struggle of polarities. I was there in the hospital when the doctor smacked your ass and you smacked him back. Reflexes I guess. I remember sitting on the bed cleaning my Mac10. You'd be lying in the dresser drawer with a gleam in your eye, reaching out begging to touch it. But that's the way your daddy made you.

May Allah help to guide you and save you. "Heir to the throne." "Young prince; here to save The Movement." The voices called out to you coronating you even before birth. I know that in your head they have not stopped. I hope that the night brings you some measure of peace. Daylight is approaching here in hell. This estate is so military. But it's not meant to reform, it is meant to break the hearts and minds of those who would dare cry freedom. Nothing is promised to you in here. Even waking is uncertain. So if this is to be our last correspondence I want you to know the truth.

"Where do I begin to tell you of my struggle, our struggle? Do I begin in Nebraska, in the house of my parents, or shall I start with the years of study and suffering in The Bay and the lessons that I learned based on them. Municipalities. By now you know of the war and all its propaganda. Perhaps the revolution and the beginning of my political activities with *The Black Panther Party*, the cause of it's collapse, and perhaps a word or two on nations and race in general. But first the development of the party and how it came to be.

The panther is a peaceful creature by nature. But what does it do when it's backed against a wall. It does not lie down. It does not retreat or surrender. It fights? Fights and dies if it must. You see there is a pride in the panther.

Can you see it?

'The man' had us under his thumb until Sister Rosa set it off. Then came the riots, Malcolm's murder; turbulent times. Stokley respected Kings non-violent approach, but we needed an antithesis to his thesis. The Government had The Agency. We needed something similar; an underground movement to recruit and fund our political aspirations. I was never a politician. Telling lies wasn't my thing.

I was and still am for truth. I wanted to be a radical. Someone that the establishment knew and was worried about; a General. So in '66 when Eldridge and Huey got it started in Oakland, I joined. The brothers had it all planned, we'd mobilize in the big cities first. Along with providing food and medical treatment for the poor, we'd demand our due. What you ask was that? Land, oil, you name it. It should've been whatever the fuck we wanted, no Governmental reparations could pay for 430 years of black holocaust,—who'd trust them anyway after the way they fucked the Indians—so we kept it simple by marching on Washington and exercising our "right to bear arms" on the steps of their precious Capitol Building where we issued:

Executive Mandate number one.

'1. We want freedom. We want power to determine the destiny of our Black Community.

2. We want full employment for our people.

3. We want an end to the robbery by the white man of our Black Community.

4. We want decent housing, fit for shelter of human beings

5. We want education for our people that exposes the true nature of this decadent American society.

6. We want all black men to be exempt from military service.

7. We want an immediate end to police brutality and murder of black people.

8. We want freedom for all black men held in federal, state, county and city prisons and jails

9. We want all black people when brought to trial to be tried in court by a jury of their peer group or people from their black communities, as defined by the Constitution of the United States.

10. We want land, bread, housing, education, clothing, justice and peace, and as our major political objective, a United Nations-supervised plebiscite to be held throughout the black colony in which only black colonial subjects will be allowed to participate for the purpose of determining the will of black people as to their national destiny.'

After that they created the *Mulford Act* and banned our weapons. That's what happens when the common man acquires *Common Sense*.

You see son, racism in America is the product of ignorance and capitalism. Therefore at its core our struggle is not a black or white one, it's a class struggle and people realized that. Our membership rose to over 2000 and after we read Mao's Red Book and adopted a more Marxist-Lenin-esque stance, we attracted the attention of non-black organizations as well. There was an unstoppable force taking shape, Brother Fred Hampton called it *The Rainbow Coalition;* but there were eyes watching.

"J. Edgar Hoover and the FBI described us as *"the greatest threat to the internal security of the country."* In 1968 he ordered the FBI to use *"hard-hitting counter-intelligence measures to cripple the Black Panthers."*

Those "hard hitting" measures Hoover spoke of turned out to be operations Cointelpro, and Chaos. Programs created for use on Communists and Terrorists. We were neither; we were supposed to be citizens. Still they hit our phones and offices with illegal "black bag jobs" they set up "swallows nests," and "ravens nests." We were surrounded by shadows, and spooks sat constantly by our doors. But we weren't the only ones. Hoover spied on everyone that he deemed to be un-American, from civil rights groups to anti-war protesters. You couldn't trust a soul, everybody was a potential agent. The SNCC committee that was our nucleus began to crumble from the inside. In six years 24 members had been murdered by the authorities and the practice continues to this day despite Executive Order 12333 of 1981 which specifically prohibits the agency from collecting Intel concerning the domestic activities of US citizens, and explicitly prohibits The Agency from engaging either directly or indirectly in assassinations. Nah man we didn't invite trouble. It just came to us. We'd run and it would run after us. There had to be a place to hide. After your sister was born I left New York, got some work, and stayed a while in Detroit, Chicago, and St. Louis. Then came the incident in 'with my sister in '76. After that I had no choice.

I came back to see you guys before I went under. It was the happiest time of my life. And the voices were right; you were a sight to see. I knew then I was bearing witness to someone special.

My son, I know that times are rough. I know of our family's condition. Your mother has told me what you are doing to survive.

I know it seems that these days a new consciousness has emerged, that all the rebels are long gone and that it's you against the world.

Keep in mind, the greatest burden you bear is to yourself; that decision you make to be true to you. No one would blame you if you chose not to take up your fathers cause. Young prince the battle is fought on many fronts, some soldiers use a pen, others a gun. Remember the one thing I always told you, "The most dangerous weapon is an educated black man." It seems these days that rebellion is frowned upon. Personally, like Thomas Jefferson said, "I believe that a little rebellion every now and then is a good thing. God forbid that twenty years should pass without such. "The tree of liberty must be refreshed from time to time with the blood of patriots and tyrants." So I ask again, what do you want to be now that you've grown up? Whatever your answer I salute you. And in the words of Soledad brother George Jackson;

"Let them never count you among the broken men."

One love, one nation. Your father, friend, and comrade,

Yoesef.

The Boy was livid.
"Aint shit funny about the way this turned out."
He read the second letter again; the one from selective services.
"Gimme a break!"
How much could one brother take? Pushed to the limit and nearly psychotic, he sat on a milk crate in the alley and began writing a letter of his own.

"Dear Mr. President,

"Please tell me what to do ..."

Minutes later at 3:18 am there was a 380 just inches from his temple.
"Stick 'em up nigga!"
J.I. had used his rough voice.
"Ok," said The Boy, "just 'cause I'm rappin' ..."

He pointed to the mini-14s stashed in the bushes.
J.I. laughed.
"C'mon, man, we gon' get this game started or what?"
"Yeah nigga, pour the Hen'."
The Boy scribbled an ending to his letter.

… and furthermore, if you aint know, I was born enlisted. Its more niggas than it is police, and we all strapped. So fuck your FBI, fuck your CIA, fuck you, and fuck peace too. If we gotta die we gotta. That's on my mama.

WAR!

Already a Soldier.

He folded the letters and stuffed them in his back pocket. J.I. pulled up a crate and dealt the cards. If we had journeyed with them inside their minds eyes we would've seen the future quietly materializing inside the dark rooms of their heads as the two sat sippin' 'yak, playing spades, and fantasizing about the things they'd grow to be.

1990

E PLURIB BUS UNUM

"This Is To Be The Conflict That Ushers In The New World Order."

(George H. W. Bush)

Imagine this. Not twenty years since the last conflict, Americans found themselves confronting yet another enemy, and *by chance* many of the players from that drug war had repeat performances in this oil war. King George sent the usual suspects from The Pentagon, and from the heartland patriotic parents sent a ripened harvest of expendable nieces and nephews to join the madness in the Middle East. If they survived the tour their rich Uncle Sam had promised to pay their way through college. In the streets, that and the prospect of training with the worlds most advanced killers had changed the minds of OG's—by now they had files on us anyway—and for some time oracular Generals had been sending their best and brightest to learn *the art of war* directly from the enemy.

SAUDI ARABIA
Near Dhahran
Thanksgiving Day

It had been four years since Staff Sergeant Laurence made the switch from Compton knucklehead to Camp Pendleton jarhead and since day one he knew he was a lifer. He slowed the humvee and allowed the M2 Bradley to catch up with him as he led the vehicle along an enormous line that had been drawn in the sand to a newly constructed and extra sterile area where the Marines of 1st Regiment Kilo Company were locked, loaded and waiting in a heightened state of readiness.

Sgt. Laurence loved his job, even missions like this one—escorting a British Television Network camera crew to the front for a public relations piece—was just another chance to lead by example and prove to the brass what the men under his command already knew, he was deserving of the title, "youngest in charge." Not a day went by that Laurence didn't pledge allegiance to the five and his family, and thank the God for the gift of the Corps.

The BTN crew wasted no time getting set up. After a few minutes the cameraman signaled for the condescending young female reporter to go to work in,

"Three, two, one, rolling."

"Hello. To the North of us is the Saudi Arabian border. On the other side of the berm lies Kuwait; a barren parcel of land roughly the size of Hawaii. It's a place most Westerners may have gone their entire lives unaware of, yet for the past 110 days nearly 200,000 NATO coalition troops have been busy battling flies, boredom and triple digit heat, but none have yet to face an enemy. In America, frugal taxpayers have begun to question the true nature of this mission and its motives. We're here on this American holiday to boost the morale of this elite US Marine Corps division and perhaps see if they have the answer to what it is exactly they're risking their lives for."

Even though all his Marines had been briefed on what they could and could not say. The reporter's questions worried Sgt. Laurence a little bit. Through his locs he assessed each member of the unit standing tall, looking good and sticking to the script; all but the last five. Recently an incident in the desert had the Sgt. watching them very carefully.

Private First Class Remus Mirra was bad-ass, a stick of dynamite ready to pop, a six foot-one, 20 year old amped-up Anglophile from Yuma Arizona. He loved skate boarding to Metallica, busting guns and banging women, in that order.

"What made you join the Corps?"
   "I wanted to be the leanest meanest fighting machine in the world. I can be that here, _____ and the uniforms are bitchin'."
   "What do you hope this war will accomplish?"
   "What? I don't know what war accomplishes but every generation has 'em, my father served in Nam, his father in W.W.II and his in ..."*What was that war?"* Whatever. I'll be glad when I get to fire my weapon. It's all this waiting around that I can't stand. I want to get some, Ooh-rahh"

"*That reminds me. Would you like to say hello to someone back home?*"

"Yeah, my brother and my girlfriend. I love you babe. Keep my oyster tight, a'ight." She knows what I mean."

Six foot three; Lance Corporal Mario Santana was a twenty-four year old Dominican Refugee from Gainesville Florida, a strong, tough, family man and a real team player who'd taken it upon himself to learn some Arabic since he'd arrived. He was exactly what the military was looking for.

"*How do you feel being a foreign born Marine?*"

I am a Marine first, an American second and a Dominican third.

"*Coming from a third world country do you feel connected to the plight of the Kuwaiti people?*"

"I've spoken with some Iraqis," he said with an accent. "I respect them but they have to realize they have been lied to. I know what it is like to live under the rule of a corrupt government. America is the country that gave me and my family the opportunity to make something of ourselves. In a democracy like America there is no censorship, you are free to choose your leaders. Only by forcing these rouge states around the world understand that, can we have peace on earth. Until then it is our job to impose Gods will. Democracy."

For each of his eighteen years Private Bobby Davenport had lived in a double-wide trailer in Odessa Texas. He was a slender, joke cracking white-boy of five-ten but he didn't know it. Every since he could remember all he ever wanted to be was a gangsta'.

"*How does it feel to be a Marine?*"

He answered with a vapid, "Oo-rah."

"*Why did you join the Corps?*"

"Sports was the only thing keeping me out of jail, and that life ended the night I broke my leg. Friday October 13, 1989, I was lying on the 50 yard line looking up at the lights and I remembered them hoes at juve' hall saying it was this or jail. I'd already been to jail so I signed up for the Delayed Entry Program on November 5th. The recruiter kept yappin' about GI bills, signing bonuses and how I'd be getting pussy all over the world. I wasn't thinking about no college but I figured that signing bonus could pay for a whole lot of pussy. The recruiter said, 'for the next three years the government is going to pay for everything you need and they're going to show you how to put your foot in a motherfucker's ass.' I said 'what the fuck!' I had to get outta Odessa, don't nothing live with my mama but a bunch of methheads and that trailer was gettin' hella small."

"What do you hope to accomplish here?"

"I'm here to get my weight up."

What are you going to do when you get back home?"

When I get that DD214 and my freedom, I'ma shoot through Houston and put some green in the air with my niggas in the 5th Ward. I'm gon' get draped up and dripped out, sip on some syurp and just trip out."

"I've been to Houston and Odessa, there's not much difference."

Davenport laughed. "See there, us Southern boys can make ya' mind play tricks. My guys is real gangsta ass niggas like the Pres'. They make six-hundred bucks a fuckin' hour, and they 'ont care 'bout nothin' but the money and the power."

Private Malcolm Cottle was a spoiled stout, husky nineteen year old narcissist from New Jersey. He considered himself a buppie until four years ago when he and his mother moved to the South side of Chicago.

"Why did you join the Corps?"

"I aint even supposed to be here. I'm *supposed* to be in College but my punk-ass parents got a divorce and blew all the money. Now I gotta do this shit. This aint me. Aint no justice, man, life aint fair."

"What do you think is America's reason for being here?"

"I don't know and I don't care. I'm just worried about getting outta here. *I've* got a life to live." Suddenly Cottle's face lit up and he began wiping away sweat. "Who all is going to see this? Maybe this can help get me out of here."

"No sir, I don't think that it can."

Cottle screamed at the camera. "Why the fuck am I talking to you then? Fuck this!" Then he broke down and water came streaming from his eyes. "Somebody get me out of here. I want to go home."

Average. That was Corporal Jahn Dough's description. A bi-racial kid from one of the flyover states, he'd never been anywhere nor done anything and the odds of anyone ever knowing his name or face were slim. All his life it seemed that a stint in the Corps would be his ticket to a world he could only dream about. He knew now that too had been conspired.

"Well. That was quite bonkers wasn't it?"

"Yes ma'am."

"But we've been watching you Corporal. You seem to be coping quite well. How?"

"By watching you. And you and you and you." He point to the other members of the crew. "I want to thank you all for being so fucking funny."

"I'm pleased we could entertain you," she said laughing, *"but can you tell me what makes us so funny?"*

"Sure, but first you tell me why you're putting on this production, asking questions that you already know the answers to.

"Like what?"

"The most important one for starters, 'why are we here?'"

"Please, enlighten us Corporal? Tell us what you think is Americas reason for being here?"

"Alright. For the longest I thought it was just about the Kings, you know, George and Abdullah, protecting their interests in oil, but something happened to me in the desert and now I see the real picture."

LIBERTY CITY
Just South of Kuwait City
7 Days Earlier

He remembered being on patrol, Mirra, Santana, Davenport, Cottle, and him. A routine patrol in grid 486755 the same grid they'd patrolled at least 150 times in the last month. He remembered there was an explosion, a big one that blew them out of the Humvee they were in. They never saw it coming, must've been an I.E.D. But the worst part was that they weren't dead yet. He remembered waking up in the sand and being blinded by the sun. His hearing was coming back and it brought with it voices, angry Arab voices, then his head was covered with a burlap sack, everything went black, and he didn't remember much after that.

"… ahn … ough … pral … ough. Corporal Dough. Wake Up!"

His body ached and his mind was misty but this time the voices he heard were friendly. The Corporal opened his eyes and found himself in a small round windowless room like the inside of a well. Other than one heavy door secured by bars the only other opening had to be twenty five feet above his head and it too was covered by bars.

Mirra gave him a canteen.

"Drink something bro, you've gotta be dehydrated."

He gulped almost all of it before asking;

"How long have I been out?"

"You've got traumatic brain injury," answered Mirra, "you've been drifting in and out for almost three days."

For him it felt more like forty. He noticed Davenport on the ground with his ear to a pipe coming from the wall.

"Where are we," asked Dough? "Where's Santana and Cottle?"

Davenport motioned to him.

"Hold that down. We're in some sort of training camp. They've got Santana and Cottle in another room. We've been talking to them through this pipe, but their in prayer now."

Dough whispered.

"*Prayer?*"

"Yeah," said Mirra, "The fucking ragheads aint gonna do shit to them. They've got them going to *madrassass*. They said they were *talib*, or brothers who had yet to learn the truth, but you, me and Davy were 'Knights on a modern day Crusade.' They said our fate was in Allah's hands."

"Fuck." Dough sighed. "Who are they Republican Guard? How did they get us?"

"Negative," Mirra replied, "They aint down with Saddam, they offered to help the Saudis get him out of Kuwait, but the Saudis went with the U.S. instead. These dudes are *Al-Qaeda.*"

"Al-Qaeda?"

"Yeah," whispered Davenport "they're part of a Jihadist network called *Holy War Inc.* Nizari Ismailis from North Africa, Hamas and the PLO from Palestine, The Taliban from Afghanistan, Hezbollah from Lebanon, HUM from Pakistan, these motherfuckers got cells all over. They told Santana they'd been planning this for weeks. We're being held for ransom."

A thought crossed Dough's mind that the others had already come to grips with.

"The United States does not negotiate with terrorists."

His hope was fading as he managed another question.

"What do they want?"

Mirra shrugged and whispered.

"All we know is some rich raghead named Osama bin Laden has declared war on America. Tell him what he said Davy'."

Private Davenport began repeating parts of the *fatwa* that Santana had been reciting to him over the past few days.

"Bin Laden said that, *for years American bankers and oil barons with the aide of their secret police and the World Trade Association have moved in the shadows desta-bilizing Islamic nations, robbing their people of food and work, stealing their resources and placing sanctions on their economy.*' He says, *'like a virus we poison their lands, murder innocent men, infect their women and besmirch the minds of their children with our filthy American values, all while we plunder oil from The Persian Gulf and conflict diamonds from Africa.*' And according to him, *'one pebble of sand at a time wicked Zionists in the pirate state of Israel steal the Holy Land from under their feet.*' He's called upon all Muslims to restore *Khalifa* and launch a raid on the infidels. In Bin Laden's words, according to the *hadiths* of the Prophet Muhammad—peace be upon him—*'Jihad is not only the duty of all Arab people, but the way of brothers from every race and religion worldwide who wish to remain free from the mark of the beast, and away from the talons of his New World Order.*' Bin Laden has sent *shaddahs* around the globe to recruit members and build training camps like this one in every city, and he vows that one day soon they will rise up, and *'you will hear about them in the media. In shah Allah.'*"

It was hard for Dough to understand what he was hearing. But even harder to comprehend was the smile creeping across Davenports face.

"You know something I don't Private? What's to smile about?"

Mirra yelled, "This pricks got Stockholm syndrome, he *likes* the camel jockeys."

"Fuck you Mirra. I said they remind me of the homies back in the hood. Besides the praying, they don't do shit but train, listen to music and get high all day, but I never said I liked 'em."

"You fucking wigger."

"Fuck you skinhead."

They squared off.

"Break it up," said Dough. "That's an order."

He wondered how they'd survived this long. Then he tuned them out, stood up and tried to get his bearings. He paced the room looking for a way to escape, trying to piece together a plan, patting himself down, looking for anything he could use as a weapon; anything his captors may have missed. There was nothing left except a tape in his inside pocket. He took it out and studied it, that's when he remembered what Sgt. Laurence said when he'd given it to him.

"It's only music, but music can bring hope when all other hope has failed."

Dough figured that time was now. He imagined he wasn't there; he imagined he was back in the rear listening to the tape while he ran laps. In his daze he put the cassette to his ear. Mirra nudged Davenport and whispered;

"Dudes lost it."

"Bro you look crazy," said Davenport, "like that skinny motherfucker in "Escape from New York." You remember that shit?" He did his imitation. *'You touch me, you die.'*

Then Mirra did his.

"You're the Duke, you're A number 1. Arhhhh!"

They all started laughing. It felt good to laugh, but the feeling went out the door when it burst open and six masked and heavily armed mujahadeen ran into the room. Dressed in a white robe the leader was waving his *jambiya*. When he realized Corporal Dough was awake he rushed over, knocked him to the ground, put the dagger to his neck and yelled in Arabic:

"Your Government has abandoned you! They have refused our demands and now the hours of your life are numbered. The next sunrise will be the last one you see!"

The tape had flown out of his hand. One of the guards picked it up and put it in his pocket. All were yelling *Allah Akbar* as they left the room. When the coast was clear Davenport called to Santana.

"What's going on man?"

"Bad news; that was the leader of this operation, Abusab al Zarqawi, he says …"

Santana stopped speaking. After a few minutes Mirra went to the pipe and asked him again. It was hard for Santana to say the words.

"He says they're going to behead you tomorrow."

The room went quiet. Hours passed in silence but no one slept. They figured they could do that tomorrow when they were dead.

Dough wished for a moment that he had never woken up. He believed for a while that he was still dreaming and none of it was real. I mean really, who's to say what's really real without something real to compare it to and reality as he'd known it had just been shattered.

He had an ineffable feeling that the rest of the world knew a secret that he and his fellow Americans didn't. The secret that the world was at war and it had been since time immemorial.

It was late the next day when the door burst open. Zarqawi gave them the sacks again and led them above ground. The Marines heard babel while walking across the compound, banter all around them that they couldn't understand. Finally one of the guards said, *"Kiff,"* and there was a knock at a door. When it opened they were treated to a familiar sound, tracks from a demo tape that they all knew well. Music from a then unknown artist introduced to them by Sergeant Laurence.

"They got us out here listening to music from 'Apocalypse Now' when we should be listening to this," he'd said!

Santana and Cottle rushed them and removed the sacks.

"You lucky fucks. You're not dying today."

Dough asked them why.

"It was the tape," said Cottle. "They've been playing it all night. They love it. They say that he is a poet, a prophet, a revolutionary and a warrior all in one. Last night they asked us all these questions about it and asked why you had it. I told them it was our favorite; it was all we listened too. Then today they said that maybe you having this was a sign and that you'd be granted *nanawati*,—asylum."

A man approached them and spoke, Santana translate.

"He said relax and eat, you're in *Beit al-Salaam*, soon we go to prayer and then to the *mafrij*."

By now copies of the tape had been circulated around the compound and it was playing in the mafrij. Located on the second level, the mafrij was more airy and comfortable than the other rooms they'd been in, but besides that it looked like an ordinary room with baggies of moist reddish green leaves, ice cold bottles of water, and a worn Qu'ran, but as they were to soon find out it was a magical place where minds were opened and *jahiliyyah* was broken.

The Marines entered and took their places in the room of *shura*, carefully observing men with complexions and beards of all sizes talking with large wads of leaves stuck in their jaws. Davenport was the first to ask, "Hey can we get some of that?"

A man they referred to only as "the tall one," answered in English.

"Yes you may."

He passed Davenport a bag and he immediately stuck a lump in his mouth.

"What is it," asked Mirra?

"Kaht," answered the man. The Marines looked at him. "It is like tobacco, but there are different kinds and each produce a different effect. That one there gives you energy."

Mirra snatched up a handful and the others followed. Soon everyone was talking, different dialects of Arabic, Farsi, Dari, Punjabi and English.

Corporal Dough couldn't tell if it was the kaht or the concussion, but after a while it seemed that they could all understand the discussion. He listened as camp spiritual advisor and *Emir, Taqi* touched the flag on his uniform.

"Tell me how you can pledge allegiance to a flag that does not respect you. We see that in your country as it is in ours your rights as humans are being stripped away. In your cities people are being jailed without due process and murdered at alarming rates, but for some reason your people refuse to fight back against these Gestapo tactics. Tell me, are they frightened of their Government? If so they have it backwards. They are only men with titles. Our people do not bow to men or their titles. You must realize that our war is not with Americans but with your leaders, murderers, warmongers, and members of a centuries old secret society called *The Brotherhood of Death*. Today they are known worldwide as *Skull and Bones.*"

The symbol was well known where Santana was from.

"You mean like the scull and crossbones on a pirate flag," he asked?

"Exactly," said Emir Taqi with an infinitesimal hint of a British accent, "but it represents much more. The symbol has been used by The Knights Templar as well as well as the Roman Legions, in fact, the area where Jesus was crucified was called "the place of the sculls, and to the Master Mason the skull and crossbones are symbolic of mortality, teaching them that death in this realm means the end of his afflictions and the entrance to a new and better life. In private, members of The Craft are often seen going about their business with one trouser leg raised, signaling that they possess a "leg up" on non-members, and a tradition of Bonesmen is to set their timepieces five minutes ahead to demonstrate their superiority in society."

"Big deal," snapped Mirra, "how are *our* leaders involved?"

"History proves that the Ivy League and Yale in particular, are production facilities for the CIA and The Establishment. Alfphonso Taft, The father of William Howard Taft, your 27th President and the creator of what eventually became The United Nations was one of the founding members of *The Order*. After spending the summer of 1832 in Germany, the other member, General William Huntington Russell returned to Yale University with the authority to form *Chapter 322*. In 1856 Skull and Bones was incorporated as Russell Trust and since then has been the premiere secret society of all the Ivy League schools. Each year only fifteen juniors are "tapped" to "accept or reject" the group. Usually none reject and at any time there are between five and six hundred active members. Under rendition we've learned from some of them that a number of disturbing rituals go on inside the walls of the structure called, "the tomb."

"Like what," Cottle asked bugeyed and chewing slowly?

"Part of the initiation process," explained the Emir, "a ceremony called "Connubial Bliss" takes place inside a coffin where the celebrant lies naked reciting his past sexual encounters.

There's another part that involves occultist chants and bloodletting, there's also the consumption of blood from a scull shaped 'Yorick,' and there are believed to be at least three sets of skulls and bones on display inside its walls. One set belonging to Indian leader Geronimo no less. Students on the campus often report hearing sounds of agony coming from the tomb."

Cottle stopped him.

"That sounds like some devil-worshipping shit."

"Absolutely. Part of their oath says; 'The Hangman equals death, The Devil equals death, Death equals death.'

"Speaking of death," said Mirra sarcastically, "is there anyone involved who hasn't been dead for a hundred years?"

"Of course," answered Emir Taqi. He passed him a book.

"Wise Men: Six Friends And The World They Made."

Handwritten on the inside cover were a list of some of the better known Bones families. Mirra read them.

"The Bundy's, of Boston Massachusetts.
    The Davison's, involved with J.P. Morgan.
    The Gilman's, of Hingham Massachusetts.
    The Harriman's, made their money in Railroads.
    The Lords, of Cambridge Massachusetts.
    The Payne's, involved with Standard Oil.
    The Perkins', of Boston Massachusetts.
    The Phelps', of Dorchester Massachusetts.
    The Pillsbury's, of baking fame.—Whoa, so they made their dough, with dough.—
    The Rockefellers, of politics, Standard Oil and Exxon Oil."

Mirra turned to Emir Taqi.

"I heard somewhere that the way they make the double x's in Exxon mean something funny?"

The Emir answered.

"It symbolizes the double-cross of Freemasonry. Please, continue."

"The Sloane's, made their money in retail.
    The Tafts, of Braintree Massachusetts.
    The Wadsworths, of Newton Massachusetts.
    The Weyerhaeuser's, made their money in Lumber.
    And The Whitney's, of Watertown Massachusetts."

The Emir continued, "Collectively they are known as 'The Boston Brahmin.' Through membership in The Order and interconnecting family ties just shy of incestuous, many Old Englanders lay the bedrock for what became New England and American aristocracy.

Much of it with the wealth they created from a of number private and criminal ventures such as slave trading and opium smuggling courtesy of ties with the infamous *British East India Company.* Every year new families are brought into the fold and from them we get names like, Dan Quayle, Al Gore, John Forbes Kerry, Prescott Sheldon Bush, George Herbert Walker Bush, and George Walker Bush, all of whom rose to power through The Order."

"I don't know about that." said Santana. "The Bushes are from Texas. They made their money through oil."

By now *Ilm* was flowing freely about the room making Corporal Dough's senses sharp.

"No. he's right," said Dough calmly. "The Bushes as well as the Pierces' claim to be distant relatives of the Windsor's. Prescott Sheldon Bush,—the former Senator of Connecticut-, and George Herbert Walker were originally settled on the east coast, and both belonged to companies that made a shitload of money from wars. Prescott Bush sat on the board of directors at the Brown Brothers, Harriman firm during the 1920s, 30's, and 40s when funds from rich families like the Dulles', Rockefellers, Fords, and DuPont's were funneled through Nazi corporations like I.G. Farben and Fritz Thyssen's Union Bank Corporation (UBC) to help finance Adolph Hitler and his SS."

The Tall One interrupted.

"That is well known, what you may not have known is that Mr. Bush and Mr. Hussein have been doing arms deals for years. Their transactions were handled through the Bank of Credit and Commerce International (BCCI), and Banca Nacional del Lavoro (BNL). So weather it is a bullet that kills you or the deadly Sarin gas, it is likely that it was sold to Mr. Hussein by your very own President. And to this very day the Bush families have interests in a business Group whose Helgian investments make those seem tame by comparison. Our lands are for sale. After their destruction many of Mr. Bush's businesses associates like Khaki, Redwater, and Holly Barton will reap enormous profits from rebuilding them."

"For real," said Davenport, masticating, "the Bushes aint real Texans. George didn't bring the family south until the late 70's when he was head of the CIA. By 1980 they had helped make Midland the richest town in America, and that's fucked up cause believe me, the rest of West Texas aint nothin' nice."

"It was all on the advice his political advisors," explained the Emir. "The Establishment saw that the average American voters were fed up with preppie, upper-crust politicians and big words that they couldn't relate to, they were looking for someone who spoke their language."

"Enter Bushspeak," said Mirra.

"Absolutely. The Bushes are no fools; they are in fact an *American Dynasty*.

Their particular brand of magick has created a totally new identity for their family in under 20 years thanks to the dumbing down of Americans and their shortened attention spans."

The Emir looked around the room at the shura and Marines quietly shaking their heads. "You know brothers; we are alike in many ways. They call us militants and racists too, but when the shit gets thick, who do they go and get? The Agency has had their eye on us for a long time. Mr. Bush knows that if he wants to throw down he'd better bring his guns because *we* would rather die than to be trapped in his New World hell."

Cottle had been studying the faces in the room too. He'd observed that without the lengthy beards and ceremonial this and that, a lot of them looked just like him.

"They call us niggers and you sand niggers," he said. "But I like in the acronym for nigga that's on the tape."

With that the discussion continued into the night. Groggy and disoriented, the Marines woke just before daybreak, their heads touching as they lay forming a circle in the desert sand. All their equipment had been restored and Zarqawi was looking down on them. He spoke just before the Land Cruiser pulled off.

"We are forever bound through *bayat.*"—An oath of allegiance—"So stay strong my brothers, and keep your heads up, they know we're fed up, and soon they *will* give a fuck."

SAUDI ARABIA
Near Dhahran
Thanksgiving Day

"It's not just them, its tyrannical Monarchies worldwide. It's all you politically correct liars, hypocrites and members of the *Black Nobility*, your Queen in particular. It's an old and evil scheme you've got going, enslaving nations and choosing who lives and who dies. You call it Democracy when it's everything but that, the United Nations, the Northern Atlantic Treaty Organization; c'mon, let's just call it all by its real name, *Rome;* and young Americans like me are nothing but its publican gladiators. What's going on here is just the next chapter in this Caesars plan for world domination. I admit for a while you had me fooled thinking that I had a place in the "republic" if I kept my mouth shut and worked toward the glory of the Empire, but I see now, I'm not a noble, my blood doesn't come from aristocrats, and even if it did, eventually there is no safety in looking away seeking the quiet life by ignoring the struggles and oppression of others.

Who am I to oppress people who were born with less just so I can hold on to my 'freedoms?' Now that I know better how could I do that?

Ho' shit like that never lasts because nobody respects someone that kisses their ass? And one day,—and you and me both know that this day is closer than most people think,—you're going to turn on them like you've done with everyone else. It's like that story about the woman who takes in the injured snake and nurses it back to health, they become friends and years later it just up and bites her ass for no reason, then as she's laying there dying she looks at it and asks, 'Why?' and it says, 'It's in my nature, bitch. You knew I was a snake.' Well, the scales have fallen from my eyes. I can hear you now; I see your forked tongue. Just like you evil motherfuckers rose to power, you will fall. And now that I know what's real and what's not, guess what I'm going to do? I'm going to make it my mission to tell the world what you don't want them to know."

The Corporal looked into the camera and gave a spirited recital of;

Pure Truth

"He is Allah, the One!
The Ultimate God.
God does not reproduce
and is not reproduced.
And there is nothing at
all equivalent to God."

Infuriated, the reporter shouted;
"Bollocks! We will prevail! Stop rolling, stop the cameras!"
Then the Corporal put a fist to his chest and called out to the *shaddahs.*
"No matter who the foe they must fall, it's us against them all."

Freeing a mind was a beautiful thing, but Sgt. Laurence knew freedom of speech didn't exist here. He stepped in to save the Marine before he wound up on the road to Guantanamo paying for his words with his life.

"Stand down Corporal. Come with me. I need to talk to you."
The Marine calmed himself a bit.
"Kind of busy Staff Sergeant Laurence, can't it wait 'til later?"
"No Corporal, it can't. Come here and talk to me. That's an order."

1991

BECOMING GOD

TENNESSE
Memphis
August 1st

"**Why are you** sitting over there? Come and talk to me."

"What's up with you, you can't hold off till later?"

"No I can't, so hurry, because I'm still waiting."

"What's the rush you and I will never grow apart?

"I know, but I wanna treat you to something right now, I've got a love jones baby."

"Ohhh', I seee', you want me to be your little plaything huh? It's a'ight, I can do that, cause I love the times we share."

Alannah Myles played on the sound system as the couple sat in a booth of *Elvis Presley's Memphis*, drinking and playing mind games. The clock in the corner read twelve pm. when the Motorola "brick" phone rang as he closed in for a kiss

"Slow up bay, my phone. _____ Go."

The caller's voice was quick and raspy.

"Yo son, this situation out here just got *real*, real, son."

"Nizuthin youzu c'zan't hizandle. Rizight?"

"Son, aint shit been built that I can't handle, but you gon' wanna hear this!"

"Thazat rizight? G'head"

"Them strays from that other side of that town just came through tryin' to fuck with the big dogs bowl, son. So I ask 'em, "You gon' bark all day bitch, or you gon' bite!" We get to spittin', the whole nine yards. Roc caught a hot one. He'll be a'ight though."

"Mezmphis Mezmorial?"

"Nah, we called up ya' man the doctor from Germantown."

"S' far, s'good."

"Anyway, I sicked the dog catchers on them strays, right. They brought somethin' back for the pack. You need to hurry, he need a vet bad."

"Szon, youz' a geznius," said A-D, with a grin. I'ma get like Mr. Blonde wit 'em! Whzere the pazarty at?"

"We with these smokers on Crump street."

"Oh yeah …" The grin dissipated and he paused. "Gzet thazat cazetcher to blzow thezem cazndles out bezefore I skazate thrzough thzere."

A-D hung up the phone laughing, but the conversation had left Jessica disturbed. Her life was on track, her g.p.a. was high, and her credit score was better. She drove a new Honda Civic and rented a nice apartment in Nashville.

As summer vacation came to an end, she and A-D had flown here from Jersey hoping to spend a few days of quiet time together before she embarked on her senior year. They'd been lounging on Beale Street while staying downtown at the Peabody, and as usual A-D had been multi-tasking.

From his very first visit to Tennessee in '88 he'd made plans to expand there. The money he could make supplying Jessica's campus with herb was crazy, not to mention supplying other parts of the state with spices. But hustling with "new jacks" from the South could be dangerous; they had a different flow. A-D didn't sweat it though. He knew that money was a dialectician and would take care of most problems from the get-go. By late '89, with Jess's help, he'd moved into a condo and traded up from a 325 to an 850i. Since '85 he'd moved from an eighth of a key, to handling five sometimes six at a time. The Commission had five members in its inner circle, and close to twenty employees who cared for the rest.

Yep, things had changed for the better. Both their lives were on the fast track. But nine times out of ten, how a relationship starts out, is how it will end.

"Jess' I'ma have to leave a lil' early today; you can drop me in The Fowler Homes. I'll get a ride to the airport from there."

Refined by college, Jessica held in her anger, sighed and looked away.

"I thought this was our time Seth. What if I had something planned for us?"

"Did you?"

"That's not the point and you know it."

"Don't start, Jess.' What's the big deal? I was leaving later anyway."

"Tonight; not now!"

"Something came up, I gotta handle it."

"What's so important? Why can't Pat take care of it?"

Jessica didn't really expect an answer; she knew he'd always plead the fifth when it came to the fam'.

"Jess, how many times I gotta tell you...."

She finished his sentence.

"There's a few things about my life that I can't explain."

A-D used it whenever he wanted to get out of a something or end a conversation. After six years the line had worn thin.

"What does that even mean?"

Jessica had taken her own bite from the tree and now *she* understood. A-D had been sinning a long time and it was too late to change his game in the ninth inning. For six years she'd been faithful, all too aware of the sex and the cheating, and still she'd promised she'd never leave him. No longer the lovestruck and blind; a new life was calling Jessica, but she'd need confidence to leave her old one behind.

"What time are you leaving," she asked?

Twenty minutes later at the hotel they packed quickly and did what they did best. Jessica let her feelings go, if this was it, she wanted to give him something to remember, she felt he deserved that.

All the while she managed to stay smoother than black velvet as she executed her plan. In the car she took a page directly from his book by playing the tape.

<u>Excerpt 41.</u>

A-D had no idea he was loosing control, for a fraction of a second the thought crossed his ...

"Is she tryin' to ..., nah, not Jess. Pull over right here," he said.

He checked out the block before he kissed her.

"See bay' everything went smooth. I hate to leave, but I got to handle this."

"I understand," Jessica said forgivingly.

They kissed again. At that moment her feelings for him were both sad and tender. "You forever my lady," he said. "I'll give you a call when I touch down."

Jessica let go of his hand. He shut the door and she watched her prince walk away. A-D glanced at the car as it disappeared down the street, unaware that a good girl was gone forever.

<u>Excerpt 42.</u>

THE HAMPTONS
22 hrs. Later

"Hit it don't baby-sit it."

Excerpt 43.

"Bitch Better Have My Money!"

The smoke from the Dutchie choked the girl just a wee bit. She closed her eyes and lay back, relaxing and giggling.

"That a girl. Now pass it on the left hand side," instructed A-D, "and *do not,* fuck up the rotation."

Christie Witney relaxed on the distressed and sturdy oak of the Ethan Allen beach furniture, enjoying the feel of this early afternoon in August but anxious for her trip to begin. She hoped it would prove just as intense, vivid, and colorful as any ergot. And who better to usher her through the gutters than New York's self-proclaimed, number one hustler.

"So what's it like where you're from," she asked?

Her curious eyes were fixed on the full lips of her guest. Her brain was waiting for the signal to put a frame around the masterpiece he was sure to paint. Indigo blue waves merged with the bleached white sand at the shore of the beach.

The intensity and frequency of those colors is what caught his eye; it was every-where, the water and the sand, the houses and their trim, the blood and skin of the residents of this gated community, ergo for generations they'd remained this way. Unspoiled. Golden and untarnished. He took it all in while sipping a rum punch and preparing his response to a question he'd soon be answering all over the states.

"Let's just say, it aint nothin' nice."

Christie couldn't accept that.

"That, I already know; why do you think I'm asking? All we ever see is what's on the news and that's filtered. I want it raw and uncut," she said, sitting up excitedly!

"I can't help you in either of those categories."

"I'm serious," she whined. "I've invited you out to my summer house, intro-duced you to my friends and told you secrets. I've been totally open and honest. You know all about me. What do I really know about you?"

"You two play fair. Christie's upset, I think she's going to cry," said the blonde exiting the kitchen; the contents of her *Abercrombie* bikini top hard like diamonds, and the bottom, smooth like pearls.

"Put the 'Chili Peppers' on," she said, flipping through her Robb Report and sipping Cristal from Williams & Sonoma crystal. "And try not to upset her too much before the *Lammas* celebration tonight. Besides, she's got a point A-D. I want to hear about it too."

"Tell us," they shouted elbowing his arms, "we want the dirt!"

A-D figured he owed them that. He'd only known Christie for a season, yet already they'd squeezed in years worth of experiences. Same city, different world. From art exhibits in Soho to clubbing at El Morocco, with Christie as the key maker doors opened that he never knew existed.

They'd met at a showing of Julie Dash's film, *Daughters of the Dust,* both questioning why the other was there. Both learning through long conversations, not to judge the soul by the skin it's in. He'd toned down the jewelry since '88, lost the gold tooth and gained a few diamonds. Christie watched him in his stiff leather and denim Exhaust outfit as they wait in the concession line. Jungle Fever or Desert Storm, whatever the weather you could count on him for a witty response.

MANHATTAN
The Village
Early '91

So what did you think of the film?"

He stared at her for a moment, wondering what she wanted with him.

"I think the women wanted to run things and when they got to they argued among themselves a lot like men do."

"Interesting; what about the way she brought the time lines together."

"Ok; why you asking?"

"Well, I could be wrong but I don't see your date, and you don't *look* like a feminist."

"See there, I'm all for women's rights. What kind of a feminist are you, Melissa Ethridge or Sinead O'Connor?"

"From where I'm standing," she said smiling, "nothing compares to you."

A-D chuckled. He liked her style.

"Is that right? So look, before I jump out the window, what's your name?

She held out her hand.

"Christie, what's yours?"

"Oh, did I forget to intr …, I'm A-D," he said shaking her hand. "You know Christie, you don't *look* Gullah.

Christie shook her head.

"I'm not. I'm a Dame of Malta and a Daughter of Isabella, but not one of the dust. I think all of us daughters have to stick together though. It's good to share in each others secrets."

A-D stepped closer, looked her in the eye and asked seductively.

"Secrets, what secrets you got?"

Christie returned his gesture.

"Take it from me, we *all* have secrets."

Christie's family could trace their secrets back to Britain. Her great grandfather four times removed had been one of the Puritan/Separatists,—later known as Protestants—who'd left England for America, and no matter how chaste and reformed they claimed to be, many of them brought to the New World their Old World ways.

EOSTRE
A Child to Magick is Born

"Rhiannon" played as they arrived in Sagaponack. A-D appraised the multimillion dollar home as the "Alpine White" Shelby Mustang kicked up gravel in the driveway.

"And this is where you 'summer?'"

Christie hung up her cellular phone.

"Yeah, the main estate is in New Haven."

Throughout the home he witnessed Brazilian wood floors, French Gaulle picture frames and Javier Marin sculptures; reminiscent of the Temple ruins at Qormi.

"Must be nice," he said.

The tour ended in her bedroom with him sipping from his third Guinness. Contrary to the rest of the house her room was a mess.

"What happened here," asked A-D?

I haven't had time to unpack. I told you. Seattle? Nirvana?"

He hunched his shoulders. "Nevermind," she said, throwing her bags in the closet.

"Here, we took some awesome pictures of the band."

A-D sift through the stack.

"Whoa! What's her story?"

He held up a picture of the black widow in desperate need of sun and a bra. Christie laughed.

"That's one of their wives, she gets sooo' wasted; you would not believe."

He placed the pictures back in the duffel.

"And what's this," he asked, holding up a large black leather bound book?

Christie's face turned white.

"Uhh you really shouldn't have that," she said, upset by her carelessness.

A-D flipped it over and saw the symbol.

"Still keeping secrets, huh?" He teased her with a knowing smile.

"What do you think you know," she asked?

A-D chuckled and tapped the book.

"Where I'm from, the points on this star stand for, love, peace, truth, freedom, and justice, but around here they probably stand for earth, air, fire, water, and spirit; and it's called a pentagram, not a star. So that would mean I'm holding your ..."

"Book of Shadows," said Christie reaching for it. "I'm impressed."

"I'm tripping."

"Why?"

A-D shook his head.

"Nobody believes in that stuff, man."

Christie touched his cheek.

"Poor child, open you eyes. The Craft, flourishes to this day." She took his hand. "Follow me; I want to show you something."

In her parents room they entered a spacious walk-in closet where Christie opened a hidden door with a skeleton key. A-D bent down and followed her up the stairs to the attic, shelves holding several chalices, jars of incense and fresh herbs lined the walls. On the floor was a large red pentagram. In the center a sword hung from a podium where she placed the book and asked;

"What religion are you."

"Nobody *belieeeves* in that stuff man."

Christie smiled and continued.

"Well if anyone asks, *I'm* a God fearing Episcopalian. But actually, like most of my friends and neighbors, I'm Wiccan."

"You mean to tell me I can find witches in the mansions next door and across the street."

Christie corrected him.

"*Wiccans!* We don't like to be called witches. It's like you explained to me about *niggers* and *niggas*." He let that slide. "Open your eyes.

We're on your block too, on TV, advertising in books and magazines. We just keep it low key. Do you know the trials we've gone through to be here?"

"What" asked A-D, "you mean The Crucible and all that Salem's Lot stuff?"

"Exactly, we call it, "The Burning Times." We were tortured and murdered by the thousands, the result of the ignorance and cowardice of a few cunning folk, that idiot King James, some Hebrews, and The Roman Catholics."

A-D had never seen Christie so passionate or upset.

"What do they have to do with any of that?"

"Everything. That's the reason I asked you about your religion. I'm not against any of them. Wiccans are pure and peaceful, we worship Selene, the waxing side of the Mother Goddess and we live by the rule of three. The Wiccan rede is "Do what thou wilt, as it harms none." But it's *them* who do harm to us, claiming we worship a "Devil" that didn't even exist before the Levites wrote him into existence. They propagated this crazy notion that magic and those who partook in it were evil, when there's evidence of an esoteric stream running through *all* religions that deals with magic and divine contact. Even so, it was our followers who were used as scapegoats for everything from bad health to bad crops. Exodus 22:18 screwed us. 'Thou shalt not suffer a witch to live.' That, plus King James's hatred of women and paranoia of the "devil" is what got us kicked out of England. James, Pope Innocent, and all his little choirboys were in bed with one another. They wanted women, Lutherans and Protestants, and anyone who was wise to the truth gone. When things got bad in America some of us started to fall for their lies, then history just repeat itself like it always does."

A-D snapped his fingers and joked.

"They got a name for people like you. Heretics! I'm going to stand over here 'cause I don't want to be close when the lightning strikes."

"Please! You're one too. So are Jews, Christians and Muslims, Buddhists and Hindus too. All of you believing stories of mythic figures like Krishna, Buddha, Beddru, Osirus, Zoroaster, Mahomet, Tammuz, Odin, Quetzalcoatl, Prometheus, *Jesus*. I could go on and on, all of them the "Sons of God," all born on December 25th!"

There was a short silence; Christie had broken through.

"You want to know what December 25th *really* represents."

"What?"

"The winter solstice. The longest night of the year. From that point the sun begins its ascent to its zenith. Symbolically it's the night when the waning side of the Mother Goddess, Persephone, awakens to find she is with child, from there she waits for the birth of the ..."

"Son of God," they said together!

"December 25th is the birthday of Sol Ivictus, The Unconquerable Son and The Light of the World. He's the god of the ancient Sumerians and their Romans descendants. All Emperor Constantine did when he "converted" Rome to

Christianity was fuse the three together; Christianity is grounded in Paganism with bits of Judaism and the story of Christ thrown in to rally the troops."

A-D asked the obvious question.

"Why?"

"Control," answered Christie, "The Roman Empire dominated over a quarter of the world's population. Constantine managed to subjugate all the provinces religious and political sects with a repackaged tool." A-D didn't seem moved.

"It's still in use today. If you don't believe me just look on the inside of the Capitol building. On the dome is a fresco entitled the 'Apotheosis of Washington.' Simply put, what all the symbolism in it means is that every president of the United States is in the 'line of Julius,' and as the Caesars did before him shall rule over the heathen deities in *far territories, north and south of the zodiacal stars ...* 'I don't know about you, but that sounds a lot like God to me."

"But what does any of this have to do with magic and witches and all that," asked A-D, still unable to see the connection?

"Wicca and many of the other Pagan religions deal with the forces of nature and the cosmos. The Wiccan knowing and willingly harnesses and influences those forces. That's magic."

"I'm not buying it."

"I'll prove it to you."

Christie opened a trunk and produced a small wooden box. She took from it a black silk scarf wrapped around a deck of cards. The couple took a seat inside the circle and Christie began speaking.

"Have you ever heard the saying, "it's in the cards?""

A-D nodded.

"Centuries ago *cartomancy* was used by nobles for divination. Even the deck you know as playing cards was based on the cosmological arts. Over time the "tarot" deck has become the preferred method of oracles. This one was designed by Elphias Levi." Christie removed The Emperor card and placed it on the floor. "I want you to clear your mind. Be serious for a moment and think of something you always wanted to know as you shuffle these cards."

Believe in it or not, A-D wasn't about to let an opportunity slip by.

"Now cut the deck three times," said Christie.

After he did that she took the cards and laid them out in the Celtic cross spread. Then she placed the first card, The World, over The Emperor card and said;

"This is what covers you."

The second card, The Queen of Cups, she lay horizontally across that and said; "This is what crosses you."

The third, The Eight of Pentacles she placed above those and said;

"This is what crowns you."

The next one, The Ten of Cups, was upside down; Christie placed it under the others and said;

"This is beneath you."

The fifth card, The Lovers, went on the left side.

"This is what's behind you," she said.

On the right side went The Magician.

"This is what's before you."

She stacked the next four cards one atop the other on the right hand side. The Two of Wands was upside down, above it lay The Knight of Swords, next lay The Two of Swords, and finally, The Devil. A-D looked to see Christie's expression. It hadn't changed. She took a deep breath and went to work on his reading.

"Your question was simple; everyone wants to know what the future has in store for them. Here's your next five years."

"I chose The Emperor for you; it best suits your character. His strengths are energy and will, but his weaknesses are pride and stubbornness. The World is a good card; it indicates the atmosphere in which the other cards will work it can symbolize change, maybe satisfaction or praise for all your past efforts, or a new phase in your life that involves travel to places you never even dreamed of. The Queen of Cups represents the earth mother, at her best when at home, surrounded by family and friends. She's loving, affectionate, and known for her other-worldly aspects." Christie smiled at him. "Not a bad person to have as around. The next card is great for you. It represents the best that can come from your circumstances. It means that with much work you can take advantage of your God given talents as an artist and turn them into a career *and* money. The next card represents your *Foundation*, the influences that made you what you are today. It's a good card when right side up, but as you can see, yours is reversed. I see lots of violence, loss, and many arguments in your past. Much of it caused by unwanted births."

A-D managed a smile.

"Keep flowin'."

"This card," said Christie, "has two meanings; first one represents a strong influence that will soon pass; most likely a lover."

"*That's got to be Jess,*" he thought.

"You want to talk about her," asked Christie?

He answered with his expression.

"Just asking. Well, chances are there will be reconciliation, but there'll also be an important decision, one that means sacrifice."

For the first time Christie seemed apprehensive as she touched The Magician card. "This card shows an important influence that will operate in the near future. Do you have any idea who it could be?"

"No, should I be worried?"

"Not necessarily, but the Magician is a powerful figure." She point to the infinity symbol on the card. "It's said that he holds the key to eternity.

He's usually young, a risk taker, and a master of skill and oratory. He's perceptive and intuitive, and has the ability to bring about the best or the worst in others. This is an extremely good card when it comes to business ventures because he will do *whatever* it takes to succeed. Magicians are the planners of life, and they are well aware of the power they wield."

"I wouldn't mind meeting one," said A-D, confirming Christies fears about the next card. The Two of Wands, ___ reversed.

"This card shows your feelings toward the situation, pride, ambition and the will to gain wealth and power by any means." Christie hurried on. "The next card affects the matter at hand, for good or ill. He is the Lord of the winds and King of the spirits of the air. He's volatile and sometimes viewed as troublesome because he often rushes in where angels fear to tread, he is The Knight of Swords." A-D seemed concerned, but Christie didn't notice. She studied the next card.

"The Two of Swords," she said. "If a situation arises this card signals a stalemate. There will be no way around it and no escaping it; you must confront it. It *will* frighten you because it stands in the way of everything you've worked for."

The last card was black and ominous; on it was The Lord of the gates of matter and child of the forces of time.

"The Devil card represents a trap, enslavement to something or someone, and although it may very well mean that someone is causing trouble from the shadows, the trap is usually of your own making. If you use caution you can break the chains, but there will be a cost, one which you may not be willing to pay."

A-D was about to speak when he heard giggles.

Christie gathered the cards as the pheromones from three wanton and sky-clad banshees waft into the room.

"Where is he," asked the first to enter?

"We came as soon as you summoned us," said another in Gaelic.

The maiden reached into the chest and hand the neophyte a green robe.

"Phoebe, Piper, Paige," she said, "I'd like you to meet A-D. Show him to the bedroom and prepare him for his initiation."

THE HAMPTONS
59 Seconds later

Excerpt 44.

Brett ran onto the deck with a box of 'Rock's' in hand. "Wait up *dog*! If this guy is giving food for thought, I want a plate. I'm riveted by tales of despair."

The mood tensed as A-D cleared the table. Christie sucked her teeth.

"You two play fair."

"Nah, It's cool Chris, I see how we working here. What's it like where I'm from?" He shut his eyes and began thumping the table like he used to in his mamas kitchen.

"A'ight. I'm there." He point to the Atlantics horizon. "Y'all right, here." He circled his finger around the deck. "No apologies for what I'm about to say."

Excerpt 45.

A-D pushed back from the table and broke into his B-boy stance as the girls applauded.

"Ohh' ho, did you get enough to eat," asked Christie?

"Brett's doing the dishes," said another guest; a health nut that'd been in the kitchen blending a protein smoothie.

He stepped onto the deck in black basketball shorts and black Air Jordan's, a Brietling watch on one wrist and a red string tied around the other, his black autographed Chicago Bulls championship jersey was flung over his bare swimmers torso.

"W'sup kids, 'sup A-D?" He slapped hands and backs fluidly.

"Freidman," said Chloe feigning disgust, "when did you get here? Shouldn't you be at Shabbats brunch or something?"

Jerry hadn't changed one bit.

He sat next to Chloe on the armrest of the bench and rubbed her back. "I came through the window last night with Brett. Problem? If so, tell me be gone."

Her phony face broke, her eyes lowered a bit and she smiled.

"No problem," she said softly.

"Good!" Jerry stood up quickly and took her top with him.

Chloe yelled, "Freidman you fucking snake. You make me sick!" She tried covering her brand new 36 C's with her hands

Jerry had heard enough from A-D, to spark his curiosity. He spun around gracefully and tossed Brett the top.

"Wipe your mouth bro. You're drooling."
Brett held it over his head, glad the torch of humiliation had been passed.
Jerry gave A-D a beer.
"Bro, let's take a walk."
"Cool," said A-D, taking one last look at Chloe.
"Christie we're taking *your* car."
Christie nodded, grabbed the top and threw it to Chloe.
Jerry grabbed a couple of apples from the kitchen as he walked to the front.
"You the same A-D from Kiluaha fame?"
"I am the one."
"I had an internship with an investment firm in London. It was big there that year. I never heard anything else. What happened?"
"Pride, greed, envy, you know; same shit that happens to all the greats."

"Well it's good to see you're still writing hot shit. What's Chaz doing these days?"
"His thing." Jerry laughed. "And never I write," said A-D. "I get into my space and say whatever I like."
Jerry admired his *chutzpas* but thought, *"you can't be that good,"* before asking; "You're telling me you *never* wrote down any rhymes?"
"Well," admitted A-D, "when I first started rhyming I didn't need to. I had a 'Magic Microphone …'"
"Hey good looking, we'll be back to pick you up later." A-D point to him. "Yeah," said Jerry, "I had a couple of those."
"When I got too old for that, there was this green notebook I used to write stuff in until the shit happened with Chaz. I stopped rhyming after that; my heart wasn't in it no more." A-D's voice trailed off for a moment. "I wish I could find it, it's probably some tight shit in there."
"Probably; because honestly, you made Kiluaha. I always thought Chaz was dead weight." An affable A-D thanked him for the compliment. "So what's up these days?" asked Jerry pointing to A-D's car. "You still spending money from '88?"
"I wish. I'm in sales now."
"Business is good, isn't it," asked Jerry, grinning as he retrieved something from the compartment of his Ducati.
"I guess so," said A-D, "what about yours?"
Jerry offered him a small red pouch and a colorful one hitter. A-D declined.
"I 'ont smoke much."
Jerry shrugged and sparked up.
"I got some good tricks out there," he said, "but I'm looking for one bad bitch so I can spoil her. I want to dump the one I got in corporate America."

"Why the fuck would you wanna do that?"

"Believe me, she's a major bitch. Boring too! Besides, it's too many good old boys' in that game for me. My primary interest is getting money. I don't care how, just so long as I do. And even though I look damn good in one," said Jerry putting his shirt on. "I don't like wearing suits." A-D took a sip of beer as he finished. "I'm a voyeur man, I love to watch. I roll with some friends who do party promotions from time to time. Now *those* bitches are sexy. I want in. To tell you the truth, I want to do what you do."

"What," chuckled A-D, "rap?"

Jerry laughed at his expression.

"Not exactly, stay with me. I'm pretty good with numbers. Rap and Dot Coms are the fastest growing games out there, but Dot Coms are unstable and rap is on the verge of going mainstream." Jerry held out his hand. "Dude, there's money there and I'm like Frank White, *"I want in!"*

A-D laughed and gave him dap. "I feel your struggle man, but I don't know how I can help you. I'm aint rappin' for dough no more ..."

Jerry was loud and brazen and did not hesitate when he interrupted.

"Then *you* are fucking up bro!"

A-D didn't know what to make of him. He was either coked up or the most confident person he'd ever met.

"You got a wife," asked Jerry?

"No."

"Kids?"

"No."

"Enough dough?"

A-D squinted

"Me either," said Jerry. "You and I are about the same age. *I've* got a little over two million collecting dust and interest in bank accounts and that aint enough for me. Wasting time is old man shit. Every moment I'm awake I'm focused on the kill. I'm looking for longevity 'till I'm seventy."

A-D liked the sound of that.

Jerry offered the pouch again.

"Trust me dude, you've never been on a ride like this before. I guarantee this G-13 will change your life, man."

A-D took it as Jerry made him an offer he couldn't refuse.

"Teach me what you know and I'll teach you how to earn better. In eighteen months I guarantee, ___ I'll triple your worth."

This time A-D's head opened up to the idea as he motioned towards the car.

"Let's ride around awhile."

Jerry dropped the top and steered the Mustang around the town before hitting the highway doing 160 mph. A-D felt like a kid again he hadn't been in this seat in a long time and was excited about what might be.

"Even on this side, this is how it be when you rolling with G's."

When they'd finished running numbers, the two compared figures.

"So what do you think of Christie?"

"That's my girl," answered A-D "she takes care of her people."

"So you're in the covenant?"

A-D kept quiet. Initiation meant secrecy.

"I'll take that as a yes. It's Ok to talk about it with a member."

A-D glanced at him with empty eyes.

"C'mon man," said Jerry uneasily, "we've known each other since we were children. I live five houses down! Our parents tried like hell for years to get us together, but whatever we had ended when I turned thirteen."

"What happened then, asked A-D?"

"I became a man, she got into Zeppelin, read Crowley's *Book of Law* and …"

"Zeppelin," uttered A-D!

Jerry peered at him through his Oakley's.

"What; don't tell me you aren't a fan?"

"I know Zeppelin," A-D assured him, but fill me in; who's Crowley and what does one have to do with the other?"

The life of *Aliester Crowley,* well known in "society" circles, may be considered bizarre to the uninitiated. Born to an English priest in 1875, he's been described as a Freemason, a Satanist, an Illuminati Magus and a member of M-I6. Tales of Crowley's exploits became legendary as he traveled the world, became a brilliant mountain climber, and enjoyed much success writing for himself and others. Some of his most popular works are, *Magick in Theory and Practice, Diary of a Drug Fiend* and *Liber 777* or *The Kabbalah Unveiled.*

"He was a character;" Jerry said, flipping through CD's "called himself 'The Great Beast' of the Apocalypse, and 'The Wickedest Man Alive.' He died in England in like 1947, but not before influencing many musicians; including Jimmy Page."

"Page, that's Zeppelin's lead singer right?"

"Right. A girlfriend of his said that Page was obsessed with Crowley, and practiced black magick."

"So the shit about hearing voices when you play their records backwards; that shit is real?"

"C'mon dude; *you* listen to a whole record backwards and you might hear anything. You've got to wonder about a weirdo who does that kind of shit anyway; and the people that said that are the same assholes that put those dumb little stickers on rap records."

"Right. So what did Page do?"

"I think it was like 1970 when he bought Crowley's manor in Bolksline England, it's old, really fucked up looking and is supposed to be haunted. You know the Loch Ness Monster?"

"Fa' sure."

"It sits right on the water where it's supposed to live, and it was built on the same ground where a church burned down with all these people inside, and later on some guy got his dome cut off in there. I saw the place. I wouldn't want to live in it and I don't scare easy."

"And Page bought it?"

"He said it was 'perfect'."

"For what."

"They say when Crowley was there in the early 1900's, he used the Kabbalah's Unholy Sephiroth to summon demons, perform magick rituals. The *other* rumor is it's the place that Page came up with the most awesome rock song of all time. Jerry put the disk in and after a short introduction, the opening chords to "Stairway" played, stirring the pit of A-D's stomach. He looked sick as the song recreated images of his lucid dream.

"Dude," are you Ok," asked Jerry?

"You want me to pull over? Don't fucking 'earl' in here with us doing ninety!"

"Man I'm straight," said A-D composed. "What about Christie and Crowley?"

Jerry calmed down.

"Crowley's phrase, "Do what thou wilt," is what led Christie to Wicca and made her a bit anti-Semitic if you asked me. The thing about that is, without *us,* there would be no "magick" or Kabbalah to unveil."

"What is Kabbalah?"

Jerry thought quickly and took a deep breath.

"What I'm about to tell you is meant to go from my mouth to your ear only, ok?"

A-D agreed.

"Have you read the bible," asked Jerry?

"Man, the only Psalms I ever seen was on the arms of my niggas."

"No matter. I'm sure Christie gave you her rant about Levites."

"Yep."

"Ok. Well the Levites are a priestly class of Hebrews."

"Hebrews and Jews are the same right?"

"No. Anyone can be a Jew. Judaism in a religion. Hebrews are a race of people who were forced out of their homeland and Zionism is the movement to create and bring them to their new home in the state of Israel. You with me?"

"Yeah."

"Ok. God taught the Kabbalah to only his highest order of angels. After Adam fell some of them taught it to him so that he could one day return to Paradise. Next it was taught to Noah, then to Abraham and his covenant and finally to Moses who taught it to a select group of Hebrew priests; male scholars over the age of forty, the Levites. After the years they spent exiled in Egypt they wrote the Torah. The Torah contains esoteric information called *Ram*. It's the apex of cosmic knowledge; very difficult to understand.

Since then it's been translated into other texts, mainly the *Sefer Ha-Zohar*, (Book of Splendor) and the *Sefer Yetsirah*. (Book of Creation) That information is Kabbalah. Judaism is what is taught to everyone else."

"So why is it so hush, hush? What's that all about?"

Jerry chuckled.

"Since the dawn of civilization, man and all his scholars, scientists and priests have tried to explain two questions ..."

"Why am I here," said A-D.

"And ..."

Jerry waited for a response.

A-D's mind had been on automatic, he wasn't prepared for a quiz, by now he was feeling the high he'd gotten from the lai.

He threw his hands up.

"I 'ont know."

Jerry answered.

"Where did I come from? Would *you* tell everyone if you had those answers?"

A-D's smile gave him away.

Jerry's did the same.

"The texts tell how God created the world by combining the three pillars, three triangles and four worlds of the tree of life with the letters of the Hebrew alphabet. *'Aleph, Beth, Gimel ...*" A-D's eyes switched on and he became alert, pronouncing each of the next nineteen letters flawlessly and in rhythm.

"Daleth, Heh, Vau, Zain, Cheth, Teth, Yod, Kaph, Lamed, Mem, Nun, Samekh, Ayin, Peh, Tzaddi, Qoph, Resh, Shin, and *Tau.* From *Ein Sof,* he combined the ten Sephiroth—*Malkuth, Yesod, Hod, Netsach, Tipareth, Geburah, Chesed, Binah, Chokmah* and *Kether*—with the twenty-two letters to create the 32 paths of wisdom that would lead the chosen few to *the light.*"

It was a miracle; an astonished Jeremiah Freidman was at a loss for words, he had trouble keeping his eyes on the road as for the next two minutes, unwavering, like a record spinning in its groove, A-D recalled things he believed long forgotten. The art of calculating Divine Names and Numbers, Characters and Letters, Holy Seals, and the miracles of prophecies and dreams.

"Motherfucker! Who taught you the secrets to "Becoming God?"

"Becoming God. If God used this to create the world, I wonder what I can do." thought A-D before answering.
"Where I'm from people think God is an old gray white man sitting on a gold throne."
"Small imaginations," said Jerry. "They limit him and themselves by placing God in a certain skin."
An ardent A-D could hardly contain himself as he explained to his new friend something he'd never told another, the story of that night in Paradise when he'd glimpsed the orchard. He took another hit and left the weed alone.
"This shits got me going!"
"Man," he said, "I been waiting fifteen years to find out what dude said on that microphone. You can explain all that to me?"
"No one can explain it all. I've studied all my life, I still don't know all that there is to know, and I never will. Remember, Kabbalah, like you and me is ever-becoming."

A-D would have to wait even longer to understand that one.

"Man it's been fifteen years; I thought I'd never know what that shit was about. I never met nobody I could …" He stopped to reflect. "Damn Jerry, that was a long time ago, and you know I can remember that shit like it just happened."

Jerry felt it was time to reveal another secret.

"Time is illusory man, and humans are the victims of a universal delusion created by their inferior minds to explain it. The future doesn't exist yet, and the past is already gone. The only thing that matters is now, *this* moment, and what *you* do with it! You want to be rich? You want to leave a legacy? Well not everyone is capable of that. You need to conquer your fears. When you find something or someone you clique with, follow it, see where it leads you, see what works are associated with it, who it's stars are, see what they were into, check their history and it may lead you to yours, _____*wherever* that may be." A-D looked at Jerry with caution. "It's funny to me, when most people wake up, smell their lives and realize where they really are, or worse, whatever's been guiding them, they piss their pants and go out like Ben Zoma did. Little bitches. Why? I say do you, then learn to control you. That's consciousness. Only with it may the flaming sword be removed and *Shekinah* revealed. She is the gate and the opening to the divine. That's where my people come in. *"… And thy seed shall possess the gate of his enemies."* I am of that seed. The tree is the key to divine consciousness, and when you've mastered it, *'Behold, the man is become one of us, to know good and evil; and now, lest he put forth his hand, and take also of the tree of life, and eat, and live forever.'"*

The car wind down the road, Jerry revved the engine, Jimmy's solo ended, and John brought the cymbals to a stop on a note as fine as a razors edge. The Mustang did the same on a cliff overlooking an omnivorous ocean view, and at that very moment Robert completed their quest.

"… And she's buy-y-ing the sta-i-ai-air-wa-i-ay, to hea-veennn."

"Honestly," said Jerry, "there was a time not so long ago when due to certain 'traits,' you wouldn't be welcome in our order, but money and power is changing us, these days all we ask is trust. We are a secret society, the *Ben Elohim* and the creators of fate."

A-D hesitate, unsure of what to do, over the years he'd run with plenty guys who told lies that sounded true.

"Dude," asked Jerry, smiling as he hand him the apple from which he'd attain *Chaigidiel,* "what the hell are you waiting for? Let's make history."

1992

THE STARS ARE BORN

CALIFORNIA
Los Angeles

They were taking place all over, unions like these, materialistic and maleficent individuals had found their way into this game of ours. This year would mark the end of hip-hops golden era; but from that first E.P. release in 87, to their multi-platinum disk in '91, Double E, Q-MD, Craig 'Rubix' Jones, Mc Villain and, Dj Sunny, had etched their names onto the clay tablets of history. Before them the hip hop culture had been largely ignored, written of as a fad and frowned upon by mainstream America. Gold albums even by "accepted" rap artists were rare; fair contracts, rarer still. When GIB's '88 release, with it's "gangsta'" lyrics sold a half-million copies in one month, the first to notice was the authorities. They tried using intimidation to stop us, when that didn't work they enlisted the help of censorship groups like Tipper Gore's PMRC. In '85 they had successfully lobbied for parental advisory labels on records that weren't under the Establishment umbrella. But it was too late, real niggas from every race knew the jig was up. Those very labels eventually helped GIB move over two million copies by the end of that year with virtually no airplay. That success wasn't lost on corporate America, music industry execs took notice. It was evident that they were taking it there, with or without anyone's help. *"There,"* was a vast, untapped market for the airing of America's dirty laundry. Rodney King's video taped jacking by one-time served as a heaven sent augury, presenting non-believers with proof of what was really going on. Some cried foul, but some of us knew that exploiting the pain of the urban experience was cyclic. It happened every 20 to 30 years after sons and daughters of the South had acclimated to their new homes and assimilate their language into styles stories that others wanted to hear. Just like their bluesmen forefathers, rappers; this generations musical bad boys, had finally been discovered. The difference was this time *they* were making money from their tales. Within months, every major label opened "urban music divisions" and placed Intel officers in the fields to recruit a few good men, but controllable ones that didn't teach and wouldn't garner the attention of The Agency. Assuming that Americans couldn't handle the truth, they returned with a bunch of McRappers,—Mc Brains, Young Mc, and Mc Hammer,—then served us a tall glass of Vanilla Ice to wash them down with. Sorry, the thugs weren't buying bullshit, by now they'd learned the prices.

What they needed for those long hours putting in work on the block, was someone that smoked like they smoked, drank like they drank, and hurt like they hurt, a voice that wasn't too perfect; someone that soldiers from around the world could relate too, so as with the British invasion years earlier, another wave was formed, and slowly, stealthily, by the end of '91 a messiah had arrived in an unlikely package, one young black male. From every jeep and every car believers bumped his music, and on the 29th day of April, 1992, when the "L.A. four" was acquitted and that city burned, as *he* predicted it would, the rioters used his words as weapons, and with them they were made hard and defiant. Screw the record label. This time The Agency went all the way to the nation's capitol. The Vice President stopped just short of banning his music, claiming the lyrics were sexist and violent; all that trouble just because he'd said what the people want.

One person who heard and understood the voice of the people was Marlon "Pooh Bear" Dark. Like Q-MD he too had grown up on the streets of South Central, escaping the trap of old school hustlers like Genie Lamp, and OG's like Ray Ray Dewitt by claiming the ghetto's other exemption. Athlete. Like Ricky, football it seemed was Pooh's way out. An all-star player in high school and college, he'd come within inches of his dream in 1987 when he was drafted by the NFL, but by 1989, he was still reaching.

"'Sup Coach you wanted to see me," asked Pooh?

The no-nonsense coach sighed.

"Yeah Dark, c'mon in. Close the door behind you." He removed his glasses as Pooh sat down. "Dark," he said, "were gonna let cha' go, Ok?"

Pooh was at a loss for words and managed a humble;

"Ok."

The coach chuckled.

"You're a funny guy Dark, and we really liked having you around, but you know how it is?"

"I'm sorry," cried Pooh.

Coach kept silent and slid an envelope across the desk, as Pooh collected himself. "You're getting' a sweet payout from your contract. What are you gonna do now?" he asked. The big man looked around the room for an answer before he stammered;

"Uhh, I … I … I think I'ma move out to Las Vegas."

NEVADA
Welcome to Fabulous Las Vegas
1991

Vegas baby! Pooh went to his apartment, packed and sped down the highway as fast as he could, choked full of true grit, and hoping to change his luck. Not yet a trendy upscale playground, Vegas in the early nineties was on the decline.

It had lost most of its Mafioso image from the Siegel era and had attempted to rebuild with a campaign billing it the perfect place for family fun, but just like today, lurking just beneath the surface; the strip offered all the seedy depravity that one could afford. That's why the unwritten rule has always been *"What happens in Vegas, stays in Vegas."* That made it the ideal place for high rollers and celebrities with fetishes, and it was their kind that eventually led Pooh to his true calling. He began his adaptation by providing protection and finding pretty women for rich men. He got cozy with them, his eyes open the whole time, looking and learning the game. Less than a year of watching his clients humpin' around convinced him that he and those cats had something in common, and at 6'3, 300 pounds he didn't need to pay for protection. After word began to circulate of the extreme measures he'd used to help out a client named Cocoa, his services were in demand. He was just the kind of strong negotiator that Q-MD needed.

At the height of GIB's success, Double E hired a business manager named Seinfeld to handle the group's contracts and finances. "Rubix" was the first to do the math. He rejected the offer, went solo, and for a while became one of America's most wanted. On Double E's orders the rest of the group threatened him and dirtied up his name, then someone handed Q-MD a calculator and he realized the numbers weren't adding up, but unlike Rubix, Seinfeld, couldn't let his alchemist go, everything Quincy produced went platinum or gold. Quincy had always tried to front, but truthfully he was soft. He took it in silence for a long time, until his boy Holiday blessed him with the formula.

"Look dog, no one can do it better than us.

I'ma stay dope as long as I can imagine, My next disk gon' be even better than the last one.

I aint frontin' or nothing, cause I'ma get mine;

But I don't think that it's funny when niggas messin' with my money.

Aint no way we supposed to be broke right now, Q'. It's time to make that move from No Mercy to Firing Squad."

Q-MD laughed it off.

"Just give me some time man, I'm gonna get our money. What's the matter, you don't trust Seinfeld?"

Holiday lay down his copy of *Marching in Place* and thought;

"Credat Judaes apella, non ego."

"You wanna stay with No Mercy," he said, "cool, I'm wit' it. It's Q-MD and Holiday all the way, but first lend me an ear and let me tell you 'bout this nigga Pooh."

Most of Holiday's secret plan flew straight over Quincy's head; all the new world talk was too esoteric. What he understood was Pooh's rep', and more important, who was backing him.

"Wait, wait, wait, wait, you got both of them dudes together," he asked?

"Nigga who am I?"

Quincy knew the answer to that question. Holiday should've been one of the best artists in the history of rap, but a slippery road and a 1200cc GXSR changed that in an instant. With his money maker gone he'd have to settle for another title, one of the most influential.

"Shit," answered Q-MD. "That sounds like it might work, and that's about the only way 'E' and Seinfeld gone let me out that contract?"

"Fuck 'em. We'll stop 'em in they tracks, and show *them* who's ruthless."

Q-MD rubbed his chin as he teetered on the edge of a decision. Holiday watched him then added this.

"The homie Pooh said if the disk is dope he can guarantee us a million a piece."

All the records Quincy had sold and he'd never seen money like that.

"How much did you say?"

Holiday decided to be his huckleberry and repeat the number.

"Whaaat," asked Q-MD with a voice that was full of lust and desire? *"A million dollars?* Nigga, I'd sell my soul to the devil for a million dollars."

MANHATTAHN
July '92

Fame could relate. He'd faced that late in '87 when his mother succumbed to cancer. Goodgame took that years shots hard, he'd lost flesh and blood and had been leaking life ever since. In '89 the Game family reached a milestone when Famous became only the second member to attend college. Goodgame's younger sister Crystal had stayed in California, gone to UCLA, and was doing big things in entertainment. In '90 Dania's family moved back to Brazil, brought a mansion and opened a business. Dioses stayed with them for a while after he lost Corinne to salmonellas in '91. This year he'd decided to divide his time between North and South America, and after twenty years in "The Life," D&G's run had come to an end and The Sons of Liberty could officially begin. Against their mother's wishes both Fame and Fourtune had been making moves on the low since high school, but they'd been drifting onto divergent paths since graduation.

Alliouisis had gotten Fourtunate into Georgetown and paid his tuition while Fame stayed in New York and tried to conform to life at Syracuse; but the Albany streets were too slow for the Harlemite. His classmates? Lames. His professors? They couldn't decipher his street slang. Even the rump shaking and coochie popping of fly girls in "Daisy Dukes" couldn't keep him on campus. Business and marketing were the only classes he ever attended, and every weekend he'd make the trip back to Harlem, in his own way still a victim of the ghetto; albeit pushing a chromed out Harley through the streets of Harlem no one saw it that way.

Last year he'd linked up with another Harlem hustler. Flamboyant for fourteen, he wore so many jewels the Feds called him "Niggererace." He ran a set around 142nd & Lennox called The Delegates; they sold it all, dope, coke, crack, and syrup; they were so thorough, on point and game tight, they could cop' em, brick' em, and re-up in the same night. For Fame looking at him was like looking at himself, pure ambition staring back at him, to top it off he was like blood; Lori and Nard's son. She'd nicknamed him Flam, short for flamingo due to her love of everything pink. Fame took him off the block and showed him how to pack coffee and wire cake; before long he was running the spot; a barbershop on Twelfth Street where they hustled fades in the front and 'dro in the back. For a while getting cake and being lionized by the streets were as high as Fame's aspirations went, until this summer when his aunt Crystal and cousin Dionne came to visit and he found himself lost at an industry party in an upscale area dubbed "Tribecca Beach."

Fame was no stranger to lavish parties, he and Fourtune would throw some of the best at the Cotton Club, catered with shrimp, lobster, and cases of Moet and Dom, but this place eclipsed all that. It was like a 30,000 sq. ft Polynesian theme park overlooking the Hudson River, equipped with lots of sand, steam from indoor rainforests, and tropical vegetation. It smelled green, crisp and clean, like a mixture of *Acqua Di Parma* and newly minted money.

Fame was bedazzled with the atmosphere and clientele, momentarily becoming a fan as he and the beautiful Dionne; a nineteen year old, slightly darker, smarter, and less wealthy version of Hillary from *The Fresh Prince*, pointed out celebrities.

"Aunt Crystal is that …?"

"The girl from *21jump Street,* yeah that's her. Don't point."

"My bad. This place is crazy. It's like we really at the beach."

"Uhh, yeah. It's like the Hamptons for people who can't afford the Hamptons." Dionne surmised

"How much it cost to open a spot like this," asked Fame?

Crystal studied the place.

"You're going to need about five to ten million to open a good club in New York."

"*That's all,*" asked Fame more serious than not?

Crystal raised her eyebrow.

"Oh, you got it like that."

"Phsst, just give me a minute auntie." He looked her way. "I could always use an investor though."

"You'd have to clean up your money before we could do business, baby."

"The old man showed me how to do that already. I've made some investments."

"I know you have," she said, "and that was smart, but I don't know of any barbershop that's making the owner five to ten million. What do you think about going into entertainment?"

"What, being a rapper? Nah not me. Besides, I can't rap."

"Well, find somebody that can. There are no shortages of rappers or singers in NY and they all need managers. That's what you like to do anyway. You think you can handle being 'in-cog-negro' I know that might be a little hard for you."

"I think I could," said Fame thinking, "… for a while at least. We'll have to see."

The family made their way across the dance floor to the VIP's section where Goodgame was relaxing with a drink.

"Where y'all been? You got me out here listening to this hippity-hop music with all these lil' thugs."

"What 'chu talkin' about, Pop? I heard you around the house banging, 'Baby Got Back.' and talkin' about, 'Can't touch this.' Goodgame's frown turned around as he pictured the video ho' in his head.

"You are *so* busted uncle, we saw the THC disk in your car," said Dionne.

"What 'chu know about that baby-girl? That's a lil' hard for you aint it."

"You're kidding right? The whole West coast is playing that. It's like, music to drive by. She closed her eyes and started to sing;

"One, two, three, four ..."

Fame cut her off.

"Jeeyeah old man, you gotta get out more, listen to Hot 97."

"*No shit?* My lil' brother got a hit on his hands!"

"What lil' brother is that," wondered Fame aloud.

"Your Uncle Larry, who else?"

Crystal jumped in before Fame could answer.

"Ooo, I've been meaning to ask you about that. So the rumors *are* true. Oranthal does have something to do with Firing Squad records?"

Goodgame smiled and sipped his drink.

"What 'chu heard, 'cause I don't pay attention to rumors sis."

Crystal rolled her eyes, "Goddamn Goodman, why must you be so difficult."

"I aint dun' nothin'. _____ Now I say again, what 'chu heard," he asked grinning?"

"What-ever," said Crystal deciding to play his game. "Ok, I heard that some big guy, an ex-football player had been running around playing Kevin Costner ..."

Dionne butted in excitedly.

"I heard he totally threw some guy off a roof."

Crystal looked at her from the corner of her eye.

"Shut-up, Dionne. It was a balcony, not a roof, and he didn't throw the boy off."

Fame chuckled at the two.

"Finish Aunt Crystal."

"Right. That boy from GIB," Crystal snapped her fingers, "the tall one ...,"

Dionne sighed, and rolled her eyes.

"Q-MD mom."

"Right. He wanted to leave the group, but his label No Mercy wouldn't let him out of his contract, so he and the bodyguard go to the little ones office with baseball bats and some of you and Oranthal's "other" family" members. After a while they come out with a release form and a new contract, and now that they have Q-MD on board, that's when Oranthal invests a million dollars ..."

"Oh-ho, Uncle Larry locked down doing big things," said Fame a little too loudly! His father told him to hold it down.

"Wait, wait, Famous, it gets better," said Crystal just above a whisper, "they still needed a major distributor, so they pitch the idea to the guys over at Periscope Records. When they saw Q-MD's track record they signed Firing Squad to a *ten mill-ion dollar deal.*"

"That's *my* brother, said Goodgame! His smile was proud and wide when he and Fame traded pounds. "Cant nothing stop us Lueders Park boys. Damn Crystal, *I* didn't even know about the ten mill'. Who *you* been talking to," asked Goodgame?

Crystal put her hand to her ear and mocked her brother.

"What chu' say? I can't hear you, say it again?"

Shortly after that, pier 25 was crowded with guys and girls dancing, industry types and partygoers mingling under the night sky. Fame watched as the Benjamins flowed faster than a *Tongue Twista* rhyme. It was 98 degrees and half past eleven on a school night when a familiar voice grabbed the mic, and every few bars, talked over the beat. "Uhh huh, uhh huh." ____Yeah, that's right."____ _ and a falsetto, "A'haa!" When the song ended a familiar face joined the voice on the stage and amidst cheers and applause, did what it did best.

"Ladies and gentleman, I'd like to thank all y'all for stepping out this evening to join in the celebration of Downtown records platinum recording artist, Da' Lover." The crowd cheered when the big man, dressed in a white suit, removed his cigar and took the mic. The guests closed in around the stage while the Game family looked on.

"Thank you, thank you. I want to thank everyone for their support, my fans, my record label, and my producers. Thank you all for coming out tonight. I hope that you all have a peaceful journey; and if you haven't picked up the album yet, you need to go out and cop that because Da' Lovers got what you need."

Back at the table Fame asked;

"Aunt Crystal, who is the skinny dude? I've seen him before at a concert."

"I don't know Fame, he …"

"Eww." Dionne frowned. "He just told me and I like totally forgot, but he said everyone calls him 'Dizzy,' because of how big his cheeks are.

He thinks he's some sort of uber-producer. Here."

She held up a business card that Fame snatched and read.

※

Yes. It hadn't taken long for the extraordinary spirit of Seth "Dizzy" Jahn to get it right.

When asked, Seth Jahn will tell you he always felt "special;" "different" from the other little kids; like he was born into "fabulouscity." And why not? His leggy mother Joyce had once worked as a fabulous model, laden with furs and designer clothes. Before his death in '73, his father was ghetto fabulous, driving a Benz to his job as a mid-level man in the same infamous crew that employed Eggo. Joyce never told Dizzy what he did.—Why should she?—Or how he died.—She said it was an accident.—Or why he and his younger sister always had it just a little better than most of their neighbors?—Just so long as their childhoods were pleasant.—

When Dizzy finally uncovered the truth years later he didn't even cry about it. Why should he? The only memory he had of his father was being tossed in the air by him, something he'd do with his own children years later.

Dizzy grew up middle class, attending a Catholic school in the 'burbs, where Joyce found work as a teacher. She enrolled him in a program for underprivileged youth, enabling him to spend summers in the pastures of the Pennsylvania countryside, amidst the tranquility of farm animals and away from the hell up in Harlem. When Dizzy was twelve the Jahn family relocated to a comfortable house in the predominantly white suburb of 'money earnin' Mt. Vernon, complete with security, front and backyards, and a pool. There is where the altar boy's alter ego began to show. Too young for a paper route, he opened a sweet shop on his front lawn, he had Joyce print up fliers and then forced the paperboys to deliver them for free, and his sister handled the transactions while he sat back sipping lemonade.

Sometimes he'd sneak and watch flicks. When he began talking dirty and slapping the ass of his teenage sitter like the actors did, she complained. Then one day she stopped, poked her ass out and said, *"Do it harder!"* That's the day he lost his virginity. Risky business for sure, but hey, sometimes you gotta say, "What the fuck!"

In high school his small group of friends flipped on him when he learned the same lesson as most other success stories, stop imitating people and go your own way. An easy task for a person many described as a selfish loner and manipulative megalomaniac. Ironically the same people described him as energetic and magnetic with an enduring charm that put him at the center of things.

Yet controversy seemed to follow Dizzy, some say that the devil chases him, and there may be some truth to that. Think about it. Wherever he goes he makes it hot.

Howard. The late 80's. A.K.A. The African-American Harvard and Olympus to a pantheon of black Greeks from Alphas to Zetas.

It's the alma mater of notables from Toni Morrison, to Taraji P. Henson.

Even as a freshman Dizzy's pace was manic, regularly putting in twenty hour days commuting between business classes on Georgia Av., and his dream job, an internship at Downtown records. On weekends he worked toward his ultimate goal; promoting himself. One day Dizzy cut his hair like Bobby Brown, donned an outfit like Kwame, and danced in a video. The Howard bourgeoisie, satiated by the non-stoppin' party hoppin' that power and wealth bring, were lusting for something fresh. Enter Dizzy, the new campus CEO. As he listened to them talk he realized, *"no matter how they front, these classy chicks love bad boys."* Though that wasn't quite him, he was courageous in his own way, plus he had daddy's rep backing him. Armed with those weapons and an organic feel for music, every weekend he'd put the Goddesses of DC, together with the mortals who ruled Antacostia in the 80's, throw in a few rising stars from Downtown and together they'd have parties that would rival Freak-Nik, and make Eros proud.

Dizzy left Howard after just eighteen months. Downtown Records rewarded the twenty-two year old for his hard work by making him the youngest VP of AR in music industry history. He returned the favor by lending them his special gifts, the ability to tap into the pop culture, see where it was headed, then steer it, that and an eye for talent were responsible for bringing the label its biggest stars; a mad band and a future queen.

In 91', his rise was slowed when he was held responsible for a fatal fire at a concert he'd promoted; it bespoke of things to come. The press attacked him; officials sent the cops, the DA, and the Feds to get him. The eleven o'clock news broadcast him throwing up the V in his moment of distress. Outsiders couldn't believe his nerve. Insiders heard his call. He'd like you to believe it was his charm and drive that helped him to get away with only a singeing, but more than likely it was his wherewithal and fraternal kinship in *The Boule,* (a.k.a. "The Talented Tenth") with the city's top official. What could mere mortals do to them? Besides he couldn't stop now. He was poised and set to present the gigantic catalyst he needed to perform his most grandiose feat yet; making the world love him.

✳

Fame felt sick, like he'd downed a gallon of 'Haterade.'

"Aunt Crystal, hold up a sec'. That skinny cat got cake like that? You tryin' to tell me this nigga is my age, running around here putting in less than half the work that I do, flossing mad-crazy, and poppin' bottles with models all from this entertainment game?"

Now the other three looked at him and laughed.

"Looks like we in the wrong business, huh Famous?"

Fame's mind was on tomorrow. He was serious as a malignant tumor when he answered his father.

"Not for long pop."

As midnight approached Dizzy entertained the guests, waiting for just the right moment to pop. When the new day arrived, Syracuse became a memory, flossing took a back seat to grinding, and Fame began his international quest for greatness and worldwide domination.

Dizzy however, was already a step ahead.

"I see it's about that time for us here at Downtown to do what we do. I don't wanna see nobody, sittin' down. I wanna see everybody on the dance floor, having a good time; cause for the next hour the Dj is playing nothing but Dowtown music ..." The crowd whooped and hollered. "... and one more thing, for those of you who don't know, my name is Seth 'Dizzy' Jahn, and *I am* the CEO of Youth Authority Records, the label that the whole world is talking about." Dizzy had to raise his voice to be heard over the clapping. "Thank you. Now, I need y'all to put 'cha hands together again, and welcome to the stage Y.A.'s newest recording artist ..."

1993

SOLACE

THE AMAZON
December '89

The Boy had discovered that a life of making records could be hectic and sleazy.

J.I finally front the money to lay the demo and after hooking up some shows at the mall he made himself manager and further proved that they come in all shapes and sizes when he blamed his artist for their problems at the same time he was using him to get richer. Again The Boy went inward, spending every second preparing for his role as what Pythagoreans would call an *episkopos* in this game that life is.

"Fuck spitting that Movement shit, dog. It's over; y'all lost. Let me on the mic. Real niggas keep it straight gangsta' mack."

Like the Goths before them, many west coast G's believed that to exercise the mind was to weaken the body.

"Nah, can't do that," said The Boy. "The main reason I'm in this is to school my niggas to the game."

Plus he'd heard J.I.'s flow.

"I thought we was in it to get paid," said J.I., "'cause that's the *only* reason I'm here; for my money."

The Boy ignored him and thought;

"See there, you know you fucked up don't you?"

He chewed the inside of his lip. It was his tell in tense situations. J.I. realized he'd said too much and turned away. To many The Boy possessed that same sort of unnerving, androgynous quality that's becoming of angels. A nearly six foot svelte frame covered by even, earthen, pliable skin. His molded face was adorned by a puffy lipped smile, centered by the glint of a golden Nefertiti, and topped by bushy brows that hovered like halos over angel eyes. It was all crowned by a curly high top fade in hues of black and brown.

"Maybe we need to chill with this for a minute," said J.I. "Let's see what these record companies are talking. I been slacking and me and my mans got a plan kicking major dust in Portland."

The Boy had expected this. But who was he to knock another brother's hustle.

"Maybe we do; but I'ma stick with making this microphone pay."

J.I. put out his hand for a pound.

"Homies?"

The Boy grasped it tight and pulled him close.

"Homies, partners, all that man. Just call, I'm down to the e-n-d."

It seemed that bad luck, the only friend that never let him down was paying him a visit again. In August there was the incident in the alley and by now both he and his fifteen year old sister had dropped out of school; to top that off she was pregnant. Marian, unable and unwilling to hide her affliction any longer had come to town and gone. Aunt Audrey had her own problems to deal with and in November she packed her things and left the kids with nothing but a note. It was December now and Marian had yet to come back to claim her children.

After the rift J.I. went north on a come up. Without his help the children who were already living in squalor went from bad to worse. There were roaches in the toaster, roaches in an empty refrigerator, and a hot plate to make their only meals.—Usually rice and beans or ramen noodles.—When it was time to sleep they shared their linen-less floors and cots with those same roaches. Cheris's boy-friend's family eventually took her in. Without her to look after The Boy threw himself into his music, doing whatever it took to get his name out there, including hanging out at after school programs for the artsy crowd. There it was cool to bum food or money, recite verses, and flirt with the females. As hard as he tried he'd yet to find another friend like his muse in Maryland. The closest he'd come was a soulful and talented dancer named Ananda. She was seventeen, chocolate chai, and passionate about her afro-centricity. After days of running game all his lines had gone in one ear and out the other until the sixteen he dedicate to the freedom of political prisoner Nelson Mandela caught her attention. After the workshop they got to know one another.

Ananda pointed to the house.

"That's it right there. I appreciate you walking with me."

"Fugetaboutit, I appreciate you letting me."

"What are you doing over the holiday break?"

"I 'ont know."

The weather was as inclimate as it gets in The Amazon. Still Ananda thought The Boy looked cold and lonely.

"Well where are you going now," she asked?

"I 'ont know," he said, chewing his lip.

Against her better judgment Ananda gave him a phone number.

"Go hang out somewhere for like thirty minutes then call here. The lady I baby-sit for should be gone then and you can come in for a while."

The home was simple but comfortable; clean, warm, and airy. A paragon of what The Boy had always wanted for his family.

"This is nice. This lady's got good taste; but I thought you said she was white."

"She is."

"Why she got all this African stuff then," he asked observing the paintings and Egyptian statues?

"Her husband is black, but she does the decorating. She's into all kinds of stuff, you'd like her. In class she calls us her 'babies.' She says she's got as many children as there are stars."

"She sounds cool. What they got to eat in here."

"Nothing fixed. I can cook if I want, but I never do."

"Why not?"

"I don't cook." Ananda's voice was filled with entitlement. "My mama takes care of all that."

"That's a damn shame. Let me see what's in here."

The Boy made himself at home in the kitchen. He fixed his specialty; turkey tacos with big chunks of garlic.

After the meal Ananda put the child to bed early and started on her second helping while The Boy looked over the family's book case.

"Damn Ananda, your girl got some really good shit here. I read some of these books and the others I wanted to read, but I aint had time for that lately."

Ananda was licking her fingers. She barely heard him over her chewing.

"Umm hmm, these tacos are fire. Where did you learn how to cook?"

"My old G taught me the basics. I picked up the rest myself. It's easy to learn when that's the only way you gon' eat. My stepfather lived in Mexico for a minute; he taught me that recipe there. It's the cumin."

"Where is your family now," asked Ananda. Why don't you stay …?"

"Don't ask me 'bout my past, it was all bad."

Ananda respected his privacy and there was an uncomfortable silence until The Boy broke it with a question.

"You smokin'?"

"No, I'm babysitting."

"That baby is *sleep*. C'mon we'll go outside and blow this joint before I break out."

"It's not that late, you can stay a little longer."

Mistaking her kindness for an invitation he pushed up on her.

"Stop! What did I tell you?"

He scoffed.

"Man, I don't believe that shit."

"Well you better get it through your big head," she said as she opened the door.

Back inside Ananda relaxed, stretched out on the couch, and played with her twists while The Boy massaged her feet and read 'February 1932' from *The Diary of Anais Nin;*

"*L' Amoure das un taxi … The big woman … the small woman …*"

Ananda was giggling. She blushed and grabbed at the book.

"Let me see it; that's not really in there."

"Yes it is. I'm telling you this chick was live."

"She is crazy. Read some more," demanded Ananda breathing heavy and fast.

The Boy read until they both lay absolutely still, hours passed and neither woke.

The woman entered her home to find a strange male asleep in her living room. Warily she made her way to the child's room.

"*Safe.*"

She followed her nose to the kitchen and found the dishes and stove clean. She unwrapped the leftovers and took a bite.

"*Good.*" she thought on her way to wake the sitter.

Ananda leapt to her feet startled.

"Mehiel, what time is it?"

"1:30 in the morning."

Her tone demanded an explanation.

"Oh I'm sorry," said Ananda. "Uhh, this is the boy I've been telling you about." She stepped on his foot to wake him.

"That's nice. Can you explain what he's doing in my house?"

Ananda hesitated as The Boy introduced himself and tried to smooth things out.

"Please don't blame Ananda Mrs. Abdul. It was bad out there tonight and she was helping me by letting me rest here for a while. Straight up, we weren't doin' nothin', just reading some of your books. You have some great books by the way …"

"Thank you. But I'm more interested in why you couldn't do that at your house."

"'The animals have their caves the birds of the sky have their nests but the son of man has no place to rest his head.' I guess you could say I'm a heretic too."

"Mehiel looked at him curiously.

"Jesus said the same thing about himself."

"So did Kahlil Gibran in that book you're reading."

Mehiel looked to the counter where the book was sticking out of her purse. "You've read *Spirits Rebellious?*"

The Boy arranged the words in his mind.

"What did he say?"

"It is the answer for every man who wants to follow the Spirit of Truth in this age of falsehood, hypocrisy and corruption."

The biggest of smiles came across Mehiel's face.

"I told you he was something special," said Ananda.

Turkish coffee kept the three awake and breaking down one subject or another until well into the morning. Mehiel listened as the eighteen year old high school drop out critiqued a panoply of philosophers.

"Camus is my man, but Freud was a fag, and who cares what Nietzsche says. He was miserable. How you gon' tell me "God is dead!" Oh yeah, well kill yourself and find out for sure."

Mehiel explained to him how she got involved with The Children's Workshop.

"My mother was a love child! She was off into the San Francisco, Haight-Ashbury scene; tie dye, Timothy Leary, Aldous Huxley, all that. When the wave broke she washed up in L.A. where she met my father. Then I came along and we moved to an all black neighborhood in Watts. This was after all the trouble and they still welcomed us. They gave me a nickname. 'Lady Me.' My mother got really involved with the community and The Movement; you know, making the world a better place and all."

The Boy could relate.

"I know exactly what you mean."

"She was always gone somewhere, or doing something like a little kid," said Mehiel. "I swear, sometimes I feel like my father raised me, and I raised her. I couldn't wait to be on my own"

The Boy spoke again.

"I know something about that one too."

"My father wrote music so there was always a bunch of artist types around. I must have been twelve or thirteen when I learned the secret of artists. Do you know what it is?"

"Nope. What is it," he wondered?

"Artists don't have secrets. They don't tell lies, and they live their lives in the open for all to see. Their work is from the spirit and that makes it timeless.

She continued talking, marinating The Boy's brain in thought. As far as he could tell, Mehiel was a five foot one, one hundred thirteen pound body of opposites; young but old, rich but poor, graceful as a gazelle and at the same time lost as a sheep.

"Oh I was totally gone when I lived in Manchester," she said slapping her thigh. "I couldn't find he fog, the Beatles or me. I sobered up and was like, 'Where's California?' That's when I came home and met Rich ... we believe it's not enough to say you care; you've got to spread the word or when you die you'll come back again."

Somehow it all seemed to work out for her. She was probably the most well balanced person The Boy had ever met.

"Look at the time. C'mon Ananda, let me get you home."

Already Mehiel had found a special place in her heart for her new "baby;" there was no way she was sending him back to the streets.

"You stay here and watch the baby."

The Boy couldn't find the words. He showered her with thanks as she found him some linens and things.

"Thanks so much Mrs. Abdul and thanks for believing me when I told you we weren't doin' nothing."

"What? I was never worried about that." She and Ananda giggled as they walked out the door. "Ananda's not interested in boys."

That morning when they woke Mehiel phoned Rich and smoothed things over with him. The Boy displayed his full range of domestic skills, performing all the tasks you wouldn't expect from a teenager, though his foremost role in the coming weeks would be that of Mehiel's assistant. His knowledge, wordplay, and minor celebrity being the link she needed to express her ideas of education and love of the arts to her youthful audience; but all that ended when her husband came home.

"Hey baby. It's so good to see you how was the tour," asked Mehiel?

"Good, sweetheart." He kissed her. "Really nice; how's everything here?"

"Great. The baby's at day care, she missed her daddy. Come here. Rich I'd like you to meet the young man I told you about."

Rich was intimidating; tall and dark as onyx with big eyes, dreads and a slight belly. He made The Boy backdafuckup when they shook hands. Rich stayed quiet for a long time, just listening as he did all the talking.

"So what kind of band you play in?"

"I'm a percussionist," said Rich. "I specialize in African music."

"Oh. ____ I'm more into Hip-Hop."

"They're one in the same to me. What they're doing now is the same as African tribes used to do to communicate and celebrate with each other. It's just smoothed out on the rhythm tip with a pop feel to it."

The Boy gave him some dap.

"I like that, that's catchy."

"So Mehiel says you're an urban poet. Let me hear something."

"Man you gon' put me on the spot just like that? A'ight, I got somethin' for you." He opened up and recite a couple of special rhymes that he'd written, to be said only for the righteous and in the depths of solitude.

Rich clapped.

"I like that man. I'm feeling it, I'm feeling it. I got a good feeling about you. You're on your way!"

THE AMAZON
1990

An obtuse and emaciated Marian arrived just before the New Year causing The Boy all kinds of pain and confusion seeing her so weak. His hero, the Queen of The Movement who'd taught him to forever be strong and never give up, now seemingly welcomed her own defeat. The sight of her drained his energy. Random imagery caused him to lose focus. He couldn't deal with those emotions now. He was chasing his dream. A few more pixels and he could touch it.

Putting to use the skills he'd perfected here; he inured his heart of glass to one of stone before diving headfirst into the river of Lethe; that fabled river that leads both the weak and the strong into an immense heart of darkness.

After less than a week he spent his last dime on her a bus ticket to her sister's home in New York. During rare moments of levity he wondered if he'd ever see her face again; not the mask she wore to hide the truth neither of them could accept, but her real face; the one that he remembered as a child, like Maria, full of grace.

His adopted family did their best to keep him positive. Rich had been planning something special. This day they glide into studio 617 on a Funk Mob baseline as rich and smooth as molasses.

"Whoa. Is that yo' band bumping the bass?"

Rich looked at him and moved his head to groove.

"You ever heard of the group Subway?"

"Yeah, but I aint never heard nothing that funky!"

Rich and Mehiel smiled.

"They're recording their new disk, my band records next door; they asked me if I wanted to fill in on a few tracks. I said, cool. Then I mentioned you. You got a meeting with their manager right now. This is it; the rest is up to you."

Rich parked the car and The Boy gave them both big hugs when they got out. Subway's manager A-Train met them at the car.

"How you doing Rich; you ready to do the damn thang?"

"Always." Rich held up his sticks. "This is my wife Mehiel, and over there peeking in your studio is the guy I was telling you about. The group walked to the door where The Boy stood with his mouth open watching the crew of Subway get naughty, squeezing and kissing a bevy of blow up dolls.

"What about you trooper, you ready?"

The answer was in his eyes.

"You want me to spit a few bars," he asked?

A-Train chuckled.

"I like this kid," he said. "I listened to your demo; well get to that later. For now you think you can handle one of them hotties on stage, because that's what we really need. It's not glamorous and it doesn't pay much but ..."

"Man I feel blessed that I got the chance. This is my passion, I'ma do it weather I'm paid or not."

Mehiel rubbed The Boy's back.

"Good." said A-Train. "Then it's a done deal." He point to some of the other members. That funny looking dude over there is G-Train. The short guy is B-Train and I'm A-Train. Welcome aboard. We're the freaks of the industry."

THE LOWER ASTRAL PLANE

Storm clouds rumbled in the realm of illusion. The cries of misbegotten entities with bloodshot eyes compete with the roar of the sea. On the shore bells tinkled throughout the great hall as the lords of karma came forth to greet.

"A'ight, one more time. I'ma take a journey through life, so I can see how I landed here."

"If home is heaven, and this aint, I got some big choices to make."
  "Blessed are the meek: For they shall inherit the earth."
  "That's too much work." "Mad dough ... truck chains ... fat asses"
  "Yeah playboy, that's how I'ma live!"
  "Fuck that bitch."
  "I heard about them cats. They went outta town and blew up, then a few months later bodies started showing up."
  "Y'all cool out here for a few, I'ma talk some business with my man."
  "You on the team now. You'll be there."

"And so I am."

"Shit seems obvious now. Can it be that I was so simple then? Has time rewritten the pages of my mind? What if had the chance to do it all again? How would I?
  First, home is where the heart is.
  Patience is a virtue.
  Nothing is ever too much—except in matters of materialism.
  The future's not ours to see.
  Honor thy mother.
  Thou shalt not kill.
  I should've listened to Ais that day outside the barbershop."

"That shit was real."

"Ok, so it was the end of '89 and I'm knee deep in the crack game. We, knee deep in it, the whole Yung Gunz crew, everybody gettin' paid, sportin' waves, and Gazelle frames. Somehow the cops always knew where to go, other dealers was gettin' popped off left and right, and we was getting all they customers. We had the avenue sewed up. We aint never wait for work. Soon as we got low, we just hit A-D on the hip, and Abracadabra! We had whatever we needed."

"Playboy A-D!"

"That nigga wasn't never hurtin'; even in the middle of a drought he was the only one with work."

"Hmm."

"I could'a been large like that. I should'a listened to him."

BROOKLYN
1989

Phat crome Anteras hydroplaned on the slushy asphalt as the jet black 850i cruised down Fulton. It stopped at Thomas's stoop. Victor jogged up to it peering through the tint.

"Yo who the fuck driving this? The invisible man." Julius laughed as the window came down slow. "Aw, y'all niggas chill, it's A-D."

Thomas got up and went to the car. Victor continued mean-mugging as the other commoners hung back admiring the king's chariot.

"Ohh, the rulers back," said Thomas! "Mu'fucka we aint heard from you in over a month. Where you disappear to playboy; shoppin' for whips?"

A-D gave him a pound.

"Maintaining; I been a prisoner of circumstance," he said, eyeing Victor. "You got a new shooter?"

"That's my nigga Vic'; the one It's holding them burners for. Nigga just came home, nowhere to stay, trying to get on. He'll have the paramedics talkin' slow and breathin' soft on 'em. You know, that "what's-your-name, where-you-from, who-shot-cha, shit?"

A-D looked ahead rubbing his chin.

"Right. What it be like over here?"

"We been made quota. I was gon' hit Theo later tonight. You want it now?"

"Nah, Nah. G'head and do that. I was just passing through. I heard it's been hot 'round here. Y'all got enough heat?"

Thomas laughed.

"Do we? We got seven mac-elevens, 'round eight thirty-eight's, nine nine's, ten mac-ten's. The heat don't end. My crib look like A'hnald's in Commando."

A-D gave him a pound.

"A'ight nigga remember the seventh commandment."
"*Seventh comma …?*" Thomas caught himself and smiled as A-D pulled off.

✳

"That's where I failed."

"*Two weeks later Five-O kick my door down talkin' 'bout, 'Where are the weapons?' Moms damn near had a heart attack. Mu'fuckas dragged a nigga outside in his drawers and socks. But I wasn't sweating it. My first time gettin' popped. They aint get but two guns. No bodies on 'em. But all the money I had stacked went to bail and I was still a couple hundred short. Moms put it up. She posted and didn't even wait for me. I aint have no dough. I had to walk all the way home from Central Booking.*"

"That's when the real trouble started."

"*When I get home Sinatra is playing and all my shit is packed.*"

BROOKLYN
1989

"Tho'mas I'm sick. I can't take dis' no more. You got to go."
"I don't have no place to go ma?"

A mother's work lasts a lifetime, and for single mothers, it's two. The years had taken their toll on Gaietta; she deserved some help and a companion. As questions of mortality began invading her thoughts, she cringed when she realized the one she'd invested in may have bore bitter fruit.

"Dats not my prob'lem. I'm tired. I don't know what to do wit' you no more. You don't listen. You do da fool ting and drop out of school to hang in da street. You want to be grown? It's time for you to go den. All my years in da' states and me own son be da' one to bring trou'ble t'rough my door. Call your pa'pa, go hang out with da riff-raff 'dere. I jus' wan' you gone Thomas!"

"Why you always doin' this to me," Thomas asked grievingly?

"Don't blame me. You do dis to your'self. *You* choose dis life."

"So did you Ma."

✳

"I took my shit and stayed at Julius's for a few days. The twins had moved and them niggas said nic's went for twenty's down in The Tarheel State. Huh. I hit A-D; he gave me a lil' somthin' on consignment and I hopped a bus."

"Power move."

"I'm down there in the "triangle" for like two weeks trying to be rich instead of seem it. That's all the time it took for them people to get to know my face."

"Popped again."

"I sat there for a spell before I got extradited to N.Y. on a vop. I aint gon' lie, hearing the slam of that great steel gate kind of set my ass straight. I think. My celly was this cool mu'fucka named Rumi. He didn't talk much; his head was forever stuck in a book. One morning I asked him what he'd learned from all that reading.
    He answered, 'The paths are different but the goal is one.'
    Whatever. But something about that shit stuck wit me.

"I couldn't go back to sleep."

"I picked up a book he had on numerology. Sixty sixties, equal one. Twenty four of those equal one. Thirty or so of those, one; and twelve of those."

"I wasn't even tryin' to see that one."

"But I was getting closer to it; wholeness, God and the universe. All that thinking had my head hurting. Rumi said I should try "The Spiritual Exercises." I never did. I wasn't on the working out tip, 'cause of my asthma. So I got my "college" education on. I learned how to mix dip and hooch, make shivs, fly kites, give tat's, draw murals, stretch grams, all that, but I couldn't stop counting. It was one thousand eight hundred and sixty holes in my steel bunk. Four hundred and fifteen bricks on the walls of our hut and sixty-six bars on the gate to it. I hadn't seen the world in two hundred and eighty six days. Then on the two hundred and eighty-seventh one."

RIKERS ISLAND
1990

"Open C74. Neece!"

Thomas's body lay in "The Bing," his eyes open and facing the ceiling.
  "Wake yo' ass up Mr. Neece," yelled the turn-key! "Let's go."
  Thomas heard his mother sing.

"Think, plot, plan, dream; make, write, dance, sing. I love you Thomas. Leave the riff-raff alone, and fo'cus on being king."

Thomas blinked and swallowed before he answered.
  "I'm wide awake."
  "Allow me to walk you to the door," said the C.O. "So how you feel leaving us?"
  "C'mon duke. What kinda dumbass question is that man? I'm trying to get the fuck up out this joint, yo."
  "Yeah, yeah; we'll see you again. It's just a matter of time."
  "G'head. I'ont know what you on, but you wont see *me* in this mu'fucka no more. Y'all niggas get ready. I got big plans. They gon' call me, "King of Kings.""

BROOKLYN
June '93

Thomas had yet to be crowned and his "college" education had lasted about as long as it took him to smoke his first L. Back on his block it was all the same, only some names had changed, but at home Gaietta was smiling and her reasons gave Thomas something to smile about.

The bright white limousine cruised down Fulton stopping at Thomas's stoop. Victor jogged up to it peering through the tint.
  "That nigga A-D dun' snapped," yelled Julius!
  The window slid down and he mean mugged the middle aged chauffeur with the thick accent.
  "Hey buddy, any of you guys know where I can find The Kid?"
  Victor stood in his usual spot.
  "Who the fuck is asking?"

A cloud of smoke spiraled from the sunroof, through it, a genie-like head and body appeared.

"Tell him it's his mu'fuckin homeboy from last night."

Victor dropped his gun

"Oh shit!"

The Kid took his headphones off, dropped his rhyme book, and rushed the car with a huge smile.

"Mr. Postman! What the fuck is you doin' 'round my way?"

"What? You thought I was on some bullshit, nigga? I told you I was coming through."

J.I. stepped out of the limo to greet Thomas with a fifth of Hennessy in hand.

The Boy followed him, their necks, wrists, and fingers, heavy with old school jewels; two scintillating figures dancing in the eyes of the seniors who peeked through their windows at the commotion as the hood went crazy. Little kids ran up calling The Boy's name. Sisters gave him kisses and thugs gave him pounds; some even asked for autographs as Thomas introduced his new friends to his old ones.

"I told you Bed-Stuy got love for you," he said?

The Boy was happy to be back.

"Good, cause I aint got nothin' but love for them; all of New York. This shit remind me of the old school, baby;

I remember gettin' fresh in my shell toes and Lee's and gettin' blitzed off tre bags with too many seeds.

Hopping the turnstile to get to the party, Red Alert on the wheels, Ricky D singin' 'La Di Da Di,' and when them niggas'd shout, 'It's Brooklyn in the house,' and throw up they hood signs, Mu'fuckers from Park Hill to Brownsville would loose they goddamn mind!"

Thomas knew that feeling too.

"I came through the door, said it before."

The Boy shouted.

"Yo, that was the shit!"

"But as we turn the page to nineteen-ninety-three," added Thomas, "niggas is gettin' smoked 'G;' believe me."

In minutes J.I. and the others had killed the fifth. "Yo Kid, where the store at? We need some mo' Hen,'" he yelled!

"And some weed too," added The Boy. "Shiiit', I'm here to *kick it*. Where the yamps at?"

Thomas ordered Victor to hold down the fort and told Julius to run and tell Tootie he'd be right back.

"Tootie. Who is that? Is that cha' woman," asked The Boy as they entered the car?

Julius looked Thomas's way and laughed as he and J.I traded war stories.

"Nah," said Thomas. "That's just a lil' hoochie I gassed up. I told her she could be lieutenant. I got her upstairs babysittin' my daughter."

Thomas gave the chauffer the destination and they pulled off.

"You got a shorty," asked The Boy?

"Yeah dog, I wouldn't be out here no more if it wasn't for her. I got too much to lose. Dizzy keep screaming, 'hold on,' Like he *En Vouge* and shit, but lil' mama can't eat no promises."

"I feel that. He aint look like he was hurting at all. My guy Roberko said his label is bout to blast off. How'd y'all get together?"

Thomas was on ten, laughing as the limo darted in and out of traffic.

"Man that shit right there was crazy. You know how jail changes a nigga. I mean they had me scared straight, I wasn't even steamin'. Soon as I got home I started writing. I was in my room for months just writing and fucking. Then my girl hit me with the news. I told mom duke I had a shorty on the way and she started bugging again. So I started hanging out in Mecca with the Nation just to get outta the crib. It's some cool brothers there. We'd leave the parliaments and go freestylin' at all the spots. I was at The Tunnel like fuckin' every night.

You know Peter Parker don't you?"

"The Dj?"

"Yeah, that's my nigga. He got a juicy lil' sister named Sasi, she 'ont stay too far from here, we should slide through there ... But anyway, Pete liked my shit.

He told me to make a tape and he'd put it out there. That blew me up. He gave it to dude at *The Source* and this fly chick named Mycha. Mycha got a baby by Dizzy. She liked it; she laid the tape on that nigga and let him know shit was real." Thomas exhaled hard. "Huh. I aint gon' lie; Playboy came through in a nick of time. I was close to sayin' fuck the world, my moms, and my girl."

Desperation breeds inspiration.

"Yeah it be like that sometimes," said The Boy.

The rapport on Nostrand and St. Johns was the same as on Fulton. There The Boy surprised them all when he bought out the spot and wanted more.

Next the limousine stopped near Franklin and Dean, at the corner, yellow tape preserved a crime scene.

White chalk and brains all over the sidewalk, while detectives questioned witnesses who refused to talk.

"I swear, I don't know *what* he looked like officer. All I know is he had a gun."

"You wanna play games, asshole? You can play 'em all day in jail. Let's go."

"Man ya'll on bullshit! What's the charge?"

"I'll think of one! The rest of you get the fuck off this corner. This is *my* corner now!"

"That's ill," said Thomas. "Let's see what happened."

Thomas led The Boy around back to a trench where the soldiers had dug in.

"Yo somebody's comin'."

Multiple guns cocked.

"Y'all niggas chill," said Thomas coolly, "it's me."

"Aww, w'sup Kid? Yo you almost caught a hot one playboy ... *Ohhh shit,* look who this nigga got wit' him.

The Boy bought out another spot while Thomas got the scoop from his man.

"... he had a hood on, but we know who it was." He leaned in and spoke lightly in Thomas's ear. There was surprise on Thomas' face when he glanced at The Boy who was busy counting out the dealer's money. Back in the limo Thomas questioned him.

"How you and Roberko hook up?"

"At a party in Miami last summer. Him and them Carol City Cartel niggas is so major out there they had me wondering how I could be down. We hung out, he introduced me to some of his boys, a flashy lil' nigga named ..."

Thomas finished his sentence.

"Treni."

"Yeah. You heard of him?"

"Every live nigga in N.Y. dun' heard of Treni."

This time The Boy read Thomas' face.

"I know about Treni *and* Glover," said The Boy. I know how them niggas do."

Thomas looked relieved.

"Long as you know. Cause word is they get shady baby."

"I know. What about Dizzy?"

"Right. So Diz' pulls up in a black 'Vette banging the tape. Me and my nigga Othello was sittin' on the stoop. I'm trying out some new rhymes on him and Diz' hops out the car looking spooked. Othello was like, 'Who is this scary ass nigga?' I'm like, 'Yo, dude where you get my tape?' I swear the niggas eyes got big as saucers when he seen me. He was like 'That's *you*? Yo, let me holla at you 'B," that's when Othello peeped the Youth Authority jacket he was wearing and flipped the fuck out. I'll never forget how hyped he was, jumpin' around screaming;

'Aww shit! My nigga finta get signed. It's 'bout to go down. We aint gotta sell this shit no more. It's over, we 'bout to be on some real shit!' After Dizzy got over how I looked, we hit it off. He said my flow was so smooth it sounds like I be singing instead of rapping ..."

"That flow is unbelievable," thought The Boy, *"Maybe better than mine."*

"... he gave me his card and I signed with Y.A. the next week."

The Boy lit a blunt and gave it to Thomas.

"That shit felt good, didn't it?"

"It did ... for like a second." Thomas took a long pull. "Othello and his people was hurting. He had two kids, his sister had four, *and* she was on the pipe. When Diz' came through, he had already planned to make a move down south on some come up shit. He left that next day. The day I signed with Y.A. I ran home to hit him with the news, that's when his cousins told me he had got moped out that morning. That shit fucked me up." Thomas threw back a big gulp of cognac and looked away. "I wanted to tell him to stay here, but you know how that go. One man can't eat off another's mans dream. I miss my nigga though."

The Boy let the windows down on both sides.

"Well don't let the liquor get like that. Tip that shit over."

Thomas followed his lead as they both poured out more than a little Hennessy.

"I went through that with a couple of my homies in Cali. I think everyone in every 'hood have. Mu'fuckas don't understand how it is when your man is lying on the pavement twisted."

"They 'ont know. That happened over a year ago and Dizzy say my shit aint droppin' till *next year*. We been putting my name out there. He'll throw me a lil' paper when he can or when we do a show. Hey, good lookin' on lettin' me rock the mic last night."

"Man fuck that," said The Boy. "I'm getting money." He went in his pocket and gave Thomas a G. "And I want all my niggas to get it with me. It's enough of that shit for everybody to eat."

"I heard that."

They traded pounds.

"So," asked Thomas, "what's up nigga? What's your story? You got albums, movies, you on TV; shit, you got politicians talking about you ..."

"That punk can eat a dick, he aint do nothin' but blow my name up. The movie thing; I just fell into that. My man B-Train was going to this audition. I went with him and ended up getting the part. Since then everybody's been throwing roles at me but I been busy trying to stay outta jail. These bitches got me crooked in all fifty states."

Thomas knew about all the cases, he was a regular in the tabloids. I know, sometimes I hear bitches shittin' on you like, 'He got all that money, why he keep doing stupid shit?'"

"I can't stand fake ass bitches like that," said The Boy angrily! "They act like I'm *tryin' to* go to jail. You know I got a price on my head?"

"Yeah," Thomas replied calmly, "it's the price of fame." The Boy realized he was right and Thomas asked; "Fuck them. How you get in the game?"

The Boy told the chauffer to drive around Bed-Stuy and waste a little time. Then with no hesitation he went straight into his past.

"You know about my mother and all that right?"

"Just the lil' bit they said in the magazine article. She seems mad cool."

"Man, don't get me started, my mama smoked so damn much ... Anyway, pops was a joke. I used to find dope in his coat, and they would always tell me not to smoke. We aint have shit, no money, no car; me and my little sister never did nothin' or went nowhere. Around '84 I started sneaking out, smoking and doing graffiti, just little shit like that. Shit didn't really get ugly till I got to Maryland. It was all these dumb shitty niggas that was always trying me cause I was skinny and on some different shit. The only thing I miss about there was the school I went to. We was doing all kinds of shit. That's where I got the acting bug. If I could'a stayed there I might've been ok."

"You know what I mean?"

Thomas shook his head.

"Yeah."

"Why you leave," he asked?

The Boy took a deep breath and expelled what had been eating at him for so long.

"It was this one nigga, stayed on Decatur whenever he seen me he had somethin' to say. One day I'm comin' out the crib walkin' to the bus stop with this chick I was fuckin' wit. This nigga sitting across the street on the porch popping shit and tryin' to holla at her. I'm thinking, 'Damn I'ma have to go over there and square off with all these mu'fuckas.' Then old girl just run up on they porch and set it off, called dude all kinds if punks and trick bitches.

Now all his homies and they girls is straight clownin' him."

"What they do to your girl?"

"Nothin'. We got on the bus and I rode her home." The Boy smiled. "You seen her too."

"Who is it?"

The Boy shook his head.

"Never kiss and tell."

"Aww, you gon' do ya' boy like that," asked Thomas jokingly? "Was it the one from last night?"

"Petula? Nah. I'll tell you about her later."

"So when I get back around the crib I see these niggas in the gas station and dude is talking big shit now. He mad than a mu'fucka he got punk'd by a girl. So he run up on me and smacks me in the face."

"Bitch move."

"Right. So I grabbed a screwdriver off the wall and go after this nigga. His boys held me back while his bitch ass ran away."

"That's some bullshit."

"I know. But it was my fault."

"How?"

"Cause I had fucked around and got soft. That school had me thinking shit was sweet. After that I aint never leave the crib without my strap."

"You ever see the nigga again." The Boy paused. He and The Kid were eye to eye.

You know it. That's when I moved to Cali."

"What's it like out there?"

"Shit. The streets out there are death row. These other niggas is copycats, Bloods and Crips is *G's!* They got blocks so hot the police won't go on 'em out there. If they on you and you get to that street, you made it cause they aint coming on that mu'fucka, not without backup and some riot gear."

Thomas smiled and passed him the L before urging;

"So how you get in the game?"

"My homie J.I. hooked us up a demo and we promote it for a minute. Then I met this white girl. Her husband got me an audition with them Subway niggas.

I went all around the world touring with them. They manager became my manager, we did another demo, he sent it to the people at Periscope and they called."

"Damn I should *been* sendin' out demos then."

"Wait though," The Boy elbowed The Kid, "this the crazy part. Them niggas wasn't even listening to my disk. One of Periscopes owners, this super rich white boy, his daughter was goin' through the bullshit bin listening to disks; *she* was the one who liked it so they signed me off that."

"How do the daughter look? Did you hit that?"

"Nah nigga, she was like fourteen."

"Damn! Dizzy always saying it be them goody-goody white girls who love our shit."

"He right. That's why when you put your single out, you always put out something for the bitches. Cause niggas buy what bitches want to hear."

"But I don't know a nigga that don't love yo' shit? I been telling mu'fuckas you the realest nigga in the game."

The Boy thanked him with a pound.

"Yo, what's the deal with the one from last night?"

"Same thing we was just talking about; little rich girl, just got to college, studying communications. Her and her girl sneaked to the club to hang out. You know who her daddy is?"

"Who?"

Thomas's eyes were as hungry as those in the limos rearview. The Boy leaned closer and answered him.

"Whaaat!"

"Guess who her man is?"

Thomas was all ears as The Boy whispered again.

Thomas yelled;

"Slow down baby! *Not Mr. Goodbar?*"

"Nigga, you better ask somebody! She came at me like, 'You know blahzy, blah?' and I'm like, 'He cool wit me.' She said, 'That's my man.' And I'm like, 'Oh, he smart enough to have you, but dumb enough to let 'chu out.'"

Thomas laughed loudly.

"Man I got the details on that buster," said The Boy. "Dude be straight doggin' her, punchin' her throwin' around the house, lockin' her up in his grandma's basement."

"Yeah, he seems like that type of guy."

"So I'm on her like, 'What's the deal baby, 'cause I only got one night in town? Can you get away?' We get to her hotel room and she throw on R. Kelly's Twelve Play, I'm drinkin', she rollin' …"

Thomas asked a totally unrelated question. He had to know.

"What's up with R. Kelly and that little girl?"

The Boy threw his hands in the air.

"I 'on't know man, he like us; still young trying to figure it all out. Nigga need to ask heaven for a hug though."

"But the ho's love that nigga."

"Yep."

"So you drinkin' she's rollin', ___ you aint gotta say no more. I saw how she was on you. What 'chu do with her?"

"Just kept it real, put that thug passion in her."

They laughed and gave each other dap.

"Stick with me Kid, I'ma help get you through this shit."

Thomas went against the third commandment when he invited him to the spot where he rest at. They pushed open the door and entered the 36 chambers.

Excerpt 47.

The second they were in Julius screamed;

"Yo Kid, the pies still wet, we can't bag yet. I'ma stick 'em in the microwave?"

"And fuck it up like you did last time. Nah. Use the hair dryer."

"Yo," said The Boy turning up the radio, "I love these niggas!"

Julius asked who else he listened to and soon everybody joined in and represent for '93.

"Y'all probably aint heard of this MC," said Thomas, "but I got to represent for my man The Prophet, he's coming."

CHEMMIS

In the sands of The Two Lands a prophet rest osmoses in Ka. The coming of Ra would mark the twentieth anniversary of this, his born day, and the start of the night journey back his phylum in the valley of the dead; his hunger for knowledge quelled by history from The Papyrus of Any, his thirst for wisdom quenched by waters from the river Nile, his *netcher* once heavy, uplifted by the angels gift of,

SOLACE

"Have we not caused thy bosom to dilate
and eased thee of the burden
which weighed down thy back,
and exalted thy fame?
But lo! With hardship goeth ease,
Lo! With hardship goeth ease.
So when thou art relieved, still toil
and strive to please thy Lord."

1994

KINGS OF NEW YORK

By 1993 whispers had reached the West. The *Ennead* rumored to restore Triumph to the East had arrived. Fearing the title they'd held since '91 was in jeopardy Firing Squad unleashed it's most dangerous MC to protect their neck. K9's disk, one that would eventually generate forty-five million dollars in retail sales, was the most sought after in rap music history. Periscope had been rescued from the brink of bankruptcy by two acts; their gamble with The Boy and their investment in Firing Squad Records. THC cost a quarter million to make and had earned them an estimated 50 million dollars in less than two years, and each day that passed meant a chance at a new case, more fame, and increased soundscans for The Boy. That year on *Samhain*, the soldier took revenge on a couple of spooks in Atlanta and basically turned water to wine for the last of the infidels who never thought that Hip-Hopers would take it that far; the ones who refused to believe that we were turning our father's dreams into markets and a living breathing economy. What quickly became paramount though was the inspiration that this Hip-Hop generation had provided the burden-bearers, in only fifteen years their peers had emerged as multimillionaires. Suddenly we had nice clothes, nice watches, nice women and rings, but some couldn't relate to those who didn't have nice things. So while the nations celebrate, we kicked back and we wait, knowing this year was inevitable. This summer? Unforgettable. The streets tweaked for weeks with niggas too geeked to sleep, arguing over who was the best MC, Thomas, A-D, or Malik.

QB

Excerpt 48.

Fatima turned her stereo down to answer the knock at her bedroom door. The apartment was quiet these days; she and Sirius had decided years ago that in order for their love to last they should go their separate ways. Bagira was grinding, he popped in maybe twice a week to drop off money and change clothes; and Malik it seemed, had just made it home.

He stuck his head in the door.

"Hey ma, you got a sec?"

Fatima took off her glasses and marked her page in *Deepak Chopra's,* Ageless Body, Timeless Mind with them.

"Sure, I think I can spare a few of those."

Malik—the adult version-entered the room dressed in jeans and a tee, Timbs and a Nike jacket. His wavy hair and chipped tooth were gleaming when he bent over and hugged his mother, "the man" momentarily giving way to a youthful demeanor that reminded her of the days when he couldn't hold himself and pee right.

"Where's Pop at?"

Fatima reminded him that Sirius was out of town. She could tell he was in one of his moods and offered her ear instead.

"What's up?"

"Nothin', can't a guy just converse with his old earth."

"You don't conversate for sport Malik; if you're talking you've got something to say. Out with it? How's my grandchild; is she Ok?"

After years of trying Karma had finally come to Malik after Chico caught a sentence in '90. For better or worse they were a couple now and their on and off again relationship had produced a beautiful baby girl.

"She's fine."

"And her mother?"

"Fine, they're fine." Malik sat in the chair next to Fatima's bed. "What's wrong with me ma." He sounded stressed. "Why cant I just be normal like everybody else, I see black people outside, living, loving, and enjoying they lives, and I be thinking. 'Why can't that be me?' I want to hang out and talk to people, but …"

Fatima comforted him.

"There's nothing wrong with you Malik. You can't help being introverted, it's part of what make you, you."

Since '89 Malik had virtually banished himself to his room in search of the miraculous. He'd taken a leave from his studies with the N.O.I. and become a spiritual nomad; his expeditions taking him out into the wilderness and back to the cradle of life where he was astonished to learn how for a period in history his ancestors were the wealthiest in the world; their continent home to the most advanced civilizations where students of all races and faiths traversed desert sands to learn from *imams* at the most distant universities in the world, the *Djenne* and *Sankore* mosques. And then there was Egypt of course, the link to Arabia, the holy land, and home to mysteries buried so deep that to this day masons, archeologists and Egyptologists are busy excavating antiquities in the valley of kings. Even more surprising was how school had taught him that Greek society was the beginning of modern culture but his teachers had failed to inform him where Alexander and the other greats had stolen much of their knowledge from. Now that he'd recovered some of it he'd come home eager to share.

"But if you want to be social," asked Fatima, "what's stopping you?"

"No one's interested in what I got to say. All people talk about around here is crimes and jail. I aint with that. To me they waste time with empty arguments; they never have real conversation. I want people to learn something from my lyrics but that aint what's selling right now."

She took his hand.

"My son the Bodhisattva?"

"What's that?"

"Buddhism. The bodhisattvas are enlightened beings. They're in line to be future Buddhas and can pass into Nirvana whenever they wish, but they put it off so that they can help others on the path. I can understand why you're lonely, that kind of compassion springs from a deeper well than most of us have. When the average person finds a little slice of happiness they run with it."

Malik scoffed.

"Really," asked Fatima, "can you blame them? What would you do if heaven was a mile away?"

Malik point to himself.

"I aint satisfied with just a slice of happiness. Success to me is the whole pie; I want my people to eat too."

"Success and failure are what each person determines them to be."

"Well," asked Malik, "what about people that say that say, 'no idea's original', and 'everything that's worth saying has already been said.' Sometimes," he confessed, "I feel like a failure for saying things that have been said in the past."

"I believe that if anyone has the ability to teach something then they should do it. If only one person learns from them how could there ever be failure in that? Maybe your job is to put information into a form that your peers can understand."

"It seems like it's a thankless job," he said, "and more than I signed on for."

"If you don't do it, who will? The ability to tell a story is a gift, and like the saying goes, 'To whom much is given, much is required.' Fatima let him consider that for a moment before asking. "So what was it that you wanted to talk about anyway?"

"Africa."

"Africa! What brought that on?"

"Me and Ais was hanging out at his crib watching cable …"

"How is he? He hasn't been around here in a while."

"He's good. We been busy running around trying to get this music done. He wanted to come through the other day and get some tchoupitoulas."

She smiled.

"Tell him he's welcome anytime. So you were saying?"

"We was watching all the stuff going on in Somalia and Rwanda. The media make our people look incompetent, like they can't govern themselves.

And why are the countries so poor, why do they depend on these other people for their survival. Something aint right.

I've read books on it and sometimes I wonder who the authors are."

"They're usually the victorious. Finding good information can take some research. Get on the Net. It's great, at school I'm on it whenever I get a chance. Anyway, there's a tribe from east Africa called Zulus …"

"Afrika Bambatta," Malik said under his breath.

"Who?"

"The guy who made Planet Rock. He founded a group called the Zulu Nation."

"Oh, I remember that song. Well the name Zulu means, 'people from the stars', they have a Sansui named Credo Mutwa, he's their official 'keeper of knowledge' and a master storyteller. If you want a really interesting viewpoint on what happened in Africa, you should look him up."

"I have," said Malik proudly. So which one you believe in, Darwinism or Creationism?

"Whew." Fatima exclaimed. "That's a long one, why don't we save it for next time?" He agreed. "And Malik," she said, "don't waste time worrying about what fools say, they'll always make jokes of what they don't understand."

"Thanks ma."

"What for?"

"Just for being there, for listening. We should do this more often, you're closer than Pop and I think you might give better answers."

Fatima tapped her book.

"I'd like that. You know your father is a good man Malik, smart too, but his music is his first love and for him to create he needs, __how can I put this, __ he needs his space. You two are more alike than you know; both sensitive people in harsh surroundings. For a long time your father had a hard time dealing with his feelings, but as he progressed as a musician he learned to channel them into his work." She snapped her fingers. "There's a case of evolution at work for you. You learned to do that much earlier in life, you're by far a more perceptive critic than he was at your age." Malik thanked her again. "I'll tell you something else you may not know. I always regretted getting you the typewriter instead of that camcorder."

"Ma don't worry about …"

She raised her hand.

"But I was sitting in the courtyard with Sheila the other day and the boys were around back playing ball and the radio from one of their cars was blasting like always, and to my surprise whose voice do I hear but yours. I've been living here for a long time and I've sat on that bench more times than I can remember, but I've never had the view I did that day; not until you painted the picture for me." Fatima had a great big smile as she wiped the corners of her eyes. "I had to leave Sheila and come upstairs." Malik touched her on the shoulder. "I came up here to your room and pulled up a chair and I opened your window and I just sat there and listened and watched as my son crafted images with his words. I thought about you and Baggy, Bill and Merlin, and my kids at school and I thought to myself, 'What a group you all are; creators, this generations improvisers and innovators.' You all are special weather you know it or not, and that's when it occurred to me, the meaning of;

The Clot:

> *"In the name of thy Lord who createth,*
> *Createth man from a clot.*
> *And thy Lord is Most Bounteous,*
> *Who teacheth by the pen,*
> *Teacheth man that which he knew not …"*

Malik was humbled and lay prostrate on the floor, overcome by her words like never before.

"Special," said Fatima, as she lift his head high. "This is your time young prophet, you joyous human being. The creation of The Believers with the blood of a slave and the heart of a king." They hugged for a long time. "By the way," she let go of his hand and gave him an envelope. "Bagira was here earlier, he said he got this from some heavy set person with glasses." Malik asked about Baggy; he'd been recovering from a gunshot.

"He's fine; back in the street like nothing happened."

"That's good, *I guess*." He read the card.

"We heard your tape, son, round the office they calling it the perfect ten. Get at me, I been searching all over for you ever since the barbeque."

"This guy's an A & R for Noise Records."

"What does that mean?"

"Artist & Relations"

"Oh! What does that mean?"

A vision came to mind of a blimp in a future time with bright red letters that read; *"The World Is Mine."*

"I think it means they want to make me a deal."

BROOKLYN
February '92

The day after the party Jerry gave his friend two gifts; his very own copies of *Liber 777* and *Hammer Of The Gods*.

"Here's my number," he said, "use it, ask questions and remember, Creation, Formation, Actualization."

Several months later A-D was still skeptical but he couldn't deny the way Christie's reading had manifest; his reunion with Jess, his hooking up with Jerry and the magick of their success.

"It's got to be something to this!"

He and Jerry had been at it for weeks, partying and getting wasted when he was reunited with a former love one night after running into an acquaintance at a club.

"Peter Parker! What's really good player?"

Ten minutes later A-D was caught in a web.

"Man you always had the flow; and shit is different now baby. Niggas aint getting jerked like that no more; they on a come up. Man, niggas is closing six and seven figure deals."

"I can't do it Pete, fuckin' with that would fuck my money up; you know I just touched down from a week in Grand Cayman right?"

"Rich nigga!"

"Yeah," said A-D smiling. "I had to make a few deposits at Castle."

"My man Pops at the barbershop told me about 'chu man. He said you fucking with large cats in Atlanta, Denver, Miami, Vegas." Peter took a tape from a wannabe rapper. "Pops a fool, he said your passport got hella stamps on it; he said you dun' racked up more miles than some Kenyans in a marathon." A-D laughed.

"You see this don't you?" Peter tossed the tape in a box behind the Dj booth. "Everybody is trying to rap and they aint got half of your skills. Aint no nigga I know can put together metaphors better than you." A-D was cheesing from ear to ear. "Check it, 'A'. You gotta think of rap money like ho' money, man, 'it may be slow, but it sho' money.'"

"Too slow."

"What if I could get you on this tour I got coming up," asked Peter? "Just for a minute. You could test the water, get your beak wet. Think about it man, you aint local no more. You gotta watch out for secret indictments, and 'B', your face is too easy to trace. If nothing else it'll be a good way for you to bleach that dough."

He and A-D slapped hands and backs.

"You always looking out for a nigga Pete."

"You just remember your boy when it's time for you to sign that deal"

A-D started opening for Smooth the next month, and though he'd never admit it, performing felt good to him. Deep down there was only one thing he loved more than the stage.

BROOKLYN
March 94

In the Howard Beach area of Brooklyn was a condo, empty except for one room; in it was a stereo, fifty-two inch TV, a king sized bed and a box with nothing but condoms in it. This is the same place where the rhymes were invented.

The furniture was gone now, relocated to an apartment in Clinton Hill. The walls, ceiling and floors had all been redone in white, and yards of raw white linen hung from the ceiling creating a Supernal triangle around an altar of white candles. For the past forty days A-D had spent the hours between midnight and noon here, invoking the spirit of *Urzla* to assist him in cleansing the space as he create, formed, and actualized a dream that he and Diane both shared.

"It's a *lovely* place, that aint it at all Seth. How did you get it?"

One should never underestimate the power of denial, *"I'll be back soon."* She remembered him saying that in '85, by '94 his underworld ties had become the subject of half of Brooklyn rappers rhymes.

"A-D sighed, "C'mon Ma don't do this, not today."

He'd paid some bills and given Diane gifts in the past, clothes, jewelry, and a used replacement for her old Buick, but memories of past times wouldn't allow him to give her cash even though she'd been clean for years.

Evret was living in Queens with a divorced vet, she had two children when they married and they had one girl together. He'd given up on his dream of becoming a barber and sold his soul; he was now a NYC letter carrier. His family could've survived on his salary, but a few years before he wed he made the mistake of fathering twins with Filani. Now the child support payments were kicking his ass.

Shirley was a manager now; she was in a good relationship with the head of security at the store. She'd recently had her first child; a boy that A-D treated like his own. Mallory, who lived two floors down from Diane, was in an abusive relationship and following in her mothers footsteps. A-D had become the black sheep of the family and Diane was hesitant to accept gifts from him, not wanting to be known as the mother of the drug dealer.

"Answer me then Seth, and tell the truth for a change."

"Alright ma, you got it. What do you want to know?"

"Right Seth, like you're really going to tell me."

"No I'm serious," he said, wanting to get it over with. "I'm tired of these arguments, I'm tired of the dirty looks I get out the corner of your eye, and I'm tired of people putting lies in your head; so cool, you want the truth I'll give it to you. What 'chu wanna know?"

"What do I wanna know?" Diane's eyes narrowed as she moved in closer. "Let me tell you something, Seth. I aint one of ya' little know-nothin peons of the street. You aint gonna stand there and play me out with none of your mind games. Can't nobody tell me shit about you. You're *my* child. As a matter of fact," she began poking him in the chest again and again. "Let me tell you what *I* know. It was *you* who tried to kill my son. It was *you* who brought drugs into my home. It's *you* who keeps me jumping every time I hear the phone ring. *You* planted that bloody knife in Jose's car and *you* told the police where to find it. *You* are the reason Shirley got that abortion, _____*And It Was You Who Sacrificed That Girls Life*!"

BROOKLYN
February 26th '93

Death and jail had come to get paid landing The Commission on their hardest times. Jersey was done and just a week ago some loose lips led to a bust and major losses in Virginia; ninety bricks to be exact, but with Jerry's help, A-D was crawling back.

A frustrated A-D had been up all night and in the same clothes for days. It was just before noon when he hung up the phone for the umpteenth time searching for anyone to make an emergency trip down south. He'd run through every number in his head looking for a mule to carry two keys to Memphis. On the bed, all too aware of the situation and flipping through that month's *Vanity Fair* was Jessica.

It was Thanksgiving of '91 before she'd agreed to speak to him again. Another four or five months of visits, phone calls, and casual sex before he could win back his title.—The only thing he really wanted.—Word around campus was during their breakup she'd made a lot of new "friends." A-D couldn't see himself loosing to them; so he took his punishment, stuck it out through thick an thin, until she'd made herself believe it; *"He love's me again."*

This time around the feelings weren't the same. A part of him wanted to forgive, but that's not the part he listened to.

"I heard you was down there givin' it away," he said! "That's how you get back at a nigga, huh, *like that?*"

Still, he set her up in his condo. For months she'd tried everything in her power to get their relationship back to where it was before and to prove to him that her love endured.

"Can I go," she asked, softly, and for what seemed like the thousandth time? "I know them down there. I'll go."

This time A-D didn't ignore her or say no. Before the split he would never have allowed her around this part of the game. But things were different now; she wasn't *his* no more. Who was she? She'd let "friends" come between them. How could he trust her? He looked at her sitting up now. Her big doe eyes waiting for an answer; waiting for the chance to once again find grace in his eyes.

"She aint innocent no mo'."

He looked at the makeshift belt packaged with coke and ready to go. Behind her the television reported news that The World Trade Center had been bombed. Security at the airport would be tight. What else could go wrong? Unexplainable feelings in his gut seemed to answer his question. He put them out of his mind. He had to get Jerry's money. A-D heard a voice that may or may not have been his.

"Fuck it, she know the risks."

That's what he listened to. He picked up the belt.

"Jess, you follow these instructions and e'rthing will be cool."

BROOKLYN
March 94

"She must've really loved you for her to be doing ten years. Don't 'chu have no shame?"

A-D reached for her.

"I love *you* ma. *If* I did all that, I did it all for you."

Diane snatched away from him and nearly screamed.

"Uhh, uhh! Don't-do-that! I am not to blame for the things you've done, Seth."

A-D stared at his 55 year old mother. With the oily strands of grey in her braided hair and her arms folded not wanting to hear or talk she looked like a weathered little girl. She reminded him of Shirley that day in the kitchen. Maybe somewhere deep inside him was that frightened little boy with the toy microphone, but what showed up today was light years away from the young man that either of them used to know.

"I admit I did some things I aint proud of," he said. "But I was young; I just wanted to live like the other kids. I had three pairs of pants, two shirts, and one pair of sneakers. That aint living. What? You think I liked selling to you? I thought I was making things better. I figured, 'at least it's staying in the family.' Diane never responded; she just looked at him. He moved toward her. She moved away. "A'ight, I'm a bastard for that one. But damn.

All my accomplishments," he asked solemnly, "they don't mean shit to you do they? Aint nothing I can do to get a kind word or a real hug from you, is it?" She rolled her eyes and he shouted; "Fuck them!" Every word was filled with vitriol. "*I* did what had to be done for *your* family; *I* did the shit that you and all your deadbeat niggas couldn't do. *I* never sat around here gettin' high or feeling sorry for myself. *I* took care of us!" A-D's face was grossly contorted when he screamed at the top of his lungs, "Fuck them other people!"

Diane's hands were shaking as she walked slowly toward him. The pain in her throat as she tried to speak made her words slow to come.

"It's not your fault Seth. You have a sickness; something that's been eating at you for a long time. Like a parasite eating a great big hole. My mother and your father; they have it too. It's like you're all … dead; dead on the inside. But it's not your fault." She recited passages from Isaiah 14:12-21. "The Lord can help you Seth; he can save you. Look at me," she pleaded. "Just look at what he did for me."

By now A-D was calm again like nothing had ever happened.

"I remember sometimes you'd hold me close and motivate me; tell me how I was the best. You'd say; 'Anything in this world you want, you can possess.' He smiled surlily as he looked into Diane's eyes and shook his head. "Now that I'm successful you pull this shit. Who you foolin' you knew I'd murder the whole world to prove him wrong and make you proud of me."

Diane's face, at first just ghostly, turned a whiter shade of pale. Oddly, it wasn't his confession that frightened her."

Gypsy was right," she thought as she removed her hands from her face. Her eyes were puffy when she opened her arms to hug him.

"Seth. Your faults as a son are due to mine as a mother."

A-D turned his back on her and walked away.

"I guess we both gotta learn to live with regrets then."

He dropped the keys on the floor.

"Happy birthday ma."

And before she could yell *"A-."* He was out the door.

HARLEM
June 18th

"Damn this mu'fucka is smooth, and it handles nice in the curves."

D'aath had taught A-D that regrets were emotions, and emotions were wasted energy.

He continued admiring the brand new SC400 as he flossed it through traffic on the FDR and listened.

(Radio Dj) "*I would say the big news today is really yesterday's news. Former foot-ball great O.J. Simpson and his long time buddy A.C. Cowlings having both been taken in to custody yesterday after leading numerous members of the California Police Department on a bizarre, low-speed, highway chase. O.J. of course, was set to turn himself in on charges that he murdered his ex-wife Nicole Brown Simpson, and her friend Ron Goldman. Mr. Cowlings was charged with aiding and abetting a fugitive. L.A.P.D. sources say the two were tracked down by calls made from O.J.'s cellular phone.*"

The buzz on his waist brought him back to full consciousness. He reached for the Nokia and pressed talk.

The voice on the other end was deep and ghetto but sexy still.

"W'sup player?"

"'Sup Ma, how you feel?"

He could care less. His thoughts were on their seven-thirty reservations at a hot new restaurant and it was now …

"*What the fuck,*"

The time surprised him.

"*6:43?*"

If push came to shove he'd have Jerry phone the hostess; but that upset him.

"*All the money I spend in there and I still can't get it done myself.*"

Respect. That's what was missing. No matter how much money he spent he was still Jerry Freidman's friend.

"*Mommy better' not be trying to check me on the time!*"

"I'm good, dada," said the voice. "What's the deal?"

"What chu' mean?"

"I'm saying; is we still on, or..?"

"Pump your brakes, Ma. I'm like, right there."

"I'm cool dada, but you know I'm with my girls and they about to ride out."

"Tell them freaks to pump y'all brakes. Them lames on that side of this town aint on shit. They can wait!"

She chuckled.

"*This cat has got some nerve.*"

He seized the second of silence before pressing the red button

"Five minutes ma."

"*I knew it.*"

It was really ten minutes or more depending on how he drove, but after the call he might make her wait. He really couldn't stand Brooklyn girls but this one had skills. Still, the thought of her checking up on him; "not cool," he said, just above a whisper.

Wind whipped his silken *Versace* short set around the cars interior. He caught a whiff of his *Dreamer* cologne as he exit the freeway in Harlem.

"These mu'fuckas."

He remembered the days of Rich Porter, Alpo, and Aize. Today Harlem belonged to ...

"Shh, don't ever mention those names. You will clash with mobsters!"

That's what Flam had once told him.

"Bird-ass nigga; what the fuck am I? Fuck him," said A-D out loud before reviewing his list.

"Doors locked, Check. *Stashbox workin',* Check. *Heat, L's, and chedda',* Check."

He turned the radio up and sang along with the hook.

"The world is mine!"

He had to admit along with every one else in '94;

"That's a hot line, but his light aint shining. Lil' homie aint ready for war."

It was 6:51 and the Seville lounge was in sight when A-D made the call.

"I'm here. Where you at?"

"Be right there."

He hit the hazards as she came out. He had to give it up; she was a thing of beauty.

"Cocky walk. Tits firm. Bangin' booty."

He kept her wrapped tight in pastel *Versace* and fresh pedicures for her *Joan and David* pumps. He watched her as she moved to the driver's side of the coupe.

"Half-black and Pilipino. Fringe benefit."

She leaned in and greeted him.

"Sup Pumpkin."

"W'sup Honey-Bunny?"

"You got a new toy. Where's the GS?"

"I'm freaking it, ma, TV's, cameras; that hot shit, since you *gotta* know."

"Poppi don't go there, you know Sasi has got her own biz to attend to, Ok. I'm just playing my part, that's all!"

She gave him a quick kiss and wiped the fifteen dollar MAC print off his lips.

One dollar for every year of her age.

"Supposed to," he whispered before brushing his hand over her ass.

"*No panties and smelling like Issey. You play it well.*"

He envisioned going in her raw for a moment.

"*Whoa!*"

He killed that thought.

"Ma, is we eatin' or what? We got a seven-thirty in Manhattan."

Sasi smiled a somewhat crooked smile.

"Let me go so say bye to my people, dada."

"Hurry up ma, you know I hate waitin'."

He watched her switch through the door. The Medusas head on her ass had momentarily turned him to stone before the bass from the small caravan of cars pulling up cracked it and freed him. He smiled at the irony of the hook. The lead car was an $80,000 yellow Acura NSX.—The drivers *Saturday* car.

"It's Ok A-D," said Fame, "you can go in, we don't bite!"

"I'd love to baby, but these new *Mauri's* is biting, hard! You'd think at $350 a pair they'd at least make 'em comfortable."

Fame laughed loudly.

"Hit me baby, we gon' politic."

"As usual," said A-D.

Next up, more irony; his security riding dirty in a pink J30.

After that came a black Range Rover; the reggae beat banged from all three.

"W'sup playboy?"

A slow, friendly drawl came from the passenger side.

"Tommy 'The Titan.' What the deal playboy?" Dizzy had changed Thomas's stage name for legal reasons. "Your first disk, huh," asked A-D?

"Word! We through mixing, its gon' drop any minute. This is number 14," answered The Titan.

"I'm feeling it. Always knew you'd blow out like an afro."

"You right behind me. I'ma kick in the door for you. But my man Dizzy here deserves some credit too." The Titan put his arm around Dizzy.

"No fu-ck-in doubt." A-D point to Dizzy. "That's Harlem's hustler right there!"

"And ya'll two," yelled Dizzy, "is Brooklyn's finest. Yo A-D, we headed 'cross the bridge to politic; you rolling?"

"Nah; tell lil' mans I said one love though."

"A'ight."

Dizzy turned up the track and peeled out in the 4.6.

"*Damn,*" thought A-D. "*I'ma be a failure. If them clowns can make it ...*"

Sasi's perfume filled the Lexus as she plopped down and put her heels on the seat. "See there, that's pride fucking wit' 'chu," she said, brushing off his shoulder. "You know you BK's finest, boo."

"If you don't get 'cha heels off that …"

He passed her the chrome 380 he'd been gripping. He knew holding it kind of turned her on. He looked at the clock.

"6:56! 8. Infinity!"

He dialed the phone, as they drove down Lenox Avenue.

"What up Jerry? Haaa! Yo, do ya' mans a favor …"

MANHATTAHN
June 18th
6:51 pm

<u>Excerpt 49.</u>

"C'mon bro,' I know you listen to Lenny?" Jerry asked with amphetamine fueled intensity. "Romeo Blue? Man, he was screwing Denise. You remember that at least?"

Fourtunate Devine was busy with his own epiphany. He'd done for his grandfather what his father wouldn't do; appear to the world as a productive member of society. He'd graduated Georgetown with a degree in economics and when the summer was over he'd begin a career with a respectable firm. Best of all he was a member in good standing with Sigma Pi Phi fraternity and the Prince Hall Lodge. Alliouisis had learned from his mistakes with Dioses. In return, he tolerated Fourtune's friends and their quest for fame, and he'd accepted Fourtune as the heir to the Devine family name. All that aside, Fourtune was pleased to be home. He laughed at Jerry—they'd kept in touch mainly through The Lodge—and turned his gaze from the Harbor as the two crossed the bridge into Manhattan.

"Whatever, asshole, you used to love her," said Jerry, tossing him the red pouch. Fourtune opened it and found "purple haze."

"Fuck no!"

He threw it back.

"You crazy? I aint going to see The Brothers smelling like fucking, Jimi Hendrix! And uhh, why you been holding out on me?"

"Holding out on what?"

"Holding out on that. It looks like amethyst it's so bright. Let me see it again."
Jerry tossed it back.

"It smells like bubble gum," said Fourtune, "You *had* to bring this it back with
you. How much you got?"

"About a half pound. My guy in customs couldn't let me through with more
than that. But bro, I can get that shit anytime you want. Why didn't you say
something?"

"Dude, its June. The last time I talked to you was New Years Eve and the only
thing I remember is K9 playing in the background, you fucking up the lyrics, and
some chick moaning in French."

Jerry grinned.

"Dude, you would've loved her, African with fucking green eyes, long brown
hair, and ass like a zebra." Jerry exhaled. "Her and her girls were dancers at the
Moulin Rouge. Hey let's call 'em, I got their numbers somewhere."

Fourtune chuckled and shook his head.

"That's why I aint say something, you been out of the country for what, like
seven months."

"Yeah, it was lovely; I was getting head all over Europe." Jerry shuddered.
"They're so nasty; and they're bumping everybody's shit. Fucking, The Ennead,
Q-MD, The Boy. Man, Periscope Records is making a killing! That's my word. I
don't know why you never go."

"You want to know why I never go. I'll tell you why. Cause it's fucking cold
there. My blood aint mixed for that, I freeze my ass off here. I tell you what, next
time I go to Rio or St. Thomas you come, and we'll kick it."

It was 6:56 when Jerry tucked the sack and answered his phone.

"You got me. Doin' me, myself and I. That's some Jew boy shit, if you didn't
know. Anything's possible. No problem, man. It's done. 8:00 pm. Is that cool.
Good. Did my guy's take care of you the other night? Good. When are you going
back to the lab? You did? Outstanding! It's all good, it's going to, be off the hook,
I know it. A'ight. Tomorrow. One."

Jerry phoned the restaurant, made the arrangements and re-focused his attention to Fourtune.

"You don't go to the fucking meetings sober now," he asked disappointedly?

Fourtune answered carefully.

"Yeah. I mean ___ I've been really studying. I'm trying to be more than just
adviser to the king. We aint all born 'elite,' you know. Like they say, 'Membership
has its privileged.'"

"Get the fuck out of here. And its *privileges,* not privileged. Fucker!"

They laughed again. One of them said; "Damn bro we got to kick it more often." "Yeah we do." The other replied.

"Fourtunate, you ever heard of this guy from Brooklyn, A-D?"

"That lightweight kid from Marcy," asked Fourtune questioning Jerry's company?

"Yeah, but first thing is he's only light here in NY. He's got half of Virginia locked down and in Jersey his people boosted the murder rate so high they sent the National Guard in to get him."

"Word," asked Fourtune intrigued.

"Word. C'mon 'G', you're slipping you should've been supplying these guys."

"As if you read my mind."

"Anyway, I was asking about him more so on the music tip."

"What, he's trying to do the label thing too?"

"Nah, nothing like that. I can barely get his ass in the studio. But, he's mad lyrical! I mean his shit is good. You heard your man Dizzy's kid, The Titan."

"Yeah? I was talking to him the other day about that kid, he's got skills but how is he going to market him? That's a risky move."

"Well," said Jerry like a child with a secret, "A-D *wrote* a couple of those tracks."

"Really? Which ones?"

Jerry stopped at the intersection. He lowered the windows and turned the a/c off. Instantly the scent of Freon and leather was replaced with heat and the smell of exhaust and cigarettes from hot pedestrians. He wanted the feel of Manhattan Island in June to engulf his prospect. He pressed the button on the console of the Porsche. Fourtune listened to the disk and tried to become present. He smiled slightly and thought of his grandfather. He knew Jerry's tactic and wasn't at all offended by it. Why should he be, they'd learned it at the same place. In years of meetings like the one they were about to attend. If it had been him he would've done the same, maybe with a bit more flair but that was due to his time spent in the streets of Harlem. Manhattan and Harlem, so alike yet so different.

As above, so below.

Jerry spoke swiftly with the precision of a skilled politician. Something *he'd* learned from the company his family kept.

Fourtune was amazed by his Brother for another reason though. No matter what drug of the moment Jerry was on his skills as an orator seemed to improve. Jerry gave him something else he'd brought back from Amsterdam.

"Open your mind," he said passing him the jagged little pill and explaining that track 5 was the song to beat. Fourtune broke it in half and gave the rest back to him. "What-a-pussy," Jerry said laughing and washing the "E" down with Evian. He rolled the windows up and listened carefully to the last song on the disk as he pulled the Carrera into the parking area of the Old Holland Lodge. One number here, two letters there; the license plates told the stories of vehicles from every country imaginable, informing the public that in a city where everyone was a star, these were the most dense.

"So what the verdict," Jerry asked?

"The lyrics are *a'ight* but I'd like to see the whole package."

"Of course. I can set something up."

"For who?"

"For you."

"Why?"

"Why not?"

"What do I have to do with it?"

"Bro. This guy is kind of ill. A partner would be a good thing. If it works out this could be just what both of us need to get in good with the old men. You know how they feel about this music. Send your friend from Uptown to feel him out, let him play the man and we'll play the back."

That's was it. Fourtune had been expecting something. He'd known Jerry for too long to take this ride as an act of pure generosity; he'd been disappointed if it were. Fourtune figured it was time to make a move. The cycle needed changing; vandals from the West had everything in chaos and the mic deserved to be rocked by proper stock. It was hot money in the rap game and he wanted all of it. Besides that, Fame had been bugging him about managing a couple of "bum-ass R&B groups" he'd put together. This could be what they needed to complete their dreams and the dreams of their fathers too; the black Rockefellers.

"Done deal," he said. "I'll set it up and get back to you."

He got his bag from the trunk.

"I knew you would," said Jerry. "Believe me man, this is going to work. You ready to see The Brothers?"

"Always."

✳

The next day at the barbershop, Fourtune found Fame already on top of things.

"Do this shit work?" He grabbed Fourtune's arm and shook it. "I'ma get you a Rolex 'B,' cause you late. I been knew about this cat! I was at the club about a month and a half ago. You know how Pete got his little side thing going ..."

"Pete who," interrupted Fourtune?

"Peter Parker."

"Spiderman," he asked, only half-joking.

"Mu'fu ..., the Dj. ___ I'm tellin' you, you late 'B'."

"Alright."

"So I was dropping Pete a package and fucking around in the back of the club when I hear him on stage giving it to 'em. The crowd loved him, the nigga was on fire. I would've stayed and holla'd that night but I had money to make. Pete slid me a tape and holla'd at him. A couple of days later I went to see dude in Marcy."

NYMP
April '94

It was a clear crisp day but Fame decided to leave the Benz at home. He pulled up alone, in a black, tinted Pathfinder. Niggas put their dice away and put their ice-grills on as he approached wearing jeans and a yellow *North Face* jacket to match his *Timbs,* chain and bracelet. Three BK bitties sat lounging, whispering and trying to start trouble.

"Y'all aint shit, y'all gon' let a Harlem nigga just soldier through here?"

Fame ignored them; he had other shit on his mind. *"... four, five, six, __eight niggas. That's like four shells each."* He kept a straight face when he spoke. "Afternoon. How's everybody feeling?"

All eight niggas all turned into mimes.

"Where can I find A-D?"

"Who wanna know?"

"Tell him Fame from Uptown is here to politic with him. Our man Peter Parker already told him what about."

Theo rest easy and motioned to Ptah, he took his hand from under his coat and ran into the building as the other niggas started shooting again.

Theo looked up from one knee.

"You riding through Marcy by yourself?"

Fame circled the toothpick around his mouth.

"Just me and the guns."

The dude next to Theo muttered something. Theo laughed and said;

"They say your crew is thorough; the best out there."

The others snickered.

"They right," said Fame, "whoever *they* are."

A-D stepped out the building in jeans, brand new Air Force Ones, and a Dallas Cowboys Parka with a matching cocked cap. He moved the rubber bands covering his Longines.

"Famous Game," he said, "you early man."

Fame wondered;

"Did this cat just call me by my Government name?"

They traded pounds as A-D looked around and asked;

"I thought you drove a platinum Benz. You creepin' up on us?"

"That's my Friday car, but I see you been doin' your homework."

They laughed together.

"You hungry," asked A-D? "I know this low spot on Amsterdam. They got great lobster *and* we can talk there."

Fame couldn't believe what he was hearing.

"You mean, *El Malecon*," he asked. "That's *my* hood man. You gon' pull my coat to a spot in *my* hood?"

"Shit, you could've been allergic to shellfish, how I'm gon' know."

Forty minutes later A-D was sitting through Fame's presentation for Prudential Records. He spoke at length about his vision for the label and what he hoped it would accomplish. How he wanted to get rich and bring jobs to people in his community and leave a legacy for his kids. How they'd pimp the music business, using it as a stepping stone before branching off into clothing, film, and anything else they could dream of.

"… and you can get in on the ground floor of something greater than yourself homeboy. I'm talking about starting a movement like they doing over at Major Federal …"

A-D studied him. They were exact opposites in demeanor.

"I'm kind of quiet but this cat can talk, he been yappin' fifteen minutes straight!"

Not about bullshit though; more like he had something to prove.

"Maybe it's his height, but he really aint short. He's ____average! Everything about him is average."

Fame could come off that way, cantankerous, but he was smart and a product of good game. A-D kept listening and soon Fame had him once again envisioning himself trenchcoated and suited up in the L-shaped corner office of a Manhattan skyscraper.

"… we not only hustlers, we businessmen, baby!" And then he said the key words, "I'm talking about multi-millions B, I mean runnin' shit like the Rockefellers."

That was it. Their avarice was the one place they stood completely eye to eye.

A-D figured having Jerry in one America and Fame in the other would bring him the best of both worlds. Fame noticed his expression and bumped his knee against the table.

"'B', you hearing me? C'mon now, I talk fast cause I think fast, stay with me?"

A-D was sold, but still cautious. He decided to let Fame manage him for a while before he signed.

THE BRONX
July 3rd

It was just after ten pm, Sunday night in a smoke-filled pool hall on one four five in the South Bronx. Fame had been waiting for the right time and this was it. The rain had held off just long enough for the city to give its fireworks show, then the clouds burst just long enough to wet up the streets. Fame had one of his acts pitted against an up and coming group from Yonkers; three youngsters that loved to battle. They were managed by The Crazy 88's, another hustling crew from Harlem with a rep for being ride or die niggas. Fourtune gave 'em their props.

He couldn't stop talking about their lead act, or the way he rolled, "he's grimy, he don't give a fuck, and he keeps his shit the hardest," according to him the nigga was *"for real."*

"Dog is a fucking problem," explained Fourtune. "No disrespect man but you better bring your whole crew."

Fame called up A-D as insurance. When he walked in, the leader of the 88's called his man who was out of state putting in work.

"Yo dog, I need you to drop everything and get up here, now!"

Loyal to the core, he immediately hitched a cab from Baltimore.

Inside the club two pool tables served as the dividing line; Prudential on one side and The Crazy 88's on the other. The crews got it started and just after one am a swarthy figure entered and quietly took his place. It was the fourth of July and everyone was on edge waiting for the big guns to pop off. The youngsters ran out of ammo and the crowd began chanting;

"Let em' loose baby they about to spark."

A-D stood on one table and the mysterious figure climbed on the other. The whole club circled them watching for almost an hour as the two locked jaws and ripped plugs out of each other. It was close to three am; closing. The club was still rowdy and still too close to call. The Crazy 88's man point to A-D and went first. The battle for New York had come down to this last verse.

"Peep this. Right there, in disguise, is a cat."
    He sniffed, and looked over at Fame.
    "Smell that right there? In your crew is a rat.
    It'll be like 2004 when you remember this verse; when you're wonderin' how in the hell, for ten years did that nigga hide his skirt."

When the smoke cleared A-D smiled and point back.

"This cat here will put you back in the dirt from which you came.
    Homie you wreak of pain; walk back to B-more, let it wash off in the rain.
    In ten years this game'll still belong to me, Fourtune, and Fame.
    And you'll be all smoked out and niggas still won't know your name."

MANHATTAN
Le Meridian
July 4th

It was early afternoon when Jerry called and said he'd be there soon. Fame showed the girls to the door and called for service to the room before asking Fourtune;

"So what 'chu see?"
    "I see a new day, Fame. A bright sunlit day!" Fourtune focused on his vision in the carafe of *Pellegrino*. "This morning I seen a dynasty dawning. Prudential Records is gon' hold that blue flame for the next thousand years."
    Fame's vision was more exoteric.
    "I see that too. Only in my vision the flame is green from all the paper we gon' burn. Life is ridiculous. Who would've thought a cat from Brooklyn was gon' make some Harlem niggas rich ___my fault, *richer*. I'ma hustle CD's like I hustle these packs, B."
    "Fame, in ten years Prudential will be the biggest thing out there and this family will be 100% legit thanks to your boy. All we have to do is work out a few kinks."

"Like what."

"Nothing serious, just a couple of industry niggas."

"Like who?" Fame's voice was high and he was looking at Fourtune like he'd lost his mind. "B, fuck a fake ass rapper. I'll make *him* famous." He cocked his Glock. "You're nobody till somebody kills you."

"I with you, but it aint just him. We got those fools out West to deal with too. You down with that?"

His looked into his brother's eyes and wondered if they were on the same page.

Before college they'd been equals, but the instant Fame locked eyes with Fourtune he knew he was being judged. And this was not a question of which car to buy, or where do I choose to call home. No! This is *the* question that answers those and more. It's for questions like these that you rely on the Pentium processor in your head and hope that it's bytes of ram and gigs are enough. Quick! Do you trust your Intel and make a move or do you wait for another vista of opportunity, *or* perhaps this instant of hesitation has already sealed your fate.

Questions like these test the mettle of men. At times like these they look through the hole in another's head and see straight into their soul.

Fourtune tilted his head slightly. And though it seemed like forever, only a few seconds would pass before Fame cleared his thoughts and did the same.

"B, *whoever!*"

"My brother," Fourtune said relieved, "our choices define who we are. The moment we stop thinking ahead is the beginning of our end, so *nothing* can stand in the way of our progress. We must always rise above."

Fourtunate poured his fathers favorite cognac into Fame's empty glass and made a toast.

"To Prudential Records!"

The glasses clinked. As they sipped Fourtune remembered a story his father had told him as they drove home from his mother's funeral. Dioses explained to him how on a cold night in a bar in Queens, he'd put his life into the hands of another man.

*

"That man asked me to believe in a dream that would change my life; a dream that would integrate our lives and make our families as rich and powerful as the Rockefellers or the Kennedy's." Dioses smiled at the recollection.

"When I was growing up, people wanted to know about John D. so bad the papers reported his every move. I don't think we got that far, but my decision that night was one of the best I've ever made. I was at a crossroad in my life. I didn't like the path I was on and I wasn't sure of the one I'd been asked to take; but Napalm and Agent Orange had proven to me what evil men will do and I wasn't afraid no more. I went into the jungle with honor and more importantly I came back with it. I called the man with me that night "Brother" because he'd done the same. I trusted him. So that night in the bar when he asked that I see his dream, I tried."

"Did you," Fourtune recalled asking his father?

"That's irrelevant son. Brothers do what must be done."

✳

Twenty-three years later each man was standing in his fathers shoes, but the roles had been reversed. Fourtunate realized this was what they called "Nobelesse-oblige." It was their turn to push forward the dreams of their fathers. He put his glass down and placed both hands together. With all five fingers touching at their tips he opened them until only his thumbs and pointers were touching. Then he peeked through the opening with one eye and said; "Fam …"

Before he could finish there was a knock at the door. Fourtune opened it.

"What did I miss," Jerry asked excitedly?

"Everything," answered Fourtune.

"That sucks. I was out of it anyway."

"Tell us something new," said Fame sarcastically.

Jerry paid him no mind. He grabbed some grapes and nibbled off the vine.

"Well Fame, it's on you. What do you think?"

"When I think of Brooklyn I think of Jordans and gold chains; niggas driving broke *Vigors* and living with they moms. My man is different, I like him."

Jerry asked Fourtune.

"What about you, bro?"

Fourtune toyed with his pinky ring.

"Well, he's definitely a hustler; whatever he can do to make money he'll do it. And the flow …"

"Most incredible," Fame shouted!

"I told you," said Jerry with his mouth full. Yet there was tension in the room. Everyone seemed to be holding something back. Finally Jerry said matter-of-factly.

"I don't trust him. He may be too smart"

"Me either," admitted Fourtune.

They looked at Fame. His mouth was full of fermented grapes when he shook his head and mumbled;

"Uhhn, uhh."

"Good," said Jerry, "for once we all agree. We'll find a way to test his loyalty."

It was time to check out. They gathered their things. In the hotel lobby Jerry's phone rang. He took a look at the number and stepped away.

"I'm going to the bathroom," said Fame.

Inside he recognized a voice coming from the stall.

"What do ya' mean, where have *I* been? I been dialing your number for fifteen minutes, it's been going straight to your voicemail. I was just about to leave. Yeah mon, I've got it. Ok, meet me in the suite; five minutes, mon."

Fame was stunned when the stall door opened.

"Treni mon' what da deal, where you been hiding ya'self."

Treni was not amused. First of all Fame did a bad Jamaican accent and second, Treni was Haitian, early thirties, five-seven, light-skinned with a receding hairline, and a rep for high end fashion labels and kinky sex.

It was guys like him that coined the term "metrosexual" after years of being called gay; even worse was his reputation for leaking information to escape the wrath of a D.A. His latest case had been all over the news.

Treni frowned; he looked around the restroom and gave Fame a pound.

"Hiding? Treni don't hide from nothing, mon. What you up to these days Famous, still try'in to play with the big boys?"

Fame forced a little laughter.

"Keep your eyes open Treni. Me and Fourtune just signed a new act, he's gon' be the shit."

Treni laughed at his optimism, fixed his clothes and moved toward the door.

"How is Fourtune? I haven't seen you two together in a long time. I'm surprised he let you drag him into your craziness?"

The water shut off and Fame went to dry his hands.

"Ask him yourself, him and his man Jerry are in the lobby checking out."

Treni gave Fame a look he couldn't quite place.

"Jerry ..." He stopped himself and forced his own laughter. "Another time. I'll see you guys around. I got some business to do."

Treni hurried out the door.

"That nigga's acting shadier than usual," thought Fame.

Around the corner he found Fourtune on the phone.

"Yo, guess who I just …"

Fame stopped talking when Fourtune put his finger to his lips and whispered;

"This is honey I met the other night at *Nell's*."

Fame searched the lobby then mouthed the words;

"Yo where's Jerry?"

Fourtune put his hand over the phone and whispered;

"He got a call; he said he'll hook up with us later."

Fourtune hung up the phone as they made their way to the valet; and not a minute too soon, Fame had to get something off his chest.

"I 'ma keep it real wit 'chu, man. I never liked dude and you know it. I give him credit. He's a hell of a business man, but he trains people to kiss ass and I aint with that. Jerry doesn't give a fuck about you or me or anyone else. You can't trust him; his only loyalties are to the dough and *his* family, that's it, that's all!"

Fourtunate had been preparing for this moment for twelve years. He'd decided to give Fame the simplest answer he could.

"That's the thing Fame, you're my brother and so is he; we're all family now."

ATLANTIC CITY
August 6th '94

Thomas hadn't seen his family, his dough, the crap tables, or anything else for that matter. Since they'd met he'd only had eyes for her. He'd come from under her spell long enough to make a call.

"Nigga where the fuck is you," asked The Boy, "I been calling you, paging you; what 'chu been on?"

Thomas laughed.

"Shits been crazy, man. I threw that pager away; I'ma give you the new number. Hold on, somebody wanna speak to you."

Her voice was laid back and sultry like she'd been steaming for days.

"Heeey, whas'suup? I can't believe I'm talking to you." The Boy wondered how she looked. "Riccardo told me all about you," she said, "He says you mad cool. We gotta get together sometime and kick it."

She gave the phone back to Thomas.

"Who was that," asked The Boy, "and who the fuck is Riccardo?"

"Riccardo is my pet name; and that was Hope, _____ my wife!"

The Boy was shocked at first but it all added up when he thought about it. He and Thomas had become inseparable. Like twins separated at birth and later reunited they were a modern day Castor and Pollux who'd had cookouts together, rocked the mic, hit clubs and laid groupies together. When Thomas and his crew came to do some club dates in Los Angeles The Boy witnessed first hand how long it took for him to fall in love.

"Dizzy aint paying for the hotel? Man, fuck that bitch; y'all can crash at my crib." And when the female The Boy was seeing at the time protested. "Man, fuck that bitch, the bedrooms is full, but the couch is yours as long you need it?"

The Boy even had dates lined up for them. Thomas's was nice and thick.

"Good looking dog. She remind me of that chick from *Xscape*, but her conversation aint all that." Yet the morning after he was ready to give her the safe combination and all that. The Boy overheard him macking as the two sipped Mo' and played Nintendo on his living room floor.

"Boo, just picture life as my wife ... "

He couldn't blame Thomas too much. He was like family and all but the truth was the truth; he couldn't have gotten much pussy. Even he'd described himself as black and ugly and Dizzy said he looked like he could rob a liquor store without a gun.

"Yo' wife! When you get married," asked The Boy.

"Like two days ago."

"How you meet her?"

"We was shootin' a video and Dizzy introduced us."

"How long you known her?"

"Almost two weeks."

"Nigga is you crazy? You finta' be paid, how you know she aint after your loot?"

"You sound like mom duke. Nigga what loot? Don't I owe you a couple hundred?

"Man, fuck that. Look 'T', I'ma give you some game I got from an OG out in Oakland. The world is filled with pimps and ho's, and you can't turn one into a housewife. *Crazy-ass man.*"

"Nah, I trust honey, she aint like that; plus she's a singer, she got her own dough."

He explained how though she hadn't asked for it he'd bought her designer clothes and a full length mink, a gold necklace and bracelet with X&O links.

"Dig it," whispered Thomas, "after I hit that she starts telling me how compared to me, no other love could measure. Now she got my name tattooed on her titty."

Thomas told some more jokes to lighten the mood. Soon they were both laughing. *"Fuck it,"* thought The Boy, *"he's a grown-ass man."*

Plus his call had been right on time. The Boy needed something to get his mind off his problems; the last fourteen months had been wrought with ups and downs. His first two disks were big hits on the underground but had yet to go gold.

He'd received critical acclaim for his roles in two motion pictures but had also been publicly fired from the sets of two more. He'd celebrated beating charges by pimp walking out of Federal court, but he'd done time on a petty case. Now the trial date had been set for his most serious legal bout yet, charges that had come from a most unexpected place.

NEW YORK CITY
In "Da" Club. Late 1993

The Boy was twenty-two; a man, but a flawed one, handsome but years of hard living had him frayed around the edges. He was going places he couldn't enter with team parkas, Fila's, and 10 karat gold herringbones.

From some directions came whispers and from others the shouts of family members, strangers and famous well-wishers with belated advice on how to stay out of trouble and make his way in the world.

"You're hanging with the wrong crowd."

"You don't belong with them anymore, you're a star."

"You need to find a new group of friends if you plan to make it in this business."

He wondered where they'd been all these years as he pondered these social conundrums. How does a loner make friends; and, to whom can you turn when society has labeled you a troublemaker? Historically this is the time when a man turns to a good woman, but there lay another dilemma.

Where do you find one of those when every parent in your new tax-bracket had already threatened their daughters?

"If you bring him home, we'll cut you loose!"

And their sons weren't much better; trust fund babies wary of the neuvo-rich'e outsider.

So where do we turn, we creatures of habit, continuously positioning ourselves in the places we feel most safe. Usually that means amongst our own kind and for The Boy that meant the have-nots, the bohemians, and the outlaws.

His advisors had yet to warn him that was next to impossible; he was a mark now that he had dough.

It came as little surprise when back in June, Treni called. He and Roberko were busy re-inventing themselves as what else? Hustlers turned record execs. Every city had a few, all stuck in the same predicament, caught between the world they'd done everything to escape and a new one that was reluctant to let them in.

This month The Boy decided to move to New York while he filmed his latest movie there. Treni and his man Glover met him on the set and promised to show him around and keep him out of trouble. All they asked from him is that he thought about doing a verse with a couple of their artists; just to help them get on. For that they'd promised to pay him well and had even put their people at his beck and call driving him around town and taking him shopping on Fifth Avenue. They introduced him to Jacob the Jeweler where he spent nearly sixty thousand dollars. There they bought him a gift; a rite of passage for East coast hustlers; his very own Rolex with a diamond bezel.

Now that he'd been laced and fit the part they promised to introduce him to a "better class" of female than he'd been known to deal with.

Each night from sun down to sun up they made the rounds. On this particular night, a Friday in mid-November, they landed at Jezebels.

The club was classy; it was the flipside of anything The Boy had seen at The Tunnel or his other haunts. At last he was around people he looked up to; people with as much money and status as him. It wasn't long before one after another pro athletes, celebrities, and beautiful women began fawning over him.

"We all think you so fly."

Elated, he was on the floor dancing when he spot her; a video vixen in a short leather skirt.

Excerpt 50.

He couldn't see her face; Chronic and *Tangueray* had him high. She danced up to him ass first. His judgment awry, he spanked it and accepted her offering. She turned around and the scent of *Bijan* was forced through her sheer top by ample breasts.

He looked down.

"Damn girl, you got some, uh, __ thighs on you!"

She licked her lips. The music in the club banged. His head throbbed. She grabbed it and led him to a dim corner. Ten minutes later he found Glover at the bar.

"Man, I need you to run me and ol' girl back to the hotel real quick."

Glover looked at her standing in the crowd with tousled hair and smeared lipstick. She looked anxious to get somewhere private and finish what she'd started.

A couple of hours later, Treni, Glover, and J.I. stumbled drunk and rowdy into The Boy's suite. J.I. crashed down on the other bed waking him up when he asked;

"Where that ho' at man, she had fat ass?"

"She looks like that freaky bitch, what's her name?" Glover snapped his fingers. "Lisa Nicole Carson!"

"You fucked her in da' club didn't you?" Treni was a bit overzealous wanting intimate details as he flicked some powder from his swollen nose. "How'd you fuck her, mon, huh? How you do it?"

Even Glover took a step back. The Boy just wanted to get back to sleep and played it off.

"Put it like this," he said, "we was in there having sex, we weren't in there making love."

✳

A day later, under orders from officials at City Hall, an army of nearly two hundred lawmen, SWAT teams, tactical units and reporters invaded the swank Manhattan hotel. On the ground floor the elevator door opened and cameras blinded him as he stepped off.

The paparazzi and hotel employees were all shouting and pointing as he walked shackled and embarrassed through the lobby. A lone policeman seemed genuinely concerned with The Boy's welfare and asked;

"What the hell you done now?"

To which he replied;

"I aint did shit officer, that bitch trippin'."

✳

On another front the so called "war on gangster rap" was on strong. As major shareholders of Periscope Records, Clockwork Enterprises was stuck between a rock and pressure from its friends in high places. Indeed Periscope's CEO's had their hands full; K'9 was facing murder charges, Q-MD was on house arrest, and the entire Firing Squad roster seemed to be headed for prison. Dozens of Right-wing conservative groups and bold opportunists seeking financial gain had band together to attack the music.

How would Periscope ever sign new artists if they gave in to pressures from their parent company or anyone else in corporate America? Guns and beat downs were a part of an image; they could put the spin on those. The Boy's new case however; that was something different. Periscope stuck by him longer than most, but after a meeting with the CEO's The Boy got the feeling they'd tired of his litigiousness and had washed their hands of him.

Meanwhile, with attorney fees piling up and his funds low, The Boy became a voice for hire communicating constantly through his pager; a musical mercenary for money spitting rhymes instead of bullets and hustling verses instead of weight. That's when he began to notice that all around him the faces looked the same, and somehow the rap game had begun to remind him of the crack game.

MANHATTAN
Le Meridian
November '94

Jerry entered the hotel with instructions on a special job for a special friend.

His friend left their meeting and went directly to another where he gave his own instructions.

"It's all set. Just put him in check, but if he get live; fuck it, y'all put his ass in dead nigger storage."

MANHATTAN
Gethsemane Studios
Days Later

"Beeeep, Beeeep, Beeeep ..."

The Boy's *Skypager* went off again. His manager asked if he wanted the phone.

"Nah, fuck him; we here now." Roberko had been calling all night trying to get The Boy in the studio to do a song; first he had the money, then he didn't. The last time they talked he'd managed to put together six thousand and someone they both knew was there to put up the other four.

"Long as the ten grand is there I'm on my way," he'd said.

But the vibe wasn't right. He'd been introduced to Treni and Glover through Roberko and early on in the trial his co-defendants had retained different council and hadn't spoken to him in months. Since then he'd received a number of veiled threats from friends of theirs, but The Boy kept his mind on the money.

"Ten grand. Ten grand!"

"Yo J.I., yo' bitch full?"

"Yeah dawg she straight." J.I. fingered her as they walked down the block. "I got that bitch right here."

The Boy's girlfriend was on a new diet; nothing but hollow shells. He'd stuffed her full of those before leaving the hotel.

The clock in Times Square read 12:17 when J.I. threw the down the last of the blunt, just then they all heard a voice from above.

"We got a gang of that shit in here!"

They looked up and saw Julius on a balcony.

J.I. yelled.

"Sup my nigga, everybody here?"

"You know it," Julius yelled back!

J.I. turned to The Boy.

"Well that says it. Dizzy and the fam' up there. We straight!"

The weed had calmed The Boy down some. He hadn't kicked it with Thomas in months. He smiled at the thought of he and The Titan getting lifted and bugging out. With the end of his trial just hours away he'd acquiesced his life to good hands.

"Only God can judge me now."

In a remote location a Japanese luxury car idled. Its driver sat watching the lobby through a telescopic camera lens. When the group entered, a man dressed from head to toe in fatigues stepped out and extended two fingers from a black gloved hand. Thirty seconds later five flashes lit the lobby of the building and the car blended easily into traffic.

MANHATTAN
Municipal Court Building
The Next Day

"Sir," **said the judge**, "you understand that you've been found guilty on the charge set before you." Then he addressed The Boy's attorney. "Council, in light of these recent circumstances and your client's physical condition, I will reinstate bail giving him a period to convalesce before his sentencing. That date is set for …"

1995

DEAD MEN WALKING

ANTONIA STATE PENETENTERY
February 14th

"The Degree to Which a Society Is Civilized, Can Be Judged By Entering its Prisons"

"Dostoyevsky"

The quote had been etched into the paint. And not a word of Russian could he relate, but the thought was very clear. The slam of the gate having just occurred, it was the slam of a gavel coupled with a man's words that echoed in his ear.

A man formed by blood flesh and experiences just like himself; yet this *man* was *his* judge. And an uncompromising one he'd been; cloaked in black, his throne exalted; to his right a Roman eagle topped mace held a gold embroidered American flag; a symbol of his supreme authority in that forum, an authority that left The Boy's supporters feeling numb that morning when he was sentenced to the maximum.

"... Five Years!" The gavel slammed. "You are to begin serving that time immediately. Good luck to you sir."

No surprise. If the statistics were correct this life had given him two choices; heaven or hell, freedom or jail. With the whole world it seemed against him, he wondered why he was still alive, as he came to grips with the possibilities, in the event of his demise.

357

CALIFORNIA
Los Angeles
Firing Squad Records

Marlon "Pooh" Dark awoke early this March morning. He'd worked out in the gym of his estate, did a few laps around the pool, showered, dressed, and drove his custom low-rider to the automobile detailing shop he owned where he kept a fleet of luxury cars. There he had crucial decisions to make, *"uuhh, let's see ____red or white, a/c or the drop."* A short time later he pulled one of the Rolls Royces's into his company's parking lot, strolled past the cameras and security guards, then past the gasping employees, leaving a trail of *Cohiba* smoke in his wake.

He entered an opulent office,—decorated boorishly in red—picked up the phone and made a call to his interior decorator, he wanted the logo on the floor changed to match his mood.

"Yeah, be at my office in an hour. I'm out."

After dealing with the years of law suits, payoffs and huge cash settlements that came as a result of his "strong negotiations," an L.A. county judge had finally sentenced Pooh for his role in a 1992 assault and weapons case. His punishment ended up being five years probation and thirty days in a halfway house; he'd left there today a relatively free man and gone right back to his life as CEO of a now billion dollar company. To the millions who were buying his records and possibly the many more who were paying attention, Firing Squad Records and Marlon Dark in particular had reached their own mythic status. They were hood heroes, the new *untouchables,* and he was the new and improved, 325 pound 'Teflon Don.' But neither wealth nor freedom nor dominating the industry could satisfy Pooh. Numerous rumors since the one about the roof proved that his true joy came from humiliating his enemies. There'd been several broken jaws, the pro wrestlers he made get on their knees and beg like dogs, some poor bastard that was made to drink his brand of "distilled" champagne, and a really wild one about Pooh knocking out the horse of a mounted policeman who tried to break up his brawl. It was all part of keeping the competition to a minimum. Before his bid he'd set in motion a plan to eliminate what the few critics who dared to write about him called his biggest rival; a scrawny little "peacock" from the East who by his own admission had modeled his company after Firing Squad, and who produced what Pooh considered to be no good knockoffs of his material. *"Fucking critics,"* how dare they mention the two of them in the same breath? In the coming months he'd undeniably separate himself from those "cowards" at Youth Authority by brazenly declaring war on them at an awards ceremony and crushing any hopes of the two ever making peace. Not since 1861 had so many prepared for battle on American soil. Pooh's declaration would have troops from north to south and East to West screaming fuck peace and choosing sides. He smiled inside; the board was set just like he'd planned it; one more piece and he'd have niggas fighting across the whole planet.

ANTONIA STATE PENITENTERY
April

"You name it, I had it man; the cars, the cribs, and the cash."

"Yeah I know her. I used to tap that back in the day when she was fine."

"You forgot about me, huh? Remember when I used to run the block back in '89?"

On D-Block few of the prisoners had futures, but all of them had pasts; and with an audience unable to escape they'd chosen now as the time to share their stories, regardless of how sad. Too stubborn to ask for forgiveness, the prisoners held on tight to their sins; for them, sins were all they had.

Determined not to share their fate The Boy had been busy putting the last four months behind him. In December he'd been judged a flight risk. His bail was revoked and he was sent to Rikers Island. For the last month he'd kept himself busy adjusting to solitude of this, level four, maximum security prison. Twenty three hours a day were spent alone in the dark, breathing the pungent smell of stagnant shit around the clock while listening to the hardest thugs screaming all night and wishing they'd stop. But that was the past, over as of this morning. This afternoon a bald and bearded, burly and barrel-chested CO walked him down the hall to the visiting area.

"So you're him

"Who am I?

"I know about you, 'Mr. fuck-a-cop'; we aint gon' have you and your Billy-bad-ass-nigger-buddy out there starting trouble in our house. I'm the leader of the only gang that matters in here."

"What gang is that?"

Captain Nokes raised his sleeve and showed The Boy a tattoo of a robed Knight rider, on it's forehead a single red eye bulged grotesquely through its white hood.

"You best be fearing that boy. That means something. You're looking at an *Exalted Cyclops* in the *Invisible Empire*."

"The shit you heard aint do me justice, did it? Ho's in hoods don't scare me. *Look inside my first disk* you'll see I got *The Malleus Maleficarum* for you bitches."

Nokes' face and neck turned a purplish red. He slapped The Boy and drew his club. The Boy dropped to the ground, covered up and waited for the beating, but instead of feeling blows he heard a voice.

"You alright over there Captain Nokes? Maybe I should call this incident in?"

Nokes frowned and put the club away.

"No Sergeant. No need for that. We'll see how tough the rich nigger is when he goes into general population."

The voice had saved The Boy for the moment. Nokes snatched him to his feet and placed him in the officers' custody before storming off. "Your prisoner, *Sergeant* Peterson."

The Boy thanked his savior.

"Sir, you should take a look around you. Think about where you are and who's in charge. This is not a game. People die in here everyday. Is that what you want?"

"No ma'am."

"Good."

She tapped the glass. The gate buzzed and in the next room another officer pointed to a table where Marlon Dark sat larger than life.

"Pooh! Damn man what 'chu doing here?"

"Came to check out my homeboy; see how they treatin' you in here."

"I been better, but I'll make it through."

"Oh I know that, you a strong brother."

✳

They'd met at a Periscope function sometime in '93. Knowing The Boy's financial troubles Pooh offered to sign him to his label; and knowing his reputation, The Boy politely declined. But Pooh was secure and could wait for the things he wanted; instead of persisting, he planted a seed.

"What you normally get for a song?"

"Normally, about 25 G's."

"Yeah?"

Pooh wrote out a check and hand it to him.

"I got a project coming up soon."

"*$250,000!*" What's this?"

Pooh pat him on the back. "That's just a portion of what we pay for talent at Firing Squad."

Since then he'd always reminded The Boy that he had place reserved on his roster.

✳

They chit-chat for a few.

"You want me to set up some conjugals," asked Pooh?

"Nah, I'm getting married in a few days. My wife will take care of all that."

They laughed.

"Man, I heard about Double E.," said The Boy. "That's fucked up."

Last month Edgar Evans had made history again when he became the industry's first AIDS casualty.

Pooh shrugged.

"What happens in the dark always come to light. It's been a rumor going 'round that him and Q' was fucking each other."

The Boy eased away from that.

"So what else is going on in the world Pooh, what people talkin' 'bout?"

Pooh's assistant removed a Wall Street Journal and a Vibe magazine from his briefcase. Pooh dropped them on the table. "You."

The Boy picked up the magazine, read through it, and dropped it back on the table.

"That's it," he said, "just like I told the reporter."

"That aint what they saying over at Y.A."

"You can't trust Dizzy, man; and The Titan, that nigga like a big ass parrot on his shoulder cosigning everything he say."

"You aint gotta tell me," said Pooh, "I don't believe shit that comes out of Diz's mouth. He like a lil' kid when you catch him doing wrong, he get all shifty eyed, looking around for something to say."

The Boy agreed.

"Maan' look; my people got some shit you should hear, but first I need you to separate fiction from fact. What *really* happened?"

The Boy figured the whole truth needed to be told.

"A'ight. It all goes back to that night at the hotel. I met her on a Friday. Five minutes after we met she went down on me in the club. I took her to the hotel and we got busy. After I saw her in the light, I aint really wanna see her no more. On Saturday me and the homies went out clubbing again. That Sunday I spent most of the day with my girl Nia and when I got to the hotel that evening, Treni, Glover and J.I. was there drinking. Treni tells me that the girl from the club called a couple of times; he keeps talkin' about how hot her body is and telling me to call her back. I had just got some pussy so I really wasn't trying to fuck, but this nigga is at me. I knew what they was on and I aint with all that gangbanging shit. I like to keep my nuts out of close proximity with other niggas. So I said, 'Maybe when I get out the shower.' I'm hoping they'd be on something else by then cause we had some business to handle later that night. When I get out J.I. tells me she called and Treni talked to her and told her to come over. I'm like, 'whatever; fuck it, that's on them.' A few minutes later J.I. answers the phone. It's her. I told him to send her up. It's tripped out when she gets there cause we straight chillin', I'm sittin' there smoking in boxers and slippers and she dressed like she going to a ball or somethin'. Anyway, I'm sitting on the couch and she come sit next to me. By this time the weed is kicking in and the whole vibe is just wrong."

"Like how?"

"I'd get up and get and get a drink, or go to the window and when I'd come back I'd purposely sit somewhere and she'd get up and follow me; plus I'm peeping how these niggas eyes is following her. You ever see that one Woody Woodpecker, "Pantry Panic," where it's winter and Woody and the kitty cat is starving they ass off, then they see each other? Well that's how niggas was looking; like they was some hungry ass Ethiopian kids and she was food. I told you, bad vibes man. So I snatch her up and take her to the room to break the tension...."

"She don't even know you tryin' to save her ass," asked Pooh?
    "Literally! Like I said, the weed had kicked in by then and she lookin' better. We in there about twenty minutes when the door open and they came in."
    "Was y'all fuckin'?"
    "Not yet. On my mama, they had to be peeking through the door or some-thin', 'cause I had just pulled up her dress."
    "You should've checked them niggas right there. I'ma keep it real; if that was me they would'a had to get they own rooms. Aint no bustas gon' be chillin' in my eight-hundred dollar a night suite."
    "You right, but I ..."
    "You aint wanna look like you was 'cakein' the bitch."
    "Right."

"So what you do when they came in."

"I kinda tensed up. Like I said I aint with that shit, but honey acted like she aint care. She aint say nothin', she just kept goin' at it in front of everybody like that night in the club. That's when I hear Treni in the corner sounding like he directing a movie. *'Move her over. Spread her ass-cheeks apart.'* I was like 'Yo, fuck this crank. I'm up.' I got up, went in the other room and passed out. When Treni woke me up I was groggy and shit was weird. I remember the radio was off and the TV was on, and all the lights were on, all of 'em. Everybody had they clothes on but me, and ol' girl is cryin' threatening me with the police and shit. All I could think was *'they gon' do me like they did Mike Tyson'*. I'm at her like, 'what the fuck are you talking about? Yo, either come here and holla at me, or bounce.' I had been through too much court to be hearing that crazy shit. Treni and Glover was like, 'We'll take care of it.' Then they went after her. J.I. rolled a blunt and we smoked for like a minute, then he was like "I'ma go downstairs and see what's taking so long." I shoulda known somethin' cause J.I. had got real close with them niggas since we'd all been hangin' out. So he left and I was the only one in the room. It was quiet and I was thinking, *'what the fuck is going on?'* Then I heard that knock."

Pooh was looking directly at him shaking his head.

"And don't nobody else knock like that," he said. "How you feel about it now?"

"What," asked The Boy, "you mean about what happened to her?"

"All of it."

"I feel bad for her, if it really happened."

"What 'chu mean?"

"I mean this shit is all twisted. Some pieces don't fit. You know they gave her a physical? They never found no DNA, they aint find no evidence at all.

Remember, I left the room and went to sleep so it coulda' happened like she say it did *or* they coulda' been in the next room plottin'.

I can't tell you what happened in there. But I *can* tell you that everybody in that room is walking the streets free while I'm in jail. That's wrong."

"You gotta be mo' careful about who you let hang around. Niggas will front like they your homies and really be some phony motherfuckers. What happened with you and The Titan?"

"A'ight, leading up to the shooting we was both real busy and hadn't been hanging out, then I ran into him and Dizzy walkin' in the Hotel with this dude Roberko."

"Yeah I heard about him. Didn't he used to run with that Jamaican crew?"

"Right, the Untouchables. So 'T' pull me to the side and he's like; 'Yo watch ya' back man, woo woo woo.' But he aint sayin' no names and I'm like; 'What's the deal?' He kept tellin' me he was gon' see me but he never did, and believe me I was listenin'. Then a week later I see jealous niggas coming for my diamonds cause they glistnin'."

That's when Pooh asked the million dollar question.

"You think he set you up?"

The Boy took a deep breath and scanned the visiting area for just the right words.

"Nah, I don't think he set me up, but he knew niggas was comin' for me. Them niggas was from Brooklyn, he had to know somethin'. And fuckin' J.I., I been taking care of that cat every since I got signed. That nigga looked like "Debo" compared to them punks. Plus he had a strap and aint do shit? Maan'. When I see that nigga ..." The Boy was all fired up and Pooh loved to see him that way. "Yo,' he better holla at me!"

He pushed the magazine Pooh's way.

"Read the interview again, you'll see what happened."

Pooh got a pencil and paper from his assistant, moved his chair closer to the table, then lowered his voice and said; "I'ma tell *you* what happened that night."

The Boy moved closer and Pooh began writing.

James Avingion   Daniel Blayloc

The Boy studied the two names for a moment. He'd never heard of them.

"You know how some people think Glover is Treni," asked Pooh?

"Yeah."

"Well Treni aint really Treni."

He started scribbling again.

In the mid eighties the real Treni Forte was large, especially in Haiti. His team had a good thing going. They moved coke and weed from South America as far north as South Carolina. From there The Untouchables took it further north and did they thing. In the late eighties the DEA started cracking down. By 1990 they had his whole operation. Niggas who know, say it was a raid in Miami and Treni got popped. James Avingion was one of his connects down there. A few months after the raid he pops up in New York with a new name.

The Boy looked over the paper a number of times not knowing what to believe. He'd been done in by people he'd called friends. Something he'd never called Pooh. *"Jealous niggas and broke bitches equal packed jails."* That's the second thing you learn in prison. *"Trust nobody."* That's the first; and if he ever forgot the gunshots wounds would always be there to remind him. He wondered what Pooh's people had to say about those.

"That explains a lot, but I aint have shit to do with that business. That aint what got me shot."

"You right. Keep up with me 'cause the ride gets tricky. I aint gotta tell you how any and everybody was looking for a way to launder they money. Some of these so called record execs is more shadier than others."

Pooh laughed to himself and started writing again.

Around the same time Treni went down, Roberko took a few bullets and caught a case. Nickel and dime shit. He did a couple of years and decided to go straight when he got out. He and Treni used to be boys in Miami when he was still James so he knows the deal. They make a deal. Treni puts up the money for the record label and Roberko supposed run it. Now it's two sides to it. If they find a decent artist then Roberko does his thing with him; that's all legit, they sign him to a bogus-ass contract but it's still legit. But if they find a nigga that's sweet, that's where Treni 'nem come in. They extort the nigga; have him paying for protection and shit like that.

The Boy sat up in his seat waiving his hand.

"They never came at me like that."

Pooh waived him back down.

"I know."

You were too big for them to be pulling that shit on. And after y'all start hanging out Treni took a liking to you; they all did, but Treni especially. He figures the best thing for him is to get in close with you so you can help put him on to other niggas in the industry and make the business seem more legit. Basically they was gon' use you."

The Boy shook his head.

"Ok, I can see that one, that's exactly what they was tryin' to do. So that night at the hotel, that was a set up right?"

Pooh laughed.

"Nah, man. Your boy is just a cum freak. Them niggas got real kinky with that bitch. I heard they had the big orange ball in her mouth and everything."

"Well what the fuck she go and put my name in it for? Why she aint ..."

"The ho' was mad," said Pooh. "Put yourself in her position. She went there to get wit 'chu and you dissed her; then that shit happens. Man why aint 'chu talk business with her instead of lettin' Treni 'nem do it?"

"I'ont know man."

"Big mistake, you should've handled that yourself."

Pooh started writing.

But when it was all said and done, it was the statements your lawyers made to the press; what they said about the mayor and city hall coming down on y'all; that was the underlying cause for your arrest. Them people like to move in the shadows."

The Boy knew that was true. Even before they became enemies Treni made a big deal about his anonymity.

"Fuckin' snitch," he said lowering his head. "I knew he was workin' for the Feds."

"You wasn't supposed to get shot. They wanted to shut you up but they aint know the rules." Pooh winked, reached across the table and bumped fists with The Boy. "There you was, a young nigga with heart and a strap. You aint have shit to lose."

Grateful for his tacit, The Boy leaned forward and whispered with eyes full of malice.

"Hey Pooh, You know the names of the niggas who shot me?"

Pooh's smile was wicked.

"Some of 'em. It's a gang of snitches workin' for the Feds; they call theyself;

"The Illuminati!"

✳

MONTH FIVE
May Day

Nia was a good girl, not a groupie, a future Cum Lade who'd made The Boy wait a couple of dates before thy did it. He decided that since they'd been together a few months before he went in he could trust her enough to make her his wife.

Father Lorenzo Cronin of the Church of The Good Thief had performed the wedding ceremony less than a week ago. Since then Nia had moved into a motel near the prison and visited as much as she was allowed. The day after the wedding Sgt. Petersen informed her that the information The Boy had requested was contraband and wouldn't be allowed in. Sgt. Petersen helped him once again when she flew a kite to The Boy via Nia, and at 11:50 pm. April 31st, corrections officer Remy Mirra pushed open his cell door.

"Follow me if you want to live."

The Boy got up and went as the guard led him to a dark and empty church where he lit a cigarette. The flame from the lighter gave life to his many tattoos. On his neck was a phoenix clutching a swastika, above it the letters DOC. On his wrist, thick, black words read Blood and Honor.

The Boy pulled out his shank. Remy pulled out his and said;

"Take it easy man. You need to listen cause we aint got much time. In ten minutes Captain Nokes and The Aryans are having a party and they plan to make you the stripper."

"Get the fuck outta here."

"No joke, my man, I am on my way there and I am letting you know in advance. Do not go back to your cell tonight."

The Boy viewed him askance.

"If you with The Brotherhood why are you helping me?"

Unsure of that himself, Mirra took a drag and tried to explain.

"I got a cousin a couple years younger than me whose been listening to your shit for years. He's all into Hip-Hop. Me and his twin brother Romulus were always ragging on him about it but he never would back down. About a year ago they get into it and Romulus ends up dead. Dumbass." Remy took another drag and forced out the smoke. "Something's wrong with Remus's head man. That Desert Storm Syndrome shit is real. Anyway, he's in a tent city in Arizona now. When he heard you were here he wrote and told me this war story he'd never told me before. I didn't believe it until I listened to your music for myself." Mirra held out his hand. "I feel you, brother." After they shook he gave The Boy a pen and paper. "He asked me to get your autograph too." Seconds after signing Remy whispered. "You can only believe half of what Cronin says, he's a *Jesuit*, and they perfected using 'blown cover as cover.'"

The Boy was befuddled. Cronin was a man of the cloth and what little he knew about *The Order of the Society of Jesus* did not fit the warning. Founded in Spain in 1534 by St. Ignatius Loyola, they'd made their reputation as the Popes most devout priests, by promoting the faith, teaching the young and providing counsel to educators, politicians and princes.

"I thought they were good guys?"

Mirra uttered 14 words.

"Don't let the cloth fool you. Traitors and Zionist collaborators is what they are." The Boy nodded and Remy continued.

"Jesuits are the agents of The Vatican. For years the Pope has dealt with charges that he's had them meddling in secular affairs, running drugs and bombing flight 103 with P2." Mirra blew his Marlboro smoke into the air. "But maybe he shouldn't be blamed. Another name for a Jesuit is an *'Ignatian,'* and an Ignatian is one who's under oath to perform clandestine services for the Society of Jesus' Superior General, a.k.a. *The Black Pope*. He is the real leader of Vatican policy, and thereby the religious arm of the Empire."

Mirra left at the stroke of midnight. The Boy found his way through the pews to the confessional. Once inside he asked;

"What's this about? Who's over there?"

"You've got friends in high places, my son."

He recognized the voice but a shadow covered the face.

"Father Cronin?"

"Perhaps it would be best if we remained nameless. Wouldn't you agree?"

"I would. What's this about?"

"It has been brought to my attention that we share a common enemy."

"Who?"

"Enigmas;" sighed The Father, "they go by so many names yet little is known about any. They lay claim to the top thirteen percent of society and are said to rule all things secular. They are the unseen, the brotherhood of shadows; you may know them as the men in black."

"You mean the Illuminati."

"That is correct. Look below you."

The Boy reached under his seat and picked up a book. *'The Art of the Illuminati'*

He looked at the cover.

"I know this. It's the Great Seal of the United States."

"To them it is known as the shining delta. It symbolizes their ability to keep watch over all things; that is why they address themselves as Gods and Kings." The Boy flipped through the pages as Father Cronin explained. "Adam Weishaupt, a disgruntled professor of religious studies at the University of Ingolstadt in Bavaria founded The Illuminati in 1776. It was meant to be a society of freethinkers opposed to the beliefs of the church.

Weishaupt had come to believe that religion and worship of God were the root of mans problems and through the process of illumination *certain individuals* could be made perfect without God."

"So they're atheists."

"They are Satanist," bellowed Father Cronin with such force that phlegm loosened in his chest! "Theirs is more than just a conspiracy against religion. They are the soldiers for Gods original adversary. You know of him, yes?"

"No."

"I will tell you a story then." The Father cleared his throat and settled down. "Once there was in heaven a particularly beautiful angel, the best and brightest of all, the angel of light."

"Lucifer!"

"That is correct. Lucifer was Gods favorite, but pride and vanity were his greatest sins. So when God formed Adam from the earth, so pleased was he with his creation that God insisted the angels submit to Adam. Lucifer, full of insolence, refused, going so far as to question God as to why a son of fire should bow to one of clay."

"So that's when his revolt began."

"Not quite. That was The Argument. For the next nine days one third of heavens angels fell. When at last God raised his hand to stop them, 133,306,668 were encapsulated in flesh wherever they were at that moment. Some became creatures of the earth, some the air, and others the waters, and there were some who by that time had made the descent into *she'ol*. They emerged from the fiery pit vile and grotesque creatures. Lucifer was one of them. For the next three days he gathered as many of his legions as possible and on the morning of the fourth day Lucifer shone as bright as 10,000 suns when he led the attack on Heaven. At the gates he cursed God, declaring war on him *and* his precious creation, vowing that if he could not rule there, he would surely be Prince here. With that, the Archangel Michael ordered the trumpets blown and the Seraphim drew their swords; and *that* is the day the war began." Father Cronin hesitated before asking; "Have you any idea what that day was?"

"None," answered The Boy.

"It was today, May 1ˢᵗ. The very day that Mr. Weishaupt chose to found his Order. You must understand that for ages Lucifer's minions had been scattered, lost souls aimlessly wreaking havoc. Weishaupt's coven gave them a home, and for nearly 220 now years they've been gathering, rebuilding, and relearning what had long been forgotten. They are now the top thirteen percent of society, wealthy and powerful individuals who have infiltrated key positions worldwide, and now that their pyramid of nations is almost complete, the time is fast approaching for their leader to claim his throne."

Mirra's warning crossed The Boy's mind.

"Why haven't I heard this before," he asked?

"Who would have told you? The people of your ghettos are not ready for this New World Order. Furthermore that information has been blacklisted. That is why for centuries whenever there were wars or invasions the temples and libraries were the first to be destroyed. It was all part of Brotherhoods plan to turn fact into legend and legend to myth. Today we live in a world that has no time for myths, but try as they may, the demons have not erased them from history. We at The Vatican possess the most extensive collection of blacklisted items in the world."

The Boy overcame his temptation to ask the Father how they'd acquired them.

"Through our Universities and charitable organizations we do what we can to remind them of the things they have been made to forget. That is why we are hated by the enemy as are you."

The Boy responded casually as he flipped the pages.

"Nah, not me. I've never been involved with any of your organizations."

"What a shame," said the Father. "We must rectify that."

The Boy ignored him.

"I'm here because I was set up by …"

"A Godless group of sycophants who've modeled themselves after another, I know," said The Father impatiently. "The demons, you see, cannot work their magick alone. They employ groups of familiars, or imps, lesser illuminaries, but no less evil or dangerous. Many, like you are self-made men, wealthy and powerful in their own right, and they believe as their employers do that *they* are now Gods, with the right to give life and to take it away. They are the ones who set *you* up as well as your mother."

The Boy was too stunned to speak, his eyes were glued to the book and the sight of the most brilliant symbol he'd ever seen, four words,—Earth, Air, Fire and Water—written in a perfectly symmetrical Gothic script. He was so taken by it that he held up the book.

"This symbol here, what is it?"
"That is the Illuminati diamond."
Father Cronin's answer brought it all into focus. The symbol was the exact one that the gunmen had made before his shots illuminated the lobby.

"That's the symbol them cowards threw up before they shot me!"

The Boy closed the book and gave The Father his full attention.
"What do you know about my mother?"

"Your mother was once a rousing speaker and an asset to her cause. Only she and her God know if the charges brought against her were true.
But it made no difference in the end. Her work with The Movement was incidental; the real cause of her persecution was you."
"Me! What did I do?"
"You were born," said The Father. "Surely you did not think God would abandon his creations. Since the beginning, prior even to religious Orders there have been those who do his work. Conduits sent by him to relay the truth to mankind. They are the artists, and you my child are one of them."
"Who are the others?"
"I am not at liberty to say. To know them you must travel the way of the astrals to the house of your father."

✳

MONTH SIX
June

The last time she'd set foot in a prison was 1987. The outcome is a one time story too personal for these pages. But a story she was sure to tell was the one of a night in 1959, the night she says led to her first trip to prison.

"It wasn't no secret. For weeks they'd been going from town to town. Each sunset brought the smell of burning crosses a little closer to us, and the sunrise made the stories of them raping little girls and hanging they mamas and daddies more vivid. Everyone knew the Klan was fed up with the niggers and Indians in Treeton, but they were so bold they posted signs with the time and place of the rally. Umm, umm, it wasn't no secret; everyone in town knew what was coming but them.

The field they chose was perfect for an ambush. One way in and one way out, and the road was surrounded by trees, but the rosewoods weren't talking that night. They was quiet, waiting while about two hundred Klansmen finished getting liquored up and tying nooses. Even though we was out numbered two to one, when your grandfather gave the signal we all opened fire on them. It was a mess, shotguns and rifles exploding everywhere. I was ten years old, your aunt Stella was thirteen. Mama had dug us a ditch and the three of us were in there. They was holding their ears and screaming. Not me. I was watching your grandfather and your uncle fight for our lives. I got my first taste of revolution that night and every since then it's been on."

Marian was born in North Carolina in 1948 to sharecroppers who'd met in the fields. Her mother Etta, a tiny, quiet, half-Cherokee girl was spiritual, unlike her father Pee Wee, a tinier, jet black, take no shit alcoholic with a mean streak who made a living gambling after they had lost their land. The girls could always tell how the cards had treated him by the way he treated them.

Marian grew up wishing her mother wasn't so passive. She wished she was more of a fighter, if for no one else but herself.

The Boy missed his mother, best friends at one point, they'd seen each other just a handful of times since he'd put her on the bus in '90. After that they'd gone an entire year without speaking. By early 1992 he'd began receiving letters telling him about her recovery, letters explaining about how after waking up one morning on Stella's bathroom floor, she'd summoned every bit of strength and checked herself into rehab. She said that she had it under control, but he'd heard that before. It would take more than words before he could trust her again. Then in '93 Marian saw the headlines from Atlanta and thought, *"What the hell has my child gotten himself into?"*

She packed her things and went to support him. In the courtroom The Boy took one look at her and found her eyes quick and bright, her face round and full of grace as it once had been. Somehow the little woman whose demons had torn her into a million little pieces had once again managed to pull herself together and find her way home. That's when he realized what he was witnessing; *the evolution of a revolutionary.* He felt lucky to have her there, he knew only she could truly understand how it felt to be in a fight against the world, but her presence also worried him. No sooner than she'd returned had she been put into these battles, and once again he was to blame.

"That's gonna be hell," he thought, *"hugging on your son from a jail cell."*

Who knew if she was ready for that so soon? And for that reason he'd forbidden her to visit him here. But as time went by, Marian could tell from the font of the letters she received that her son may have gone a little crazy.

Neither one could hide the joy on their faces that morning when they met in the visiting room.

"Ma! What are you doing here?"

"I came to see you," she said as they hugged.

"Well I made it," he replied, "top of the world."

The conversation started of light as the two caught up. Marian told him all about her beloved garden in the country house he'd brought for her before he went in, and he explained to her just how big a following he had in the prisons. A few hours later The Boy introduced her to her daughter-in-law when she came to visit. Nia left early and let them have some time to themselves. By the afternoon they couldn't dance around the real topics any longer.

"Hey ma, when I was in elementary did you ever think I'd end up here."

"Truthfully, yeah. Everyday I prayed against it, but with our family history all you needed to do was slip up once and I knew what was waiting for you. So tell me *really*, how are you holding up in here?"

"There are times when all I can think about is suicide, but when I hold that steel to my neck all I can see is your eyes. All I can hear is your voice telling me not to be a punk."

Marian closed her eyes and wondered as always how good of a parent she'd been.

"I'm glad you made the right decision," she finally said. "I need you here, your sister needs you here, and maybe you've forgotten but your fans need you too. They're waiting for some of that thug shit; at least that's what they tell me."

"The music is over, Ma. I aint wrote nothing since I been in here. I can't write. I can't get a moments rest. I told you in the letters how I've been having these, ___ I guess you'd call them crazy dreams." The Boy watched as Marian's cigarette began to shake in her hand, she knew all to well the content of crazy dreams. "But that's the thing," he said, "they cant be dreams because lately I've been having them with open eyes."

Marian flicked away her ashes.

"I had my share of those when I was in here." She said, steadying her nerves for what she was about to say. "But I know what you're saying can't be true, your music is as immortal as the angels that walk with you." Then she focused on her reflection in the window as she recalled.

"It was May of '71, the night before my trial and I had the weight of the world on my mind, I hadn't slept, I hadn't ate, the only thing I knew for sure was that I was going to jail for the rest of my life and I had no idea what would they would do to you. The night guard," Marian cringed, "I'll never forget his name, or his face or his breath; he was on the floor beside me talking, constantly. He never stopped talking. Even when he wasn't there I could feel that foul, rotten breath whispering on my face, telling me to stop fighting, to give up and he would make all my pain go away. The radio in the hallway was playing, *"When the Music's Over,"* by The Doors. She cringed and chuckled again as she shook it off. "All that psychedelic shit about "the girl in the mirror", and what they'd "done to our fair sister," I swear it was like; _____ like the song was talking to me. I *know* they were talking about me." She was rocking from side to side. "I couldn't take it. I was suffocating, there was all this pain on my chest, like something was on me, and you were kicking my stomach so hard I thought you were going to tear your way out of there. I was in so much pain."

"What did you do?"

"I didn't know what else to do. I closed my eyes and prayed. I don't know how many times I said the Lords prayer. I just kept saying it over and over and when I opened them my eyes." She stopped her rocking and sat still. "It all felt so strange, it was very surreal, like the room was the same yet, _____ *different* somehow. I tried to move but I couldn't. I was paralyzed and that's when I noticed Eblis had become this mass of smokeless fire, and the flames looked like they were fighting these two balls of light."

"What was I doing?"

Marian was all choked up. "Nothing. You weren't moving at all. And when I realized that, I remember screaming so loud."

The Boy looked into her glazed eyes. "But there was no sound," she whispered. "It was like the scream, _____ of a butterfly."

She mumbled incoherently.

The Boy tugged gently at her arm.

"Come back Ma."

She focused on him.

"I'm here."

"What happened," he asked?

"I saw Eblis running into the hallway yelling something about wanting the world and that's when I looked down and saw the light."

"What light?"

Marian smiled at him.

"Your light. My belly was glowing, and you started moving again."

"And the next day you beat the charges," he said.

"Yes," she replied, "we did."

Visiting hours were at an end. He kissed his mama goodbye and wiped away the tear seeping from her eye.

"I'm glad you came to visit today. You know you are appreciated."

"So are you."

They hugged, and after a moment a C.O. stepped forward to break their embrace. Marian took her sons hand and said;

"People don't believe this, but until we've given back more than we've received our lives don't belong to us. In this life we all have an obligation to fulfill. Mine was giving birth to you."

"What 'chu think mine is?"

"I can't tell you. But I've seen you give your life to this music. So if you asked me you don't owe nobody nothing and that includes me. Whatever you accomplish from now on should be your hopes and your dreams. But let me warn you baby, like your father once told me, the gods reserve a special place for folks crazy enough to try and fulfill their dreams."

✳

MONTH SEVEN
Independents Day

Emancipated by her visit, the last three weeks of sleep had been the best

The Boy had gotten in months, but now his crazy dreams had been replaced by the unanswered questions about his father that had plagued him since a child.

This July 4th after the lights went out, and before he laid it down to sleep, he prayed the Lord his soul to keep, soon after he was startled by the approach of a figure that vaguely resembled Sgt. Peterson inside his cell.

"What the ... Who are you?"

The figure didn't speak. Instead it an offered him one end of a red knotted bandanna. The Boy understood. He took it and followed the figure through the cell door and on a night ride to the very heights of the prison, to a tier from which no tear would ever fall, known throughout Antonia as The Mountain. At the pinnacle Surya stood ignited at the entrance to The Old Mans cell.

"Greetings Prince."
  "Greetings," replied The Boy.
  "One request," said Surya, *"go easy on The Old Man. Long ago he was full of big dreams and plans. Believing he could be or do anything that he wanted, he decided to change the world. So he dreamed up a plan that to this day unfurls, only to find out later that between what we dream and what we do lays this world."*

The Boy had prepared his whole life for this, yet he was hesitant, his stomach queasy thinking about the times when he'd lost faith in his father and questioned his means, and even worse, the times when he'd put his hopes and dreams on the scales of a triple beam.

"Not to worry," said Surya. *"All was permitted because nothing was true. Your sins are forgiven; you had the spirit of a Thug in you."*

The Boy remembered Marian's promise as he entered the cell.

"One day you'll get to meet him."

He did. And that's the one memory that he kept just for him.

But when his initiation was over, without warning his surroundings changed, the floor of the cell gave way and for an instant he found himself in good company, drifting amidst the stars of Empyrean. Then came the fall. And he fell longer and farther than he'd ever imagined he could. And when he awoke in his cell he did so a new man, his mind set on new dreams, and his sights set on new plans.

✳

MONTH EIGHT
August

He read.

"A man who might want to make a show of goodness in all things necessarily comes to ruin among so many who are not good. Because of this it is necessary for a prince, wanting to maintain himself, to learn how to be able to be not good and to use this and not use it according to necessity."

(The Prince: By Machiavelli)

And he wrote.

✳

MONTH NINE
September

Pooh had come to visit every month since April and each visit had been laced with a tempting offer which The Boy had always refused, but nine months gestation in the belly of the penal colony had metamorphisised a military mind.

"Yeah I know what I said before but believe me, you fuckin' with a changed man. I'm a General now. Your enemies is my enemies, Pooh. They can kiss my ass from here to," he pointed through the window and across the street, "over there. Fuck them, it's on. I'ma destroy them cowards. When I get free …" he moved in closer, "peep game nigga, let me tell you 'bout my ambitions as ridah'!"

✳

MONTH TEN
October

Their alliance was as frail as the tissue it had been written on, but their signatures meant that the contract was binding, for how long he didn't know, and now was not the time for legalities, not as the freedom bell rang. Nokes and his henchmen looked sad, as if they hoped he'd never leave. The voice of the prisoners was deafening as Peterson walked beside him, her body language seeming to question the means of his departure. Just beyond the outer walls was a fully stocked limousine waiting to sweep him off to the airport where a red and white G-4 was prepped and waiting to deliver the newest member of the Firing Squad family to his new home in Los Angeles.

The limo door opened as they neared, Pooh got out with a big smile on his face and a bigger cigar in his hand.

The General smiled back, tempted to scream, "Free at last, free at last, thank God ..."

But God hadn't freed him from his inferno; instead it had been a Faustian pact with an underworld chieftain. The future was in his eye when he shook hands with Peterson.

"Don't go celebrating too hard in L.A.," she said, "remember you're out on bail."

He stopped chewing his lip long enough to smile and assure her.

"That aint even in the picture, what I look like celebrating when I'm living on borrowed time; umm umm, I got too much work to do."

On the plane Kleinfeld and Pooh were noticeably more enthusiastic than he; even more so as the liquor flowed and they worked together constructing plans for Firing Squads future with The General in command.

"You really have no idea what a great decision you've made joining the organization," said a clearly intoxicated Kleinfeld. "All those legal problems you've dealt with in the past no longer exist. My firm will take care of those. Were going to make your appeal a top priority. We'll get your conviction overturned or at the very least get you off with time served; that you can count on, just ask Pooh here."

Pooh nodded and asked for Kleinfeld's attaché case. Kleinfeld went inside and handed Pooh stacks of crisp hundred dollar bills. He peeled off a few, gave those back to him and gave the rest to The General.

"There go a lil' somethin' for your pocket," said Pooh, "and it's plenty more where that came from. You aint gotta be running around hustlin' songs and all that old crazy shit. You aint gotta worry about money no more period. I want your head in the game. I want you in the studio doing what you do. I got you the best security too; you aint gotta worry about a thang, you a member of the family."

Kleinfeld chimed in.

"You heard of La Costra Nostra?"

"Yeah, the five families, The Vallachi Papers, and all that," answered The General.

Kleinfeld smiled.

"Exactly."

"I told you this nigga was smart," said Pooh.

"Good," said Kleinfeld, "well let's just say my firm's history goes back to the old country, and you and Pooh should consider yourselves friends of ours."

Kleinfeld held up his glass and said a toast that he ended with, "To Strict Observance." The glasses clinked and Kleinfeld drank as The General asked what that meant.

"Aww, that's just some Jew boy shit he always sayin'," explained Pooh. "What's that other thing "*Mishpucka,*" I think the motherfucker got him a little gang goin' or something.'"

They drank some more and Pooh had the flight attendant roll The General some green as he got comfortable while phoning his loved ones to tell them the good news. When he'd finished, Pooh made a call and hand him the phone.

"Remember that lil' problem I told you I was havin'. Here, see if you can talk some sense into this nigga."

The General took the phone.

"Who dis? Dis Q'! What's up nigga? Guess who?"

Pooh had kept the news on the low. His plan was to light a fire under the asses of his other artists.

"Whaat? W'asup baby, what's the biz? Where *you* at," wondered Q.

"Nigga I'm free like O.J. Me and Pooh 'bout to touch down in Cali. Hey, you know we family now, right?"

"Word?"

"Oh yeah; and you know all eyes is on me to see what I'm about to do. I need you, Q. Meet a mu'fucka' in the studio with some of them bomb ass beats."

Q whined in protest.

"Right now?"

As of late most of his time had been spent in the bedroom of his suburban mansion with an endless stream of avant-garde personalities. It was a running joke in the industry about how it took him years to finish one song.

"Yeah, right now! Get off yo' ass nigga, I need some hits!"

✳

Quincy obliged and Pooh made good on all his promises. With his every need met and a bottomless cache at his disposal The General took flight. His destination? *The Aeon.* That place where energy and thought meet and dreams are brought to fruition. His return was welcomed; for ten months he'd been bound and unable to reach it, he basked in its glow and bathed in the ebb and tide of creations flow. His mind was like a flower in bloom, his mouth emitting pollination for people. In every track laid were fertile thoughts captured as both producers and artists fell by the wayside attempting to keep up. In just six weeks he'd fulfilled his promises. With material for two disks already complete, he formed his own group, *The Eternals*. Seven loyal soldiers blessed with power to speak and reach the peeps on every street.

Pooh was pleasantly surprised in the recoupability of his investment. Not since the last Great War had there been a General like this one, one with the blood and guts to say what he meant and mean what he said or one who'd made a vow to return and did. Just to be in the presence of him inspired the average person to do better by forcing them to look in the mirror. That's why Pooh's uneasiness was allayed, when at last a request from The General was made; a sacrilegious request that Pooh was more than eager to grant.

QUEENS

"**C'mon 'G'**, let me get at this nigga. I'ma rock the bitch to sleep."

"Yeeahh! That's the shit I'm talkin 'bout nigga! Soldier, straight soldier! But this shit is personal. This motherfucker gon' die, by my hand."

"Revenge is like the sweetest joy . . . "

Or so the saying goes. So many thoughts, words, and memories were going through his mind. But it was his words, the ones he'd written exactly six months earlier that he focused on. Ironic he'd thought, how on the first of May he too would begin the vendetta that he hoped would bring about their end. Irony or something more? Questions like those always arise when speaking of plans. He knew now that his plans as grandiose as they may have seemed were just a modicum of another's; but what then of theirs?

"If that's the case," he thought, *"then everybody's got to play their part."*

He hit the Thai twice and passed the rest to Stella's son who was rolling with him. His lil' cousin Kay, he too was a ridah' now.

"'G,'" said the young cadet choking of a long pull, "we gots to stick to the plan."

The General chuckled a bit.

"Nigga you aint know? This was the plan all along. You just drive. I got this bitch."

He tossed the last of the blunt and all caution into the wind.

How did it come to this? He remembered seven years ago, then tried hard to shut the memories out. But of course they kept coming. It's said in hindsight your vision becomes 20/20.

"Fuck that!" You gone remember some shit, remember all the times that nigga lied! Remember the block and all the three in the morning oaths you and that nigga took! Remember them times when that nigga was supposed to be on the corner looking out and you looked up and there was five-o half way down the block. Remember them lame excuses he'd give!"

"'G'", they was on some real creep shit, plus, you know it's kinda foggy and shit!"

"I knew that fuckin' trick was sleep," he said lightly. *"It's that extra long smile they always give, to hide the trace of hate."*

And through the years the smiles had gotten longer; especially as The General's star began to shine brighter than his.

"And I still showed that nigga mad love. Got to pay more attention to the signs."

But close to seven years ago both of their visions were cloudy as they stepped across the threshold to make their weekend a dream come true.

INSIDE THE MINDS EYE

The Boy had been shopping his demo for a while and had finally hit pay dirt in the form of a one album deal with Periscope Records. He'd taken J.I. along with him to sign the paperwork and to try and get him something; anything. Why? Cause that's the rule. Leave no one behind. If one man made it it's his duty to throw back a line. And though his deal was less than stellar, he succeeded in getting his homeboy some guest spots and production credits on two songs. That was on a Tuesday afternoon. By Friday morning when they picked up their advance checks J.I.'s smile was extra long.

"Damn," thought The Boy, *"I did my best."*

"You go ahead and handle your business with yo' cheese," he said to J.I. as they left Periscope's offices. "Re-up, hit ya' people off, get your rims. I got us this weekend."

J.I. seemed to be genuinely touched by the act.

"Man that's real, thanks 'G.'"

"Till the end that's how it's gon' be," said The Boy. "You aint never had a friend like me."

THE AMAZON
August '89
3:33 am

"POW." One shot and a second of silence, followed by six more in succession were enough to shatter that dream about the day they got signed.

The Boy got off two shots then fell off the milk crate into the cognac and cards. He tossed that pistol to J.I. who was fumbling with the safety on his 380.

"I'm going for them 14's in the bushes," he yelled!

J.I. let off the last four shots in the twenty-two while The Boy got the big guns. Two black 'nina's' came out the back of the car. J.I. tried the 380 again. "TAT, TAT, TAT!" A fiend someone was serving screamed and ducked behind a dumpster as bullets from the 14's shattered the back windshield and blew out a rear tire. Blood squirted from the window and onto the street. Gunfire and sparks from the 'duece and a quarter' lit up the night. J.I. had managed to hit the passenger door with a couple of shots before the car sped off.

"Punk beeyaches," yelled The Boy! "I'll get you fuckers back before I'm buried!"

A troop in green basketball shoes ran toward the scene yelling;

"Y'all niggas straight?"

Two more soldiers followed him; all were strapped.

"Yeah," said J.I. wide eyed.

"Hell yeah," said The Boy squeezing off two more rounds. "I got that trick in the back seat."

Smoke from the fire, from the guns and tires filled the air as police sirens neared.

J.I. was overwhelmed when he began speaking.

"Nigga! If you aint come with …"

"Fuck that dumb shit. He came with it like he always do," said green shoes.

The Boy and J.I. gave each other a quick pound and an even quicker hug.

As the five troops scattered into the abyss, three of them took an oath to stop street dreaming and to get this entertainment shit moving; and most importantly, to always have the others back.

Ignorance or innocence?

Youth, I'd say. Youth is a beautiful thing; beautiful and fleeting.

"So dawn goes down to day ..."

(Robert Frost)

✳

QUEENS

Now, close to seven years later the streets of New York weren't the only things that had grown cold. December was just over twenty-four hours away and holiday cheer was spreading throughout the boroughs. But in some parts of the city cheer never spreads and death knows no holidays. Over time some parts of the oath had blossomed beyond their expectations, others had died like their friend with the green shoes. It had been years since he'd been murdered in the streets but The General still couldn't let go. With his eyes getting blurry he loaded the clip and thought;

"Damn, why they take another soldier? I remember my oath. Now let's see if this trick remembers his."

Soon a faded memory would be all that remained of the oath.

A black Acura Integra sat empty at one end of the block, at the other end sat a red Chevy Camaro, both stolen. Four men sat in that vehicle, but if the measure of a man is the quantity of his heart, the Chevy was just as empty. More soldiers willing to die for the cause; maybe not the exact same cause, but they were loyal and would follow his orders. He'd learned there was power in numbers; but again this was personal and he'd ordered them to stay in the car.

Truth be told, ten months in prison had taught him many things. One lesson was;

"To thyself be true."

He gave final instructions to his young cadet. In his heart he prayed the two of them would never come to this. With his entire being he hoped that this would be his last tour. He knew his time was near; he'd felt the shadows depth exactly one year ago tonight when Judas finally revealed himself. The night he'd set him up to get stuck up. The night he'd heard the guns bust but the shots could not shut him up. He thanked them for those five bullets. They'd slowed him down long enough for him to get a question answered; the question that should be first on everyone's list. And fuck getting the answers second hand. He'd gone to the source and asked for himself. The answer had startled him only because he'd known it all along.

"We're All Soldiers in God's Eyes!"

"Now," he said lightly, "it's time for war."

Kay approached Judas from the back as he left a building and walked toward the corner store. The General shook his head at his former comrade's predictability.
    Kay spoke first.
    "Big man, you know what time it is. Run yo' shit!"
    Judas turned to run and stopped, wide eyed once again as the General stood in front of him with his gun drawn.
    "I always told you that late night drinking would get the best of you."
    Judas's eyes dropped to The General's feet.
    "Look 'G' …"
    The General cut him off.
    "Nah *you* look, ___ 'G'! You remember the oath, nigga?"
    "Yeah," said Judas softly.
    "Give a bitch nigga a little power, time, and money, and all of a sudden he think he a god. Your new friends got you thinking you a god," asked The General?
    "Nah 'G,' Judas said suddenly emancipated, "I just work for him." He smirked and hit the blunt he was holding.

It's true. You never feel more alive than when you are about to die.

Kay slapped Judas with his gun.
    "You weak minded bitch. We 'bout to do you a favor. Maybe in ya' next life you'll come back as a man!"

The General wanted to laugh, scold, and congragulate him all at the same time.

"Nigga you sound stupid," said The General. "I used to tell you all the time, all the answers is written somewhere. All you had to do was look. But nah! You wanted to take this route. You spent your whole life being foul and wilding out.

Now after all the dirt you done you think you just gon' gracefully bow out? Aint but one God, Judas; and that nigga you running with aint him!"

"Nigga you the stupid one. These cats is rich, they got troops; *we are legions!*" cried Judas. "They already peeped ya' plan 'G.' I hope you been reading your verses, tithing and being a good Christian, cause they coming for you."

The General lift the blunt from his fingers and took a long pull before giving it back to him.

"Father, bless me please. This thug life is gon' be the death of me, J."

For a moment the city that never sleeps fell silent until at the corner a car door opened and through the woofers a soldier received his orders.

Excerpt 51.

Tears swelled in both their eyes. Judas moved back silently begging for
   Mercy. The General sniffed and grant the last wish of what was once a friend.

"Get on the wall. Close your eyes, J." He did. "Now get on yo' knees and pray."
   The General put the gun to his head. "You lie, you die …"

"… Nothing gold can stay."

(Robert Frost)

1996

DIVINE TIME

VIRGINA
Camp Peary
February 14th

Benjamin and Alliouisis were both in their seventies and rarely made unexpected trips. They'd surprised Jerry when they interrupted his training at *The Farm,* but even more surprising was the order they'd come to deliver. Standard procedure within The Agency's hierarchy had him unaware that The General was a target was on the elder's radar.

"Well," said Benjamin, "I'll be the first to admit when I'm wrong. Never in my life did I envision a threat to national security by one of these, Hip-Hopers."

"I'm with his kind often." Jerry explained to them. "They love to talk, that's their thing; but it's just talk. Aside from killing each other they couldn't kill a plant. Trust me father, he doesn't have it in him."

Alliouisis agreed.

"I can't believe they have the resources to pull off an Op like that."

Benjamin wasn't giving in. The General was already on record for having made Presidential threats, plus this request had come from a high ranking member of The Order to whom he owed favors.

"On the contrary," he said, "review his history. His words have proven to be authentic. We believe his ambitions are seditious and no less than revenge on the agents that played him and anyone else that was down with them." Benjamin paused a moment. "*And,* if that isn't enough, this could turn out to be very lucrative for us."

"How so," asked Alliouisis?

"As a major share holder in Clockwork Enterprises I am privy to some Insider information. Consumer polls are showing that sales of the targets next release; his entire discography for that matter, would increase dramatically if he were to meet with an untimely demise. Put simply, he's a nuisance that is worth more to us dead than he ever was alive. I've taken it upon myself to share this information with a Brother and litigator friend of ours on the West Coast, one Francis Kleinfeld."

"Oh no," Jerry exclaimed, "not the Italians. You guys worked JKF; you know how sloppy they can be."

Benjamin was fuming when he looked at Jerry. "Silence!" he yelled in Hebrew. "He is on of us, *B'nai B'rith*. Fortunately that is more than I can say of the company I hear you've been keeping."

"They're business contacts," Jerry said defensively, "nothing personal."

"And so are my orders," said Benjamin. "Working together the two of you should be able to come up with something foolproof. Oh, and after that Agent Freidman, I'd advise you to distance yourself from all of them."

There was silence at the table until Benjamin who almost never raised his voice finally did.

"This nonsense has gone on long enough," he said, "I want him added to the list with the other subversives!"

A list that went on and on and included performers like, Cass Elliot, Jimi Hendrix, Brian Jones, John Lennon, Bob Marley, Sal Mineo, Phil Ochs, and Peter Tosh.

Jerry quickly agreed and made an attempt to placate him.

"Don't worry father. I've been grooming a familiar who is both venal and malleable. He will serve us well."

Alliouisis passed Jerry a folder.

"Well there you have it," he said. "This Black Op is a go; do what must be done"

✳

LOS ANGELES
Pelican Bay State Penitentiary
April

Fame and his father boarded a plane the same night Juanita called with the news. This visit promised to be the hardest for Goodgame to take. He watched as the corrections officer pushed Larry-O through the visiting area to the table. After seeing him wheeled across the room with a bandaged hand and bruised face, Fame was ready to hurt something too.

When Juanita was finished with her kisses and hugs, Larry-O greet his family.

"Y'all didn't have to come all the way out here for this," he said.

"I told them you'd be Ok," said Juanita.

"A little battered and bruised but I'll bounce back."

"Who was it Uncle? Please let me know, I got some assassins on my team that will shut them the fuck down!"

He hugged Fame again.

"I bet you do nephew, but I've got it covered."

"Yeah son, the old men still got some tricks up their sleeves."

He and Larry-O laughed as he sat down.

"Real talk," said Larry-O, "them dumb shits better hope they never get out of the SHU."

"I can't believe some Crips did this to you man," said Goodgame looking in disbelief at his childhood friend. "Them bitches gotta' get they names crossed out."

"No doubt. But that Crip shit is just smoke and mirrors," explained Larry-O. "This is Kleinfeld's Work."

"The Lawyer," wondered Goodgame?

Juanita nodded.

"Mmm, hmm."

"Yeah man. I didn't speak on it because I didn't want it to get this far, but I've been having problems at Firing Squad."

"All the money they makin'," asked Fame, "what kind of problems?"

Larry-O looked at him deadpan.

"The mo' money you get, the mo' problems you gonna' have nephew."

"I dun' told him," said his father.

Larry-O took a deep breath.

"Firing Squad is in trouble," he said, "not only are they under Federal investigation, but the fame has gone to Pooh's head. He's got stacks of law suits 'cause he aint paid nobody over there, me included. But I can't put all the blame on him. Pooh is damn near a puppet. Kleinfeld got his hand all up in his ass."

Juanita agreed.

"See Pooh aint from the streets," she said. "He got his pull with the Bloods from Larry and his pull with the Crips from Kleinfeld."

"Yeah, I remember you told me that before," said Goodgame. "Now he out here acting like he Don Coreleone or something."

"I bet it's gotten worse since they signed The General," said Fame.

Larry-O answered.

"You know it nephew."

That lit a fire inside Goodgame.

"That boy's snapping hard, aint he!"

"Blood," said Larry-O, "the first song on the first disk; they can't play that in here, that shit starts riots."

"Yeah, I can imagine," said Goodgame, "The lil' nigga is making fight music."

"Yeah but who's he fighting with," asked Larry-O? "I don't know how true it is, but over at Periscope they tell me he got Q-MD kicked off the label and after his next record he's planning on leaving and starting his own thing. K9 and The Kennel is solid but they aint got it like them two. Q-MD is what got me to invest, and as far as I'm concerned, without him there is no Firing Squad Records. That's what I told Kleinfeld; I said to him, 'Look Francis, you been giving me the run around for months. Now I hear this.' I told him that wasn't what I signed on for so just give me back my million dollars with interest and we could call it even. Then he tried to doubletalk me again. That's when I told him I'd see him in court."

"What did he say to that," asked Fourtune?

Larry-O looked him in the eye.

"You see me don't you?"

"See," said Goodgame nudging his son, "what did I tell you about you and Fourtune's business situation with that boy?"

"Nephew, I'ma tell you like the warden told me, 'Kleinfeld and the people he runs with are as smooth as they want to be and just as vicious given the situation.' Watch your back if you're doing business with them."

Fame flashed him that same sign that he'd been flashing since he was a little boy.

"Until the moment I'm deceased. I will."

Larry-O flashed it back.

"Blood, what we gonna do about Pooh and Kleinfeld," asked Goodgame?

"Aint nothing nobody can do for 'em now," he said, "them bustas got dollar signs on they heads."

They all knew what that meant. Bounty Hunters would hunt 'em till they were dead.

NYMP
June 4th

Four million disks in four months made it official; The General wasn't just king of the streets, he was king of the world. Fastidious New Yorkers however, had cast their votes asunder. The Prophet's disk had been an instant classic placing him amongst raps elite. A truly phenomenal feat since to date it had sold only two hundred thousand copies, while his unofficial rival, The Titan had sold over two million. Both were in the studio hard at work on their sophomore efforts. Of all his peers The Titan's rise had been the most meteoric, but success and good times had been overshadowed by rumors and accusations courtesy of his estranged friend. Since his release, The General had been on a mission to publicly eviscerate him and evince to him what death really was. Thomas had tolerated a slew of threats masquerading as late night phone calls and ignored countless interviews deriding him. Dizzy's PR machine decided it would serve them best if they turned the other cheek. Fresh out of cheeks and feeling more tiny than titanic, Thomas and a handful of less fortunate New York rappers planned an underhanded response to The General's latest diatribe on wax.

"What! What we gon' do about this cat?" Thomas sounded like a three hundred-fifty pound Baby Huey. "Maaan', this mu'fucka *keep* shittin' on me. Psshht! This nigga don't know what beef is; I'm telling you, he don't know beef! These are sup-posed to be good times for me man, but this nigga keep shittin' on my crown." He puffed away on his blunt thinking about better days. "I can't believe I used to have love for this cat 'A', I mean he used to be my man."

A-D sat in the car, his attention divided between bobbing his head to The General's music, and for reasons he couldn't quite explain actually feeling sorry for Thomas.

"That's the way things go in The Life 'T'; love changes, a thug changes, and best friends become strangers."

Inside A-D knew Thomas was right. This should've been the time of his life, yet the offer he was making was one of a desperate man. An offer that crossed a line they both knew he wasn't fit to cross. A-D made an attempt to steer him back.

"'T' you positive you wanna do this; I mean you sure this' the only way? You know to make a nigga die bleeding is nothing, when you make him die breathin' then you saying something."

He couldn't quite put his finger on it. Had Diane's evangelism paid off? Was it because Prudential had given him prospects that he'd never had before? Maybe he was going through a midlife crisis; he couldn't be sure. What he did know was for the first time in his life he was getting money, but it was like his conscious was eating at him.

As of late, he'd taken to sitting on the edge of his bed, zoning out for hours to the thought of friends and faces, people and places that were no longer there.

Mayor Giuliani had turned the lights on and made niggas disappear.

He'd ordered Bratton's bone crushers to take back the streets, and every borough harbored beasts with nothing to eat.

Suddenly Five Percent predictions were what they'd all come to fear.

Beset by so many agents that even civilians could see things clear, for the New York City drug kingpin, the end of an era was near.

Thomas insisted.

"Somebody's gotta die! That bid fucked duke's head up yo', and he wasn't all there to begin with." He point to the stereo. "You hear this shit. Dude aint even rappin', that shit is more like a tirade. I 'ont think he know what he be saying." A-D laughed. "I'm serious; you remember what J.I.—God bless the dead—told us, 'When that nigga get high he get to running off at the mouth and when he come down he don't remember half the shit he said.' Duke aint lie. I seen the nigga in the booth plenty of times. That nigga don't even be there; I mean his body be there but that nigga be gone; flying, he stay in the wind ..."

"Your stairway lies on the whispering wind."

A-D automatically tuned out Thomas's rant as he recalled. 95, 94, 93, 92, 91.

"He is the Lord of the winds ... If a situation arises this card signals a stalemate. There will be no way around it and no escaping it; you must confront it. It will frighten you," A-D shuddered but Thomas didn't notice, *"... it stands in the way of everything you've worked for."*

A-D tuned into Thomas again.

"… disrespecting me and my bitch and fucking up my cheddar.

I'm too old for that man, plus I got expenses, so whatever! If I gotta do it like this I will, cause the thought of being broke at thirty gives me the chills."

A-D put his fist out.

"That aint no lie. I mean it 'T'; I plan to be multi before I die."

They took a moment to laugh before Thomas continued.

"Hope got twins on the way." A-D looked at him, everyone had heard the rumors that the kids weren't his and that his girl was a ho, but Thomas was in love and refused to let her go. When he heard the rumors about Hope and The General he'd wondered; *was him or his fame, good dick or good game, whatever the case; I'll bet he screamed "Weestsiiide", when he came.*"

"She swore to me that shit wasn't true," said Thomas before thinking out loud. "And even if it was, why would he shit on honey like that?"

It didn't make since, Thomas had always known The General to be an honest man. "Why would she do some dumb shit like that, when she know what I'll do to her?"

"It's The Life," said A-D.

Thomas looked at him puzzled as he explained.

"C'mon 'T', ho's be knowing the deal. Why do we do what we do when we all know how the story ends? It's the same for them. They claim they love us, but really it's this life we lead."

"And the dick," Thomas added.

"That too; but mostly it's The Life, it blocks out the death."

"And when you think about it," said Thomas, "all niggas in the hood got to look forward to *is* The Life and death."

"Right, right!" A-D chuckled and they bumped fists again. Satisfied with Thomas's conversion he took his first pull. "Think about it, he said blowing out the smoke," these jiggy broads wasn't checking for me twelve months ago. I was 'so ghetto', but look at 'em now, I'm all they know."

A-D watched Thomas's face for a reaction. He got none. Thomas sat there staring into space as his man A-D dropped another dime.

"I'm the king of this city, 'T'. Yo, the city is mine."

Thomas didn't want to admit it, but the word on the street said A-D was right. The General's attack had hurt him bad and Prudential was gaining ground. Effete and running out of breath he thought of Rumi and The Spiritual Exercises but figured it was too late for him now. He remembered Matthew 24 and the advice his father had given him in the bedroom years ago; he blew that off too.

"I aint got the time for no praise the Lord shit." thought Thomas. *"Nowhere else in the world is your burn quicker than here. What's fifteen minutes anyway _____ especially when they're New York minutes?"*

He cracked a weak smile as he thought about passing the reigns.

"Shit. I never really thought it could happen anyway. A black ashy nigga from the gutter with no father and an immigrant mother. Look at us now."

Thomas had sent Gaietta to the best doctors, and with her cancer in remission she was all smiles pushing her new Acura through BK and modeling furs to the hospital. He'd even put her in a few videos and given her the gift of fame that she'd always desired. And at last, he'd been crowned king.

He was done; this was as high as he could dream.

He'd always looked up to A-D; he'd always been the man around town.

This was the way things should be, it was time he wore *The Crown.*

A-D could feel Thomas' energy giving out. His hypnotized mind was easy to read, and *Harab Serap* was in the air as he considered the possibilities.

"Don't take this the wrong way "T", but this is pretty big what 'chu asking. How you gon' bankroll it if you don't want Dizzy knowin' what happened?"

"C'mon man, I took care of all that. Dizzy paid me a quarter mill' when I sold him back my half of the publishing rights. I got somethin' put up. Plus I got Dizzy to guarantee you a spot on the next disk, playboy. I aint forgot what I said, or how you love the dough."

A-D smiled and The Titan stuck out a weak fist.

"That Brooklyn bullshit?"

A-D's pound it down.

"We on it."

LOS ANGELES
Summertime

And the living was anything but easy. Factions from both sides wanted to see them dead. They'd put prices on their heads. So now when Pooh and The General slept they did it with rottweilers and big girls in their beds; and they all ate lead.

Pooh decided to splurge on an island vacation to regroup and get his "family" away from it all. With everyone tipsy and frolicking about a rented beach house and yacht, drinking champagne and margaritas with models and having the time of their lives enjoying his previously unheard of generosity,—he'd passed out stacks of hundreds and diamond rings bearing the family crest on the plane—it was turning out to be a good idea. The General felt especially alive as he cast his troubles aside and part the ocean while skipping across the waters on a wave runner.

That particular day the summer sun shone brighter on him than ever before, melting his heart and warming his skin, setting his soul on fire like the kiss from an old friend; and when he opened his eyes to Petula giving him mouth to mouth on the seashore,—the victim of a freak riptide that almost took his life—it had also seared some indelible images into his brain; and they weren't of her, nor were they of Pooh, or K9, or The Kennel, or The Eternals who all stood around him waiting for a sign of life with baited breath. The images were of a face he'd seen but had not met, a portentous glow on a hand in the distance, and most vivid was a passage from a book that he'd read in prison.

Excerpt 52.

Petula may as well have been a princess; her parents were the equivalent of Royals in most circles. All throughout his prison stay and annulled marriage to Nia she and The General had remained close. They'd been together since the day after his release, traveling and getting closer. He'd even made it onto the estate to meet the parents, and ever since they'd returned from a romantic vacation in Italy she'd been hinting at marriage. But right now what was most important to The General was the group lists in her *Startak* phone. She called it her "black book" and in it were what amounted to bi-coastal files on all sorts of characters, from big time realtors to up and coming drug dealers. After she'd made some calls, The General made another request that Pooh was more than eager to grant.

NEW JERSEY
Teterboro Airport
Several hours later

"C'mon G, you gon' let me in on this or what?"
"You sure you up to this Kay, you aint having second thoughts is you?"
"Do I gotta say it again? "'On my grandmamma, I will.'"
The General gave him a pound.

"A'ight then. Get ready, its gon' be a long night in the field."

A short time later the taxi they'd taken from the airport dropped them in front of Ponce funeral home in Marcy where The General opened the door to a vehicle that was parked in front.

"What the fuck is we doing in hearse," asked Kay, "and how you know it was gonna be here?"

The General whispered.

"Pooh got family all over the world, man." They smiled and trade pounds before he hung up the burn-out and continued. "A'ight, this how we gone play it. I found this nigga.

One of Petula's girls knows someone who fuckin' him; she knows where he at right now. After we catch him we gon' cuff him and search him. If he strapped, you keep that. Then we gon' make him get …

BROOKLYN
Greenwood Cemetery
11:41pm.

Inside the coffin, his mouth tied with the Generals rumal, A-D knew he'd already made what could turn out to be his fatal mistake. He chanted furiously attempting to invoke the aide of the Baphomet. Little did he know that with every stroke of the clock his chances for survival increased, as by memory alone he performed the rites of the Masonic thirty-fourth degree; the satanic ritual *L'Air Epais* or The Ceremony of the Stifling Air.

"Why am I here? What is the meaning of this?

It is if a strange and overpowering summons intrudes upon my rest. A curse must be upon me yet …

… The world rolls round forever like a mill: it grinds out death and life and good and ill; It has no purpose, heart, mind or will.

… All substance lives and struggles evermore, through countless shapes continually at war, by countless interactions interknit:

If one is born a certain day on earth, all times and forces tended to that birth, not all the world could change or hinder it …

… Oh brothers of sad lives! they are so brief; A few short years must bring us all relief:

Can we not bear these years of laboring breath?

... Without the fear of waking after death ...

The hearse was parked deep in the heart of the cemetery. Inside the coffin A-D could hear footsteps in the gravel, outside The General could hear his muffled rant.

"Wha' 'shu wan' 'wigga? Wha'? Ca' I liff'? Huh, wigga? 'Ca' I liff'? Oo 'ow wha' we 'eed 'oo 'oo? 'Wes 'wop 'whayin' ganes. Wes' 'way 'wor 'weal 'wigga! 'Wes get it on!"

The General laughed at him.

"Stop bitching, nigga, I'ma let 'chu outta there. Huh. I bet 'chu sold out already didn't you?"

Kay held his gun on A-D as he opened the coffin and ordered him out. He stayed posted by the vehicle and The General led his prisoner to an open mausoleum. Once inside he ripped off the rumal and A-D spat on the floor.

"Y'all niggas is finished," he yelled, "y'all the past bro, our time is now!"

The General let him know.

"You must've been poppin' that X if you think you can touch us. We got every ghetto in the world backing *us*, mu'fucka."

"That means aught," A-D said seething! "C'mon man, proceed with the dialectic for this evening."

A-D perceived surprise in The General's eye.

"Yeah Mr. President, you think you well read? Well I know a lil' bit. Look at me. You think ho's was beating down my door? Your future's my past yung'un, I been here before. See you *think* you deep, but you have no idea."

"Nigga you a bitch, end of story," said The General. "One of my young dawgs introduced me to ya' girl Sasi. Oh yeah, we kicked it a long time, she way too pretty to spit rhymes that gritty. She told me about you too. Nigga how old are you? Fuckin' pedophile. I heard your lil' album too. I'll give it to you, you a'ight; but you aint *him*. *You* a trick and a thief. You stole mad styles, mad lyrics, The Prophets hooks, The Titans ideas; and tell me why I hear my life in yo' shit. But it's a'ight, 'cause I'ma tell you this right now. You can rap 'till Kingdom Come but it won't matter. They'll never love you like they love me. They won't follow you. They know I'm the realest. You weak dude. Ya' ass would be dead now if you'd dreamed the shit I dreamed. And oh yeah, one more thing. Tell your boys Treni and Glover they right; niggas in jail do got some horrible stories to tell. Even so, I passed all *nine degrees of wisdom*. What about 'chu? You aint even a Novice and no matter what 'chu do you'll never be King."

A-D was silent; his hateful eyes were burning holes in The General's clothes. The General didn't flinch.

"Just accept it; being a stand up nigga aint for you. See, this shit is bigger than us. It's bigger than East and West. It's about the prestige and the factions we represent. Imposters like you spinning the public, keepin' 'em off track, making money off the hood and not giving nothing back. Uh, uhh. Not while I'm alive. That's against the rules of the game. This is war, and on my side we take this war shit deeply."

"What rules?" A-D asked anxiously. "Nigga aint no rules, aint no parameters, aint no ethics. It's those played out morals and dogmas that have always held us back. Not me! I'm gettin' mine." The evil genius looked towards heaven and gave the middle finger to the Lord as gripped his balls. "Fuck y'all." he shout. "Runnin' 'round screamin' war; y'all niggas should want more." He chuckled. "I guess you didn't get the call homie, God is dead, and *this*," A-D maneuvered his hand into his pocket and pulled out a handful of Federal Reserve Notes, "this is what killed him." He tossed the bills on the ground. "He who follows him has lost." Then he tried his best to sound sincere. "But if you would just bow down and play this game right we could both get paid. Just keep quiet and stop trying to save people that aint worth being saved.

The General looked into the eyes of his adversary for some saving grace but found none. There was not one single solitary drop of compunction in him.

"Them devils got cha' mind." He said sorrowfully. "I know for a fact that God aint dead. I talk to him. As a matter of fact the nigga is walking right here beside me, and you know what he's saying? He's says that the reason he created Hip-Hop was to save them people; to take the secrets of the rich and share them with the poor?"

A-D shook his head, truly bewildered.
    "This aint a movie dawg." After that he snickered. "And tell me how you gon' help the poor if you one of them? Did niggas help you when you was locked down? What about when you was shot bleeding." A-D's snickers turned into full blown laughter, so amused by his next thought that he could barely get it out. "I guess you like, 'his one begotten son', huh; speaking for the poor in spirit. Ahhhhh." He let out a long breath and calmed himself. "C'mon man, you know better than to believe in shit that don't exist. We make our own plans. *I'm my light.*" He

paused. "Why can't you just admit it; you on an ego trip, right? I can admit mine; I'm on a power trip. So let's do this; let's get together and we can make the world believe in *us*. You can even play the star; my plan has always been to fade to black anyway." A-D stopped and gave the proposition a moment to sink in before he continued. "That's the blueprint for success homie; that or quit the game. Cause otherwise ..." he hunched his shoulders. "I gotta say, God bless."

The General entertained the thought.

"Quit rap," he said after a moment, "I don't know how to do nothing else."

"Me either."

"And I," said The General firmly, "aint gonna do nothing else."

"Me either."

There was no conversation left. It was *Conspirara;* they'd said it in the same breath. Both their thoughts were racing; bad blood was boiling from too many cant remarks.

"He'll never change; he's too stuck in his ways."

Each one knew that the other was right.

"It's either my life or your life."

"You got a lotta nerve, to play me." The General swung at his enemy with his free hand. His anger had him off balance and A-D patient and nimble under fire all but dodged the jab, but the ring that Pooh had given The General caught his lip and drew blood from the corner of his mouth. A-D smiled at him and licked it off.

"You too eager."

The General smiled, aimed his weapon and put pressure on the trigger.

"God bless. That's what they gon' say at your funeral. Bang nigga, you dead!"

"Whoa!" A-D threw up his hands and revealed his last trick. "Hold it, hold on a sec. I almost forgot." He was still grinning, still playing it cool, like he wasn't staring down the barrel of a Desert Eagle. "You want to hear this, really."

The General watched him closely as he spoke.

"They said this message, comes directly from the GM. I was told to give you this, if I was ever compromised."

With his hands still in the air, A-D maneuvered them to unclasp his Bvulgari. He was nervous but he didn't show it. He gripped the watch tight between two fingers when he shook it.

The General's hands were steady; he took the watch with his left and held his arm with his right. As he reached, A-D got a good look at his watch and thought about Treni and Glover.

"*Them aint Rolex Diamonds. What the fuck they dun' did to that?*"

"You gotta twist the bezel first, then flip it," he said.

The General, suspicious of a trap, smirked and tossed the watch back.

"Think you gone catch me sleeping, he asked? "What Marley say, 'Sleep is for fools, I'm 'bout me faddah's biz'ness.'"

A-D's brain was flipping every possible script, back and forth, looking for something he may have missed. Perhaps losing the watch meant his time was up. Maybe it had been wired to explode, killing them both; he knew he too was expendable. He fumbled with it.

"Wait," ordered The General. A-D stopped and The General backpedaled to the door. Pushing down on the latch he opened it from behind and stepped back a few feet. "Now open it."

"*Shit.*" A-D was pissed; The General was reading things like he'd written this chapter. There was nothing left to do but hope his gods had heard his call. He followed procedure and laid the watch on the ground where it produced a fast whirring sound like that of a tiny drill. Then on the mausoleum wall there appeared a faint blue apparition. The General thought, "*A hologram,*" as he walked to the doorway and listened.

"So there's been a breakdown in negotiations exactly as I had foreseen. The spirit of your father is strong in you. It's enabled you to live a charmed life, so to speak. But it's of no consequence; you are but a man and man has no time. From conception he is racing to beat time; to find his destiny before that destiny overtakes him. The age of man and his ridiculous dogmas is passing as gerontocracies such as yours are blown away like leaves from a lifeless tree. The new Millennium is upon us, and when it arrives and my heir takes his place in Jupiter's earthly abode; take my word for it; *this scourge will stop*!

My emissary here believed we could have used you. That led many in my Order to question his programming. Nevertheless," the image turned, its eyes seeming to focus directly on A-D, "I had faith in you my child; after all; we are our fathers' sons. Now as your journeys merge I have some prudent advice for you both to ponder here at the end of your lives. For my adversary; never go to war without proper funding, trust me, it's an area I have some expertise in. And for my aide and advocate; 'Behold our secret'. It's about *time* we welcome you to illumination.

May its keeper assist in your transmogrification.""

A puff of smoke seeped from the inside of the watch. The image on the wall began to cackle as it shifted shape and form; a sight that left The General stunned but focused, and left A-D crunching the numbers faster than ever.

"Advocate, illumina ..., transmogrifica ..."

He shut his eyes tight and dove for the corner. Just then a light more brilliant than 10,000 suns exploded in the tomb. Laser-like rays broke through every crack in the structure as a single clap of thunder brought the end of the calm and the start of the storm.

The General had been blinded and was grunting in pain. A-D who'd barely been able to make out shadows himself followed the whispers and tore past his captor out of the tomb and into the world of tomorrow. Outside colliding clouds released a deluge as The General pursued. A dense fog besieged him as he let off two shots at point blank range; they missed. He emptied out his clip, never stopping to aim. A-D heard footsteps behind him like hellhounds on his trail. He was scrambling like a quarterback searching for some safety when he found himself directly in front of the cemetery wall. With his hands still cuffed he scaled a large tombstone and leapt for it. Loosing his footing on the mossy concrete, he slammed down on the wall and watched as his breath float away. His life was in the balance, his body open to vessels of inequity. Just then lightning struck illuminating the whole show. He pushed up on his elbows and gave Kay a perfect shot at his head. A-D sensed the danger and turned to face it; lightning struck twice and showed him in his proper form. Kay hesitated in the face of d'evils, and A-D smiled.

"Fire!" ordered The General.

Kay squeezed instantly; but it was not meant to be. For time waits for no man. At the stroke of *High Twelve,* gales swirled and evil tempests roared, sending shrubs slamming against them and knocking the soldiers to their knees. A-D was sent over the barrier that separates the world of spirits from the world of matter, his body radiating energy as he fell from the sky like Apollo, in *Evening Fall to Earth."* This time he wasn't afraid, and this time the moment wasn't lost on him; he knew he'd narrowly escaped his death. The powers that be had granted him a new lease on life and new breath. His transition was complete.

So is the price of knowledge, the death of the old you and the birth of the new.

The Agent ran for over a mile before slowing down. As he approached a taxi, the driver noticed the handcuffs barely covered by the sleeves of his shirt. He waved him away and tried to pull off but the Agent blocked his path and said;

"Be merciful my friend," It startled him when it came out in Arabic.

"I was kidnapped and barely escaped with my life. Please, take me to Marcy,"

A-D point to the ring on his finger. "That's five carats; take it as your reward."

The driver accepted, watching as his passenger sat silently in the back of the cab. As strange as things seemed to him they also made since. Through the whole ordeal, even while staring death in the eye, he'd kept his head. He felt he was being guided by something, but he'd had those feelings nearly all his life. He remembered what they'd told him that night in Paradise. *"It's true."* He thought, realizing he'd seen this play out long ago, his, theirs, ours, *"Life is but a jumble of dreams."* With his dreams rejuvenated. He laughed out loud thinking, *"Immortality!"* Then saying the words he made it his reality. "I Can't Die."

✳

Back in the hearse The General knew he'd fucked up, The Prince says that;

"Men must be either pampered or crushed, because they can get revenge for small injuries, but not for grievous ones. So any injury a Prince does a man should be of a kind where there is no fear of revenge."

"I think I should expect some revenge to come from this," he said to himself, "and it won't be minimal."

While some will say he wasn't fit for the job, others will say he let curiosity get the best of him, while I myself believe it was compassion, perhaps even a bit of regret. Whatever the case, a maelstrom such as that provides no time for either. To deny a dying man his last wish may have seemed ruthless to a man of morals, but what is often mistaken for ruthlessness may in actuality be clarity of the mind; and clarity must be acted upon, in the present, as it happens.

They were in tune not long ago. The General wondered if the tie had been severed. Once settled onto the plane he tried sending a message, but there was someone else on the line.

"Vengeance Is Mine."

A-D heard the voice loud and clear and dismissed it like that of an old fool. "You said it better than all."

That night he went to work on a piece to capture the moment, and though it would be years before he completed it, he wrote the hook while it was fresh in his mind.

"How art thou fallen from heaven, O Lucifer, son of the Morning?"

With that he'd sworn his will and allegiance to dark societies. Then he made them a promise.

"He is I, and I am him. They outta here, my Lord. With rhyme and reason I will chase them off of this earth!"

✳

Before his feet ever touched the ground The General had made some changes, because now every single, tiny, microscopic little thing had to go exactly according to plan. Immediately he exorcised the last of the demons from his circle in order to test the mysteries of the mystical numbers, forty, thirteen and seven, and the theory of what could be accomplished in the span of seven days. Could a single person fulfill his life obligation, keep his promise, and destroy in seven days what had taken 220 years to build. Against all odds he head once again to the Aeon, spending a full 168 hours adrift in creations flow. Members of The Eternals who were there said they felt blessed to have witnessed the blitzkrieg of that one week in August when his spirit was purged. The result of those studio conclaves? A dizzying body of work. 53 songs produced; an amazing 33 of which even they had never heard. The General's lost scrolls in the event that he was ever overtaken by the shadows.

LOS ANGELES
Hollywood Hills
September 1

Petula was an emotional wreck. She'd just flown in from New York to visit The General on the set of his latest project. On a break from filming he dropped the top on the Rolls and cruised to a quiet place where he could calm her down and get the latest Intel before going back to the set for the interview where he'd finally unveil the political aspirations of the newly formed *Independents Party*; the undying dream of The Old Man an the elders to elect the first Hip-Hop endorsed President by the year 2012.

"What's going on? Everybody's so tense. I could barely get any of my friends to talk to me, and when they did it seemed like they were trying to get information out of *me*." For the very first time this thought crossed her mind. "W-What if they're informants?"

He eased her head to his lap, put the blunt in her mouth and continued reading.

She took a pull and jumped up.

"Ba-byyy! They're saying all these people want to kill you. This is so fucked up. I don't know who to trust. People are saying that you would've been safer in jail, and since you fired Kleinfeld, *the mob* is after you."

"Phsst. You believe that?"

"Maybe. Pooh has been acting funny ever since we came back from the islands. What if we can't trust him anymore? This is *so* fucked up. For heavens sake, this is the music business; it's not supposed to be like this. What are we going to do? I've got a bad feeling; maybe we shouldn't go out of town next week." Petula started weeping. "Where did all this come from? Never in my wildest dreams did I see us like this."

"How do you see us?"

"Everyone is after us," she cried. "It's like were outlaws, the '96 versions of Bonnie and Clyde."

"*We,*" wondered The General? "Yeah," he said turning the page, "them people really wanted me to rot away in jail. I found out they threatened anybody who tried to get me out on bail. Pooh was the only one with enough nuts to say, fuck 'em. If it wasn't for him I'd still be locked up right now; I gotta respect that. Plus I gave him my word that I'd go." He finally looked up at her. "You gotta respect that."

A summer breeze carried the faintest hint of hyacinth through Petula's mahogany hair. He ran his fingers along her wavy red highlights then grabbed a handful of them, pulled her head back, pressed his lips to hers and blew. When they part, she moaned a light but guttural moan, like she'd been waiting to exhale. Her eyes opened, she'd never felt like that before, but he had.

In the sky ten years of clouds passed by in single file.

Lately his dreams had been of carefree days as a child.

Back when he didn't know what was in the hearts of men.

He would've given anything to be that innocent again.

Being in LA he thought about her from time to time.

But too much thinking could lead to doing and finding answers that he wasn't prepared to find.

If she'd wanted to see him he should've been pretty easy to call, with him being the biggest rap star in the world and all.

But to this day she had yet to pick up the phone.

Sometimes he questioned her motives, but that never lasted long; sure that one day soon a starry night would lead them home.

Petula was shaking; he could hear her heart beating fast. He wondered what exactly had her so paranoid, was it the threats, the weed, or the life he'd soon leave. He closed his book,—*The Bank of America of Louisiana*—and tossed it in the backseat.

"Shh, baby. Rest your head." He kissed it, gently pulling her hair between his lips. "It's too pretty to be dealing with shit like that."

She covered her face.

He moved her hands.

"Baby, look at me. Promise me something. Promise that whatever happens, whatever you might hear you won't shed no more tears. Remember what I told you when we were in Milan. Just hold your head, '*The Book* will absolve me.'"

SIN CITY
September 7th

"Hell was empty, all the sinners were here."

(Shakespeare)

Especially when the Champ was in town, and it made no difference to them if the bout went the distance or if he made quick work of a bum; it was the spectators who made fight night something to remember. The atmosphere was at once a Trinidadian carnival and a G-8 summit for the streets. Tonight all the heavyweight contenders were in attendance, and while the Haitians from the east had a score to settle, the west refused to bow down. The Midwesterners from Chicago and Cleveland wanted to avoid conflict and thug in eternal harmony and the south was set to rise again as the boys from Texas went through a resurrection, their leader remained untouchable. ATliens had emerged from the dungeon of the 213 with a mob, while soldiers from N' Orleans had cash money and knew no limit; even the mafia from Memphis had arrived with their cousins from Orange Mountain; no longer on the outside looking in.

Yes. The world was watching on this starry night as The General made his way through the city, the first of many stops on his campaign to be elected Commander in Chief.

10:42 pm. The fight was over and five east coast hustlers sat comfortably in the Suburban, taking shots of Louis the XIII and awaiting a party, occasionally glancing at one of the TV screens, but mostly paying attention to the money changing hands in a stripped down game of poker they called "guts". Through the open windows they tried out pickup lines on the city's B-list nymphs. A-D was unusually anxious; his mind elsewhere, Fame noticed him surreptitiously checking his watch or cell phone once a minute like he had somewhere to be.

Their man Alfredo was a Philadelphia hustler riding in Prudential's jet stream.

"Yo A-D, check it, there go old girl from earlier with the honeydew tits."

He yelled at her, "Yo, put them things away ma, they out of season."

Hours earlier at the strip club A-D had dissed her double D's.

"Too much scar tissue," he'd said, "I'ma find her doctor and get *my* money back."

Now all of a sudden he had a change of heart.

"Damn 'Fredo, why you so hard on the ho's? I'm out."

He put his cards down, snatched up his winnings and got out of the vehicle.

"Yo' 'B'," asked Fame, "where you goin'?"

"I'ma get a private show this time; get my money's worth. I'll be back before the party." Then he followed honeydew into the hotel.

"S'cuse me miss."

"Yes."

"What's your name?"

"Dominique," she said, handing him a card.

"I wanna apologize for my guys …"

She mentioned something about being an actress as they shook hands.

He wasn't listening, he glanced at his phone. ***"10:47."***

"That's what I'm saying, let's have a quick drink and talk about it."

By **10:55** he was pouring champagne. His phone vibrated and he answered.

"It's underway," said the voice on the other end.

It was the call he'd been waiting for. He sighed, looked around then hand Dominique a "grand."

"What's this," she asked?

"That should buy me some time, right? Order us a lil' sushi roll or somethin'. I had chips on the fight, I'ma check on 'em real quick and when I get back you can tell a nigga how you want it, a'ight."

He walked away, turned a corner and jogged through the hotel kitchen and out onto the loading dock where he ducked into a waiting black utility van. Several blocks away, an agent in a black one piece coverall exit the van, ducked into the backseat of a waiting white Cadillac and donned a black ski mask. It was **11:04.**

Minutes later on Golgotha street, the driver of the Caddy slowed and wait for the chaos to catch up to them. The traffic was sparse where the vehicle was now, the disorder distant, it was darker here too, almost serene as the gauntlet of lights from The Strip had dwindled to nearly nothing here on the edge of town. Just blocks away, the Cheop's forty billion watt illuminated capstone could still be seen prowling the darkness of the desert sky.

11:08. The Caddy's other three occupants remained silent. Crouched in the back seat The Agent closed his eyes and listened to the sounds of excitement creeping up through the void; engines purring, horns honking, bass, treble and voices intertwining to fuel the revelers who screamed adulations at the mere glimpse of their heroes. The Agent could feel the target approaching. He looked at his watch, *"11:12"*. He gripped his pistol tight and took a breath; this was it, time for his star to shine.

At the center of the spirited procession, in the passenger seat of Pooh's plush car, his body marred by battlefield scars, sat The General. His ringing ears and dimming sight told him that a spell wasn't far. He didn't fight it. He glanced at his *Omega* and then gazed out the window in an attempt to make sense of his life as a ghetto star. In under five years he'd done everything he'd set out to do and accomplished more than most would in a lifetime, but as his brother had once brilliantly noted, it had all come at a price. He was tired of this life; he felt he'd given enough. He focused on an oasis and something he hadn't seen in years, waterfalls, heaven, and a red desert rose swaying on Paradise Road. The inside of his head felt like vacuum, he let the vibrations lead him to specters from his present and past. There was Marian smiling peacefully in her new home, content at last, Cheris and her children living a better life than they'd ever had, Yoesef, The Old Man and all the political prisoners of The Movement, eternal inspirations; their flesh may have been scared, but their spirits were still going, their voices still flowing; all Generals in war, forever spitting the knowing.

"This is it? Imortality is what I wished for?"

He thought back to the time and how at one point he would like to have lived a long life; he knew that longevity had its place.

He also knew that since ancient times the number twelve had been linked to perfection and grace.

From the twelve tribes of Israel, to the zodiacs twelve signs, for centuries the number twelve has been seen as divine.

But time had moved on, it was **thirteen** past the hour, and superstitions just as ancient linked it to cults and covens, bad luck and evil power.

From The Last Supper, to the tarot, to the curse of the Templars, for centuries the number thirteen and death have looked familiar.

11:14. Inside the Quarter to Eight, the flash of the paparazzi snapped The General back to life. His fans surrounded him with shouts and showed their love. With his vision still blurred as he smiled and gave it back. Then;

Pooh turned at the corner, and not a half block ahead, hanging from a cable, the streetlight turned red, exposing underneath it, in the lane on the right, a black hand and a Caddy, that had been veiled in white.

Empirically navigating the void, The General moved towards the light, exiting the gates of this realm, and entering his next life.

At **11:21** the four men ditched the Cadillac in the trailer of an eighteen wheeler. From there the black van sped back to the hotel.

The kitchen was on and popping as A-D walked through, by this time news of a shooting was coming in. Outside in the Suburban the hustlers sat, mouths open and minds spinning, they'd barely had time to digest the fight before they began dissecting this.

Fame already had a theory.

"11:32. He's been gone forty-five minutes."

He got out of the SUV.

"Yo, y'all chill. I'll be right back."

Seconds later he was holding his key card as he slid through the hotel traffic on his way to their suite.

"This nigga better be there."

He left the elevator, turned the corner and made a dash for the room. He slid his card through and the light from the lock cast a green glow on the door, behind it the stereo played *O' fortuna*—the goliards theme. Cautiously Fame made his way around another corner where he was equally weirded out as he was relieved to find A-D leaning against a wall, Cristal bottle in hand, grinning mischievously as Dominique, in nothing but a La Perla thong, danced lasciviously around him flashing the Prudential symbol. Fame shook it off and asked;

"B, whathefuckyoudoin? You aint heard the news?"

"News," said a drunken Dominique. "Fuck the news!"

Fame glanced at her.

"It's over for you, ma. Put cha' tits away, go home and feed your kids."

A-D chuckled and made a wisecrack about knocking.

"Fuck knocking B. Yo, your boy just got popped, yo!"

"Whaa ..." A-D's voice trailed off as he recalled his moment of clarity and those storied three shots. "You mean the presidential candidate? Is he dead?"

"Shit, he might be by now; I came up her to find you."

A-D grinned and pointed a mock gun at Fame and said, "Politics as usual. Pow!"

Fame sighed and shook that off too.

"C'mon 'B', you playin'. Shit's about to get hectic. The streets is calling 'B'."

Dominique dressed quickly. At the elevator A-D suddenly had a million questions for her.

"So ma, what's your name."

"My name ..." she slurred, "is A-D."

Fame looked at her. "'B', what did you give this ..."

A-D waved his hand and cut him off.

"No hon', *my* name is A-D; what's yours?"

She could hardly stand.

"Oh, riiight, you're A-D, I'm ..."

"A ho who can't handle her liquor," said Fame.

A-D helped her out.

"Your name is Dominique. We had a ball these last few hours, right girl?"

She smiled and touched his face.

"Yeaahh, you got that good shit ..."

The elevator door opened and another couple who were just as out of it got on. Dominique began rambling through her purse.

"Daddy, if you're ever in L.A. come see me. I've got some cards here somewhere."

"Is that what you're looking for," asked A-D holding up the card case. "They fell out cha' purse when you were dancing. I hope you 'on't mind, I took a few."

"No, that's fine." She yawned. "I'm so clumsy." She burped and took the case. "Ooo, excuse me everybody; I'm a little drunk too."

The woman who'd just gotten on giggled.

"Don't worry," she said, "we all are; no one will remember any of this tomorrow."

A-D reassured her.

"Its a'ight ma, we all been drinking a lot, but a good actress never forgets her lines." The elevator door opened and A-D elbowed Fame to stop him from laughing. "A'ight ma, this is it," He hugged her before sending her off again. "I'ma call you a'ight!" Fame was doubled over laughing as she wandered away. A-D followed her for a few steps. "Be good. I know where to find you, a'ight!"

Fame noticed Fourtune and the rest of the crew moving toward them.

"Yo, where y'all niggas been," asked Alfredo? "Everybody is headed over to Golgotha."

Fame called to A-D.

"C'mon man, leave her drunk-ass alone."

They moved towards the others, still laughing as he brushed some specks of black lint from A-D's head, specks that in Fame's mind would forever leave a trace of *reasonable doubt.*"

"You wild 'B', but yo, what's all this black shit you got in ya' hair?"

✳

Six days later, with the music seemingly over, members of the intelligence community received a transmission.

```
ATTENTION! CLASSIFIED! ATTENTION! CLASSIFIED!

Memo: OPERATIONS COINTELPRO & CHAOS

Operation: "Premature Assassination."
Successful.
Subversive threat:
Terminated.
Public Enemy Number One: Alias: The General:
Executed.
Threat of intended political coup:
Eliminated.
Instructions to field operatives; The Untouchables
and The Commission:
```

Maintain Surveillance of remaining insurgents and enemy combatants;
aka. *The Movement*.

At the bottom of the transmission was a picture of a black rose.

EPILOGUE

THE HAVANA COUNTYSIDE
Near The Millennium

The sun was setting over the island. A beautiful day had become a beautiful evening. Selma was busy catering to the diners in the restaurant and Juan and Carlos were still at their game. The White Book was mine now. I studied it, turned it back and forth and flipped through its pages trying to put together the information that had been given to me. My father smiled as he waited for my response. My mother, who had recently joined us under the tree, was more sensitive to what must have been a bewildered look on my face.

"The H.I.P.-H.O.P. nation is one of survivors," she said. "If we've learned anything from the movements before us it's to keep pushing forward; to take existing concepts and hopefully make them better. For example; since the truth is that one cannot exist without the other, like Ormazd and Ahriman, *GOoD An d'EVIL* will always be with us."

My father joined in.

"The Old Man and the others knew that, long ago they combined the "good" of the number 40 with the "evil" of the number 13 to bring forth a new holy number, *'53'*."

"And," continued my mother, "if people had looked closer or better yet *listened* closer; well now, surprise, surprise! Fifty-three days after that fateful one when a rapper was turned into a martyr, they'd find, his music, the theory of seven, and the spirit of The Movement, not dead, but *alive.*" From her chair she bent down and kissed my father's head. "And buried in his fifty-three songs," she said, "are the answers to some questions that many have harbored for a long time."

"Answers," said my father, "to why some feel the need to justify their thug."

"And," Mother said, "wise words that have often been quoted in times of poverty and wealth and in times of war and peace. We pray those and all other harmonic influences will forever assist in providing inspiration to not only you, but our entire young Nation."

The last words were reserved for him. And like magic; instinctively I knew that they too were true.

"Never forget," he said, "I write for you, I rhymed for you, I'll roll with you; it's all been for you."

Imagine that.

Excerpt 53.

978-0-595-42498-6
0-595-42498-8

5300417R00232

Printed in Great Britain
by Amazon.co.uk, Ltd.,
Marston Gate.